JESUS CAME AGAIN

THIS IS NUMBER ~~3~~ 30 ~~-~~
OF A SPECIAL PRINTING OF THE FIRST EDITION
LIMITED TO FIFTY COPIES AND MADE FOR

Opal Laurel Holmes

Vardis Fisher

1956

Vardis Fisher

1961

Vardis Fisher

JESUS
CAME
AGAIN

A Parable

ALAN SWALLOW, *Denver*

AUTHOR'S FOREWORD

"It is a serious fact," wrote Professor Archibald Duff some years ago, "that virtually all men are wondering just what Jesus was." It is a curious fact that they should wonder, for the truth of it was given by a great Jew nineteen hundred years ago. "Yea," cried Paul, "though I had known Christ after the flesh, yet now would I know such a Christ no more!" There it is, all of it, and the truth of it still endures.

"It is an unpardonable historical blunder," said Weiss, "to suppose that the faith of primitive Christendom was based on the impression of the earthly image of Christ." The same thought, Paul's thought, has been stated by many other scholars. "We must not confound the Nazarene," said Professor Guignebert, "with the ideal which he has come to represent since the birth of Christian dogma." "The religion *of* Jesus," said Professor Bacon, "must be accepted, if at all, on authority. The religion *about* Jesus is eternally self-verifying because it is a religion of the Spirit." "He is beautiful, strong, and good," said Couchoud, "because of the multitudes of men who have given him the best of themselves."

What did O. Müller tell us? "If one who invents the myth is only obeying the impulse which acts also upon the minds of his hearers, he is but the mouth through which all speak." "I believe," said Otto Rank, "that the idea of hero formation (i.e. including savior-gods) . . . was strongly influenced by the discovery of the man's share in procreation. . . . The nucleus of all mythical religious tradition is the nobility and tragic fall of the hero who comes to grief through his own presumption and the guilt arising therefrom. That is the myth of humanity, ever recurring in the various levels of development."

G. Stanley Hall defined many of these matters with superb clarity: "He is at bottom what we most profoundly feel him to be. Nor in invoking art to reinstate him need we imply that he is only the consummate artistic creation of the folk-soul in the past, although even if one held this, he might today be most radically Christian. . . . If he be conceived as the greatest projection that the folk-soul ever made, his figure and story are the most precious of all things, perhaps more potent as an ideal than as antique reality. . . . If unconscious man-soul evolved him in the travail of the ages, he becomes thus in a new sense the 'son of man!' . . . If I hold him a better and purer psychological being than any other, although made warp and woof of human wishes, and needs, and ideals, I insist that on this basis I ought to be called an orthodox Christian."

But it remained for Albert Schweitzer, himself so like the ideal, to give us Paul's deep truth in poetry: "He comes to us as one unknown, without a name, as of old, by the lakeside, he came to those who knew him not. He speaks to us the same word: 'Follow me,' and sets us to the tasks which he has to fulfill for our time. He commands. And to those who obey him, whether they be wise or simple, he will reveal himself in the toils, the conflicts, the sufferings which they shall pass through in his fellowship, and, as an ineffable mystery, they shall learn in their own experience who he is."

That each of us must still learn in our own way who he is, this surely is all we need to know.

I

He was plodding along a rocky and dusty road, a Jew named Joshua, a little taller than most of his people, thin and sad and ascetic, with a boyish face, almost delicate, and soft smoky brown eyes and thin sensitive hands. He stopped for a moment and looked over at two men hanging on crosses. He had seen men on crosses before. He knew that all over the Roman world rebellious slaves were crucified and the sight of them was common enough, hanged on trees to be the accursed of God, with no painkiller at their lips, no merciful soldier standing by to break their thighs or thrust a lance into their side to hasten death. He knew that these men were not yet dead. Even from a distance he could see the ghastly anguish in their faces and bodies as they hung suspended from thongs at their wrists, with a piece of wood under their crotch to ease the burden on their arms and to prolong their agony. While he looked at them there was in Joshua's bowels the sickness he felt when in diarrhea after voiding he still strained. There was in him pain and despair for the wickedness and the evil in men, who could hang their fellows up in the heat and the flies to suffer as men could suffer only on the cross.

He glanced round him and saw no man or woman. He then moved slowly toward the tortured ones, his gaze fixed on their naked forms, twisted into the shapes of unendurable agony; and while he was going toward them, slowly and afraid, he heard a sound of pain or horror in a thicket on his left. Moving toward the sound he wondered if it had been made by man or beast. He peered into the thicket and saw a human form there, a woman in a ragged garment, bowed over her lap and swaying back and forth, weeping bitterly.

After looking at her a moment Joshua asked softly: "What is your trouble?" The woman looked up and in the tree-shadow he saw her face, a thin face wet with grief and drawn with fear. In that moment he saw that her eyes, wet and clouded, were blue. "Why do you weep?" he said. "Is one of them your man?" When she gave no reply he stepped in among the trees and stood before her. "My dear woman, why are you here?"

"Please go away," she whispered.

Then he saw that just behind her was a babe, wrapped in a piece of coarse cloth. It seemed to be asleep.

"Is this your child?"

The woman made a frantic movement as though to flee. She swept his face with a terrified glance and sank back helplessly and said, "Yes!"

He supposed she had lied. She was of fair complexion but the child was dark, with night-black hair. He suspected that she was a slave. "Is your man out there?"

She looked up again, fearfully, but at once her gaze fell and again she made a convulsive movement of terror. She turned and drew the child to her breast. She bowed over it and began to rock and hush it gently, her loosed hair falling like a cloak to hide it. Joshua sank to his knees to look at her more closely.

"I'm not a spy," he said. "You can trust me."

Again she swept him with a brief wild look.

"I'm a Jew," he said, using the term with which the Roman world designated his people. Softly he touched her hair. "You can trust me. You have run away from your master, haven't you? But why are you here?"

With sudden fire in her soul that startled and confused him she tossed her hair up and with a hand flung it over

8

her shoulders. It was long brown hair full of dust and leaves and the odor of burning wood. Meeting his eyes her own eyes opened wide and full and were steady and deep blue and at least for a moment unafraid.

"You've come to take me," she said.

"Oh no, not I. How could a Jew do that?"

"Then why do you ask me questions?"

"I know who you are," he said in that gentle voice. "You're one of those Isaiah mentioned, the prisoners who have sat in darkness, yet will be brought forth out of the prison house. I the Lord, he said, have called you and will hold your hand and keep you."

"You're mocking me!" she said.

"No, woman, I'm not. You've fled your master and somewhere you found this child. But where are you going? Have you no husband, no children of your own?"

He saw her draw the child close to shield it. Then she met his gaze, trying to fathom his motives and his nature.

"Where is your husband?"

"You know."

"Out there?"

"Out there."

He stood up and looked down at her. He said: "I'm going out there but I'll be back soon. Please don't run away."

The sickness in Joshua's bowels came up to his heart and throat and suddenly his eyes were blind and wet. He stared round him and searched until he found a stout cudgel and with this in his hand he left the thicket and looked everywhere, to learn if spies were watching him. He then went to the men on the crosses. As he approached them he saw the slobber running from their lips and the blood from their nostrils but their eyes were shut tight and he knew that they did not see him. He supposed they were too sunk in pain to see anything or to be conscious of anything but the death that held them transfixed and would not let them die. Like most crosses these were low, the feet of the men being only a little above the earth.

9

Joshua faced one of the men and raised his cudgel to strike, saying to himself, if I strike him across his forehead he will die soon. But when he realized that one of them in his agony was trying to speak his grasp relaxed and the club fell from his hand. He turned away and went back to the thicket, his whole body trembling with the shame of it.

The woman looked up when she heard him. She said simply, "The gods will bless you."

"There is only God," he said and put an arm to his forehead. He was sick and he turned away to vomit but he brought up only a taste that was bitter. He knelt and bent over, his skull filled with the agony of the men, his soul filled with the pain of human evil. The woman moved over to him and sat at his side.

She whispered: "I've been sick that way."

Joshua's hand groped round him and found grass to wipe the slobber from his lips. "We must go," he said, resting on hands and knees, his eyes closed. "We mustn't let them find us here."

"I've no place to go," she said.

"You'll go with me."

She shrank away from him, for she knew that Jews did not like Jews who talked to women. She was trying to tell him that when, wiping his mouth, Joshua said:

"In the kingdom that is coming we'll all be brothers and sisters. We'll lay down our burdens and even the weariest will find rest."

The woman saw again that his garment was of fine fabric. "In the kingdom?" she said.

"The eyes of the blind will be opened. The deaf will hear. The lame man will leap as the hart and the tongue of the dumb will sing."

She stared at him, wondering what sort of man this could be. In the kingdom! "But not for slaves," she said. "There's no kingdom for them."

"The slaves will be first," said Joshua. He stood up but he did not look at her. She saw that his face was bloodless

10

now and his eyes inflamed but he was very gentle and kind. She had never known a man like this man. "What is your name?" he said.

"Lucia."

They had been speaking in Greek, the universal language of the Roman world. "You're a Grecian," he said, which was the name by which in Israel Jews called non-Jews. "Come now. We must go."

She clasped the child to her and they went out into the light. Joshua then looked at her white face, her blue eyes, her great mass of hair and said: "You're very beautiful."

"Oh no," she said. She was confused and frightened. "I —I'm only a slave."

"You're beautiful," he said. "Come, we must go."

"But where?" she asked, for a moment suspicious.

"To the kingdom. The one we have waited for is coming."

"The—who?"

"The mashiakh," he said. "The king. We'll go to Israel, for he'll come there."

She had no notion of what he meant. He was a strange man and she was afraid of him. To Israel? "How far is that?" she said.

"Not far." Thousands, yes, tens of thousands of people, he said, were going to Israel. Word had gone abroad that the end of the world was near, that the messiah, the king was coming; and whole villages roundabout were being abandoned as people left homes and shops and fields and moved toward Israel. Lucia did not know that Joshua was only one in a tremendous migration. She did not know if Joshua was telling her the truth.

She looked up at him a moment in profile and said: "I have no food."

"God will provide," said Joshua. "With the kingdom so near do we hunger for food or righteousness? You were beautiful a moment ago but when you speak of food you're not beautiful."

Lucia knew that she had been chided and she was

shamed but she was also a little angry. For a moment, which afterward she was to hate when remembering, she wondered if this man had a demon in him. Again she glanced at his face and drew her child more tightly to her. No, he had no demon in him, his face was gentle, all his ways were gentle and in his eyes there was none of that coldness she had seen in the eyes of men. She had been very hungry an hour ago, because for days she had eaten almost nothing; but now she felt strong, strong enough to walk all day and all night and all day, on the road leading to the kingdom. Joshua took the child from her arms, saying that he would carry it for a while; and they left the dying men, though once or twice Lucia glanced back, and took the dusty road south, a river-road that led to Galilee. The time was early spring. The vegetation along the river was lovely, the birds were singing; and for the first time in many weeks Lucia felt free and light and almost unafraid. What a miracle it would be if the messiah took slaves into his kingdom!

During the long afternoon while they walked, Lucia barefooted and with only a rag to cover her, Joshua in sandals and a cloak, the babe asleep in his arms, he talked about many wonders that were new to her. He did not talk to her really—she knew that—but to the sky and the earth and the river and to all the things that were listening. Lucia marveled, because nowhere in the world did the common people, and the slaves least of all, share the blessings conferred by religion—not even in Israel, where the wealthy Sadducees, and the Pharisees learned in the Law, looked with scorn upon the ignorant and the poor. If the things Joshua spoke of were miracles she was not surprised, for in the world of her time miracles were as common as white birds from heaven. She knew that Augustus Caesar had risen from death and ascended bodily to heaven; that sometimes the dead were awake in their graves; that rivers rolled back and cities fell to the ground at the spoken word. She knew that demons could be cast out, and the sick healed with the touch of a holy hand.

She believed all things because the need in her to believe was as deep as her motherhood; but she had never heard such wonders as Joshua was telling now.

Not the things which edged his voice with scorn: not the mysteries in religions that were supposed to confer immortality on the soul: no, he did not believe this, nor did she, because he did not believe. In Thrace he had seen the wild and frenzied worship of the god Dionysus, who was no god at all but only a myth. Only a myth! she thought, forming the words with her lips after watching his lips form them. He had seen the people carrying torches and pounding on kettle-drums and striking infernal music from cymbals; he had seen them dance and shout and sing until they were out of breath; whirl round and round in mounting delirium, clad only in foxskins or in deerskins with the antlers still attached. He had seen them so abandon themselves to their orgies that they sank exhausted at last, babbling in strange tongues, belching great sighs, fainting and falling and rolling over and over like tormented things in the underworld. All that, he said, was not religion at all, and with her lips Lucia said it was not religion at all. . . .

The god Mithra indeed, born at midnight in a cave! What was this? When the sun was hidden at dusk his worshipers offered prayers and then celebrated all night; and at dawn they hailed the sun with shrieks of joy. They put the initiate to trial by water and fire and scourging, by hunger and bleeding and branding and mock death; and on the initiate's forehead was set the mark of Mithra, a cross. They took the flesh of a lamb, the lamb of the god, and baked it in round cakes of bread and ate it. This Mithra, they said, had a seamless robe and a mystic rock and he turned water into wine. But he was no god, said Joshua, and this was not religion; and, shaking her head as her eyes watched his face and lips, Lucia formed the words, no, this was not religion. . . .

Now and then the spell of his words broke and she came out and she looked at her child, afraid that Joshua might hold it too tight, unaware of what he was doing; for when he expressed scorn of these other religions he seemed angry. Or she would look ahead at the misty land of Israel, where the messiah, Joshua said, would soon appear, as the ancient prophets had foretold. She wanted to ask what sort of person he would be but she did not dare to interrupt Joshua. And besides, he was telling her about Isis and she was no goddess, no goddess at all.

In this woman's rites, Joshua said, his smoky brown glance darting round him, his forehead puckering a little with scorn, the initiate wore on his head a garland of flowers and held aloft a lighted torch. The garland had rays sprouting out to represent the glory of the sun. Thus clothed and adorned with many symbols the initiate stood on a pedestal in a temple court, before the goddess, and curtains were drawn aside and a multitude came forward to bow and acclaim his as a god. But he was not a god and Isis was not a goddess and all this, Joshua said, was not religion at all. All this was not God.

Walking in awe at his side and understanding so little of what he said, Lucia had a thought that at first startled and then shocked and stiffened her. She tried to put it away. She tried to be glad that he was holding the child and to be silent but after a while in a voice barely audible she said:

"But don't some men become gods?"

His shrug was slight. So the worshipers of Mithra believed. They said to the initiate that he should come as a child; and he came and took his place in a rock-womb and was born again. But what was this? And Lucia thought scornfully, Yes, what is this! As the god died and rose on the third day so did the initiate, a new man or a god-man or a man-god. He ate a sacred meal. He was baptized with blood. He was marked with the sign of the cross. He was given secret words with which to unlock the gates of the seven heavens. He was told that as surely as the god died and was born again so he would die and be reborn, to live forever. Hail! they cried to him, you have suffered the

14

Passion! Rise! they said, for you are now one with the god and no longer like mortal man! For you are I and I am you; your name is mine and mine is yours; I am your image and you are found in me. But was not all this folly?

Joshula turned to her with a faint smile. "A Jew is not so easily saved," he said.

She did not know what he meant. Shyly she asked, "Why not?"

"We are saved with good deeds, not with rites and sacraments."

"You mean only Jews will be saved?"

Again he lightly touched her hair. "All will be saved who come to God."

"Even slaves?"

"Those first of all, the arrogant rich man last."

She had choked up with hope and longing and she was trying to get the question out of her throat. "And—and women?"

"Women more than men, for in them is more love."

Her mind went back to his other statement. Good deeds? she said—she had none. She had been a slave all her life.

"This," he said, looking at the child. "Do you know what men do with lost children?"

"Yes," she said. She knew at least that much. She knew that they raised them on slave-farms and sold them when they were grown in the slave-markets.

"Do women," he asked, looking at her, "do such things?"

She did not know. She did not know that all over the world women were held in contempt by men. She did know that here was a man holding her child who seemed to feel no contempt for women. Maybe Jews did not. She asked the question.

Most of them did, he said.

"But why do men have contempt for us?"

"Because of some wickedness in men."

"Will the messiah? But no, you said he would not."

"He will come with love for all creatures, for the sinner

15

as well as for the saint, yes, even more than for the saint. And for the slave more than for the master."

She almost spoke and was abashed by her boldness. She had to ask the question. She struggled with it but it would not be put down and at last she let it come out: "For the whore more than the mother?"

He turned and gave her what she thought was a queer look. He did not meet her eyes. She thought he glanced first at her chin and then at one of her cheeks or ears. He moved the babe to the cradle of his arm and said: "The mother above all."

The mother above all! How her heart was singing! She wanted to ask if Jews, like other people, had a divine mother but she thought he might not like the question. She was becoming more and more confused by the things that clamored in her for answers when Joshua again touched her hair lightly and said:

"You are one of the chosen."

Lucia gasped and thought she would faint. Her senses swam and she turned dizzy and sank, her knees collapsing under her and her hair spilling. Joshua then sat by her and looked at her and saw that her hair was streaked with gray and her face deeply lined. He saw that she was weeping. Then he looked down at the babe and was startled to find two round black eyes staring gravely up at his face. This was not a Jew-child, he thought. Still, the masters of Jew-slaves sometimes left infants to die of exposure, as other people did all over the world. Looking more closely at the child he thought that possibly it was a son of Israel, or a daughter: many Jews had mixed with other people, as Joshua's had done: his name was Joshua ben David but he was not all Jew though he thought of himself as being so and was glad to be so.

He turned to Lucia and said: "Why do you weep?"

"I don't know!" she gasped.

"Are you so unhappy?"

"I—I'm very happy now."

"Then come, for we must go."

16

He helped her to her feet and she trembled when she felt his clasp on her arm. They followed the river-bed and before dusk came to a village; and Joshua gave the child to her and sat and plucked at the seam of his robe. He extracted a coin and said she was to wait here while he went to the village to buy food.

"What shall I get for the child?"

She could think of nothing.

When he was out of sight she looked at the child and wept again and thought of Joshua and his words of light and his kindness; and of the coming of the kingdom and of herself as a chosen one, set apart before God. She did not want to be set apart and she was shamed for having allowed the thought. Anyway, who was God? She had heard of gods, of Dionysus and Pluto and Osiris and Hermes and Apollo and Jupiter and Mars; and of goddessess, of Demeter and Cybele and Isis, all the great mothers; but she had never heard of a god or goddess who cared a husk about slaves. Slaves as she had known them had no religion, no divine protection, no divine parents or love; yet Joshsua said this was not so. Possibly Joshua was wiser than all other men. Possibly he would lead her to the kingdom in which there would be no more suffering, no more scourging, no more husbands on crosses or babes lost in thickets—no more, O God, no more!

She was drying her eyes when Joshua returned. She went with him to a grove of trees, to be away from the people thronging the road and to be near running water. Lucia wondered what he had fetched for the child, if goat-milk or barley for gruel. Joshua sat by the water, with the food on his lap; and he looked at the food; and at last he glanced at her in his strange way and said: "What would you like?" His gaze lingered a moment on the hunger-lines in her face and the dark areas under her eyes. "What have you been eating?"

She sighed. "Roots," she said. "Locusts when I could find them."

Joshua looked away, as though thinking about locusts.

17

He said they were all right when fried in flour or in honey and olive oil. What, he asked, had her child been eating?

Her child! He had called it *her* child! She hoped God would bless him for that. "Nothing," she said.

"Do you nurse him?"

"No," she said, embarrassed.

"I've bread and honey and curd and some beer," he said, looking at the food. "Did you ever drink beer?"

"No, my lord."

"Don't call me lord," said Joshua, frowning at the food. "Which of these things can your child eat?"

"The curd, that would be nice."

"What have you named him?"

"I haven't. Would you choose a name?"

He passed the curd to her, still frowning.

Lucia arose and went away in the grasses and reeds and returned with a green hollow stem. She filled her mouth with curd and gave the babe a dry breast and when she had chewed the curd into a liquid she let it run down the hollow reed, the lower end of which was in the child's mouth. As the infant sucked and fed she patted it.

Joshua had been watching her while eating bread and honey. His gaze made her feel self-conscious and ashamed and she looked nervously round her, seeing nothing, her confusion piled like fog on her senses. Her hand patting the baby was still.

"Shall I spread honey on bread for you?"

"Please. And thank you."

When she had fed the child she accepted the bread and honey and after she had thoroughly chewed a mouthful she pressed her mouth to the child's mouth and fed him again. Only when the child would eat no more did she feed herself, her eyes glancing at Joshua now and then, full of blue wonder and fright. Joshua gave her some beer and another piece of bread covered with golden honey.

"Thank you," she said. Her gaze darted from his face to the child, to the woods, the sky, the water, to the far mists of Israel, to Joshua. A little while ago she had wondered

if he was a god but now he was acting like a man. She
could not understand what had changed him so. Still, he
seemed not to know that he was eating: when his hand was
empty of bread he put it to his mouth and then seemed to
have difficulty in realizing that no bread was there. She
suposed that he was thinking of God and the kingdom and
of so many things that were strange to her.

"We'll follow the river to Galilee," he said at last, not
looking at her. "Then we'll cross Galilee to Samaria but
we won't go through Samaria, for they would kill us. We
must follow the main roads or brigands will kill us. We
must go to Judea."

She had never heard the name. "Will the messiah come
there?"

Yes, Joshua said, he thought the messiah would come
there, for the holy city was there. Was it far to Judea? It
was a long way, he said. She then asked how it was known
that the messiah would come soon and Joshua told her
that the wise men among his people had figured it out.
Every person in the world knew that the year five thousand
would usher in the millennium. Some learned Jews had
spent their lives trying to calculate the exact year, even
the month, yes, even the day and hour. But the wise men,
Joshua went on, speaking as if the matter deeply troubled
him, did not agree among themselves. The Book of Daniel seemed to give six different times for the coming; other
books gave still other times, and among the wise men it
was known only that he would come, but not when.
Joshua was sure that the time would be soon, because
there was so much wretchedness and misery, so much brutality and despair and sickness over the whole earth.

He wished he knew on what day the messiah would appear. A few of the wise men thought he would come on
the 14th of Nisan, for on that day the children of Israel
had been redeemed; but others thought it would be in the
month of Ab or of Tishri.

"Will he come down from heaven?" Lucia asked in a
whisper.

19

Joshua's boyish forehead drew into a frown. Well, some said he would come in the clouds of heaven; some, that he would come with fire and a sword; some, with prayer and forgiveness. Some thought he would enter the holy city riding an ass.

Lucia forced herself to say: "What do you think?"

"I think he will come with forgiveness and love."

She looked up through leafwork at the sky. "Will there be signs?"

Yes, Joshua said, there would be signs. The sun and the moon would turn to blood, the stars would pitch down from their courses, great whirlwinds would march upon the spheres and the earth would shake like a woman in childbirth. There would be heavenly trumpets blowing and the glory in the sky would blind all who looked upon it. The earth would darken. . . .

Feeling afraid, Lucia moved a little closer to him; and in a whisper, for she was so suffocated she could barely breathe, she asked what the kingdom would be like. Joshua said that in this also the wise men did not agree. Some thought that Israel would be the crown upon the world and that the holy city of Jerusalem would extend from Joppa to Damascus and be raised to a height of nine miles. All its windows and gates would be of precious stones and all its walls of silver or gold; and its streets would be of gold also, smooth and golden and shining like the streets of heaven, with millions of jewels scattered over the gold for people to gather, as they now gathered corn that fell from the sickles. Food would grow in wondrous abundance; a vine that now had a cluster of grapes would have a thousand, every tree bear its fruit daily, wheat and barley would grow as tall as oaks, with heads as long as a man's arm; water would turn instantly into wine, and fish while you beheld them would multiply in the seine. That was what the wise men said.

Lucia gasped as she took the wonders in. "Is that what you think?"

"I am only a humble man," Joshua said.

"But you seem so wise to me."

His smile was brief and thin. He was sure, Joshua said, that there would be no more disease, no cruelty, no punishment and no death. Righteousness, peace, justice, love would come down from the heavens, though Rome, of course, the Harlot, the new Babylon, would have to be destroyed, to be wiped from the face of the earth; and all the enemies of God, the iniquitous, the wicked, the miscreated and misbegotten, the diabolic and hellish and infernal, in whom there was neither repentance nor love nor mercy nor kindness, all these would perish, so that the kingdom would come into its glory. No longer would the righteous be oppressed by the wicked, nor the rich spit upon the poor, nor the learned scorn the ignorant, nor the slave be scourged by his master; for was it not said in the holy writings that he shall stand at the right hand of the poor?

"The king?" Lucia whispered.

"The king who will rule over the earth for a thousand years."

"He'll stand by slaves like me?"

"So it is written. For I am poor and needy and my heart is wounded in me, but he shall stand at the right hand of the poor, to save them from those that condemn them."

"For a thousand years?"

"Yes."

"And I'll live all that time?"

"Those who repent before he comes will never die."

Never—die! For a moment she had trouble breathing. "I'll repent," she said.

"You'll be among the shining ones."

"Oh, but I'm not a Jew!—Am I?"

"In the kingdom there'll be neither Jew nor not-Jew."

"I'll repent if you'll tell me how."

Night had fallen. Insects were singing around them and a bird was talking and the river was making music over its stones. Joshua said they would sleep and they would rise at daybreak to walk again, for the 14th of Nisan was near and Jerusalem was far away.

21

Glancing at her, his eyes in that moment blinking hard, he asked: "Do you pray?"

"I try to."

Jews, he told her, had many prayers, favorites among which were some of the psalms and hymns of faith and thanksgiving. Turning toward Jerusalem he stretched forth his hands and prayed, and such a prayer Lucia had never heard before. Breathless, she looked at him, her whole body listening.

. . . and a man shall be as a hiding-place from the wind and a covert from the tempest—as rivers of water in a dry place, as the shadow of a great rock in a weary land. I the Lord have called you in righteousness and will hold your hand and will keep you, and give you for a covenant of the people, a light for the heathen, to open the blind eyes, to bring out the prisoners from the prison, and them that sit in darkness out of the prisonhouse. Sing, O ye heavens, for the Lord has done it! Break forth into singing, ye mountains, forest, and every tree in it, for the Lord has redeemed Jacob and glorified himself in Israel! Drop down, ye heavens, from above, and let the skies pour down righteousness, let the earth open, let them bring forth salvation! Sing, O ye heavens, and be joyful, O ye earth, and break forth into singing, O ye mountains, for the Lord has comforted his people and will have mercy upon the afflicted and will stand on the right hand of the poor!"

Joshua lay down in his cloak and put a cheek on one arm and was soon asleep. For a little while Lucia stared at his face, her own face grave and motherly and touched with wonder; her soul asking by what miracle this man had come into her life. The thought came again, and again she put it away. She moved over with her back to a tree and with the babe on her lap and for hours she did not sleep but turned over and over the marvels and portents and holy things whch he had told her. She thought of the wonderful prayer he had uttered and again and again she whispered the few phrases that she could remember: Sing, O ye Heavens! . . . them that sit in darkness out of the prison-house . . . . Sing, O ye earth! . . . the Lord will have mercy and will stand on the right hand of the poor! She would look over at Joshua's sleeping face, a face so sensitive and delicate and even in sleep so sad; and at the outline of his wasted form under the robe which he had drawn around him; and at his two long pale hands clasped together before him, as though he had been praying when he fell asleep. How radiant his face had been when he said, Sing, O ye heavens! How boyish he had looked when the prayer was finished and the music fading . . . .

Lucia slept at last and she was in heaven with her child, who wore a crown of jeweled light and a white robe of pure linen. They walked the golden streets and her child seemed to be Joshua and for a moment she seemed to be Demeter or Cybele; and they saw the trees laden with fruits, and the great rock, and the open and empty prisons, and the rivers of life where people drank to restore their youth; and they heard infinite joy and the music of great choirs singing. Her ears were filled with blessings and her eyes with heavenly visions when, just at daylight, Joshsua touched her lightly; and on looking up she had the foolish thought that he was the messiah.

"We must go," he said.

She arose, feeling shamed and frightened, as was often the way with female slaves. She wanted to tell him that in her dreams her child had been crowned and she had been in heaven. She wanted to say that she had looked over the whole earth and there had no longer been the shadow of a great rock in a weary land. But she said nothing, for again his behavior startled her. He had turned to her with a quick impulsive movement and in that moment she had sensed with a woman's intuition that he intended to kiss her on the forehead or cheek. But in that moment he swerved and turned his head downward and kissed the child.

"Come," he said, "we must go."

23

II

They entered Galilee just above Kadesh and crossed over to Lake Huleh, where they turned south, following the Jordan; and the hour came when they stood on the sea of Galilee between Bethsaida and Capernaum. Horror had been growing in Joshua as he saw more and more people and their loathsome condition in poverty and filth and disease. All around them, he said to Lucia, gesturing, were the signs that the king must soon come, for God would not leave his children in such wretchedness as this.

During the preceding two centuries there had been little peace in Israel. There had been a long war, followed by rebellions, riots, court intrigues and assassinations, with an incessant flow of blood, until most of the stronger stock had been destroyed, leaving the land to the crippled, the diseased, the insane. Israel had only two classes, the rich and the poor; the wealthy landlords with huge estates and a cynical and worldly aloofness, with the priesthood, supported in luxury with a multitude of taxes; these two together, and the common people, the tradesmen, beggars, slaves. For the poor, locusts when they could be found were a comon food, along with sycamore figs and carob pods, the latter a coarse legume used to feed livestock. These common people were ignorant, illiterate, dirty, uncouth, frightened, and sotted with superstition. They had been so oppressed and beaten down, so leached of their humanity, so despised and humbled that few of them, indeed almost none of them but the Zealots, dared to speak aloud about political matters. Everywhere around them were the spies and secret police: it could be discerned in a man's rags or in the marks of his trade whether he was an honest fellow or a villainous tax agent or spy.

Joshua was telling her about tax agents and spies as they walked toward Capernaum. They came to a man lying full in the sun, with wounds in the exposed parts of his flesh and with black flies swarming over the wounds. Touching Lucia's arm Joshua went over to the man and looked down at the filthy creature, whose odor was vile but whose large eyes were intelligent and humorous.

"Why don't you lie in the shade?" Joshua asked.

The man drew an unclean hand from his ragged garment and gestured. "If I lie in the shade it will take the tax-eaters only a little longer to find me."

Joshua bent over to scatter the flies. The man said: "No, don't drive them away. They're half-filled with my blood but the fresh ones would be twice as hungry and eat twice as much. Look, the villains have taxed me off my land. They taxed me out of my house. They've turned me over to the flies."

Joshua was looking at him and Lucia was looking in turn from Joshua's face to the man's. "You're a son of Israel," Joshua said. "Haven't you heard that the messiah is coming?"

With both ragged arms the man made a sweeping gesture of impatience. "How long, O Lord, has he been coming? Haven't we waited for generations?—and still he doesn't come!"

"He'll come soon," said Joshua, looking into the man's inflamed eyes.

"So you say. Others have said it before you."

"You'll be one of the chosen in the kingdom."

"Look, I'm only a man whose luck lies in his trough and his trough is empty. The emperors' tax-eaters, may they rot in their baths, are worse than the flies—and this idea of a coming king is worst of all. It has deluded and deceived us for centuries."

Joshua turned away and as he carried the child and

walked again with Lucia he told her the story of taxes in Israel. In no other land on earth, he said, was the burden so crushing. Here there were civil and religious taxes, each independent and contemptuous of the other. Of religious taxes the faithful Israelite paid or tried to pay sin- and thanks-offerings, the firstfruits of his harvest, the best of all the fruits of field and orchard and vineyard; and the tithes, first and second; and the firstborn of all animals; and the redemption money for firstborn sons; a part of the fleece, and the breast and right shoulder of all beasts slaughtered—as well as other fees and extraordinary payments and various freewill offerings.

And the Roman tax system, Lord, O Lord! What a marvel of ruthlessness and efficiency it was! Land was taxed one-tenth of all corn, one-fifth of all wine and fruit; and besides these there were import and export taxes levied on road and sea; bridge and road money and a duty on everything bought and sold in the towns. There was a poll tax, consisting of an income tax and head-money. Did she think all these were the worst of it? Roman knights formed stock companies which bought up the revenues of a province at a fixed sum. The company then resold at a huge profit the right to gather the taxes; and those who bought the rights, the publicans, were privileged to squeeze out of the people as much as they could in excess of what they were entitled to. They also levied import and export dues, and tolls on bridges and roads and in towns; and no matter whether a man was a farmer, a tradesman or merchant he encountered at every turn and almost every day of his life the arrogant and predatory and thieving tax-collectors. Their decisions were arbitrary, often punitive and from them there was no appeal, because the very judges to whom the appeal might be taken were being enriched by the loot.

Joshua gestured at the world before them and glanced at her face. What was there now but these two classes, the great majority who had been robbed of most of what they had and were being systematically filched of what remained, and the small minority, the wealthy landowners and merchants and the priesthood, who were living in luxury upon the shoulders of the poor.

"Look," said Joshua and looked round him. "All over the land of my people it is like this. There's a saying which I have heard, that it'll be easier for a camel to crawl through the eye of a needle than for a rich man to enter the kingdom. Can anyone doubt that the messiah must come?" And since there was a land tax and a poll tax on all males over fourteen and females over twelve, with only the very old exempted, was it any wonder that many of his people cursed the day they were born?

Looking at the wretched creatures struggling along the road or sitting by the road in clouds of flies Lucia shuddered, for not even among slaves had it been worse than this. Where were these diseased and feeble things going? To Jerusalem, he said.

Joshua was carrying a little food with him and he had been thinking about the food. He now turned and went back to the man under the flies and gave him the food and blessed him. Observing, then, others no less miserable he wondered where he could buy food for them, wondered how far it was to Capernaum; and he went back to Lucia and took the child and they walked again.

Just outside the city's gates they came to two old persons stretched out on their backs, and a young woman sitting by them who had red hair. Joshua looked at them a moment and then said to the young woman: "Are they dying?"

"Dying?" asked the voice of the old man. "Man born of woman—what does the book say?" He had a huge arched nose, heavy lips that looked leprous, and bulging eyes under brows that had once been black but now were snow-white. His big hands were scabrous and mottled. His deep chest rumbled with scorn.

"We're just resting," said the woman with red hair.

Joshua looked at her with interest. "What is your name?"

"Sirena."

27

"You're a Greek?"

"Yes."

"Where are you people going?"

Wearily the woman said: "Where are they all going?"

"The king is coming," the old man said.

Joshua bent forward to peer at him. "Are you sick?"

"I have a demon in me," Aza said.

"He grumbles and grumbles," said his wife Sarah. "I got a demon too." At once she began to groan and twitch.

Looking up at Joshua Aza asked: "Can you drive demons out?"

Before Joshsua could reply Lucia cried, "I'm sure he can!"

"For shame," said Joshua, chiding her. "I have no such powers." Looking for a moment into her eyes he said: "Would you bring the spies against me?"

"Forgive me," she said, humbling herself.

Joshua looked again at the wealth of burnished hair on Sirena's head. "If you are a Greek why are you here? Are you going to the holy city?"

"She came to comfort me," said Aza. "The demon was like hell in me."

"He always complains," said Sarah, looking up at Joshua. "Hah!" she cried, like one suffering terribly. She began to twitch all over and to strike her head up and down. She was searching round her with clutching hands. Joshua was looking at her and now saw her eyes roll upward until only the yellowish white was visible.

"It's mama who complains." said Aza, his big eyes looking with mock horror at his wife. "I suffer much more. I suffer when alone but mama suffers only when someone can see her."

"You old fool," said mama, striking her head and twitching.

Lucia had been staring anxiously at the two old people and wondering why Joshua did not use his heavenly powers to drive the demons out. She was a little impatient with him, for he seemed to be interested in the Greek

woman. Lucia had observed that though rather good-look-
ing her nose was short and humped as if it had been broken
and one upper front middle tooth lapped over on the
other. She had a wide forehead and was wide between
her eyes. Lucia thought her eyes were green.

"Are you going to the holy city?" Joshua asked her again.

Sirena gave a little shrug and glanced at the two old
people. "They want to go to the city called Jerusalem but
they cry when they walk."

"Mama can walk," said Aza cheerfully. "But me, may
the Holy One have mercy! There's a demon in my knees
and I can hear him cracking his fingers when I move.
When I walk he jumps up and down inside and chokes
me."

"How long," asked Joshua, "have you had this demon?"

"A long time," said Aza.

Sarah said: "They jumped out of pigs and ran into us."

"Two pigs," said Aza. "The pigs died."

Joshua looked at them and was thoughtful. He had
read a little in the philosophers and knew that the wise
men disputed over the nature of demons, their motives and
powers. Some said they were the hideous progeny of the
sons of God who lay with the daughters of men, but others
believed that the most cruel and vindictive ones were the
spirits of persons who had died before their allotted time
had run or who had not been properly buried or who had
been neglected after burial. The wise men also said that
their depraved and lawless work was not confined to human beings, but that they also tormented beasts and birds
and practically everything that lived. The whole world
was filled with their crimes of violence. There were demons of frost and hail and snow, of fire and wind, of the
four seasons; and of adultery and greed, injustice, envy,
hate, jealousy, lust, fear. Every house, the wise men said,
was full of them, for they lurked in crevices, under stones,
in dark places; and when persons sat to eat or when they
slept or when they voided then demons tried to enter
them. It was said that if a demon entered you, you at once

felt pain and turned dizzy and vomited and had splitting headaches and diarrhea; and in extreme cases, when the demon was especially malignant, you were caught in a violent passion and you shook and cried out with strange wild words, or you were seized and convulsed and you turned rigid.

Joshua had no doubt that there were demons in these two old people but he was not a holy man and he had no power against them. He knew that Rome's spies were everywhere, waiting to hang on a cross those who pretended to such power. Still, certain prayers were said to abash and frighten them and force them from their hiding-places. He knew of no Roman law that forbade prayer.

He moved close to Aza and Sarah and in a low voice he said: "Holy One, deliver us from all evil, let your great might deliver us from evil men, from evil chances, from evil companions, from hard judgments and hard adversaries, and from Satan the destroyer, and from all evil things that afflict and tear and rend and maim and destroy and torment." He then waited, looking down at them but there was no sign of relief in their faces. They both stared at him, hoping for stronger magic, for they had been prayed over before, they had touched holy things, they knew that these demons were strong.

"Do you say the Shema before you sleep? Demons don't dare approach anyone who says the Shema."

Aza's big strong eyes were looking up with contempt. "Would I say the Shema, an ignorant son of Israel, a goat-herd who can't read and had no father who could read? Would mama say the Shema, who is a hundred times as stupid as I am?"

"You old fool," said Sarah. She then spoke up to Joshua: "No person in all the world is as stupid as papa."

"For shame to talk about one another this way! Shall I teach you the Shema?"

"The Shema!" Aza grumbled. "It's for priests, so let them have it."

Staring at them, Joshua wondered if it was demons after

30

all, or merely divine punishment for some wickedness. Had someone sold Aza a theriac, an antidote against all poisons and a cure for all diseases?

He turned to Sirena. "Has he been taking medicine?"

"Why ask her?" demanded Aza. "Has my tongue been cut out?"

"No one would think it," said Sarah, still twitching. "You talk all the time."

"May the Holy One hear!" cried Aza. "Nobody in the world talks as much as mama."

"I don't know," said Sirena, looking up at Joshua. "I met them only today."

"Where were you going?" Joshua asked Sarah.

"To the holy city, man. The messiah is coming."

"Isn't it true?" asked Aza. "Or have the priests lied again?"

His soft brown eyes blinking rapidly Joshua said, "It is true. The kingdom of God is near."

"I told papa," said Sarah. "But the old fool has no faith."

"Let the Holy One hear!" cried Aza. "Did I leave my house and my goats and my vines and set off hobbling and groaning because I had no faith?"

"I begged you," said Sarah.

"Did I set out leg over thigh—"

"Oh, papa, be still!"

"Did I leave my cistern—"

"He talks all the time!" cried Sarah. "Only God will ever shut him up."

"They were in a group," said Sirena, "but the others left them behind."

"Everyone in Wadin," said Aza. "We all set out, leg over thigh, but look, they are gone and we lie like two beggars by the road. Are we in Israel?"

"Yes," Joshua said.

"Then God be praised. I feel better."

"Can you get up?" Joshua asked and reached for Aza's hand. It was a huge gnarled hand with lumps on the knuckles and with lumps standing out on the wrists. Aza groaned dreadfully as he struggled to his feet and then stood bent over, one hand behind him pressing on his lower back, the other clutching a knee. That he was in terrible pain was clear in the ghastly pallor of his features and the tremors that shook him and the sweat bursting from his forehead.

"Can you walk?" asked Joshua.

"He can," said Sarah, "if he will." She was still flat on her back, her short thick lower legs exposed to the knees.

"You get up now," Joshua said to Sarah, "and let's see how you feel." He took her extended hand and helped her to a sitting posture, and there she sat, a woman so thick and square that she seemed to have no legs but only feet attached to her torso. When Joshua again pulled on her hand she said no-no and shook her hand free. Turning over to her hands and knees she first thrust her huge rump up, like a cow rising, and then, after standing for a moment propped on feet and hands, she slowly rose. Anyone observing her might have seen her face turn white and moisture dampen her brow. Nobody saw anything strange until she toppled over, not suddenly, not like a gross inert weight, but slowly like a thing with heavy ballast in its feet. She had fainted dead away.

Sirena knelt by her. No one thought to bring water to cool her brow and pulse. No one would have thought of something pungent to smell. No one thought to chafe her wrists. They all believed that the demon had momentarily overcome her and was triumphantly leaping up and down inside her. When Aza saw his wife fall under the attack he began to groan in terror and to mutter that in a fading garden there was no water. He broke off his muttering and made a hideous unintelligible sound and with a heavy hand smote himself hard blows across his lower ribs. Then he lifted his right leg and tried to swing it on its knee-hinge and it cracked once like the snapping of a dry twig. With a grimace of pain Aza took his leg with both hands and gently set his right foot on the earth.

Aza said he thought he could walk a little. He took a

few difficult steps, bent over, stiff-legged, his whole face grimacing. Sirena sat by Sarah, waiting for her to come to. Lucia hugged her child to her and kissed it, her blue eyes clouded by wonder and fear.

Hours later, when the day was drawing to its close, this group of persons could have been seen sitting together in the dense vegetation on the north shore of the sea. The atmosphere was humid and oppressive, even so early in the season, and the odors were saturated with heat. The sea or lake of Gennesaret or Galilee lay deep under sea-level, and this evening there was no breeze blowing down from the cool snows of Hermon. They sat in the shade of oleander brakes but they were all bathed with moisture, including the child, which Lucia fanned with a palm leaf. Joshua had gone to the village to buy food and while walking alone he wondered why women liked to attach themselves to him. It had always been that way. Lucia, who for all her ignorance and confused emotional states was a shrewd judge of people, was wondering why Joshua, who had seemed to be in such haste, had taken on the burden of these two old people. O Lord, when would they reach the holy city now! Was he interested in Sirena, with her irregular nose and teeth?

Joshua returned, bringing goatcurd and figs and roasted barley.

After they had eaten and Lucia had lain down with her child and Aza and Sarah had fallen into angry dispute over their pains and woes, Joshua and Sirena sat apart, listening to the gentle waves on the beach and the evening industry of birds. Sirena had told him that she could read and write, that indeed she had read a great deal, being familiar with many of the philosophers, including Zeno of Elea, Pythagoras and Plato. Joshua was astonished. He had known few women who could read, and none who had been interested in philosophy.

"But why do you come to Israel? Did you come alone?"

Yes, Sirena said, she had come alone. In Damascus she had heard that many people were going south to the Land,

the name which pious Jews gave to Israel; that the world
was coming to an end; that many signs of the end had already been observed; and that those who were in the Land
when the end came would inherit greater blessings than
those who were elsewhere.

"Is that true?" She spoke, he thought, in the tones of a
lady.

"It's true." Looking at her but not at her eyes and
blinking his own eyes in his rapid frowning preoccupied
way Joshua asked: "Where are your people?"

"Gone. I have none."

"No husband?"

"I'd rather not talk about such things," she said. "Please
accept me as you see me."

Joshua, whose sensibilities were delicate, never again
spoke of her past. He now changed the subject.

"Over there," he said, looking toward the city, "are
thousands of people going south—the poor, the lame, the
blind, beggars and the sick, runaway slaves—all, all going
to meet the king. In their hearts they know that he is coming."

"All the way from Damascus the road was alive with
people."

"Yes, and the other roads."

"In my language he is called the savior. You call him
a king?"

"My people do not agree." For some, Joshua said, he
was the root of Jesse, another David, a powerful king who
would rule over the whole earth. Shammai, a great rabbi,
had said that he would sweep away the Romans with the
breath of his mouth and would destroy all of Israel's enemies. But Hillel had said no, he would be a prince of
peace. It was written in one of Solomon's psalms that all
the nations would stand in fear before him, that he would
smite the earth with the word of his mouth forever. Still,
there were some who said that the words meant Israel, not
one man.

"Haven't there been many false messiahs?"

Glancing at her hair Joshua said yes, he had heard that there had been many. Even Herod, that monster, had pretended to be the messiah. Had she heard of Bagoas?

"No."

Well, when this eunuch-prophet announced that the messiah would beget children Herod had had him slain. "For Herod, you see, pretended to be the messiah. That monster! May the jackals contend for his liver!"

"You sound bitter," Sirena said.

"Haven't Jews a right to be?"

Ignoring the question she said: "Some say Augustus Caesar was the messiah."

"I've heard it."

"And some say Cyrus, and others, Alexander. Still others say that Socrates was, or Plato."

"And some, Simon the Maccabee."

"What do you say?"

He did not see the faint amusement in her eyes. "I'm not a prophet, I do not say. There are those who say he'll be of the seed of David, a conquering king gifted with divine powers. In a book by Enoch it is said that he'll be a celestial messiah, who sat with the Ancient of Days in the heavens and has been waiting these five thousand years to come to earth and judge it. Some rabbis believe in Daniel, that he will come down in clouds of heaven as down a staircase, with glory around him. But others say he will be a meek and lowly one who will enter the holy city riding an ass."

"You tell me what all these others think but you still don't tell me what you think."

Joshua looked away at the sky. "I think he'll be a prince of peace."

"A Jew?"

Again his gaze swept her dark red hair. "Does it matter? He will be sent by God our Father, who is One."

"He could be a non-Jew?"

"Does God think of his children as Jews and non-Jews?"

"I've had no way of knowing what God thinks. I'd like

to know how you think. Will he be a king?—that is, king of Israel? Will he be the anointed one, that is, the christ? In my language christ is the anointed one, that is, the king but not like other kings."

"I think of him," said Joshua, "as a very great man who will love the humble, exalt the poor, reward the righteous, and in all ways manifest God's meaning in the souls of men. The last on this earth, the sick, the slaves, the outcasts, will be first I think in the kingdom. Anyway, I hope so. I just feel it will be like that. Those who are first here, the rich and proud and haughty, will be last there. So I feel."

"This woman Lucia?"

"Yes."

"While you were gone for food she told me something."

His head turned and his gaze, lowered, swept her chin. "What?"

"She thinks maybe you're the messiah."

"May God protect me!" he cried and seemed about to rise. "Does that foolish woman want me hung on a cross?"

"No, Joshua, no. That foolish woman loves you."

"Doesn't she know what the Romans do to the false messiahs?"

"I didn't ask her."

"Then talk to her, please. Get that blasphemous thought out of her soul. Tell her for me—"

"Joshua," she said, touching him.

"Yes?"

"I have known you only a little while but I have a thought that will not be put away. May I tell you what a student of Antisthenes told me?"

"Was he a Cynic?"

"Don't the Cynics say that virtue is the only good?"

"Didn't Socrates say that?"

"Not quite. He said virtue is the highest good but not the only good." Thinking that her gentle correction had offended him she said, "Forgive me."

"There's nothing to forgive. What did this student say?"

36

"It's what the philosopher Antisthenes said. He said men create gods and then destroy them."

"But there is only God."

"He said more. Shall I tell you?"

For one swift moment he met her eyes. "Tell me," he said.

"He said men must destroy their gods or become their slaves."

For a little while Joshua seemed to be considering her words. At last he asked, with a touch of bitterness: "You don't believe there is only God, do you?"

"Maybe. But that is not what I was telling you. Most people have many gods. What Antisthenes said—"

"Yes, yes," said Joshua impatiently. "He said men must destroy their gods or become their slaves." ·

"Do you think that is a deep thought?"

"I think is has nothing to do with God."

"Will you think about it further?"

"Well yes, if you'll think about God. Look up at the heavens. Can you doubt it? The Lord our God, the Lord is One, from everlasting to everlasting. There is no other. People invent gods and I suppose that kind should be destroyed, shouldn't they?"

"You refuse to understand," Sirena said. "So let me ask you a question. When the messiah comes will the people destroy him?"

Her question aroused in him violent agitation. He leapt up abruptly and looked down at her and in a voice shaken by emotion he said: "How could they?—for he will be too powerful."

"You said he would be a prince of peace."

"Yes," said Joshua, "so I did."

Sirena arose. She was trembling. "Why did you look at me that way a moment ago?"

"Why do you ask a foolish question?"

"Joshua, listen. You say he will be a man of peace. If so, then what will he protect himself with?"

"Love."

"Love? But the philosophers say that people don't like such princes. They say—" She broke off confused and helpless before the hurt and the outrage in his sensitive face. "Again forgive me if I offended you. I hope he is a prince of peace and love. I hope that Hillel is right. But I'm afraid."

"Of what?" he asked, his hurt eyes blinking.

"Of people. Oh, they have such awful passions in them! I have seen it. They destroy what loves them most. I have seen it. People—Joshua, can't you see this?—people don't want love but hate, for hate gives them strength, but love makes them weak before their enemies."

"Weak?" he asked.

"Yes."

"Love—" he began but broke off, feeling heartsick. "Love makes people weak? Did you say that? Who are you anyway?"

"Sirena."

"Love makes people weak? Did you say it?"

"I said it. It made me weak before my enemies. Now I have nothing."

"But was it love?"

"It was all the love I had to give."

"And you say enemies? But there'll be no enemies." His gaze swept her face and his voice rose in anger and reproach. "I tell you there'll be no enemies!"

"Oh, Joshua! How foolish can you be?"

Abruptly he turned away. He went down to the beach and sat there, with his naked feet in the water, thinking of this strange woman and of the strange things she had said.

III

Lucia's notion that he was possibly the messiah and Sirena's that if a prince of peace were to come the people would kill him left Joshua deeply shaken and troubled. He wanted to flee from the group and go to Judea alone but he could not find in his consicence the right or in his will the strength to leave them. While he was brooding over the matter another woman added herself to their number. They were going west around the sea from Capernaum, covering only two or three miles a day, because Aza and Sarah moved with great difficulty and in constant pain; when, one evening, while they were sharing their simple meal, Joshua looked up and saw a woman staring at him. She was regarding him with such intent and unhappy eyes, such morbid and distrustful eyes, and she had round her mouth such a bitter sneering smile, that he was instantly afraid of her.

All his life Joshua had been a little afraid of women, and particularly of aggressive and single-minded women who fixed upon a man an unshakable infatuation. Though thirty years old he had never married.

"Greetings to everybody," said the girl, for she was barely twenty. "My name is Zillah though some have called me Evadne, for I'm the wife in the play who perished on her husband's funeral pyre." She bowed, mocking them.

Her words and her tone disconcerted Joshua. No ordinary woman ever made remarks so pointed in their irony. Joshua glanced up at her mocking face and tried to think of something to say and was silent. Disliking this intruder instantly, Lucia hugged her babe closer and looked anxiously at Joshua. Sirena looked at Zillah with cool appraisal.

Then Zillah smiled, her smile embracing all of them, and there was an astonishing transformation in her face. She had been scowling and sneering and mocking, her lips twisted and her eyes hateful and mean; but when she smiled, revealing perfect white teeth, her face was all girlish innocence and light and her eyes were innocent.

Joshua saw her smile and was again disconcerted and glanced hastily at Sirena. The smile left Zillah's face as suddenly as it had come and the sneers and the evil returned and the cold light to the eyes.

Almost spitting at Joshua she said: "Why are you so attracted to her? Is it the red hair or is it her nose?"

"What do you want?" Joshua asked.

"Tell me, do Jews like red hair, who so long have thought black hair the most beautiful?"

It was Lucia, the gentle and timid one, who came to Joshua's aid. "Please go away," she said to Zillah. "Why do you bother him?"

"You old grayhead!" She was scowling at Lucia but the instant Joshua looked at her she again opened her soul in an unbelievably sweet and innocent smile. When he looked away her face changed and became dark and evil. Sirena, closely watching her, had observed that when Zillah smiled her eyes were beautiful with light and kindness.

"For days I've followed you," said Zillah, speaking to Joshua. "I saw you buy food and give it to the poor. I saw you help this old man and old woman to walk. I saw you bless the one who was dying. I saw you carry this child and smile upon it as though it were your own. But it isn't, is it?—or is it?"

"Please go away," Lucia said.

"Two nights ago," Zillah went on, dismissing Lucia with an impudent gesture of her elbow, "you went away from these people to humble yourself before God and weep. You reminded me of the story about Moses. Do you remember it? While feeding the sheep of his father-in-law in the wilderness a lamb ran away. Moses followed it and found it drinking at a well and he said to it, I didn't know you ran away because you were thirsty. He carried it back to the flock and God said to him, Because you have shown pity you will lead my flock. I," she said, looking at Joshua, "am the lamb that ran away."

There was silence. Zillah smiled at Joshua and when he did not return the smile her eyes became hurt and wicked and she looked like one about to strike or burst into tears. She moved a little toward him and then sat, dropping awkwardly, and looked at him.

"Are you a daughter of Israel?" asked Joshua.

"A Jewess. Why don't you say the word?"

"But you have fair hair and skin."

Zillah's shrug ran down her arms and into palms spread open. "Not all the sons of Jacob have lain with Jewesses, nor the Jewesses always with them. Hadn't you heard that it is so?" She pointed her insolence by refusing to look at Sirena when she said: "One of my ancestors had red hair like hers." Again she gestured contemptuously with an elbow, as if to say, The woman somewhere out there. She smiled again, that open and childlike and astonishing smile, and said sweetly. "Maybe the messiah will be a woman. Had you ever thought of that?"

"A woman!" cried Aza, appalled.

"Don't you think so?" she asked Joshua.

"No."

Zillah was delighted. She had breached his defenses. She had pierced his armor where it was weak. For the sheer delight of hurting him she lifted her brows at him and asked: "Why not?"

"Not a woman," said Aza, muttering. "May the Holy One save us from that."

"Pull the skin over your teeth," said Zillah, and made an evil face at him. "You old leper-lip."

"Here, now!" cried Joshua angrily. "These are my friends. If you speak to them—"

"Your friends! You stupid Jew. I saw you when you picked this old man up—and her," she said, gesturing with an elbow at Sirena. With childlike gloating she looked into his face, saying: "I've watched you when after dark you talked to this redhead. The one there with the color of a babys' diaper. I've seen you loving her when she didn't know you were loving her, for she's awfully stupid. And I've seen this grayhead move her lips in prayer when she looked at you."

There was a gasp from Lucia. Sirena, who had been listening with open astonishment, arose abruptly and stood a few moments, head cocked sidewise like a bird's, looking at Zillah; and abruptly sat again. Aza was appealing to his wife for understanding and aid and muttering in his gray beard that the Devil himself was in this girl.

They were all thinking that Joshua would soon send her away but Joshua said to her: "Will you eat with us?"

"You *are* sweet!" said Zillah and moved so close that she almost touched him. She gave Joshua the smile of an angel and in the next moment turned and looked at Sirena like something out of hell. "That woman," she said intimately to Joshua, "has dyed her hair"—and with her elbow she gestured.

The next morning Joshua was awakened by this imp of a girl. She was tickling him with a spear of grass across his upper lip, his nose, his ears. When he opened sleep-filled eyes and looked at her she gave him that heavenly smile and said, "It's time the shepherd was up." She looked up at the sky. "Have you seen any signs?"

"Not yet," he said.

A little later the group moved away, with Aza and Sarah supporting one another and grumbling, with Lucia cradling her child, Sirena walking apart, aloof and unhappy, and Zillah trailing them like a lost thing, now looking morose and sullen, now opening her whole face in radiant light if one of them looked back at her. All of Joshua's

42

senses were fixed on the country and on the swarms of people moving around him.

He thought Galilee the loveliest part of Israel. He knew of a Roman who after visiting it had said that it was one enormous garden; for besides its many kinds of grains and vegetables and fruits, its olives and dates and palms, it had acres and acres and here and there whole hillsides of roses. It was a fragrant land.

Galilee, Joshua recalled with a touch of bitterness, had never been a stronghold of the Law, nor favored by priests and the wealthier Jews. There were no Sadducees here. There were no Pharisees, save those who passed through. Joshua had heard that the Zealots were here in considerable force, these members of a secret and illegal organization, whose sworn purpose was to kill as many Romans as they could. Romans called them the Sicarii because they carried daggers. Joshua was not sure that he had seen one of them. He did not want to see them, for they believed in force and violence, he in peace and love. He belonged to those who accepted the parable of the lion. This beast once devoured his prey—so the story ran—but a bone stuck in his throat. In his agony he promised a large reward to anyone who would remove the bone. An ibis with its long beak removed it and then demanded the reward; and the arrogant lion said, Congratulate yourself, you stupid thing, for having withdrawn your head from a lion's jaws! Jews like Joshua said, We should congratulate ourselves on having escaped from Rome's jaws but if we insist on literal fulfillment of promises there will be none of us left. That was before it was known that the messiah was coming. Now everything was changed.

But the Sicarii, he had heard, who carried concealed daggers and made assassination their principal work, did not believe that the messiah would come. Did the Essenes? At this moment he was looking at an Essene, walking a little distance from him. It was easy to recognize the members of this strange and secret sect, for they carred a little shovel with which to dig holes, in the manner of a cat, to bury their excrement . . . Joshua had long been interested in these people; they bound themselves in loyalty to one another with a dreadful oath, which called on them to be righteous, to practice justice toward all men, to despise wickedness, to be compassionate toward their inferiors, to love truth, to denounce liars, to keep their hands clean of theft and their souls of unhallowed gain, to have no secrets from their own members and to keep their common secrets even under torture, and to bequeath unchanged all their principles to their children. Abjuring marriage and pledging themselves to complete celibacy they had no children of their own, but adopted such waifs as they could find and brought them up in their order. Joshsua was also interested in them because they were communists: they had no slaves and such possessions as they had they shared in absolute equality. He liked the delicacy of their feeling in all matters relating to the functions of their bodies. They always wore an apron, for instance, even when alone bathing, because they thought their genitals impure and never to be revealed to the eye of God. But their punishments Joshua thought too severe. If, for wicked conduct, an Essene was cut off from his fellows, and even though he then kept his oaths, he was to eat nothing but grass until he starved to death. No, he did not like such drastic punishments but he did admire them because they were communists and celibates and wonder-workers and mystics and forecasters of the future. He admired them because they spent a part of their lives traveling among other people to teach and heal and comfort them.

A friend had once said to Joshua, "If you're not an Essene you ought to be. For in what way do you differ from them?" "I don't carry a shovel," Joshua had said. "No, you don't unless it is hidden; but you've never known a woman, have you? You believe in a community of property and interests, don't you?—and in their austere self-denial and their monastic withdrawal from the wicked world?" "But not their utter contempt for women." "Oh, do they have that?" "Nor in their fanatical devotion to the Sabbath. Why, on the Sabbath these Essenes won't empty their bowels or bladder, even if the pain kills them. Was man made for the Sababth, or the Sabbath for man?"

He smiled, remembering. He knew there was a lot of the Essene in him and he was not sorry. He would have been sorry if he had found in himself any of the Sadducee, for he abhorred these worldly and wealthy Jews who enriched themselves from the toil of slaves and were sycophants before their conquerors. They denied fate, these people, and the resurrection of the body, even the immortality of the soul, maintaining that the soul perished in the body's death. They said that good and evil lay in the choice of men, that human beings themselves were the cause of their misfortune or their prosperity. The Sadducees loathed the Pharisees and the Pharisees loathed the Sadducees. Joshua despised both.

In this moment he passed a Jew who looked on him with distaste and suspicion. The look was so cold and malignant that Joshua turned to look back at the man and at once Zillah's face opened in a heavenly smile. In the next instant she turned to make a horrible face at the Jew who had passed. Joshua shrugged, feeling as he had felt so many times that he was an outcast from his people. He knew why the man had given him the evil look. It was because he was journeying with women. For most Jews a woman with her hair uncovered was shameful—and Joshua now glanced round him at the women and saw that all their heads were bare. For most Jews a woman who dared to sing was unchaste. Lord, he had heard Lucia singing to her child, he had heard Sirena singing with the birds and he had thought both women nobler for it. In Judea, yes, in Judea but not in Galilee, a bridegroom was allowed to pass one whole hour alone with his betrothed before marriage. Yes, but not in Galilee! What a strange thing a Jew was, and how strange that he, a Jew, should be journeying with women, and with women whose heads were uncovered at that! He wondered where this strong prejudice came from. It was so strong that every trade and profession in which men had to be associated with women was looked upon with contempt if not with horror. No unmarried man could keep a school: it might be visited by the mothers! No observant Jew would have dreamed of apprenticing his son to the trade of goldsmith, wool-carder, handmill-borer, perfumer, weaver, cupper or bath-heater, because in all these men were inevitably degraded by the presence of women. He remembered hearing as child, hearing all his life, that Jewish thanksgiving: Blessed be the Lord our God who did not make us a woman!

He looked over at Lucia, walking at a little distance from him and crooning to her child. He glanced back at Zillah, and again she opened to him with heavenly grace. It occurred to him now that she had come to him and was determined to follow him for no reason but his tolerance of women. If so, what a trivial thing it was! He glanced back again and at once Zillah hastened forward and boldly walked at his side, looking now at his feet and adjusting her stride to his, looking now at his face, smiling if his face looked kindly, frowning if it looked stern.

"Do you worry about that dog?" she asked.

He glanced at her, his brows perplexed. "What do you mean?"

"That dog who hated you because you walk with women."

"I wasn't thinking about him," he said .

"You kept looking back. Joshua, you're in Israel now. You're not supposed to be seen with women in public."

"I know it," he said.

"Why don't you go ahead and leave us?" Sirena had come up to listen. Zillah turned to her and said, "Go away, you witch."

Sensing the crisis here, Lucia behaved, as she always did when deeply agitated, by making queer clucking sounds in her throat and darting her gaze round and round,

46

seeing nothing. She had seen Zillah's nostrils twitching. She had seen evil things in her eyes.

Sirena's fair face had turned as red as her hair. "Why," she said to Zillah, "are you so disagreeable?"

"Why are you such a snoop?"

"I am not snooping. I also saw the way the man looked at him. I also think that he should go on and leave us."

Joshua felt weary and he knew that the old people were very tired. He looked round him and saw a leafy tree and said, "Let's go over there and rest a while."

They went over and sat under the tree and Lucia came with her child and sat, her gaze on Joshua. Aza and Sarah sank by the roadside to wait. Zillah, again consumed by hate and furies, did not go all the way to the tree, but stood looking after them, her young body stooped and sullen, her thoughts lighting up her face. After a few moments she reached out and plucked a weed and toyed with it. Her eyes were fixed on Sirena.

Sirena was saying: "I don't know much about your people. I've seen a number of them look at you with hate and if it's because you're with women you should leave us."

Joshua glanced at her chin. It was not his way to meet a person's steady gaze, and Sirena's gaze was always steady, searching, and sometimes amused. It was not because Joshua was sly or evasive; he was so absorbed by his own inner thoughts, so sunk in mystical reflections, drawn so deep into his own unresting emotions that the stark meanings in human eyes confused and troubled him. He would meet a gaze briefly, his brown eyes opening wide as though startled, or as though they saw more than he had wished to see; and then he would look away, and back, and away, not to meet the eyes again but for his gaze to touch lightly the chin, the hair or the throat. He glanced at Sirena's chin and saw again that it was aggressive and a little too large. She had a mole on it and two pale hairs stood out of the mole.

"I'll stay," he said quietly. "I don't mind contempt."

"But you must think of yourself." Her face relaxed into a selfconscious smile and colored a little. "You have four women now. Before you get to Judea will you have a multitude?"

"I think your question is foolish," he said.

"I think the real question is why women are so attracted to you."

He met her eyes a moment. "Are they? I hadn't noticed." He glanced at the mole and thought there were three hairs instead of two. He was afraid of this woman. Under her quiet manner he sensed that she was unyielding—not hard but resolute, not ruthless but uncompromising, not cold but indrawn. "Do you like me?" he said.

"Of course I like you. We all like you."

"Women never have," he said. "Not even my mother. She thought I was—well, a little queer."

"Have you ever given women a chance to like you?"

"Why, of course," he said, surprised.

"Have you never loved a woman?"

"You don't wish to talk about your past," said Joshua, a little sharply. "I don't wish to talk about mine."

"I'm sorry," she said.

"I'm sure I love all people," said Joshua, looking at a purple thread in her garment. "All men, all women but I suppose I love children most. If a man loves all people can he love just one woman? When love is confined doesn't it become preference? That, I sometimes think, is what is wrong with my people. They have great capacity to love but they love themselves most."

"You surely don't mean you love all people. Not *all*."

"They're all God's children."

"Well, then he has some pretty wicked children. Do you think God loves all his children equally?"

"As a father, yes."

"But human fathers don't."

"They try to. I've never known one who didn't try to."

"It isn't easy to love wicked children."

"Ignorant," said Joshua, correcting her. "There are no wicked people, only ignorant people."

"A Greek said it," said Sirena. "Joshua, you'd make a wonderful teacher. See all these thousands of poor people around us. Why don't you teach them?"

And Lucia said quickly: "Why don't you?"

"What would I teach?" he asked, his eyes blinking fast and hard.

"What you have already taught us, and more. Look," she said, turning to the road where a group of beggars in rags were shuffling along toward the holy city. "Everywhere the people wait for teachers. You should be one."

"Why don't you teach?"

"People don't listen to women. Besides, I'd teach what I've read in books, you what you have read in the human heart."

He looked over at Zillah, still toying with the weed. She made a hideous face, bunching her nose up as though Sirena were a vile odor.

"There's Zillah," he said, "in whom there's too much love."

"Oh?" said Sirena. "Is that it?"

"Hadn't you known? Is there so much love in you?"

Sirena colored again. "I don't know what you mean by love."

"That is what he should teach," Lucia said.

"If he really loves all people," said Sirena, "he certainly should teach us how to. For I don't. Do you?"

"I try to," Lucia said.

"How could I teach you," said Joshua, chiding her, "for you don't believe our Holy One is the only god."

"The philosophers say there is no god."

"The Cynics," he said.

"Oh, the Stoics and the Epicureans also."

Lucia moved impatiently. She hated Sirena when she seemed to show off her knowledge to embarrass Joshua.

Joshua said: "If you don't believe in God there's nothing I can teach you. For if you don't believe in God you can't believe in love."

Sirena drew a long breath and looked reflectively at

49

the sky. She had been nettled. She said at last: "Well, you can tell us what the messiah will do when he comes. You can tell us what the kingdom will be like. You can tell us what Hillel meant when he said whoso makes great his name will lose his name. As a man sows, so shall he reap. You can tell us what that means. You can tell us why there is so much evil in the world and what people must do to win against it. You can tell us if being saved means just that, the conquering of evil. You—"

"But you have no faith," he said.

"Oh," she cried, "you've said that before! Did Julius Caesar have faith? He believed in none of the gods but he never entered a carriage without addressing some words to them. Augustus scoffed at the gods but he was miserable all one day because by mistake he put his left shoe on his right foot. If I have no faith why am I here in Israel?"

"Because your mercy is good, deliver me, for I am poor and needy, and my heart is wounded within me. I am gone as the shadow when it lengthens, I am shaken off like the locust pod." He glanced at her face. "Maybe that is why you're here."

"Maybe."

"They shall run and not be weary, they shall walk and not faint."

"Maybe," she said, thinking of his subtlety.

"Is that why?"

"Maybe." She looked over at Aza and Sarah. "Do you know what is worrying Aza? You said the last will be first. He's wondering how high he'll be in the kingdom. Since he's one of the least here he thinks he may be very high."

"What do you think?"

"I don't know. What could he be high in?"

"Love."

"Does everything come down to love?"

"Up to love," he said.

She thought a moment about that. "Aza wants you to teach him."

"Do you know what happens to teachers?" He gestured at a multitude shuffling along. "They expect them to work miracles and wonders and if they try to do these things the Romans hang them on crosses."

"When the messiah comes will the Romans try to destroy him?"

"He will be too powerful."

"In what way?"

"Love."

"Love?" she said, cocking her head like a bird. "You mean wicked men can't destroy love?"

"If you don't know that wicked men can't destroy love what do you know? But ordinary men like me they can destroy. Where is the man who said he would roll the waters back on the Jordan? He is dead. Where is the man who took a multitude into the desert to work great wonders? He is dead. Where is the man who said he would make the walls of Jerusalem fall down? He is dead."

"But you don't have to make foolish promises."

Joshua gave her a thin wry smile. "It's the teacher with the biggest promises who has the largest following."

"Well, then, is it love people want or to see a river roll back?"

"Eyes they have but they see not. They have ears but they hear not. So it has been written, so it still is."

"I suppose so," said Sirena, looking at him curiously. "I suppose people want a messiah with a sword rather than with love. They want to hear the cries of their enemies, don't they?"

At this moment Zillah tossed her weed aside and came boldly up and looked at them. "Don't tell me," she said, sneering at Joshua, "that the Grecian is educating the Jew!"

Sirena looked up at her, recalling what Joshua had said. Was it true?

"Have you so much love," asked Joshua, "and no one to lavish it on?"

"Love! My God, did you say love?"

"I said love."

"I hate," she said. "It is not love. There is no love in me. There has never been love in me. I had no father," she said, her voice rising in bitterness. "I had no mother. I had no brothers and sisters. Love? No, I hate!"

"You don't hate," Joshua said. "You love almost too much, if a daughter of God can love too much."

He glanced at her and saw that she was trembling, that her eyes had filled with tears. With a cry so heartbroken that it was not human she flung herself to the earth before him, and clasped his feet, spilling her hair over them and washing them with her grief.

IV

Toward dusk the next day Joshua and his group approached a town, first crossing a moat and then entering at a massive iron gate which, when shut, was secured with strong bars. Above the gate stood the watchtower; and just within the wall on the right was a shady grove where the elders sat, or where citizens met to transact business or to discuss the affairs of the world. Beyond this was a large square on which the streets converged. Peasants in from the country were hawking the produce of field, orchard and dairy; and along the streets merchants had exposed their wares. In the square was a fountain where those got water who did not have a cistern in their homes.

The moment he entered the gate Joshua knew that some wealthy persons lived in this town. He saw that the grated or latticed window-frames of the houses along the cleanest street were carved and inlaid, the woodwork being of olive and cedar. He saw that the street before these houses was paved with white stones and that the walls were whitewashed. He observed next that a number of houses standing close together each had a stairway, leading up from the street, which went to the flat roof, on which the lord of the house spent a part of his time, for the roof was the coolest and sweetest part of his house, particularly in the evenings. Joshua wondered if these houses were occupied by Jews or Romans. For two or three days now he had been feeling anxious, feeling as if he were under the steady gaze of spies, possibly because of the way Lucia looked at him or some others had looked at him. Twice this day a man had left the throngs and come up to Joshua and stared hard at his face. He was a filthy man in rags but Joshua knew that spies disguised themselves in many ways. Sirena had thought the man looked at Joshua to see if he was the messiah, for she had observed that many people, especially the old and sick, went up to any likely looking man to stare at his face and speculate on his nature and powers.

Joshua did not like to spend the night within walls. This town, he saw, looking round him, was already filled with people, nearly all of them the wanderers moving toward the holy city and hoping to find a wonder-worker who could drive demons out or cure their ills. At the fountain Joshua and his group paused to drink and to wash their hands and feet and to fill two small water-pouches. Beyond the retreat of the elders Joshua saw a lone tree where he thought they might spend the night; but Sirena said no, for delicate reasons of her own. She had learned that there was almost no sanitation in these towns and that often they were filled with sickening odors, even though by law the tannery and bakery and dyer's shop and livery stables had to be fifty or more cubits beyond the wall. The odor here was of things that had been dead a long long time. She suggested that they should go into the country where the smells were sweeter and where a person could in some way attend to his needs without going to a foul public latrine.

Nodding assent Joshua went to the venders and bought a few things for their supper. They then left by the south gate. As soon as they were beyond the gate they smelled the dreadful stench from the tannery and stables. Supposing that to get away from this odor they would have to go a mile or more Sirena turned to Aza and found him groaning horribly and limping and grimacing. He was tired, he said, terribly tired, and he bent a knee for them to hear the hinge crack.

"You're not as tired as I am," said Sarah. "You complain more, that's all."

"See how my feet are puffed," said Aza, and balanced unsteadily while holding one up. "Look!" he said and pretended himself to be horrified.

"It's your soul puffed up," said Sarah. "He thinks he'll be the biggest angel in heaven."

Sirena offered Aza an arm and he accepted it, mumbling, "The pitcher is close to the cistern." He took a few painful steps and groaned and said, "Judah shall plow, and Jacob shall break his clod."

"It's all your blab," said Sarah, "that keeps you weak."

Aza looked slyly up at Sirena and said: "Mama loves me."

Joshua had gone ahead of the group and Zillah had followed him, with Lucia struggling forward to keep an anxious eye on Zillah. Since clasping Joshua's feet Zillah had not spoken a word. When she looked at Joshua her eyes were childlike and tender but when she looked at Sirena they brooded in deep sullen horror. If he would have allowed it Zillah would have trailed Joshua like a lost dog, content to wash his dusty feet, to accept a crust from his hands, while striving in all things to anticipate his wishes and his needs. When Joshua paused at last and turned, waiting for the group to come up, with Aza leaning heavily on Sirena and with Sarah clucking contemptuously, Zillah never took her eyes off Joshua's face. Joshua knew that she spent most of her time looking at him and he was annoyed but if he rebuked her she wept.

They went beyond the tannery and stables and left the road where it ran close to the blue sea, along a terraced precipice above it. This was to be the hottest night they had yet spent together. There was no breeze. Even the cloud fleeces looked hot. They were nearly four hundred feet below the level of the coast and they were all drenched with sweat and dust and weariness. Aza was breathing hard when Sirena, who had exhausted herself supporting him, sank to a limestone ledge.

"There's a road down there," said Lucia, pointing to the beach.

"There's a road here," grumbled Sarah. "It's not a road we need."

Aza, looking at her, cried suddenly: "Mama, don't you sit down! If you do you'll never get up."

"Muzzle your big mouth," said Sarah. "You old hypocrite, you pretend to be weak so this woman will put her arm around you."

"This is wicked talk," Joshua said.

Sirena arose quickly, saying, "Let's go over here" and struck out across the roadway to a big dusty palmtree behind which, in a dense thicket of bramble, stood two olive trees that were very old.

"We haven't enough water," Lucia said.

Sirena said: "I'll go back for more."

"We'll get along," Lucia said. "You don't need much to drink if you sleep." She went beyond the trees to gather soft grasses or lichen or moss or anything she could find to cleanse her child.

Weary through and through and deep in his bones Joshua went over to the tree and set the food down. As usual, it was curd and fruits and a thin slab of hard unleavened bread. Taking charge of the meal, as had become her habit, Sirena broke the bread into six pieces, five of which were almost equal and the sixth larger for Lucia and her child. On each piece of bread, about a thin finger in thickness and as large as her own hand, she put a portion of curd and dried fruits and offered it to one of the group, serving Joshua first, then Lucia and the two old people, and Zillah last. Zillah tonight, tense and brooding, was watching her, and the moment Sirena offered the piece with one furious blow Zillah struck it from her hand. From the others came cries of dismay and astonishment, for how could anyone be so wanton as to waste food in a world where so many starved! Before anyone cold move Zillah was clawing at her hair and spitting and crying out, "She handles our food but she is unclean!

She was born unclean! Everything she touches is unclean!"

Joshua set his food aside and stood up. His thin sensitive face had turned white. The others had broken off in their eating and were now looking up at Joshua and Zillah, all of them stirred by anger or nausea or shame. Spitting out her venom Zillah was distorting her face hideously and behaving as if out of her mind.

"Look," Joshua said to her, his gesture embracing the multitudes north and south. "People everywhere are coming to the messiah, yet in this moment, with the end of the world near, you can think only of yourself."

"It's not myself," she said, her lips trembling, her eyes half-lidded. "You know the laws of our people."

"I don't believe all of them," he said. "Do we become unclean when we touch the heathen or when we hate him?"

"But why do you let her serve our food?"

"I'm not clean in the way you're thinking. Neither are you or any of us. If I obeyed all our laws I'd not be with women, not even with you."

Zillah stared at him, her eyes still half-lidded, her body tense. "Yesterday was the Sababth but you didn't know it."

"Of course I knew it."

"Then why did you profane it?"

"I didn't."

"It says in our holy books—"

"The Sabbath," Joshua said, "was given to us as a memorial but these are not ordinary times."

Lucia had risen and come forward. She said to Zillah: "Why do you argue with him? He knows all these things."

Zillah swung to her and said, "You slave!"

Joshua moved so quickly that it was hardly by any will of his own and he was deeply sorry a moment afterward. With the palm of his hand he slapped Zillah across her mouth.

The others expected Zillah to redouble her fury. Swiftly she stepped back and threw her head up, tossing her loosened hair away from her eyes; and she looked at him, her eyes at first wide and astonished, then childlike and innocent and almost tender. She looked as only a child can look. Obeying one of those strange and deep and unpredictable impulses that were her master she came forward, and when she knelt she tossed her hair up and over, so that it fell as a curtain to hide her face. She knelt before him. Joshua looked down at her and thought she was praying.

"I'll pray with her," he said, speaking to the group but not looking at them. He knelt by her and they heard him say: "Repeat the words after me. Our Father in heaven, holy be your Name—"

"For what has man of all his labor and of the vexation of his heart?"

"—may your kingdom come and come soon; may your will be done, as in the heavens, so here on earth."

Sirena and Lucia had exchanged glances and now they exchanged glances with Sarah and Aza. At first in their faces there was wonder, then incredulity, then astonishment. They all bent forward to listen.

From under the cloak of her hair came Zillah's words: "For all his days are sorrows and his travail grief; yes, his heart takes no rest in the night."

"Our bread for this day give us today, and forgive us our debts as we forgive our debtors."

"Then said I in my heart, As it happens to the fool, so it happens even to me; and why was I then more wise?"

"Lead us not into trials and sorrows but free us from all evils."

"For there is no remembrance of the wise more than of the fool, seeing that which now is in the days to come shall all be forgotten."

"For yours is the kingdom and the power and the glory through all the ages. Amen."

"Therefore I hated life; because the work that is wrought under the sun is grievous unto me: for all is vanity and vexation of spirit. Amen."

Joshua arose, with his head turned away, so that he would not have to look at the astonishment in the faces or show the grief in his own. Zillah remained bowed over for a little while. When at last she moved her first gesture was to throw her head up sharply, flinging her hair back from her face. She looked calmly at Sirena and said, "Forgive me." She then got to her feet and went over to the precipice and sat there, looking up at the stars and down at the sea, or at the beach where hundreds of pilgrims lay sleeping.

The women now talked about Zillah but Joshua was turned away and did not listen. He thought he knew why she was so violent and unhappy. She was an am-ha-aretz, one who did not purify his non-holy food or tithe his friuts or recite the Shema morning and evening or lay the tefillin or wear the zizith or have a mezuza on his doorpost. According to the Pharisees such Jews were more unclean than the beasts. They were despised for their boorish ways and uncouth manners and speech; and if one was bold enough to rise in a synagogue to ask a question or expound a meaning he was cried down because of his illiterate pronunciations. Slavery was a horrible plague in Israel. Zillah knew it and hated it, and was not that the reason she had taunted Lucia? It seemed so to Joshua. The poor were sinking deeper into beggary year by year—and Zillah came from the poor. Indeed, to be poor in Israel was a disgrace and a crime, as it was in the whole Roman world. As for illiteracy, if an ignorant and unclean Jew approached the temple he was stoned.

"Poor Zillah!" he murmured, thinking of her with pity. She had no home, no family, no people, no friends. He was thinking of her as a kind of symbol of all the friendless and homeless when he heard Aza saying, "Joshua, am I right?"

"About what?" he asked, turning.

"That she is very sinful."

Joshua shrugged. "Aren't we all? Who among us would dare to cast the first stone?"

"Does she have a demon in her?"

"Yes, the demon of loneliness."

"It's not that kind," said Aza, who fancied himself as an authority on demons. He knew—he supposed that men everywhere knew—that all diseases, all ailments, all the wickedness and evil, the war and torture, the slavery and beggary was the work of evil spirits.

"Who are we to judge?" Joshua asked, glancing at him. "Judgment is reserved to our Father."

"It's a big demon," said Aza. "Bigger than the one in me."

"Papa," said Sarah, "how you do lie. I've seen you act just as bad."

Aza looked round him slyly, feigning astonishment. "The truth has always been in my mouth," he said. "How can the wife of my bosom, my only vineyard, say such things?"

"Your vineyard!" Sarah snorted. "You're the fox among the vines."

Over Aza's big rough face played the light of his slyness. He looked at Lucia and winked.

Sirena said to Joshua: "Shall I go to Zillah to see if she'll come back?"

"When you have a wish to be kind do you ask then if you may?"

"Be careful," said Sarah. "She might jump off the cliff." She looked up at Joshua. "Didn't you say the king might come on the 14th of Nisan?" When Joshua gave no reply she looked at Sirena and said in a stricken whisper, "It has passed."

"Passed?" asked Lucia, horrified.

"It was the holy Passover," said Sarah. "But we didn't see any Passover feasts."

"What's the next day he might come?" asked Aza of no one.

Lucia whispered: "Joshua says the ninth of Ab."

"O Lord!" said Aza. "How long is that to wait?"

"Three or four months," Sarah said.

"God help me!" Aza groaned. "Three months with this demon jumping up and down in me."

Joshua was looking away to the south. Glancing at him Lucia said in a low voice: "He might be there now."

"Who?" asked Aza hoarsely.

"The messiah. He might be in Judea now."

"With all the damned rich Pharisees," said Aza.

"Joshua says they're not all rich."

"I never knew that," Aza said.

"You could talk all night," Sarah said, "about what you don't know."

"Mama is my vineyard," said Aza, again winking at Lucia.

Joshua went off a little distance and sat to be alone, and Lucia kept her eye on him. Sirena was telling them—for she had heard Joshua say this—that there were seven kinds of Pharisee, five of whom were fools and hypocrites headed for hell. There was the one who ostentatiously paraded his virtues, which were of his own imagining; the wait-a-little Pharisee who was forever telling people that he had important religious duties to perform; the bruised Pharisee, who bore wounds from his haste in fleeing from women; the pestle Pharisee, who had the false humility of a pestle with its head in mortar; and the Pharisee who was always asking, What is my duty? Besides these five there was the God-fearing and the God-loving. Most of them were pompous and arrogant; but the great Hillel, Joshua said, was a woodcutter; Shammai was a carpenter. Other great Pharisees had been tailors, shoemakers, potters or smiths.

"But never a weaver or a tanner," said Aza. "Imagine a Pharisee letting his son go where women work."

"That," said Lucia, still watching Joshua, "is because a woman brought sin into the world."

Aza looked with sly triumph at his wife. "My vineyard, did you hear that?"

Sarah said: "She certanly brought sin into the world when you were born."

Sirena asked: "Do Jews really think a woman brought sin into the world?"

61

"The holy book says Adam was godlike before Eve made him sin."

"I thought that was a myth."

"Well, then, how did sin get here?"

"Men *would* blame a woman," said Sarah.

"With a symbol such as the serpent," said Sirena.

Sarah did not know what to make of that. She looked at Sirena with distrust. "Why do they blame women?" she asked, almost angrily.

Sirena said blandly: "Because man was pure before a woman tempted him."

"Mama, did you hear? I was pure until you tempted me."

"You goat!" said Sarah. "You were chasing the nannies when you were only a boy."

"I just got it figured out," said Aza, with the expression of one listening to the turmoils and meanings inside him. "The demon in me is a woman. Only a woman could torment a man as I'm tormented." He groaned and stretched a leg out to hear the knee crack. He held a swollen hand up and gently moved the fingers. "It's a woman," he said, "and I could almost name her." He turned to his wife. "You remember Naomi?"

Sarah shrugged as a wife might whose husband has bored her for forty years.

"Small and black and as mean as the Devil," he said. "I never liked a real dark woman after she died."

"Why should she be in you?" asked Sirena, looking at him.

"Because," said Sarah, "a part of him was so much in her."

Aza looked genuinely shocked. "Mama," he said, "you got the worst tongue a man ever listened to. This Naomi," he went on, appealing to Sirena, "I never even—"

"Excuse me," said Sirena and jumped up quickly. "I'm going over to Zillah."

She hastened away and almost at once those who remained sitting were shocked by a dreadful scream. Joshua leapt to his feet and started running toward the river, and Lucia followed him, after handing her child to Sarah. Joshua thought at first that Zillah had thrown herself or fallen off the precipice but as he drew near he saw her, standing, and Sirena rushing up to her.

"What happened?" asked Joshua, coming up.

Zillah pointed. Close to the spot where she had been sitting was a deep narrow crevice in stone. Out of it, she said, a demon had come. She saw it leap out in a long narrow grotesque shape, as though it had been squeezed between stones when emerging; but at once it had shortened and struck out with its arms like a swimmer and she saw then that is was in the form of a woman with a red wound in her throat. It shot upward and vanished beyond the trees.

"Are you sure you saw this?" Joshua asked.

"Of course I'm sure. Can't you smell it?"

Her eyes met his with childlike candor. He thought she had answered a little too promptly, without fully understanding his question. He was sure that she was lying.

But Lucia was now babbling hysterically, and Aza, who had come limping over, said, "I can smell her. She smells like Naomi." He was bent over a crevice and he was sniffing. He said he could smell the sulphur odors of the underworld and they all gathered around him and sniffed, turning this way and that. They all knew that when a spirit escaped from its underworld torments it had about it a strange and unearthly odor, like something that had been scorched with fires and scalded in vats of hot oil.

"Yes," said Joshua, blinking hard, "there is an odor."

They all agreed that there was a strange odor. It was of sulphur and of hot smoking salts. Lucia sniffed at her naked arms and said she could smell it on her arms. Joshua bent over and thrust his head deep into the crevice and breathed deep and said he could smell it far down. That was enough for all of them, even for Sirena; for if the smell of Satan's regions was in this area none of them would have dared to sleep here.

63

"Was the wound bleeding?" Lucia asked.

"Yes," Zillah said. "It was wide like this"—she showed them with her hands. "Blood was pouring out of it."

Joshua looked up and all the way around the sky. He thought this might be one of the signs, that the terrified in hell were beginning to flee before the coming messiah. They went down the road and two hours later were huddled together under another tree, subdued and silent, all but Lucia, who was softly weeping.

V

Most of them slept a little but all night Joshua was awake, his gaze sweeping the sky for signs or his ears listening for rumblings in the earth or his sensitive nostrils sniffing; and at daybreak they set forth, anxious and fearful, all of them looking up at the heavens or round them at the earth. Joshua led, as was his habit, and this morning Lucia walked on one side of him and Sirena, carrying the child, on the other. It was a remarkable child, for seldom did it cry or fret, and it seemed to thrive on the thin diet which Lucia gave it. She kept it clean, and this, for Sirena, was a miracle in itself. When Lucia came to water she would take the babe out of the coarse cloth in which she swaddled it and lay it on grass and wash the garment. Then she would wash the child. She gathered soft moss to cleanse it or to use as a diaper; and sometimes, anticipating its need, she would take it out of the garment to let it void. The child's eyes were round and back and full of good humor. Its cheeks were rosy with health. Privately to herself Lucia called him Pastor, having heard that this was the name of one who spent his life in the service of others. If she had dared she would have called him Joshua.

Behind the four walked Aza and Sarah, assisting one another, complaining, bickering, or now and then sinking to the earth to rest their aching bones. Zillah was with them. She was morbidly quiet today, her gaze veiled, her emotions indrawn. They passed through Magdala which stood on the plain of Gennesaret and late in the afternoon

65

approached Tiberias. Joshua knew that devout Jews shunned this city, for it had been built upon the ruins of an ancient settlement and upon a graveyard. Herod had chosen this site for his capital city because it stood on a hill which could be easily defended and was close to the hot baths just south of it, famous throughout the Roman world. It was a large city for Galilee, with some splendid structures amidst the slums. Old human bones, unearthed in digging the foundations, were scattered everywhere, and heathen images looked down from the walls.

Two miles north of Tiberias were some ancient wells, whose water was sweet, and here Joshua and his group spent a night. All around them during their journey was the traffic moving north or south or coming in from the west—wealthy merchants dashing by in their carriages; carts and asses laden with produce; various petty officials, including the publicans; and around them all, over them all, smothering them all the unclean rabble of the poor, the diseased and homeless, looking for the messiah. These now were coming in on roads from the west and across the sea from the east, to swell the multitudes; and Joshua wondered how many there would be, for besides those whom he saw every day there were hordes he knew to the north coming down, and only God knew how many to the south, pressing toward Jerusalem.

From a cart-vender Joshua bought bread and fruit and honey for their evening meal. At a well they washed their faces, hands and feet and Lucia cared for her child. Aza was so stiffened in his spine that he was unable to touch his feet, and so Sarah had to wash them; and this she did clucking hatefully and telling him that he was more helpless than the babe. His feet, like her own, like those of all people who went unshod, were soled with thick hide and browned over like tanned leather. When washing his feet she spread his toes two by two to search between them for tiny stones and briars.

"Mama!" he would yell. "You tickle!"

She seized a toe and yanked it. "You big helpless no-good man."

"Look," he said, appealing to anyone who would look. But nobody would look, for they had heard all this before. "Listen," he said. He bent forward. He turned his head from side to side and there was in his neck the sound of brittle things snapping. "Maybe it's a dog," he said. "I can hear barking."

"It's no dog," said Sarah. "It's Naomi."

"Ugh!" said Aza, shuddering.

Joshua was quieter this evening, more subdued, his countenance, Lucia thought, touched by a deeper sadness. It was a riddle to him how so many persons could indulge their whims in idle talk, in bickering, in efforts to be witty, when the hour stood imminent and the whole world trembled in the balance. Had they no sense of the catastrophic changes that stood just beyond the next week or month or possibly the next morning? Were they unable to imagine the majesty and wrath of God when, looking down at his children, he shook their world and convulsed the spheres and flung his might through the whole shuddering universe? Well, yes, Lucia had a sense of it, dear faithful Lucia, whose anxious eyes were so often on his face. But what was Sirena saying?—that souls were carried to heaven by eagles, which Assyrians called birds of the sun; that Plato had said that God had made as many souls as there were stars and that a soul mounted its star as it might a chariot. What was Aza saying?

"How does a soul know its star?" he asked, craning his neck at the heavens. "One of them must be mine," he said, staring hard, gazing at the brightest ones in spite of the fact that he felt very humble.

"Yours is so dim," his wife said, "that you'll never see it. Don't get the crazy idea that some bright star is yours."

"Whose are they?" asked Aza, staring.

"Great men, not herders of goats."

"But Joshua says the first shall be last and the last first. Mine must be one of the bright ones." Slyly, to torment his wife, he pointed to the brightest star in the sky and said: "That's mine."

"That's Joshua's," Lucia said.

"You've been so wicked," said Sarah to Aza, "that you don't even have a star. You'll just find a hole and go down."

"Where?" he said.

"To hell, of course."

"And what'll I do there?"

"She can tell you," Sarah said, inclining her head slightly toward Sirena.

Aza looked at Sirena and winked, and catching his spirit of sly teasing she said: "You'll be like Tityus, forever eaten by vultures; like Tantalus, dying of hunger and thrist, reaching out to water he can never grasp, to fruit that hangs above him. Or like Sispyhus you'll forever roll a stone to the top of a mountain, it will fall back, you will roll again. Or you'll have to carry water from one place to another in a leaking bucket and when you get there the bucket will be empty and you'll go back, always back and back."

Joshua turned to look for a moment at Sirena.

"No faster than I can walk," said Aza, "it wouldn't have to leak much. I'd rather roll the rock. I could kneel doing that."

"Monsters," said Sirena, "will eat at your bowels. They will flog you with whips and chains, they'll throw you into vats of boiling lead."

Lucia's eyes were wide and horrified. "Unless you repent," she said.

"I'm repenting fast," said Aza.

"If you're a hypocrite—" Sirena said; and Sarah said: "He is."

"Then they'll turn you inside out, with your bowels on the outside and you'll go around eating one another. If a miser, they'll douse you in a lake of boiling gold and drag you out and throw you into pools of ice and drag you out and poke redhot iron pikes through you. If a blas-

68

phemer they'll hang you up by your tongue. If rich you'll have to walk forever on redhot stones."

"That's one thing I won't have to do," Aza said.

Joshua turned again to look at Sirena. It seemed to him that she was scoffing and this was no time for scoffers.

"The killer," said Aza, "how is it with him?"

"They put him in a cave full of venomous snakes and they eat on him forever and ever."

Lucia was moaning a little. "Please," she said to Sirena, "don't tell us any more."

"If you've been a glutton," said Sirena, looking at Aza with relish, "you'll enter a big fat hog. If you've been lazy you'll live in a fish."

"In a fish," said Sarah, "that's where you'll be."

Grinning, Aza looked up at the bright star and considered. "I'd rather be in a fish than carry a leaking bucket forever."

"If you've been an adulterer," said Sirena, "your soul will never be able to leave your corrupt body. It'll just be stuck there, like a dog by its dead master."

"You hear that?" Sarah asked him. "And Naomi, she'll be right there with you."

"She is already," said Aza.

"The poet Virgil said, Aliae panduntur inanes suspensae ad ventos, aliis sub gurgite vasto infectum eluitur scelus, aut exuritur igni."

Zillah made a dreadful face and then, as though to shut out a horror, covered it with her hands. Joshua again turned to look at Sirena, thinking, The Greeks don't believe any more, they are all scoffers and atheists.

Aza said: "What does all that alley pandey spensee mean?"

"Some souls are hung up lightly in the winds, but others are corrupted by sins and washed away into deep chasms, or are destroyed by fire."

"I'll be a soul in the winds," Aza said. Looking slyly down his long nose at Sarah he added: "I've had enough of the deep chasms."

69

Lucia gasped. Sirena colored a little and Zillah put hands to her face to hide her laughter.

"What I want to know," said Aza, "is how I can get to heaven. Joshua says repent. May the Holy Name bless me, I repent all the time. What else should I do?"

"There are three ways to get to heaven," Sirena said. "Get on the back of an eagle or fly with your own soul-wings or climb a ladder."

"A ladder," said Aza, looking up. "It would be a long ladder."

Lucia said: "Joshua says the way to get to heaven is to repent."

"Who?" asked Zillah, sneering. "There's no place in the kingdom for women. *We* put the world's light out! *We* tempted Adam, the dull stupid imbecile! *We* brought sin into the world! Men were happy and pure until we seduced them!"

"When I listen to you," Sarah said, "I can believe it."

"I should be quiet," said Zillah, making an abject face. "We women are not supposed to speak."

"That's true," said Aza. "It's too bad you women can't remember it." Then, trying to smooth things over, he said: "My vineyard here has decided that my soul will enter a hog."

"Or a jackass," Sarah said.

Joshua got to his feet and turned away, with Lucia's gaze anxiously following him. He was wearied by the talk but it was not that alone that sent him over to the road, to stand there, looking at the pilgrims all around him, talking, sleeping or wandering restlessly, their gaze on the heavens. He had a sense of things imminent, of changes, of signs, of new orders; and while he was standing by the road, almost oblivious of things around him but busy with his own inner sensations, a man came up and looked into his face. He was a heavy square man, thick, solid, dependable, with steady eyes and a strong mouth. He looked at Joshua without speaking, searching him, appraising him, and Joshua was not at all disconcerted, because many persons had come up to look at his face, as they looked at other faces, to see if by chance this was the king and messiah.

"You going to the holy city?" asked the man.

"Yes," Joshua said.

"And all the people," said the man, his gesture encompassing all of Galilee. "The city won't hold so many."

"They can sleep beyond the walls," Joshua said.

"I've just come from there," the man said. He moved an arm slowly in a level plane clear around him. "All the way from here to there it's like that—and bandits and brigands everywhere."

"Brigands? You mean along the river road?"

"The river road, from Jericho to the city, everywhere. Tell me, when do you think the king is coming?"

"The ninth of Ab," Joshua said.

"Well, some say then, some the Day of Atonement, and some not till the next Passover."

"I don't think God will wait that long," Joshua said.

"Have you seen any signs?"

Joshua hesitated. Had he seen signs, or had he only felt them? "No," he said.

"Down there," said the man, pointing toward Jericho, down the river, toward the holy city, "they have seen signs, many signs. But I myself have not seen any."

"What signs have they seen?"

"They have seen the moon bloody but I did not see it. They say the south wall of Jerusalem has fallen. I did not go out to see. They say the jackals are coming in from the wilderness close to the towns, being afraid, and that they cry all night and will come right up to a person and lick his hand. They say that the river in places has been rolling back. They say it rolls back a cubit, two cubits, and then boils up in a great wall and bursts and spills. So they say, but I have not seen it."

"The signs are very close," Joshua said.

"But you have seen none."

"Not yet."

"Well, I must go now. May your memory be for a blessing and may your light shine on. And watch out for the bandits, for they would kill you for the robe you wear."

Joshua stood a few moments, looking after the man, thinking of what he had said. Then he returned to his group, deeply troubled, and they all saw that he was troubled and they were silent. He stood before them, not looking at them, but covering them with a swift glance now and then, his boyish face very grave, his eyes blinking hard. At last Sirena said:

"Is there some trouble?"

"They are seeing signs," he said. He moved his body toward the south. "Down the river."

"Signs," said Aza. "Then he'll soon come." He leaned back so that he could look up at Joshua without trying to bend his stiff neck. "Maybe he'll come before the ninth of Ab."

"I don't think so," Joshua said, his face so earnest and guileless and furrowed with thought that Lucia's mother-heart yearned toward him.

"Have they seen many signs?" asked Sirena.

Joshua glanced at her quickly, perhaps to see if she was scoffing. "Not many yet."

Aza said: "But won't there be a lot of signs before he comes?"

Joshua nodded yes. "We'll see many strange things, many wonders and marvels. We'll see the earth darkened when the sun is overhead, and the night as bright as daytime; and we'll see the lame walk and the deaf hear, and the dead will rise from their graves." Again his glance swept them, as though to see if they mocked. "The rich will throw away their treasure and cling to the skirts of the poor, for so it is written; and tyrants will throw themselves in the dust and cry for mercy and jackals will come to the cities."

Each chose from the words those whose meaning was brightest for him. Aza stretched a leg painfully and said:

72

"If the lame will walk, then I guess I'll know about when he comes. Won't I?"

"You!" said Sarah with disgust. "Of course of all the men in the world you would know."

"But I'm lame," said Aza, "and Joshua says when he comes I'll be lame no more."

"But the dead will rise," she said. "Maybe Naomi will tell us."

Joshua looked round him and chose a spot for his rest and lay down but for a long while he did not sleep. He was looking up at the sky: one of the wise men had said that the first sign would appear there and it seemed to Joshua that it would, for a sign up there all men could see. They could not all know about a wall tumbling down or a river rolling back but every person on earth could see the moon if it turned to blood, or the stars if they pitched downward in their courses. But the sky tonight was as serene and untroubled as perfectly still water; the stars winked in their old way and from outer darkness stars appeared a moment to wink and vanish and a pale golden half-moon was the moon of his childhood and youth. It was a firmament of deep peace.

But before morning all this was changed, suddenly, and with a dramatic intensity that brought him wide awake. He had no idea of what had happened and he lay without moving, his eyes open, all his senses alert and waiting. Then it came again and he could hardly believe it. He was moved or rocked or swayed—how was it?—with infinite cosmic gentleness, about a foot or two feet, back and forth, two or three times. Then again he was still. It was the most weird sensation he had ever had. He felt gooseflesh on his scalp, down his neck, over his shoulders, and then realized when he choked and gasped that he had been holding his breath. He lay very still, trying to think about it, to feel his way into it and around it; and while he was thinking and feeling and wondering the movement came again, so soundless, so deep and still, so infinite in its gentleness and power, as though the earth had become

73

a cradle, with God's hand on it. He knew that he had seen, no, *felt*, one of the signs, and he waited to see if it would be repeated but it did not come again. He lay on his back, looking up, and felt a slight sensation of nausea; it seemed to him that there was a slight but gently insistent back-and-forth movement in the earth under him but the sky still looked the same.

In a little while it was morning and he stood up, shaken, and paler than usual. He was sure he had felt the sign but he wanted to be doubly sure and he glanced in turn at the members of his group as in turn they awoke and sat up, to see if in their faces . . . Yes, it was there, in Lucia's.

She was looking at him, her eyes wide and frightened and deep blue in the morning dusk. "What was it?" she whispered.

He did not reply. He glanced at Sirena. Her eyes were not wide or frightened and they were a hazel-green. "Did you feel an earthquake?" she asked him. "I felt something in the night. Is this hot springs area volcanic?"

"Wasn't it a sign?" Lucia asked.

"Yes," he said. His gaze swept them, seeing them darkly in turn, one and another. The time had come when he must choose one among them. "Lucia," he said, "give your child to Sarah and come with me."

VI

He knew the time had come when he would have to get rid of the gold coins sewed in the hem of his robe. If he did not the brigands would take them, though it was not of brigands that he was thinking now. He was thinking of the words written in the holy book, that the rich would throw away their treasures and cling to the poor. He was not and had never been a rich man; he had only a little gold but no man but a fool would face the messiah with gold in his robe. He would bury most of it.

He went away and Lucia followed him. He wandered around, looking for landmarks or signs that would not be changed by man or forgotten by Lucia; and chose at last a huge palmtree that stood in plain sight of Tiberias. Swiftly he sat and opened the hem and took the coins out and after handing a half-dozen gold pieces to the astonished Lucia he swiftly dug a hole and buried the remainder. He then sat with her by the tree and for a minute or more looked all around him, casually, like one talking to a friend; for he wanted to be sure that no one had observed him. Lucia meanwhile stared at him, too overcome to speak. Joshua scattered old leaves and dry earth over the buried treasure to make the earth appear undisturbed and then said to Lucia, "Come with me." They went away from the tree a distance of fifty yards and Joshua said: "Look all around you and choose your own landmarks, so you'll know the tree. See, the city is there. Mark the distance between the tree and the road . . . Are you fixing these things in memory?" She nodded. He went with her beyond the tree in the opposite direction and he scowled at her in his boyish way that sometimes looked fierce but was not fierce at all; and he said with a touch of impatience: "Lucia, don't look at me. Look around you and fix that tree in mind." Lucia gasped, "My God!" and thought she would faint, for an intuitive sense of him had almost paralyzed her mind. "See that other old palmtree," he said. "From here the two are in line with the west tower in Tiberias. Do you see?"

"Yes!" she gasped. And within she said: O my God! She was weeping.

His gaze swept her face. "Why do you weep?" he said.

"Oh, Joshua!"

"Come," he said, "we must go."

Joshua summoned Zillah and asked her to walk with him and while they moved slowly toward Tiberias he talked to her about the roads in Israel. Great highways crossed Galilee and Samaria here, from north to south and from east to west. One road left the plain of Gennesaret and climbed to the plateau above Tiberias, passing thence between Tabor and the Esdraelon hills to Megiddo, to Sharon, to Philistia and Egypt. Another road followed the sea down to Bethshan and from there the traveler could cross over to the route to Egypt, or go through Samaria to Judea, or follow the river to Jericho. A little north of Bethshan there crossed the Jordan another great road from Damascus, which went west over Esdraelon or north to the plateau above the sea, and thence past Cana to Acca. The great west road from Damascus was called the Way of the Sea.

The Jordan river poured downward to the Dead Sea, over the poisonous salts of an infested jungle. Many wild beasts were there, and tropical heat, Joshua said, glancing at Zillah, and terrible fevers. Most of the multitudes going to Jerusalem were taking this route. Joshua thought it would be safer, from every point of view, to cross the forty mountainous miles of Samaria, though devout Jews would not enter this land, preferring brigands and fevers to this hated people.

"The trouble with Samaria," he said, "is that it's farther. We might still be there when he comes."

Zillah was deeply flattered. He had chosen her to walk with him and he was talking to her. She knew all about the roads and the wild beasts and the fevers, for she had lived all her life in Galilee; but in a woman's way she let him think that she did not and she opened her eyes on his words, if he looked at her, as though they were filled with wonders.

"But you said he won't come till the ninth of Ab. We have plenty of time."

"Yes," Joshua admitted, frowning. "But the sign. He may come sooner."

"What did the sign mean?" Zillah asked, not because she was interested really, but to keep him talking while alone with her.

It meant, Joshua said, that the underworld was deeply disturbed. Hell was convulsed. They might have expected the sign, had they only thought about it; for had not a demon come screaming out of a fissure a little earlier, indicating that terror had struck in hell? He looked up at the sky for other signs but the day was cloudless and serene.

"But won't he come on some special day?"

"I'm sure he will."

Zillah knew her religious calendar well. "What special day is there before the ninth of Ab?"

Thoughtfulness covered his whole face with a deep frown. "I can think of none," he said.

Zillah glanced back to see if Sirena was pressing forward, but no, she was walking with the two old people and Lucia with her child was just behind them. Zillah wanted to speak to Joshua of a matter that was like lead in her breast. She fell back just a little to study his profile: his beard was very short, silkly and curled. His hair was also very fine and his ear was so thin that it was almost transparent. He had a good nose, a good chin, not rugged, not granite-like: he was boyish really, but quite manly in his way; he was—and then it came to her—he was about what the son of God would look like if God had a son.

"Joshua, may I speak about a matter?"

"Of course," he said, his glance darting over her face but fixing on no part of it.

"It's about Lucia. You know what she really thinks? She thinks you're the messiah."

"No!" he cried, horrified.

"But she does. And she has heard Sirena say that when the messiah comes the people will destroy him, if he comes with love instead of a sword. This greatly worries Lucia."

"You remind me," said Joshua, "of trees. A forest tree once asked a fruit tree, Why is the rustling of your leaves not heard at a great distance? The fruit tree replied, We do not need to rustle to manifest our presence. Our fruits testify for us."

Zillah turned pale with anger and burst into tears. "Why do you hate me so? I only told you this for your own good!"

"Zillah, I hate no one. The waters of the Euphrates run smoothly and are not heard. So it is with the pure in heart: their deeds like a deep river speak for them."

"You mean I'm just a noisy mountain stream. All right, Joshua, if that's what you think. But remember this—"

"Please don't say it."

"I will say it. Lucia more and more—"

"I won't hear it," Joshua said and he turned back. He took the babe from Lucia's arms and looked at its bright face and kissed its two red cheeks. Then he walked again, with Lucia at his side now, but now and then he glanced back to be sure that Zillah was coming. After they entered the city he turned to Lucia and said: "How many coins did I give you?"

"Six, Joshua."

"Give them to me." Lucia gave him the coins and for a moment he looked at them. "They are all of the same worth," he said. "Lucia, here are two for you and your child. Here is one for Aza, one for Sarah, one for Zillah, and one for Sirena. Go buy the things you need or—" and they all missed his slyness "—you want and we'll all meet at the south gate." He gave the child to Lucia and turned away.

Tiberias, the women were to learn, had magnificent bazaars. Beautiful garments could be bought of silk or of Pelusian or Indian linen, and coarse garments of cotton or Cilician haircloth. There were colorful displays of capes and mantles and girdles, and of sandals, including Greek, Persian and Laodicean; and of ornament and headdress from all the lands roundabout. There was also a variety of underwear, though in this torrid climate most people wore only a loose cloak like the Greek chlamys, or the chiton, or a combination of chiton and cloak, or a peplos with girdle, or a sagum, a mantle that left the arms free and was favored by soldiers and artisans.

Joshua bought nothing for himself. Indeed, he had no money now, not even a copper coin. He went straight through the city, observing that it was filled to overflowing with pilgrims, and just outside the south gate sat by a wall. He hoped they would not be too long, for he was all the more eager now, having had a sign, to get to Jerusalem. He thought it possible that the messiah might be there now. He knew of nothing in the holy writings or in the words of the wise men that said *all* the signs must manifest themselves before the king appeared. Still, if he had not yet come Joshua could not believe that he would come before the ninth of Ab, and that was about three months away.

He sat with his knees up, his arms on his knees and his face resting on his arms, and he wondered if he ought to speak to Lucia. Surely she was not foolish enough to think *him* the messiah, a very ordinary and humble and untutored man; yet he had observed, more especially of late, the way she looked at him, her blue eyes full of hope and heaven. As he approached the holy city the spies

79

would be more numerous and much more alert. He would find himself in deep trouble if the rumor went around that he was thought by some to be the long-awaited king. Yes, perhaps he ought to speak to her.

The first voice he heard was Sirena's and slowly he raised his head and then looked her up and down. He suspected at once that she had spent all the money he gave her. She had bought a himation, a huge rectangle of fine linen with a handsome colored border; and a pair of expensive sandals with thick soles and strong straps of soft brown leather. Because Greek women were proud of their hair and took great pains in arranging it, but even more because her beautiful hair was her glory, she had bought a blue fillet within which she now confined her burnished tresses. She looked like one who had prepared herself to be a queen's maid instead of to journey across endless miles of dusty hills.

She must have read the disapproval in Joshua's eyes, for she said: "I'm a woman and women are vain."

"To everything there is a season, and a time to every purpose under the heavens."

"You mean I should have bought sackcloth?"

Joshua leaning against the wall had closed his eyes. "Before people enter the kingdom they will give what they have to the poor and turn both cheeks to the enemy."

"You mean we're to enter the kingdom naked?"

Without opening his eyes he said: "Does the seed of the lily enter the earth naked or clothed? It is put naked into the ground, and look how it comes forth arrayed. So it will be with the righteous when they rise from death."

"But we'll be alive," said Sirena, nettled by his parables. "Are we to cast our garments away and go forth naked? When you do so I'll do so. But the messiah won't appear before us naked, will he?"

Joshua felt too weary to reply. "Are the others coming yet?"

"I don't see them."

Zillah came next and she also had spent her money.

80

She had bought a light sleeveless cloak that fell almost to her feet and had bound it in with a girdle. She had draped the girdle so expertly that her figure, which was lovely, was quite fully revealed, including her full breasts. She had also bought sandals and a fillet. She came up, looking Sirena up and down.

Sirena said: "Zillah has come."

Joshua opened his eyes and looked at Zillah. Then wearily his lids fell. The two women, both standing, were gazing openly at one another, their eyes full of challenge. Zillah stood erect to show off her full firm bosom, for she knew that Sirena was almost flat-chested; and then with slow and proud and disdainful movements she walked around Sirena. She looked into Sirena's eyes, her own wide open and innocent; then her gaze fell, pausing, as her lids lowered, with significant emphasis at Sirena's breast; then fell to her waist, and her brows shot up, as though with astonishment; and then to her sandals; and at last, again open and childlike and full of feigned wonder, rose slowly to her face and rested on her hair. In a voice that could not have been sweeter she said: "A woman with such hair needs nothing else."

Sirena was astonished. "Thank you," she said.

"A bundle of myrrh is my well-beloved unto me; he shall lie all night between my breasts. Behold, you are fair, my love. Behold, you are fair."

All night between my breasts! Sirena was trying to fathom the woman's purpose when Aza and Sarah and Lucia came through the gate. Aza and Sarah had spent a part of their money but had spent it wisely: they had bought homely but rugged garments and sandals and food for all of them for supper. Lucia had bought nothing but a simple robe for her child. She still wore her ragged garment and her feet were still bare.

Joshua opened his eyes and looked at them in turn. Then he went over and gently touched Lucia's hair and took her child, saying, "Come, let's go."

They went down the road toward the baths, Joshua lost

in a subtle mood of anxiety, Lucia glancing now and then at his face. There were pilgrims ahead of them or behind them, for the road was filled now as far ahead or as far back as they could see. The two old people were walking together and behind them were Sirena and Zillah, talking.

Zillah was saying: "Joshua didn't like what we bought."

"I know it."

"He doesn't understand women, does he?"

"I don't know."

"You know well enough but you're afraid to say. Wasn't Adam the fool instead of Eve?"

"Maybe," said Sirena, looking at her.

After glancing behind her Zillah said in a low voice: "Lucia thinks Joshua is the messiah."

Looking at her again Sirena said. "How do you know that?"

"I heard her telling her child. I heard her say it when she was praying."

At about this moment a small earnest man with staring eyes came up the road, his gaze fixed on Joshua. When he came abreast of Joshua and Lucia he stopped and turned and walked with them, on Joshua's right with Lucia on his left. While he walked the man stared at Joshua's face and Lucia stared at the man, resenting him, suspicious of him, afraid of him. Joshua seemed not to be aware of the man's fixed gaze, nor the man of Lucia's. She felt at first that there was menace in the situation but on sharpening her gaze she saw that the little man's face was gentle, his eyes wide, eager, expectant, his mouth hopeful—and while she was looking across Joshua at him she heard birds singing. Or was she sure of that? She looked left toward the river and around her at trees and was sure she could hear larks singing and more than larks, for there was a whole choir of birdsong, as if in heaven. She was so startled and confused that she dropped a parcel of food that she was carrying; and on recovering it and hastening to catch up she saw that the man was walking in stride with Joshua and still gazing at him. Did Joshua know it? Did Joshua hear the birds singing?

Aza was saying: "You know, mama, if we soak a while in these hot baths maybe we'll feel better. Joshua says people come to them from all over the world."

"Maybe," said Sarah, limping, panting, using all her strength merely to stand upright and walk.

"We'll just lie in them and soak like hogs."

"They're probably full now," Sarah said.

"Then we'll wait."

"And after we leave the baths we'll feel worse, so what's the use?"

"But every day, mama, the messiah is nearer. That's all that keeps me going."

Zillah was saying: "If we don't marry before the kingdom comes will we be allowed to marry then? And if not, are we to live forever and ever without children? Would you want that?"

"No woman would," Sirena said. "But the kingdom, Joshua says, lasts only a thousand years."

"What woman wants to live a thousand years without a baby? Lucia is smart. She hustled around and found one."

"It isn't her own."

"She loves it just as much. You know, I've been betrothed three times but the men all backed out. They said I was wicked. And so—but should I tell you this?"

Though sunk deep in whatever it was that troubled him Joshua became aware at last that a little man was walking at his side and staring at him. His gaze swept the man's face and took from it an impression of two large pleading eyes that asked a question. He turned toward Lucia and she said: "Can you hear the birds singing?"

"Birds?" said Joshua, frowning, blinking. "Who is this man?"

"I don't know," Lucia said softly.

Joshua turned again to the man and his gaze, full and strong and unblinking, met Joshua's eyes and overwhelmed them; and Joshua blinked hard and frowned and said to him. "Who are you?"

"I am Levi," the little man said.

"Why do you look at me that way?"

"Master, how is that? I look at you—"

"Don't call me master. My name is Joshua and I am on my way to the holy city."

"I have come from there," Levi said. "In Galilee they say, Go to the holy city, the messiah will be there. In the holy city some of them say, Ah, but he is in Galilee now."

"He will come to Jerusalem," Joshua said.

"But what man knows? At the baths they said he was in Tiberias and at Tiberias they say he is at the baths; and as some of them describe him he looks much like you."

"Like me?" cried Joshua, horrified. "Why do you say such senseless things?"

Lucia felt suffocated. The whole world was singing now.

"I only told you," Levi said gently, "what they are saying."

Zillah was saying: "Joshua said that the dead can bury the dead. Do you know what he meant?"

"No," said Sirena and sniffed politely. She wondered if Zillah had also bought a scent.

"It is an old Jewish saying. But the greatest was Hillel's, Love your neighbor as yourself and do nothing to him that you would not have him do to you. Joshua says that covers everything. What a man sows, said Hillel, he shall reap, and by his fruits we shall know him."

"He must have been a fine teacher," Sirena said.

"The greatest of them all, Joshua says. Oh, but Joshua loves Hillel! For Hillel never prayed, Blessed are you, O Lord our God, King of the Universe, who did not make me a woman. Hillel never said it and Joshua has never said it."

Joshua was saying: "He is not in Galilee. He is not anywhere around here. He will come first to the holy city, for that is the world's navel."

84

"There are more poor in Galilee," said Levi, still peering hard at Joshua's face, still unconvinced that this was not the messiah. "Won't he come where most of the poor are and most of the sick and the old and the outcast?"

"The wise men say he will come to the holy city."

"But who are the wise men but Pharisees and where do the Pharisees live?"

"Mama," said Aza, "may the Holy One forgive me but I have to rest a while." With his staff he poked at the roadside to learn if it had hidden anthills and then with a groan let his aching bones sink to the earth. After deliberating a moment Sarah went over and sank down at his side.

"They're resting," Sirena said, looking ahead at the old people, and left the road.

"I can smell the baths," Zillah said. "How long is it since you had a bath?"

Again and again this girl's questions flabbergasted Sirena. She looked at her now and could think of nothing to say.

"You know," said Zillah, going over to sit with Sirena, "only the wicked can be honest. The good have never learned how. I admit that I bought such garments as will show off my breasts and body but you wouldn't make such admissions. You're simply not aware of your motives."

"Let's not quarrel," Sirena said.

"My dear, we're not quarreling. I'm just facing the reality, that's all. If the messiah doesn't come till the ninth of Ab, that's almost three months; if not till the Day of Atonement, that's five months. That's a long time," said Zillah, thinking of what a woman could do in five months. "A woman could marry and have a child on the way. Would the messiah bless her for that?"

"Joshua doesn't seem to think so."

"But do you see how he kisses Lucia's baby?"

"Yes, I have seen. Look, they are going on."

"Please," Joshua was saying to Levi, "don't go tell anybody I look like the messiah. Nobody knows how the mes-

85

siah will look. See me here," said Joshua, shrugging his shoulders, "I'm only an ordinary man."

"No," said Levi, "I'm an ordinary man. Look at me."

Too disturbed to say more about it or to hear more Joshua suddenly strode on ahead, leaving Lucia and Levi together. Levi now looked at her, in the same guileless eager expectant way, as though nothing remained of his life but the emotions in hope and waiting.

"Is he?" he asked her.

Lucia put a finger to her lips and lightly shook her head no and after a moment of hesitation she said softly, "No," but she knew that he did not hear, that nobody at her side could possibly have heard, in a world where so many heavenly choirs were singing. She was straining to the music and looking ahead at Joshua's back when down under the bird-choirs she became aware of another sound, of the murmuring babble of many voices, and of crying and wailing as from babies and sick people; and she hastened ahead to catch up with Joshua and then stood with him, looking upon the greatest multitude she had ever seen. Before her and to the right and to the left and as far as she could see were hundreds or thousands of people gathered at the baths.

VII

There were many hot sulphur springs here, a few of which flowed away in smoking currents past Tiberias itself. All the finer baths, set aside in one area and fenced, were for people of wealth, chiefly the aristocracy from distant lands; but there was one enormous pool open to the common people and a few springs adjacent to it in which they could soak their feet. Convinced that the messiah would not come before the ninth of Ab, Joshua had decided, even though eager to push on, to pause here a few days to let the two old people rest and immerse their bones. When he walked ahead with Lucia and saw before them the scattered rabble of the sick, the blind and lame, the old, many of them almost naked with only a rag covering their loins, many of them so emaciated that they were little more than hide and bones, and some of them unable to rise from where they lay, he wondered if Levi was right. Perhaps the messiah would appear here first, for it looked as though all the homeless and unfortunate of the earth had gathered here to wait for him.

He went among them, followed by Lucia, and a little later by Sirena and Zillah, and saw creatures so ravaged by disease, so infested by running sores, that they were unable to stand but crawled like beasts, their sunken eyes, still kindled with hope, staring up at those who passed them; and others barely able to walk who hobbled along in their filthy rags, begging every person who would listen for news of the messiah; and some with parts of their bodies or faces eaten away, with eyes gone, or ears, or a part of their nose and mouth; and a few, unable to move at all, who seemed to be dying. Yes, in the name of God and his children, why should not the messiah come here first and why should he not hasten!

Joshua was staring at a man lying by the pool when a little old thing hobbled over and looked up at his face. He said this man had lain there for twenty years, reaching out and down with his shrunken hands to touch the healing waters, eating anything that was thrown to him, and praying day and night. "Poor man!" Joshua murmured and then pinched his nostrils, for the stink of these people filled the whole area and was so dreadful that Sirena had turned back. Of such as these, Joshua reflected, would be the kingdom of heaven. For such as these the messiah would come. Feeling great compassion he turned to the horrified Lucia, hugging her child and looking out from half-closed eyes, and said, "What have you there? Give it to him to eat and I will pray for him." Joshua took the little parcel of food and gave it to the prone man, and he looked up, his old eyes luminous with thanksgiving. With a finger that was nothing but shrunken bone and hide he touched Joshua's garment as Joshua stood above him and blessed him, and then pressed the finger to his lips.

Joshua learned that a false messiah had recently been here, haranguing the people, and that the Roman police had come and taken him away. This man had promised to throw down the walls of Tiberias. He had promised them that manna would fall from heaven until the earth would be white with it. He was taken away and some of his disciples went to find him; and they returned to tell this story, that when the Romans tried to crucify him he uttered the secret name of the Holy One and the soldiers turned to stone and the man ascended bodily to heaven. Well, Joshua reflected, the poor and the sick, God bless them, lived for wonders and miracles, and there were many wonder-workers who had phenomenal tales to tell. But when he walked among these people he saw only one question in the eyes of all: Are you the messiah, and if not, when will he come?

Joshua and his group spent the night at some distance from the baths and the stench. They had for supper only the food that Sarah had bought and in giving to each his portion she acted like one for whom this food would be her last. In Sarah's angry mind there was, of course, the thought that while she and Aza had denied themselves and bought food for all, Zillah and Sirena had spent all the gold that had been given them to adorn their vanity. This feeling was so plain and candid in her large unhappy peasant-face that Sirena set her portion aside and left the group, shame deep within her.

Sarah interrupted her eating and stared at the portion Sirena had left, as if by looking at it she could decide what to do about it. It was a segment of bread covered with honey and a small piece of cheese.

"Does anyone want it?" Sarah asked, looking at the bread but not at any of the faces.

"Maybe she'll eat it later," Lucia said.

"What I wonder," said Sarah, though what she wondered had for some time been plain in her face, "is what we'll eat when no money is left."

"Our Father will provide," Joshua said.

"I've heard that all my life," Sarah said, "but every crust I've had I've worked for. Except this," she said, looking at the bread in her hands.

"Don't worry about it," Lucia said. "I have some money."

"We all *had* some money," said Sarah and resumed her eating.

Joshua spent a restless, an almost sleepless, night. He had expected another sign, in the earth or in the skies, for it seemed to him that God would manifest his signs here, of all places, where two or three thousand people were anxiously waiting. He scanned the skies, he turned all his senses downward to the earth, but everything was serene above and below and there were no signs, save possibly the choir music which Lucia said she could hear. Now and then Joshua would hold his breath and listen but he could hear no bird-song, only the distant babble of voices, only cries of pain in the night.

The next morning he arose at the break of day and went again among those gathered around the pool and springs. He soon learned that there were teachers here and that each teacher had a group of a few or a score of persons who followed him as he went from place to place, striving for a larger audience. Joshua paused to hear what one of them was saying.

This teacher was a tall cadaverous man, with a grotesquely long arched nose, very narrow and thin, the point of which came down to the plane of his lower lip. His nerves had been shattered by long suffering, his mind filled with ghostly counsels and legends, as his eyes burned upon the vision that consumed him. He told his listeners that in Smyrna, long years ago, he had been stricken, and no physician in the city had been able to tell him what his illness was. From one to another he had journeyed to the temples of all the gods, to Chios, to Pergamum, to Cyzicus, to Epidaurus, to Athens, to Rome, to Alexandria —he had gone to all of them, racked by tumors and fainting spells and palpitations, tortured by pains that made him bend over like a bow. The physicians had prescribed fresh air baths, exercise, fasting, holy waters, sexual continence, purgings, blood-lettings, emetics and enemas, but not one had done him any good. He became so sick that he thought he would die and he suffered so dreadfully that he prayed for death.

Joshua moved closer, both ears open.

Before his presence, said this teacher, what had the oracles done? Why bless you, they had fallen silent. Was there wisdom in Dodona, Delphi, Ammon? Only the wisdom of a dull child or a foolish old man. Was there wisdom in Lebadea? Bah! It had told him to be gone. Cicero himself had consulted the Pythia and it had been tongue-tied. The shrine of Apis at Memphis had been dumb.

Had the shrine of the Paphian Venus cured the sick? "Listen," he said. "I knelt before it, I beseeched, my face wet with tears and it was silent. Then one night I lay down in a dim place and dreamed, where I could smell only the goat and the ox and the ass; and when I awoke I knew myself to be an agent of divine powers." His dropsical and dyspeptic symptoms, he said, had vanished; his tumors had shrunk and died; and he was no longer racked by fevers, coughs and bloatings. Since then he had been traveling over the wide world, healing those who suffered, consoling those who grieved, merely with a touch of his hand or garment.

When this man was done with his tale people crowded in to touch him, some of them crawling, some walking on those who crawled. Joshua moved around, closely observing all those who touched the man's garment but he saw none that was healed. He did hear some say that this was the messiah and he thought, How difficult it is for the common people to know! How many will be hanged before he comes!

What, Joshua wondered, moving slowly toward the pool, did all these people eat. Perhaps officials came out from Tiberias with food but he had seen no sign of them nor sign of food or of eating: it was as if all these people were suspended in their wasted frames between earth and heaven, hungering and waiting. Those who moved him to the deepest compassion were children. There were not so many of them, compared to the number of adults, but still, they seemed to be everywhere, the poor scrawny things with their sober eyes full of questions and their pale faces like masks. He was looking round at one and another when for a moment a child caught his gaze, a small girl, possibly seven or eight years old. At once she moved toward him, fearfully, her eyes on his face, her two hands hanging clenched at her sides. She came up to him and looked up at his eyes, her thin little face so grave, her brown eyes so full of wonder, her head tilted a little this way and then that, in the manner of a bird, as though tilting it gave her a fuller view of him or a deeper view. He knew what she was thinking and he did not like it. She was wondering if he was the messiah; and after she had studied his eyes and for a moment his mouth she looked at his robe and down at his feet.

"What is your name?" he said, made self-conscious by the intentness of her gaze.

"Mary." She met his eyes again. "What is yours?"

"Joshua."

"What will the messiah's name be?"

"I don't know."

Mary turned and looked across at a man and said: "He says there will be no messiah."

Joshua happened to glance at her hands and was startled. Her little fists had been enfolding two handfuls of sand and now, with the fingers relaxing, the sand was spilling down between the fingers. He had heard that the poor among his people sometimes clutched sand that way and pretended that they were paying tithes which they could not pay.

"We won't believe him," Joshua said. He had seen the old Cynic, a man who, like all those of his fraternity, announced his presence with a long beard, a coarse cloak and a staff. Cynics took as their badge ragged garments, poverty, unwashed bodies, uncombed hair and beard. Among them were hypocrites, dabblers, charlatans, sycophants; but this old man was sincere. It was a genuine principle with him to avoid marriage and labor, to scorn fashions, to denounce governments and priesthoods and thieving parasites, to scoff at oracles, wonder-workers, gods, angels, heavens and to pity those who believed in a life beyond death. When his day's teaching was done he was content with a jug of water and a piece of black bread.

Joshua moved toward the old Cynic, without looking again at Mary and ashamed that he did not again meet her eyes, yet knowing that if he gave her the slightest encouragement she would attach herself to him, as so many others would, to him or to anyone who would offer solace or listen to their woes. From another direction he saw Sirena approaching and observed that she had removed the fillet and let her golden hair down.

As Joshua and Sirena drew near to the Cynic's handful of people he was saying that there was no soul, no resurrection, no life after death. Such beliefs were fables for children and madmen. "My body is no longer pledged for my rent. I enjoy the free and perpetual hospitality of the world out-of-doors—"

"What is it like below, Charidas?"

He turned to Sirena and looked at her. "Ah, very dark."

"And what about our return from death?"

"Lies, all lies."

"Then I am done for?"

"Woman, you are done for."

Sirena had lifted from memory a famous epigram and was delighted to find him familiar with it. She was enjoying the moment when a little old hag gave an unearthly cackle and slapped her hindend. "Hoo-hoo!" she cried, her strange eyes giving Sirena the lie. "You red-headed devil! Wheeww!"

"Don't mind her," said the Cynic. "She's waiting for the messiah."

"Aren't we all?" asked Joshua.

"My good man, for countless centuries people have waited for a savior. He does not come."

The little woman, stooped over, her rump thrust out, was ambling around Sirena like a duck and making grotesque faces at her. Sirena moved so close to Joshua that the woman could not encircle her.

"Virtue," the Cynic was saying, "that we seek and cherish. There's nothing else worthy of all our sufferings in this nightmare of horror. Suffer we shall and must and alone."

"You don't believe God will leave his children in such misery as this?" asked Joshua.

"He has since time began. Is there anything new here?

Haven't disease and suffering and famine always been with us?"

Other people were coming up. They would stare at the old Cynic's face, at Joshua's, back and forth, their own faces as solemn as death.

"You're an evil here," said Joshua, "for you would take religion away from these people. You would leave them—"

"Man, what do you mean by religion? Romans worship their emperor, only a mortal man and usually one of the worst. Is that religion? It is for them. Is Augustus now worshiped as a god? Was it religion when Empedocles offered to make the winds blow or abate, the sun to shine or darken, old age to vanish and the dead to rise? People worshiped him. Was it religion when the Athenians built altars and shrines to him and appointed priests to worship him?

"No, don't interrupt me," he said lifting his staff. "You are ignorant and I would teach you. Thucydides tells us that the people of Amphipolis offered sacrifices to the Spartan general Brasidas. Because he had slain so many? Plato agreed with Hesiod that departed heroes become angels."

"Can you prove they don't?"

"I can't prove that you'll die but do you doubt it? Come, come now. The Roman senate enrolls the Caesars among the gods. Is that religion?"

"Not for a Jew. We don't believe in gods but only in God."

"The Father. And why in heaven's name do you have a Father but no Mother? Man, look around you. All these people are waiting for one they call a messiah, to overthrow their sorrows and lead them to eternal bliss. But that is illusion. All this—"

"Would a human father leave his children in such misery?"

"Many of them do. Look round you," he said, gesturing with his staff, "at these people rotting and groaning and dying. Does some father care for them?"

94

"Some father will, yes. He'll send a king to punish the wicked—"

"Oh, what vain hopes. A messiah, you tell me. Generations will wait and die, wait and die and he will never come. All over the world today they are waiting for a savior. Here you call him a king. Jews—"

"What would you have us do?" asked Joshua.

"Grow up, be adult, learn to get along without your father and your mother. Learn to accept the kind of life we have here. A great Jew said it: All things are full of labor, yea, man cannot utter it, and what has been will be again, and there is no new thing under the sun. Behold the tears of such as were oppressed, and they had no comforter; and on the side of their oppressors there was power, but they had no comforter. Better is a poor and a wise child than an old and foolish king. This also is vanity and vexation of spirit.

"My good man, what do you strive for? Some strive for fame, some for riches; but you seek eternal life for this wretched arrangement of flesh and bones that I see before me. Have you never sensed how colossal your vanity is, how childlike your hope? In your language madman and holy men are the same word. Come, I'll show you."

He took Joshua's arm and went with him, followed by those who had been listening, until they came to a tree, where a man lay on his back, his eyes open and staring. "This may be the kind of teacher you prefer, so listen to him. My good fellow," the Cynic said, prodding the man with his staff, "tell him what happened."

Blowing slobber from his lips the man gasped: "I went to heaven!"

"Very well, you went to heaven. How was it before you went?"

Twitching, shuddering as tremors moved through him, the man with great difficulty managed to say that he had been sad, he had wept, until there came a blinding light. . .

Sirena pushed through to look at him and saw that every

exposed part of his body was moist with sweat and that the ghastly pallor on his face was that of death.

Gasping the words out the man was telling them that he flew, he ascended, he entered vast worlds of light, he saw the heavens, the first, the second and third, the fourth, where everything was heavenly white light; and peace took him in as a child and God touched him with forgiveness and he shone like the heavens. . . .

It seemed to Joshua that the poor emaciated creature, naked but for a dirty rag across his loins, was in dreadful pain; for his fleshless arms were thrust out and twitching and even his eyes flickered from the tremors. He said to the Cynic, "Why do you torture him? Let's leave him with God."

Joshua went away and some of those who had heard him followed him. He did not want people to follow him and stare at him, for he knew that there were Roman spies here. He did not want to speak out, yet felt now and then that he had to speak; he did not want to remain here, yet when he looked at the pain in the faces of Aza and Sarah he knew that he would have to remain a little while.

He found them at the mud baths and they were so grotesque and in a way so happy that they forced Joshua to smile. There was mud and mire and swamp grass where one of the hot springs flowed across the pool, and there Aza and Sarah were buried, all but their faces. They were like hogs in a mud-wallow. Aza was next to the bank and he had one hand on the bank clutching their garments. Nothing was visible but the hand and forearm, his face, and Sarah's face just beyond him.

"How you feeling?" Joshua asked.

"Better," said Aza's lips, which were barely above the mud. His big eyes were winking in the sun.

Like some kind of weird aquatic beast that had surfaced, Sarah said, her lips moving just barely above the mud: "We both feel better."

Aza said: "I don't think Naomi likes this stinking hot mud. She isn't jumping around in me now."

Joshua gave a little laugh. Sarah was to reflect later that she had never heard him laugh before. "That's fine," he said. "Feel better as fast as you can, then we can go sooner."

"Any more signs?" asked Aza's thick lips.

"No signs but misery. That is sign enough."

Joshua thought he had shaken off the old Cynic but the next morning just as daybreak he sought Joshua out, a thick gray man in a hemp robe, wagging his beard and gesturing. "What do you think of whores?" he said. "Will they be in the kingdom?"

Joshua was rubbing at his eyes.

"There's a whore over here who tried to drown herself. I fished her out, though there is no reason for it. Someone will have to care for her or she will die."

Sirena had come up. "We haven't the food for her," she said.

The Cynic looked at her handsome garment. "For one with no food for a dying woman you dress well."

"Bring her to us," Joshua said.

The Cynic brought her over, a thin pale woman of unearthly loveliness. Her eyes were hazel, her skin fair, and her hair, hanging matted down her shoulders, was as black as night. With one hand she clutched a small linen bag. She looked at Joshua with her strange haunted eyes, unashamed in her wet garment that clung tight to her, revealing every curve of her body.

The Cynic said to Joshua: "She says her name is Sibyl and she is from Migdal."

She was looking at Joshua. "Is he the messiah?" she asked the Cynic.

"My dear, I've told you there is no messiah. Now conceal yourself somewhere and wring your clothes out and dry them."

"I feel the love of God here," she said and put a hand to her heart.

"Yes, dear. Now go dry your garment."

She reminded the Cynic unpleasantly of the Pythia at

Delphi, who fasted three days and chewed laurel leaves, when, intoxicated, and standing over a vent from which issued noxious vapors, she shook until her hair almost stood on end, while out of her convulsed and frothing mouth came the answers to questions.

"Over there behind that," he said to Sibyl, indicating a bramble hedge. When she was out of sight he turned to Joshua, his eyes twinkling. "A philosopher when asked why he never married said he was too fond of children. I never married because I have too much respect for whores." He looked at Sirena, as if to see what she made of that. Then he took Joshua's arm, saying. "Come with me, I want a word with you."

When they were out of hearing the old man faced Joshua and said: "You're in danger here. Do you know it?"

"In danger?" said Joshua, blinking fast and hard.

"I wouldn't let the notion get around that you might be the messiah. I saw one of those poor fellows crucified. You're too nice a person to be hung on a cross for the crows."

Joshua was astonished. "The messiah? Are you having fun with me? Who in the world would think I'm the messiah?"

"A lot of those people," said the Cynic, nodding toward the pool, "might think it of almost anyone. Sibyl thought it. The trouble is that once the idea gets started it's like a fire in a wind. Don't let it get started."

"What can I do about it?" Joshua said.

"Let everybody know that you're not. Rome has spies here, you know, but you can't tell who they are. They may be dressed as beggars. But you can be pretty sure, Joshua, that they have their eye on you."

"But why on me?"

"Man, are you as naive as you seem? You spend most of your time here with the poor and if you have been over the world you know that the poor are held in contempt everywhere. Yet you have been heard to say here that

98

the poor will be first in the kingdom. Can you imagine what the rich would want to do with a man who says that?"

"I hadn't thought about it," Joshua said.

"It might be well to think about it before you get into trouble, rather than afterward. The spies have already observed that you seem to be attracted not only to the poor but to the dumb and the blind, the epileptic and the paralytic, the insane, the leprous, the old, the sick. Roman officials don't want such people to make trouble and they have no mercy for any man who incites them to trouble."

"But have I been inciting them?" asked Joshua, blinking at the old man.

"Not deliberately, Joshua. But when you tell them that the messiah will soon come and the kingdom is near and that they will be first in the kingdom and all that you make them restless. You make them want to throw off their oppressors." He gestured with his staff and said, "Joshua, look. Thousands of people have left their homes, their farms, their jobs. Every day still more of them set out for Jerusalem. What do you think the Romans are going to do with all these mobs who think they are going somewhere to meet a king, a king who is going to overthrow Rome? And look at them, most of them don't even have anything to eat. Why, man, this whole land is moving toward anarchy."

"It will be all right," Joshua said, "when the messiah comes."

"I'm not going to argue that with you. I thought at first you were an impostor and I confess now that to test your sincerity I brought Sibyl to you." He looked at Joshua, waggling his old gray beard. "I hardly know what to make of you but it's because I like you that I give you this warning. You'd better be careful here. No man knows how many of these false messiahs they have already crucified."

"Thanks," Joshua said.

"One other thing," said the old man, his shrewd eyes studying Joshua. "There is a man here dressed like a beggar who has or pretends to have a stiff right leg. He

99

drags it this way," the Cynic said, showing Joshua how the beggar walked. "I think he's a spy. If you find him watching you that should be warning enough."

"Thanks again," Joshua said.

VIII

He was so deeply disturbed that he stayed away from the rabble the remainder of this day and he seemed so unhappy and withdrawn and strange that Lucia could not hide her motherly concern. She sat and looked at Joshua, shaking her head gently now and then, talking to herself a little, as a mother might who grieved for a child yet felt powerless to do anything for it. Joshua became aware that she was looking at him and he did not like it. Suddenly, losing all control, his temper exploded and he shouted at her, "Why do you stare at me that way? What's wrong with you?"

Astounded, speechless, Lucia could only shake her head oddly like a hen, her gaze darting but seeing nothing, all her emotions scattered into blind confusion.

"I'm sorry," Joshua said. "Forgive me, Lucia, but please don't look at me that way."

"What—what way?"

"The way you do."

Meanwhile the Cynic had found Sirena sitting on the bank talking to Aza and Sarah and had asked her to go to the shade of a tree and sit with him. "I'm worried about Joshua," he said.

"Why?"

"You're not a stupid woman," he said a little sharply. "You must be aware that the Romans have crucified quite a number of these messiahs. But first tell me, do you believe this folly?"

"Folly? You mean it's folly to believe that God will not leave his people in such misery?"

"You actually believe you will live again? If you never suffer can you ever be happy when free of pain? Can you—"

"I know all the arguments," she said. "But I also know there is more in life than formulas and syllogisms and philosophers. If there is no nobler meaning than what we find here, then it is all nightmare of such evil that we should all wish to be dead."

"Don't we?" he asked, twinkling at her.

"If you do then why don't you drown yourself?"

"My good woman, it's not my intelligence that clings to this wretched life. It's my irrational and unreasoning body. But no matter. I wanted to talk about Joshua. You women are going to get him into trouble."

"You've said that before. What do you mean?"

"Have you heard of Simeon? Well, no, I see that you haven't. Simeon was a good man like Joshua. He had no contempt for women, no scorn. He loved all people. -Some disciples began to follow him around and they began to think he might be the messiah. Then the Romans came and that was the end of Simeon. *Was* he the messiah?"

"You mean—"

"I mean the Romans crucified him. It seems that no matter what people they live under the Jews make trouble. Look yonder at Tiberias. The Procurator is there. He hates Jews. Not long ago he ordered his troops to march into Jerusalem carrying banners with the image of the emperor. Then what? The Jews, a whole vast multitude, went to Pilate and begged him to have the emblems removed. He wouldn't. For five days and nights—I was there and I saw it—those thousands of people before his residence wept and beseeched him. He decided to ambush and destroy them. He told them to go to the Hippodrome, where he had soldiers concealed. He then spoke to the Jews, saying, Every Jew will die who doesn't pledge his loyalty to Caesar and return at once to his work. And what did they do? The whole multitude fell down on their faces

102

and begged to be slain rather than have their city desecrated with the emperor's image.

"My good woman, you can't do anything with a people like that. I'll tell you another thing. At this very moment Pilate is building an aqueduct to Jerusalem. To pay for it he took some of the temple treasure. What did the Jews do? Wailed and clamored and made such an infernal nuisance of themselves that he dressed his soldiers in peasant garb and told them to murder every wailing Jew they could find. And they did. Hundreds were killed that day."

He touched her gently with his staff. "Do you pretend to understand them?"

"Not very well."

"Take this messiah-king who is supposed to come. Do you know what it would mean if Jews were to acclaim some man as their king? Why, bless you, they would revolt against Rome, as they may some day anyhow, and they'd all be killed. If the Romans are to have law and order they have to destroy these messiahs as fast as they appear."

"You're talking about impostors. When the messiah comes he'll overthrow Rome."

"Are you mad? There'll never be any messiah more genuine than Joshua. Try to make a place in your foggy skull for that thought. And don't forget Simeon."

"Oh yes, I understand all that. But if Joshua is law-abiding and doesn't offend anyone—"

"Did Simeon? He was all love and kindness. If Joshua were to sit inside a pig and blaspheme the Holy Name he couldn't be more offensive to devout Jews than he now is. He mixes with the unclean. He pays no attention to the Sabbath. He accepts all people as his brothers. He—"

"I mean if he doesn't offend the Romans."

"Did Simeon? It was his goodness that was the menace. Is that truth too simple for you, or too profound? It's not evil that people really hate. It's persons who make them conscious of the evil in themselves."

103

"I've told Joshua that it is love that makes us weak before our enemies."

"Fine! You said it very well. And what did he say?"

"He said that love will conquer."

"So it may, alas, some time. Without hate can there be strength? These Jews are a strong people. Even their enemies must admit that. They hate as no people in the world hate. Their whole land is inflamed with suspicions and anxieties and the Zealots are trying to stir up a rebellion. I tell you a man doesn't have to offend God to get hung up. This whole land is explosive."

"All right," she said impatiently, "what do you want me to do?"

"Do you love Joshua?"

Sirena shrugged. "I don't know what you mean by love."

"You're a pretty arrogant woman," the old man said. "Perhaps you love only Sirena. But you're moving toward a tragedy—"

"Yes, yes, so you tell me but what can I do?"

"Persuade Joshua to go on."

"There are other spies in other places. He says the messiah won't come before the Jewish month of Ab or maybe the Day of Atonement. He seems to like to be with such people as these."

"He seems to draw the unfortunate to him." By moving the muscles of his chin he wagged his beard at her, admonishing, chiding. She looked into old eyes that were fading, smiling eyes, the eyes of a man who had seen much and understood a part of it.

"A philosopher once said that people destroy their gods. Is that what you are saying?"

"Well, yes, in a way I suppose it is. People try to absorb the ideals they create. The ironic thing, my good woman, about the whole thing is this, that the only kind of messiah who won't be destroyed is the kind some of the Jews expect, a mighty king with armies and banners. Those

104

who come with peace never last long and are soon forgotten."

"Then what do we live for?"

"Not much. Well, I must leave you now. All we can do is to admonish Joshua. He must decide the thing for himself."

After the old man had left her Sirena felt ill. She felt a great fright inside her and the presence of evil all around her. There must be God, she thought. There must be some reason for the beggar's filth, the leper's sores, the slave's torments—some purpose, some eventual good, some higher guiding will. For if there was not, life was all nightmare and a curse.

Should she try to persuade Joshua to move on? Would he be safer in another place than here?—or less safe perhaps, because the spies were more vigilant and numerous the closer they drew to the holy city. Joshua wanted to teach or at least to console and comfort the multitudes of suffering people but Sirena as well as the old man knew that he could do it only at the risk of his life. So what, she wondered impatiently, should she say to him, or should she say anything at all?

She went to the spot where they camped, a fairly secluded spot fenced on three sides by a high bramble hedge and overhung by a very old palm tree. Lucia was there with her child, and Sibyl, looking more pale and angelic than when she was drenched and half-drowned.

"Where is Joshua?" Sirena asked Lucia.

"He went off that way," Lucia said.

Sirena found him after a few moments. He was sitting alone by a tree, his knees drawn up to him, his arms around his knees and his chest sunk forward, his eyes looking away toward Jerusalem. His eyes began to blink hard and fast when he saw Sirena approaching and when she stood before him his gaze swept her face and his forehead drew into a deep frown. She knew that he was very unhappy and that he wished to be alone.

"I'll be only a minute," she said, sinking to the earth

an arm's length from him. "I've been talking to the old Cynic."

"I know it," he said.

"No doubt you know what he has been saying. He thinks you should go on."

"He means there are no spies in the holy city!"

"How long would you like to stay here?"

"I don't know," he said. He did not want to talk about it.

"If Aza and Sarah are ready are you ready to go?"

"I suppose," he said, looking away at the sky.

"Shall I go see if they feel strong enough now?"

"If you wish to."

"Please don't resent me so," she said. "I did not wish to bother you with this but the old man thought I should."

"That's all right," he said. "He means well."

Sirena got to her feet and stood, hesitating, looking down at him, wondering about him. "I'll see what they say," she said.

She found Aza and Sarah lying prone in the hot water and mud, their faces looking almost benign.

"Aza, are you asleep?"

He opened his big eyes and blinked in the sun. "I was just about," he said.

"Are you and Sarah ready to move on?"

"Mama, did you hear? You think we can walk to Jericho?"

"Is that where the wonders are?"

"Have you heard about them?" Aza asked, turning a little and blinking at Sirena. "They say there is a great wonder-worker on the Jordan near Jericho."

"You hear about wonder-workers all over Israel."

"Mama, shall we go with them or shall we stay?"

"You old fool, if we stay what shall we eat?"

"What'll we eat if we don't stay?" Between winks his eyes were appraising Sirena's robe. "Does Joshua want to go?"

"We all think mabye we'd better move on."

"Well, mama, I guess we have to walk again."

This night Sirena slept only a little. How, she wondered, did people sleep anyway lying on the hard earth without blankets or pillow? Perhaps it was all right if you were fat and cushioned but she was rather angular and she could find no position in which all her bones were at rest. Aza slept on his back and snored like a hog. Zillah usually lay on her left side with her knees drawn up. Sirena lay on her back and looked at the stars and listened to the sleep-sounds of those around her and tried to imagine what the next weeks or months would bring. Would there be a messiah after all?

It was understood that in the morning they would all depart. Everything was settled. Everyone was agreeable. And who, Sirena was to ask herself afterward, who then made a dreadful mess of the whole thing? Who precipitated the matter almost to the brink of disaster? It happened this way. . . .

Having slept only a little Sirena was irritable when morning came and unhappy and short of temper and eaten by doubts. During her time here she had heard a number of the philosophers and all of them, like the old Cynic, had heaped scorn upon the idea of messiahs and saviors. Before they left the area of the baths there was one thing she wanted to say to him and just at daybreak she slipped away. She wanted to say to him, "In one of Plato's dialogues Alcibiades is asked, Would you accept dominion of the whole world in exchange for your soul? And he said what all intelligent persons must say: If I lost my soul of what use would the world be to me?" She wanted to say to him, angrily, scornfully, "You say there is no soul! How, then, are we any higher than the beasts?"

But while she was looking for the old Cynic her attention was drawn to another teacher, a disciple of Buddha, a small sunbaked man with bright animallike eyes and a high thin voice. He was talking to a few persons and in passing she heard him say: "A woman can become a mother without pleasure in sex."

Her temper flared. She was getting awfully tired of men who spoke with complacent scorn of women. At once she hastened over and hurled the challenge: "How would you know? Are you a father? Are you also going to tell us that children are born in sin?"

"They are," the little old man said.

"If motherhood is base, then the world is too wicked for anyone to care what happens to it. If noble, how dare you say children are born in sin?"

He put a finger in his short beard and scratched and considered. "Well," he said at last, "we have to distinguish between acts that may be evil in themselves, and acts which, while seeming to be good, may produce evil. The Jews have a saying that all bastard children are unusually bright because produced with such intense raptures." Deep in his throat Sirena heard a chuckle. "If adultery produces intelligence is it wicked? The great and wise Buddha taught us that all life is pain and pain comes from our passions. When we destroy our desires we shall be wise."

"You mean," said Sirena, "when we destroy the human race! You mean that when we destroy in women the desire for children we shall be wise!"

"Woman, be patient and I will tell you. Buddha said, Now this, O monks, is the cause of pain: that craving which leads to rebirth, combined with pleasure and lust, finding pleasure here and there, namely, the craving for passion, the craving for existence. This, he said, is the way to wisdom: right views, right intention, right speech, right action, right living, right effort."

"What a fine circle to round around on! Who determines what is right?"

The Cynic had come up to listen. Other people were gathering, attracted by Sirena's shrill angry voice.

"Buddha said the great evil is sexual desire, for that leads to birth, which perpetuates suffering. Among his five moral rules the fifth is, Let nobody be unchaste."

"This Buddha must have been an awful fool! You're

telling us he believed in the extinction of the race. Isn't a woman unchaste if she mates to have a child?"

"Why of course she is."

"Then your Buddha taught race suicide."

"Oh no. He said suicide would be useless, because the impure soul would be reborn, would have another in- carnation."

Tossing her flaming hair Sirena looked round her. "What we need," she said, glancing at the Cynic, "is the extinction of all male philosophers. This Buddha didn't like women, did he?"

"Buddha—"

"Answer me! Have you ever known a philosopher who liked women?"

"The Master taught us to overcome anger with kind- ness, hate with love."

"Why should we love what we don't want to perpetu- ate?"

"Buddha—"

"Answer me!"

"Very well, woman, but don't shriek at me." He re- garded her thoughtfully a few moments and said: "In re- gard to women, I do recall now that his disciple Ananda once asked him, Master, how shall we conduct ourselves around women? And the Master replied, By not seeing them, Ananda. And if we do see them, said Ananda, what shall we do? Don't talk to them, Ananda. But if they speak to us what shall we do? Keep wide awake, Ananda."

Sirena sucked her breath in. "Well!" she said. "That's plain enough! He had contempt for women, this Buddha, and so have you. What a pity it is that you men can't be born without us! How wonderful if every one of you were an hermaphrodite so that you could beget your image without assistance!"

"You are bitter."

"We women have a right to be. We are not to have children. We're simply to wait and die and everything will be fine!"

109

Zillah and Lucia had come over and Lucia was tugging at Sirena's arm, trying to draw her away. Without looking to see who it was Sirena threw the hand off. She turned and met the Cynic's eyes and cried at him, "Why do men hate women? And if the passion in mating is sinful why place the whole burden on us?" She was outraged, deeply outraged, angry, bitter, almost beside herself. Her whole face and throat were almost as red as her hair. Her eyes were so inflamed and challenging that no man at whom she looked would meet her gaze, and least of all Joshua, who had now come up.

"In the holy books of the Jews," she went on, "there's a story. It says that man was happy and godlike until woman seduced him into sin. It's a vile and stupid and contemptible story and it was a vile and stupid and contemptible man who invented it! It's a *man's* story! What would the story be if a woman had written it?"

She waited, and lowering her voice a little said: "I'll tell you. Woman would have been happy, devoted to her children and their welfare. But man made a whore of her. Men put her in their temples to mate with men, so her shameful earnings could support a priesthood—*of men!* Men took her as his woman, concubine, slave, property, chattel; mated with her when he pleased; cast her off when he pleased." She drew an angry hissing breath. She shrugged like one who disliked clothes and would preferred to stand forth naked. "Today on Delos, in Rome, in Antioch, in a thousand places men sell women into whoredom. And you have the incredible gall to say that *we* brought sin into the world!—we, the mothers, nurses, slaves! Buddha! What a nasty creature he must have been! Plato! What a prodigious fraud! Even Socrates, Euripides, Aristophanes, Aeschylus—they have all left the record of their contempt!"

She tossed her flaming hair back; and her eyes, wet with the tears of rage, looked round her at the men and at last saw Joshua and softened a little. Lucia was softly weeping. Zillah stood back, her eyes lidded, studying Sirena's face

110

and gestures. A lot of people had gathered around now and they were all looking at this woman.

"You men have no answers but the brothel. You'll go on with your damned contempt and abuse, degrading us, trying to shame us, making us the playthings of your lust, making us ashamed to be mothers, ashamed to conceive our children in joy, while you have your gods born of virgins; you will go on listening to your queer half-man philosophers until we women get enough of it. Then we will hate you and O God how we will hate you for having done these things to us, your wives and mothers, your cooks and nurses and your only tenderness. If only I could be alive when that time comes! If only I could help destroy you as you are destroying us! If only we could find a way to have children without you! And we will, God help us, we will!"

She was close to hysteria and collapse. Her violent passions had aroused her audience and there were murmurings like those of beasts getting ready to stampede; and while she stood there, shaken and trembling and turning white as her blood drained away, there was a profane shriek and an obscene cry and the little old hag rushed in and smote her and spit up at her face and turned, slapping her round plump buttocks and her overhanging belly.

IX

She did not walk erect, this queer little woman, but trotted in a strange beastlike way, bent forward, her rump thrust out, her spine sagging, her small bright eyes peering up at people and hating them. She now hastened away from Sirena, as though afraid of attack, and stared up at a face and cried, "No, it's not you!" She trotted to another and peered and said, "No, it's not you!" The multitude that had been listening to Sirena's tirade now fell apart and transferred its interest; and rumors at once began to run from tongue to tongue. What did she mean by saying, It's not you? Had this queer creature the power to recognize the messiah?

Like a bentover witch, her skinny hands clutching her garment and her gray head shaking as with fever, this woman hopped around like a grotesque toad and peered and cried, "No, it's not you!" People began to follow after her, and other people at a distance, seeing the excitement, began to move over; and the woman kept hopping and crying and peering and slapping until she again came to Sirena. There was then an astonishing transformation. She moved round and round Sirena, bent over, studying her, her ridiculous rump thrust out, her head turning from side to side on her scrawny neck, her eyes birdlike and suspicious. Sirena rushed at her angrily and told her to go away but the little thing paid no attention at all. When Sirena then moved to slap her or to push her over she hopped away like an ungainly toad but with surprising agility.

But she was back in a moment, her eyes peering and calculating; and after hopping toward Sirena and back and toward her, like one whose mind could think only when its body was in violent motion, she gave a shrill and blood-chilling cackle of triumph and gloating and began to gesticulate. "It's her!" she shrieked. She was pointing a finger at Sirena. "It's her!" She swung and slapped a buttock at Sirena and loped away; swung again, and placing two fingers in her mouth gave a shrill whistle. "It's her!" she cried and hopped away, slapping her rump with both hands. Then she began to prance in the most grotesque way, her buttocks rolling as though they half-turned in sockets, her pendulous belly jouncing up and down and her arms flapping like broken wings. "Hoo-hoo!" she was shrieking, and to some she sounded overjoyed and to some in torture. "Hoo-hoo!"

A great throng of people was watching her and some were suggesting one thing and some another. Some thought she was a witch who was laying on Sirena a horrible spell or curse and these people were watching Sirena to see if she would fall over convulsed or give up the ghost and die. Joshua had just seen the man who dragged one leg and he wanted to get away from here. He beckoned to Sirena to come with him but she did not see him and she still stood alone, redfaced and dismayed and angry, while the disfigured and slouching old harpy grimaced around her and fixed upon her the attention of everyone present. She was shouting, her voice now thin and ghostlike. She was dancing right up to the paralyzed Sirena and poking at her with dirty fingers as the hellhag chanted, "Hoo-hoo, it's you! . . ." Turning suddenly she slapped her right rump, swung the other way and slapped her left, and with each slap she hoisted the side of her that had been slapped; and presently she was alternately slapping and hoisting, all the while keeping up the chant, her whole being pos-

sessed with an ageless coquetry so shrewd that it was time-
less.

Out of the throng now there rushed another old woman,
a hag still more decrepit and sordid, who began to imitate
the one who was laying the spell on Sirena. Her voice was
shriller, wilder, her movements and gestures less graceful;
and she hopped around, slapping madly at her rear and
emitting a shrill cry with each slap. Sirena's dulled and
fogged senses realized that these hags were mocking and
rebuking her because of something she had said—something in defense of women? But how could that be! Still,
these were not women, these creatures, but only things that
had once been women; and now there was a third, a fourth;
and then they were hopping and loping by twos or in
small groups, as more and more emotions were sucked into
the vacuum and more and more people took up the dance
and the cry. It was frightening for anyone like the old
Cynic who was still in possession of his senses. Round and
round they went, these things that were neither human
nor beast, slapping their rumps and shrieking. Some of
the men now began to prance, even old men who for years
had walked limping and bent over in pain; and swiftly the
mob became so hysterical that the Cynic came up to Joshua
and seized his arm to draw him away. As for Sirena, she
was now completely fenced in by these hopping people
who were shrieking and mocking and slapping their
hinders at her.

The first of the old hags was not to hold her dancing
choir together very long. Creative impulses were surging
up in the mob, old yearnings, hates, bitternesses were boiling at the surface; and one and another began to improvise
as the spirit moved him. A tall thin man with a deeply
pocked and scarred face and a bald head began to dance
alternately on one leg and the other, hopping three times
on one and chirping, "Up—up—up!" and chirping again
while hopping on the other leg, the unused leg meanwhile
bent on the foot drawn up to the thigh, his eyes staring
up, his thin gray beard romping up and down his chest.

114

Some fell to their hands and knees and chased around or back and forth, squealing or barking or grunting, sniffing, scratching, pawing, or trying to mount one another in the way of beasts or to smell out the rutting odors or to nip at shoulders in the way of studs. Among those rushing and squealing on the earth was a big man with a beard that reached almost to his hands. The old hag who first danced around Sirena came rushing to this man and sat astride him as though he were a horse; and when she smote him and encouraged him to gallop he did his best, his eyes glazed, going on hands and feet with his rump high in the air and with every leap almost pitching the old woman over his head. . . .

The hysteria spread like a contagion and the whole area rang with the wild animal-like sounds. Some of the people did things that caused those with more delicacy or more presence of mind to avert their faces. Some yielded so completely to passions that had long smouldered deep within them that they were besides themselves and ran squealing or howling or leaping, their emotions touched off and fired by what fell upon their sight or ears; somersaulting and rolling, trying to kill or falling under in submission to the killer, trying to drag one another down. Some of them were making copulative movements, monotonously and mindlessly repetitive, like automata in a tableau. Others had fallen exhausted, their mounths open and wet and their eyes turning feebly in their skulls.

Zillah was sitting. Joshua happened to glance at her and thought she was acting strangely, for she seemed to be shaking all over, seemed to be strangled by an unholy passion. He went over to her and reached down to take her arm, intending to lead her away, but at once she threw both her arms around his legs, clasping him and clawing, baring her teeth and biting. With both hands he tried to fight her off and break her grasp.

"Zillah, you fool!" he said, angered and astonished.

Lucia then saw what had happened. She ran to the Cynic and thrust her child at him and then flew to the attack.

She first seized Zillah by her hair and tried to drag her off. Joshua fell or threw himself down and began to kick with his legs, struggling to be free. But Zillah was hanging on with all her strength. She was not biting him now. So far as the horrified Lucia could tell she was trying to kiss his legs and to draw them snugly against her, into the valley between her breasts. While the three of them fought, Sibyl also dashed in and seized Zillah's hair and the two women pulled and yanked at her and kicked at her but Zillah had her face buried firmly against Joshua and she was not to be moved.

"You wicked woman!" Lucia cried, breathing desperately against her. "You wicked wicked woman!"

Despairing, Lucia relaxed her clutch on Zillah's hair and looked round her for a weapon; and she might have found one and knocked Zillah senseless if at this moment Sirena had not leapt in. When, standing close and looking, she had seen the pain and disgust and passion in Joshua's convulsed face she flung herself on Zillah and began to bite and gouge with every weapon she had, including her toes. With her toenails she tried to rake the girl up and down her bare legs; with her fingernails she was tearing into Zillah's plump breasts, which she was reaching to under the garment; and with her strong and slightly outthrust teeth she fixed on one of Zillah's ears. And so they struggled and fought, Joshua the prisoner of four women, three of whom seemed wildly bent on killing the fourth.

The old Cynic held the child and chuckled.

Lucia at last leapt back and looked round her for a club or stone, her head jerking, her eyes darting in the queer way she had when she was churned in her emotional depths. The old man stepped forward to restrain her.

"Look," he said, "are you women or beasts?"

"Save him!" Lucia begged. "She's killing him!"

"I don't think they'll hurt him," he said.

"Please help me!"

"Strange, strange," he said, grave and reflective. "Women will fight over men, from the humblest whore to the haughtiest princess. Yet this Sirena has been saying—"

"Will you do something?" Lucia begged, clutching his arm.

"My dear woman, why should I? In such moments as this the philosopher learns most. Here's your child."

"Zillah!" Joshua was crying, his voice choked with shame.

Sibyl had withdrawn from the fight, exhausted. Zillah was still clasping Joshua's legs, now bared almost to his crotch, and Sirena was still gouging at Zillah, determined to make her let go. The Cynic went over to look at the two embroiled and desperate women and then rapped Sirena smartly on her skull with his staff.

"Woman, have you no brains? Virtue, said Aristippus, restrains us from excesses of passion that degrade us. Do you find pleasure in this shameless and ragpicking barbarism?" He rapped her skull again. "Sirena," he said, taking a handful of her long red hair, "if you don't desist I'll yank your scalp off."

He yanked, gently and then more severely, and Sirena got to her feet. Her handsome garment was torn, her tangled hair was filled with earth, her face was distorted by the ugly passions still beating loud in her heart. She flung her hair back and turned a white and distorted face on the Cynic.

"Why are you always snooping around?"

"I'm like Israel's Elijah, for whom they set the chair. I try to be where I'm needed most." He again grasped her hair, saying, "Haven't you run with the dogs long enough? You'd better go to a mirror and look at your face."

He turned to Zillah and told her to get up but Zillah was not Sirena. For a moment she was quiet and he thought she was preparing to obey; but then, suddenly, with all the wild fury of her being she was up and hurling herself at him, her fingers like talons and her feet like clubs. Dismayed, he backed off, trying in gentle ways to defend himself; until, convinced that she intended to kill him, he smote her with his staff. She paused and staggered, her eyes rolling.

"My God," said Lucia, "you've killed her!"

"Well, that's only what you were trying to do. The wicked don't die so easily."

After staggering around, Zillah toppled and fell and rolled over, twitching; but whether she was senseless or acting the old man was not able to tell. Joshua meanwhile was lying back, panting, done in, his eyes blinking at the sky, his whole face alive with tiny spasms.

The Cynic went over and looked down at him. "You'd better get up," he said. "Somebody has to control this mob or it will get out of hand."

Joshua sat up. "Why?" he said, blinking.

"Man, look round you. Over in the pool one is floating who fell in or jumped in. A husband for what he calls love of his god is beating his wife to death. The passions of these people have been aroused. They are dangerous."

Joshua got to his feet. "What can I do?" he said.

"What can any man do? Perhaps nothing at all. Sirena is the one who started them off. Perhaps we should put the burden on her."

Some of the people had fallen so completely under the power of demons that they took the posture of beasts and ran or hopped or rolled around barking and growling and hissing and fighting among themselves like a frightened menagerie turned loose. Others were wildly singing or prophesying in unintelligible tongues. Others were weeping or praying. The hysteria was so loud and becoming so violent that the Cynic said:

"If Roman officials happen along and see this they'll have to find a goat. And you, Joshua, might be the goat. Can you do anything to quiet them?"

Joshua found the thought repugnant. He had never thought of himself as a teacher or guide. "If I tried to do anything," he said, "I'd only make it worse."

"Then perhaps you should leave now."

"That would be cowardly," Joshua said.

After a little while of thought he did go over to a hysterical group of almost naked persons who, exhausted by their frenzies, were weeping.

"Let us pray," he said. He bowed his head above them, saying, "Suffer not, O Lord, that we should be led into sin, or into transgression, or into disgrace; put away from us all evil thoughts, in order that we may attach ourselves to those that are good—" He broke off, feeling that he might as well drop snowflakes into a raging fire. None of the prostrate people were listening to him. They continued to weep and wring their hands and moan over one another, like mourners at an open grave.

Lucia had come up. She said: "Pray a simple prayer that they can understand."

"I know only the prayers I was taught."

"Make one up," she said. She stepped forward to hide a man's shame by drawing his rag over him. She turned back to Joshua and said: "Tell them about the kingdom."

Joshua looked round him for the man who dragged one leg or for the approach of Roman officials. He saw none of them. He did see the Cynic standing apart, watching him.

Lucia had left him to go among the people, saying, "Come, a holy man is here who will tell you about the kingdom!" In a lower voice she said, "See, over there he stands. Please come, for he will tell you. . . ." And one or two or a half-dozen went over to Joshua, followed at last by another and still another, as Lucia continued to entreat and arouse them; until he was surrounded by a group, some standing, others on their hands and knees. Lucia slipped up to him and whispered: "Now tell them about the kingdom! Nobody can tell it the way you do!"

"Tell us!" a man begged.

Another asked. "Are you a Jewish rab?"

A third gestured despairingly at the heavens: "How can we tell when the messiah will come?"

Forgetting to be prudent, knowing only how to be gentle, Joshua explained to them that wise men, using the sacred books in which the whole future had been foretold, had determined these things. The wise men of Israel had learned that the world would endure only six thousand years. They had learned that the six thousand years would end soon and that the kingdom would be ushered in. . . .

Other people were coming over as Lucia hastened from group to group.

"When will the messiah come?"

"Yes, in God's name, tell us that!"

"If you know, tell us, if not, don't waste our time, for we have traveled the length and breadth of Israel and we have listened to fools."

Nobody, Joshua told them, knew the exact day. It was believed that he would come on a holy day, on the ninth of Ab or on the next Day of Atonement or in the time of the next Passover. . . .

Sirena had come up and was now staring at the people on the inner circle—at the leprous, blind, lame, dumb; at old harlots, castaways, pariahs, escaped slaves, beggars, drunkards; the kithless and homeless and estranged, the lonely and forgotten, the feebleminded and insane—they were all here, ragged, emaciated, stinking. Covered with vermin they spent a part of their time scratching themselves or peering into one another's hair. They urinated or made wind with the lack of self-consciousness of the beasts.

To comfort them, Joshua was telling them what the wise men said about Israel—that its very air was a blessing; that there was no learning anywhere in the wide world like that in Israel; that merely to live in Israel, and particularly in Judea, was equal to the observance of all the commandments in any other land; that one, any one, who lived in Israel was sure to inherit life in the next world. Ah, what a glory it was! There were wise men, the great rabs and teachers, who said that anyone who dwelt in Israel was without sin; that whoever was buried in Israel it was as though he were buried under an altar; that on resurrection day those buried in Israel would be the first to see

God; indeed, that those buried in Israel would rise from their graves a whole month in advance of those buried in other lands. . . .

But they did not want to hear these things. They clamored and shouted at him, demanding to know when the messiah would come and what their rank and privileges and blessings would be in the next life. Raising his voice in the din Joshua told them to repent, to accept the glad tidings, to do the will of the Holy One, to love their neighbor as themselves. He told them that the poor would be blessed, the humble would be exalted, the sorrowing would be comforted, the pure in heart would see God, and the peacemakers above all others would be his children. Here before him, he said, were his brothers and sisters, the salt of the earth. If they laid up the treasures of good deeds on earth they would have in heaven treasures more precious than pearls and rubies. They had only to humble themselves and ask, and they would receive. "For as the light of the body is the eye, so the light of the soul is the pure thought. You'll be judged there by the love in your heart here. . . ."

But where was God? they wanted to know. Had he forgotten his people?

Where was the messiah? they wanted to know. Would he never come?

God, Joshua told them, was everywhere. He was in the lilies, in the feeding of ravens, in the flight of birds, in the number of hairs on their heads and in the number that had fallen. He saw all things and knew all things and was in all things. Even at that moment he was listening to every word spoken and looking into every heart. He was measuring their good deeds against their evil deeds; for with the measure that they measured to a neighbor, so it would be measured to them. He was a God of mercy and compassion and lovingkindness. "He takes the hand of the penitent, he forgives the sinful, he lifts up the weary and the heavy laden, he bids us all come. . . ."

His audience was growing. Among those standing close

to him were two sightless old men who held their heads high like people who could see. The deaf, sensing the spirit of the meeting, stood tense and expectant, like people who could hear. The dumb were making efforts to speak. The golden promise of Joshua's words was shining in many faces; and even the old Cynic, who had come up to listen, seemed, Sirena thought, to be affected by the simple story of divine forgiveness of the weak and redress of human wrong.

Joshua was now telling them that a great and mighty one would come, the root of Jesse, a son of David, to establish the kingdom on earth. For a thousand years he would rule, while all nations and tongues bowed before him. Satan, the prince of evil, would be overcome and cast down; and goodness and peace and joy would prevail over the whole unhappy earth. To share in this infinite love and glory the people had only to confess their wickedness, to repent, and to acknowledge the one and only God. . . .

A man cried out, "There can be no salvation for me! I killed my father!" A loathsome thing, all skin and bones, with patches of hairy hide showing through his ragged cloak, he had put both trembling arms across his forehead, as though to shut out the sky.

He had only to repent, Joshua was telling him, when a shrill old woman flung a hand his way and silenced him.

"Can I be saved? Rab, look at me, this thing of sin!" She flung out her skinny arms, prodded wantonly at her withered breasts, kicked out with her shrunken legs, shrieking, "See this thing of sin!"

"Repent—"

"Rab, O holy man, see this thing of sin! Listen to this foul tongue that has done things you have never dreamed of! I have lain with ten thousand men! I have drunk—"

"God damn you, shut up!" a man said and clapped a hand to her mouth.

She struggled and broke away, crying, "Son of man, see me!"

"Don't call me the son of man," Joshua said quickly but the mischief had been wrought.

People turned to one another, asking, Is *this* the son of man?

They looked into the eyes of one another, thinking, Is this the one mentioned in Daniel who will come on the clouds?

Was this the perfect and eternal man, the messiah-king?

A voice was shouting, "Master—"

"Don't call me master!" Joshua cried angrily.

"Master, are you the son of man? It is written, I saw in the night visions, and, behold, one like the son of man came with the clouds of heaven and came to the Ancient of Days—"

"No, no!" Joshua said, horrified.

But the man would not be put off. "And there was given him dominion and glory and a kingdom, that all people, nations and languages should serve him—"

"Silence!" Joshua shouted. "I am only a common man like you. I—"

"Don't be a fool!" Sirena said to the man.

"This, then, is the son of man?" a distant voice asked.

A woman was yelling: "Master, hear me!"

"I'm not the master!" said Joshua despairingly. "Will you people listen—"

"Master, hear me! The sin I sinned—"

"If he's the son of man let him perform a great wonder! There are sick here. Let him heal one of the sick."

"Master, tell me, have I been a wicked wife?"

"Let him perform a wonder!"

"Master, here is one who would confess. Hear him!"

"I'm not a master!" Joshua cried helplessly.

Sirena pushed forward. "You fools shut up calling him that!"

"Who is this redhead?"

"Perform a wonder if you're the son of man! Give us a sign so that we shall know!"

123

A woman's voice was yelling: "I can see the light around him!"

"You old fool!" Sirena said.

"Master, see this thing of sin. I have drunk—"

"Oh, God damn you, you old whore! Cut that foul tongue out!"

A man was now standing above the crowd, his feet on a stone. He had bulging black eyes and he was very angry and he was waving both arms to get attention. "Listen to me!" he bellowed. "Listen, you wicked impostor! Who in hell are you that you should come here and judge us?"

Hands pushed him off the stone and a man smote him, crying, "You son of a pig! Shall a teacher cast his pearls before such swine as you?"

"Master, hear this woman!" A number of hands were hoisting her and voices were entreating for silence. She was lifted to the shoulders of two men, and when the din subsided, so that she could be heard, this old grandmother, without a tooth in her head, and smacking her lips together as she spoke, uttered the following in a singsong voice:

"Calamity follows on calamity . . . and wound on wound . . . and sickness on sickness . . . and frost and cold and fevers and chills and torpor and famine and death!" She smacked a time or two. Then: "Sons will kill their fathers, fathers will whore their daughters! These are signs that foretell the kingdom! All these—"

There was a surge from behind and the old woman slipped and fell. Others were clamoring to be hoisted. Others felt the tongue of prophecy. Astonished and appalled, Sirena had slunk back a little from the multitude but Lucia stood bravely by Joshua, now and then begging the people to let him speak. But the people wanted to speak, not to listen. The man who had been toppled from his stone had climbed back and was again flinging his arms.

"You foul and blinking impostor!" he roared, choking with fury. "You blinking bat! You well-greased liar! You don't know when the messiah is coming any more than I do! And by the living God you'd better cease your lies,

124

you blinking pig, or I'll have a Roman official hang you on a tree! For you lie and lie—"

A blow fell on his skull that sounded like stone on bone and he was dragged down and silenced.

Sirena had heard him. She now rushed up and seized Joshua's arm and tried to draw him away. Lucia then shoved at her and begged Joshua to look down at a little old woman who had crawled forward to ask a question. Joshua stared down into a pair of faded black eyes and saw that her neck was horribly twisted to one side.

"Master, I have sinned dreadful sins. Is there hope for me?"

Because of the great din and clamor Joshua had to bend down to hear her words; and the moment he did so she touched his garment and moved to kiss his hair. Switfly he drew back, and again felt Sirena's hand on his arm and heard her voice entreating him.

Another angry man had pushed through the multitude and was shouting at Joshua and threatening him with clenched hands. So he boasted that he could cure people of their ills?—and cast out demons?—and raise the dead? If he could not do these things then why did he have the gall to claim to be the messiah?

"He doesn't, you idiot!" Sirena cried in his face.

With a powerful arm he swept her away. Had not the Most High wrought great wonders, turning the seas and rivers back, stopping the sun, shaking walls down, hurling thunderbolts, destroying the Egyptians with plagues?

"Can you raise the dead or not? Answer me, for these people want to know."

"You fool!" Sirena said at his ear.

Joshua struggled to back away but he was now surrounded. A man stepped up and struck the one who had challenged Joshua and cried out, "Master, is this pig my brother?"

The other man said: "Let him raise the dead or make the blind see!"

"Is this pig my brother?"

The more tragic ones had been creeping forward among the legs of those who stood, and some of them now crawled close to Joshua, striving to reach up and touch him. Feeling a hand he looked down and saw a creature horribly mutilated. Possibly this was somebody's castoff slave: his tongue had been torn out and his whole broken unsightly face was patched with scars. Crawling with him was a little old woman, toothless and blind, and when she reached out and was unable to touch Joshua the man guided her hand. He was trying to back away from them and was feeling shame for trying: had these been created in the image of God, this half-naked woman with inflamed sores over her face and throat, this man dragging hugely swollen legs and feet, this youth with the sacred disease who was now convulsed and after a moment shrieked and turned rigid and collapsed? Or the old hag there, looking at him with one eye in a face a part of which had been eaten away? Were these the children of God? Yes, Joshua thought, feeling pity for them, these were his brothers and sisters, these hideous things crawling with lice, creeping over the earth to find the messiah. . . .

Men now broke a path for a woman who was coming to him, a woman with the falling sickness. In her periods of seizure her emotions would overpower her and she would turn dizzy and sick, and all her senses would meet in one channel of dark wild swimming; and she would then fall over, dead to the world. She came up timidly, her gaze on Joshua, and stood waiting and watching; and the moment he looked the other way she rushed up and touched his robe. In the next instant she reached up and touched his hair. Then, with a hundred persons watching, she flung herself down to kiss his feet, and when Joshua backed away from her she arose and stood very still, looking at him.

She turned and looked at the faces that were waiting and said, "It has gone away." She looked at Joshua and said: "The evil spirit has left me." Sensing what tragedy such words could lead to Sirena grasped Joshua and tried

126

with force alone to take him away. To convince the people that this man had wrought a miracle, that the power to cast out demons was in him, the woman went through the mob, pointing to herself and crying, "He has the power! This man is holy!" The people who had watched her now saw that she seemed to be healed. Most of them were now convinced that he was a great wonder-worker and the messiah, and with a babble of tongues they beseeched him for more signs and greater miracles or they went running to their friends to tell the good news. Those who gathered round him begged him to cast demons out, to heal wounds, to open the eyes of the blind, to raise their friends from the dead, and to bring manna down from heaven so that they might eat.

With Sirena crying to him that his life was in danger, and with the old Cynic alarmed, now that the people were yelling for signs in the sky and wonders on the earth, Joshua was trying frantically to break through the circle that hemmed him in. But it was too late now. Like starved wolves that had tasted blood, these hundreds of people who had gathered, believing that a miracle had just happened among them and that the messiah or the messiah's forerunner was here, were not to be denied now. They were pushing in and trampling one another and they were demanding at the top of their voices that this wonder-worker show his powers by turning water into wine and multiplying a loaf and a fish, in the manner of pagan gods; or that he take all the blind here and all the deaf and cure them; or that he go to the pool where one floated who had drowned and raise him from the dead. . . .

And then above the infernal babble there was another outcry. There was a stronger voice, a sharp and officious voice, as one in uniform clothed with authority came in, followed by two more in the pay of Rome. These men as they came heard women crying that Joshua had cast a demon from one of them. They heard men saying that the messiah was here, the one who would overthrow Rome and set Israel above the world. They came in, hurling the people out of their path, striking them down, beating their way through the mob until the leader of the three stood face to face with Joshua.

X

He did not speak at once. He stared hard at Joshua as though to record his face in memory. Joshua had not seen him coming, nor had Sirena, but they were instantly conscious of the menace and the danger the moment the man spoke.

"Are you this king the Jews are expecting?"

Bewildered and for the moment speechless Joshua could only look at the man. He could think of nothing to say.

"Listen, Jew, did you hear me?"

"I hear you."

"Are you this king?"

"No."

"Then who are you?"

"My name is Joshua."

"What are you doing here?"

"Just resting, while journeying south."

"Are you pretending to perform wonders?"

"No."

"Say sir to me. Do you hear?"

"Yes sir."

"Have you been stirring up this rabble?"

The Cynic had come up to listen. He studied for a moment the face of one of the men and thought, How spic and span today, who only yesterday was a beggar dragging one leg!

A woman now spoke up, saying: "He has been telling us about the kingdom to come."

The Roman official looked at her several moments before turning back to Joshua. He moved a step forward and looked into Joshua's face. "You mean the kingdom that's going to overthrow Rome?"

"I told them to forgive their enemies, to love and pray for those who commit evil against them."

"You mean that Rome is commiting evil against these people?"

Sirena now stepped forward and stood before Joshua. "This is a good man," she said. "He has done no wrong."

The official looked her up and down. "And who are you?"

"My name is Sirena. I'm a Roman citizen."

"Oh?" He looked at her more sharply, for he knew of course that citizens of Rome had special rights and privileges that were denied to all other people in the Empire. "If you're a Roman citizen why are you with this rabble of thieves and beggars? Aren't you aware that a lot of these people are Jews?"

"A Jew is a human being. A Jew—"

"I didn't come," he said, interrupting her with a sneer, "to be instructed by a woman. I want to know what this man was doing and what his plans are and if I don't learn at once I'll take him away. We know what to do with trouble-makers."

Aware that she had gone too far, Sirena said, as graciously as she could: "We are going south, we only paused here to rest."

"Has this man been telling them that a Jew-king will overthrow Rome?"

"No sir. He told them to be meek and humble and fulfill their duties as citizens. He said that they should respect the laws and those who govern them."

"Well now, that's a little better." He turned to Joshua. "Is that what you were telling them?"

"No," a voice said.

"Who spoke there?"

"He told them—" Sirena began but with a furious gesture the man silenced her. He turned to see who had spoken, and then to Joshua.

"What did you tell them?"

"I told them to repent—"

"Man, come to the point. Did you tell them that a Jew will overthrow Rome?"

"No sir."

"Do you think one will?"

"No sir."

"I think you're lying," the man said. He looked round at the hushed people. "Did he tell you that? Did he tell you this Jew-king will overthrow Rome?" For a few moments they were all dumb. Most of them were only creatures who had had all the spirit and pride beaten out of them.

But a man spoke up, saying, "He's an impostor. He's not the messiah."

"Have you pretended to be the messiah?"

"No sir."

"Have you told them not to sacrifice to Caesar?"

"No sir."

He turned to the man who had spoken. "Did he?"

"He pretends to perform miracles," the man said. "There is a woman here—"

"Do you?"

"No sir."

"Bring the woman over here." The woman with the falling sickness was brought. The official studied her a moment and said: "What did this man do to you?"

"He drove a demon out of me. There was an evil spirit—"

"That's enough," he said and turned to Joshua. "So you pretend to be a wonder-worker, do you?"

"No sir."

Sirena said: "He didn't pretend to cast the demon out. He was only—"

"Woman, will you be still?" He merely glanced at Sirena but almost at once he looked at her again, with sharp interest this time, with a sly smile touching his features. "By the way, have you made offerings to Caesar lately?"

Sirena lied. "Yes sir."

"It'll be bad for you if I find out that you lied. Do you accept Tiberius Claudius Nero Caesar as the master of the world, who stands above all creation, and the one god above all others?" She looked at him, hesitating, and he barked, "Answer me!"

She was trapped. She gagged at the thought of telling a lie so repugnant but after a long moment of terrible indecision she said weakly, "Yes sir."

"Do you believe in this god of the Jews?"

"I—I—"

"You don't have to gasp and stutter. Just answer the question."

"I don't know."

"Oh, you don't know." He looked again at Joshua. "There are a lot of these impostors who claim to be a king mightier than Caesar. The bones of some of them still hang on crosses. The bones of some of them have fallen. The bones of still others will hang there. If you pretend to be working wonders, if you are arousing this filthy stupid mob—"

"Sir, I am not."

"Then why does this woman accuse you?"

"She was deceived."

"If you didn't arouse this mob who did? And don't lie about that. We had spies here who observed it."

"I did," Sirena said.

"You did. And what did you do or say to arouse them?"

"I defended women."

"Oh, you defended women," he said, sneering, his raised brows showing his incredulity.

"The old philosopher here will tell you I did." She turned to the Cynic.

The official turned to him also and looked at him. Then

he turned to Sirena. "Woman, I'm going to investigate you. I'll find out if you're a citizen of Rome or a liar. Where were you born?"

"In Antioch,"

"What was your father's name?"

"Hylas."

"What was his trade?"

"He was a merchant."

"Is he alive or dead?"

"He is dead."

"Is your mother dead?"

"Yes sir."

"Have you ever been married?"

She hesitated an instant. "No sir."

"I think you're lying again. Is this man your husband?"

"No sir."

He looked round at the people, as one might who suspected that he was among liars and conspirators. He looked at Joshua, at Sirena, at the Cynic.

"Where are you going?"

"To the holy city," Joshua said.

"Are you journeying alone with this woman?"

"No sir."

"Who else is with you? But don't bother," he said, raising a hand, his face again touched by a sly smile. "We've been watching you for some time. What are you going to do in this place you call a holy city?"

"My mother lives there," Joshua said.

"Why do you keep lying?" the man said. "We know where your mother lives."

"Well," said Joshua, his sensitive face turning red, "she lives just a little way from the holy city—"

"That's all right. We know where she lives." He glanced up at the sun. "Be on your way out of here before dark. Do you understand me?"

"Yes sir," Sirena said.

"And you," he said to Joshua, "watch what you're doing. Don't let us again find you stirring up the rabble or pretending to cast out demons. Now be on your way."

"Yes sir," Sirena said and took Joshua's arm.

XI

They took the road south. Sirena walked ahead like one
who had taken command, and Zillah was last, held again
in the pain of deep and sullen frustration. Lucia with her
child and Sibyl and the two old people walked together.
Joshua walked behind Sirena. In all of them there was a
sense of haste and menace.

It was midafternoon of a clear day and the heat was
stifling. The road here was deep under sea level; the atmosphere was heavy and shimmering and the sun was un-
bearably huge and hot. The path under their feet was
deep with hot dust. On their left the blue water was dot-
ted with the sails of small fishing boats, and along the
beach people were lying, with a part of their bodies immersed. Sweat was pouring off poor old Aza's suffering
face as step by step he put his stiff legs forward. Sweat was
pouring off all of them, including the child. They had
not gone far when the little man who said his name was
Levi caught up with them and walked with Zillah, until
he learned she would not speak to him, and then with
Lucia and her group, and at last with Joshua.

Looking at Joshua's back Lucia was thinking, He *is* the
messiah but for some reason he doesn't want us to know!
For her, the glory of God was upon Joshua: he had healed
the sick, he had created a wonder, but why was he hiding
from them? Was he waiting for the signs before announcing himself? She concluded, very sensibly, that he was
obeying orders given him by the Father and would make

himself known on some holy day, when all the signs were right. She glanced at those walking with her, wondering if they had guessed the secret. . . .

Looking ahead at the sky Sirena was recalling many things. One of the wisest of the philosophers, the Cynic had told her, had decided that man was crawling back into the womb and hacking away at the mother's liver, the seat of life. It was a strange and terrible thought but the Cynic was a strange man. "If I were to love my neighbor as I love myself," he had said to Joshua, "I would pity him and think him a dreadful person; for though I cannot help loving myself I can find no rational reason for it, and in my more lucid moments this great fondness for myself fills me with unspeakable weariness." Well, yes, she reflected, there was plenty of truth in that. "In you," he had said to her, wagging his beard, "self-love is an awful disease." And with his eyes twinkling to take the sting out of it he had told her that he was only another Jonah, forever fleeing back to the womb. "My outrageous love of self I can rebuke and control only by feeding it black bread and water. My mind tells me that is more than it deserves."

What mirrors the old man held up to self-love! What flame he had brought to Joshua's face! He had said to Joshua, "You talk more about love than any man I've ever heard but you never mention mother-love." It was the Father, Joshua had said; and the Cynic had exploded: "By the heavens, man, you must also have a Mother! Didn't you love your own?" Then the color had drenched Joshua's face.

His mother, he had confessed, was a typical daughter of Israel and religion for her was a matter of rules. Hillel had said the Feast of Lights should last eight days and on each succeeding day a new candle should be kindled; but Shammai had held that all the lights should be kindled at once. Joshua's mother had always preferred Shammai. Shammai had said that the Shema ought to be read at night while the person was lying down, and in the morn-

136

ing while standing; but Hillel had said that it should be recited while you sit in your house and walk by the way. Shammai had said that all persons converted to Judaism were naturally and incurably wicked. Hillel had welcomed and loved them. Shammai had said that the wicked would go down to hell and suffer eternally but Hillel had said that God would never pitch his children into fire.

"My mother," Joshua had said, his face burning, "always accepted Shammai. Because Shammai spent most of his time preparing for the Sabbath my mother forced me to do likewise and I came to hate it. Hillel said if a non-Jew accepted our faith and had been circumcised as a child he did not have to be circumcised again. Shammai said no. I saw such a man die. I saw hypocrites washing their hands while hating their neighbors. I saw hypocrites reciting the Shema while their eyes lusted after a passing woman. If I talk so much about love maybe it's because I had so little."

Poor Joshua! she thought, glancing back at him. What *did* he mean by love? "Love," he had said, looking at Lucia, "is there, in the way she holds her child. Love was in her heart when she picked up this abandoned waif and gave it her motherhood. Love was in her when she fed it, giving it her empty breast and chewing the food for it and feeding it through a reed. Love was in her when she saw men hanging on crosses and wept. You can see love in her now, in every gentle part of her face. . . ." But it was always mother-love that he talked about. Had he no sense of man-woman love, no sense at all?

"Love, love, love!" the Cynic had cried wearily. "You Jews seem to have only one kind of love, love of God, which means love of self, since you have created him in your image. Love your neighbor as yourself, yes, but first convert him to your prejudices. I love you, a man says to a woman, because you understand me. I love God, Joshua says, because he is a father who watches over me. But don't you people ever love anything that doesn't promote your love of self?"

And then the Cynic had taken her aside, his head wagging mysteriously and his eyes twinkling like windows that looked upon secrets. She did not know if what he had said to her was sense or nonsense. In a hoarse whisper he had said, "The Father of all men! Ah, that's the wound in us! That's the rib, the garden and the serpent. And here it is in a contemporary version, in a man named Joshua whom women pretending to love would destroy. But hardly in me, a foolish old fellow who left his wife because she thought a philosopher's writings proper fuel for the frying of his bacon. When you get down there, Sirena, tell Joshua to be kind to his mother. If women are now wasps and shrews or hellcats smelling of sulphur have we men anything but our vanity to blame?"

"Farewell now," he had said, facing her only an hour ago. "If you would teach Joshua something, teach him this, not to say the Father of men but the Mother of men, for it is women who have love. If we men are not destroying with war or staring fascinated at philosophic conceits that seem to make us triumphant in a universe that can't distinguish between us and ants, then we are trying to crawl back in and hack at the Mother's liver. Farewell, my friend, farewell!"

Her eyes had been moist when she turned away.

While thinking of Joshua and trying to understand what love meant to him her mind turned to Sibyl, a woman delicately ethereal and not of this earth, a woman so lovely that she was hardly human, and yet a whore. What could you make of that? Sibyl seemed to be unaware of the heat, the hot road, unaware of hunger and thirst. She walked like one who was blind but guided by an inner vision, her body tense and poised, her face upturned and expectant, her gaze on the hills or the sky.

They journeyed until dark, covering four or five miles, and halted for the night just before the city of Taricheae, at the southern end of Galilee's sea. This Greek name meant pickling places, and here were large plants for curing and pickling the fish that were famous over the whole

138

Roman world. The beach was littered with the materials of ship-building, and many artisans had just laid down their tools.

While Sirena looked for a spot where they could talk or sleep unmolested, Lucia left her babe with Sarah and entered the city for food. Day by day she had been spending a little of her precious hoard but day by day she had bought less and less, and tonight she returned with only half a salted fish for each person, and for each about four ounces of bread. When all her money was spent what would they eat? O Lord, and now they had this man Levi on their hands and he was a beggar too! But she supposed that Joshua would provide for them, if this was all right with the Father: he might create food, as wonder-workers were said to do, or multiply one loaf into many, as saviors did in distant lands.

Almost nothing was said this evening. Levi stared hopefully at Joshua, as though expecting wisdom or miracles; Lucia cared for her restless child; Sibyl sat like a thing only half-alive, her gaze on the sky; and Sirena took her fish and bread and went off by herself. Early the next morning they followed the river-road south, and two days later came to Scythopolis, the ancient Bethshan or House of Security. Across the Jordan three different highways led to eastern lands; and on the west was the valley of Jezreel, lying upward to the plain of Esdraelon in the northwest. The valley of the Jordan was eight or ten miles wide here and two roads ran through it to the south, both at some distance from the river. Because Scythopolis, one of the ten Decapolitan towns, was Greek in its architecture, Sirena wished to tarry—to explore the arches and forum and temples and theater and baths; but Joshua was eager to press on. He had spoken hardly a word since the Roman official had threatened him and he looked harassed and miserably unhappy.

And so they pressed on, taking the westernmost road of the two down this infested valley of tropical heat. Eight miles south of Scythopolis they came to five large springs of pure sweet water, with only a short walk between them, one after the other; and because the old people were weary and pain-wracked Joshua was persuaded to spend a day or two here. There were many people by these springs, most of them pilgrims on their way south. Sirena went among them but saw no one who looked like a Roman official or one of Herod's spies.

Hungry, indeed, almost starved, she was exploring in the area roundabout for wild fruits or grain or roots or anything they could eat when she came to a man lying alone in deep grass; and at first she thought he was dead. She bent over him and spoke but there was no response. She knelt and clasped his head and turned his face to the light. Then she recoiled in horror. The face looked bloodless and ghastly and dead but the eyes were alive. The eyes were open and they looked at her but they were so feeble and dull and sightless that she would not have known they were alive if she had not seen the lids move. She ran away to find Joshua.

"Over there," she said, pointing, "a man is dying."

"A man?" Joshua said, blinking.

"A man, he is dying. Please come."

With Zillah trailing, Joshua went with her and looked down at the man. "Is he wounded?" he said. "Will he speak?"

"I don't know."

Joshua now observed the man's garment, and a small shovel lying at a little distance. "He seems to be an Essene," he said. He knelt by the man and asked, "Can you speak to me?" The lids moved slightly but there was no other sign of life.

Joshua stood up and looked round him. "I guess his brothers have cast him out. He looks as if he has been living on grass."

"Let's bring him food and drink."

Joshua shook his head. "He wouldn't eat it, not if he keeps his oath." He bent forward to study the man's face.

140

He turned to glance at Sirena and said, "I think he's dying."

Lucia had come over. She took in the situation and knelt at once and began to chafe the man's wrists. She put her ear down but could not hear the heart beating. Looking up at Joshua she said plaintively, "Why don't you cure him? You can!"

"Don't talk like a fool," Sirena said.

"But I know he can."

"I'm no wonder-worker," Joshua said.

"You healed the woman."

"I haven't healed anyone."

"You have to stop such silly talk," Sirena said. "Do you want the Romans down on us again?"

Lucia said sharply: "But I saw him heal the woman."

"You saw nothing of the kind. If you don't stop—"

"We all saw it," Lucia persisted. "You saw it. And the woman herself said he did."

"O my God!"

Lucia was deeply offended. She went away.

"What shall we do?" Sirena asked.

Joshua knelt by the man to whisper holy words in his ears. "Then said the Lord unto Moses, Behold, I will rain bread from heaven for you; and the people shall go out and gather it and eat." He was watching the man's eyes but there was no change in them.

"What are you saying?" Sirena asked.

"And when the dew that lay was gone, behold, upon the face of the wilderness there lay a small round thing, as small as the hoar frost on the ground. And when the children of Israel saw it—"

"Joshua!" Sirena said, peering at him. "Don't waste time talking to him. Let's do something."

"If he's about dead," said Zillah, "why not let him die? He'll then be out of his misery, which is more than we'll have."

Joshua turned to her. "Is there no pity in you?"

"It is pity that says let him die."

Sirena whispered: "I think there is a man coming."

"Where?" Joshua said.

"Don't look but it's over there. That way," she said, holding a pointed thumb down against her thigh.

Zillah turned boldly to look. "Another Roman son of a dog," she said. "Still—"

"He looks like a peasant," said Joshua, following her gaze.

"He's running!" Sirena cried shrilly. She seized Joshua's arm. "Come!"

"And leave this poor man?" Joshua said.

The man came running across the open spaces and though he was garbed as a Jewish peasant he was in fact one of Pilate's spies. He rushed up, shouting, "What are you doing here?" He looked first at the man and next at Joshua.

"We were trying to help him," Joshua said.

"I'm an officer of the law," the man said, looking at them in turn and at last fixing his gaze on Sirena's hair. "What are you people doing here anyway?"

"Nothing," Sirena said. "We just happened to see this man, who seems to be dying."

The spy went over to the man and thrust against his ribs with a foot. "One of these damned filthy Essenes!" he cried. "Look, will you?" He flung the garment back from the man's feet and lower legs. The man had been tortured; he was lacerated, broken, burned.

Joshua went forth to look at the feet, which until then had been hidden. Every toe had been unjointed and was now discolored and swollen. With torches a part of the flesh had been cooked halfway to the knees. Joshua turned angrily to the spy and said: "Who did this?"

"It's none of your business who did it."

"Romans!" Joshua muttered.

"Do you intend to let him lie there and die?" Sirena asked.

"Well, do you want him? Would you like to have an

Essene to take care of who eats nothing but grass and won't talk?"

"But why do you torture him?" she asked, her eyes flashing at him. "Is that a part of your duty?"

"Why didn't you kill him?" Zillah said.

"Look!" the man said, losing his temper. "It seems to me you people have very glib tongues. As for you," he said, turning to Sirena, "you'd better keep that broken nose of yours out of things that don't concern you. And as for you—"

"All right," sail Zillah, "let him lie in the flies and rot. That's Romans for you."

"What did you say?" the man asked, narrowing his eyes and advancing.

"I said let him die!"

"Oh, let him die. Very well." The spy looked round him until he found a stone and he was picking it up when Sirena cried:

"Joshua, in God's name, come!" She seized one arm and Zillah the other and they were taking him away when they all heard a dull heavy blow. Sirena began to weep.

Zillah said: "That's the end of him the poor bastard."

The three of them were moving along, sickened, fearful when the spy again came running toward them. "Just a minute!" he cried. He came up to Joshua and studied his face. He said: "Aren't you the one who caused a lot of trouble at the Baths of Hammath?"

"I caused no trouble."

"Were you there?"

"Yes sir."

"I'm glad you don't lie about it. You were there and you were stirring up trouble. Now you are here and stirring up trouble seems to be your purpose. Just what were you doing over there with that Essene pig?"

"Just feeling sorry for him," Joshua said. He put a hand to his brow and felt sweat on his palm. He was sick with the brutal horror of it, sick and angry and helpless, and he was sinking to the earth, his senses darkening, when the spy seized him and shook him.

"Stand up, man! Have you no respect for Caesar's officers?"

"I'm sick," said Joshua, trying not to vomit.

"Can't you leave us alone?" Sirena asked, her eyes hating him. "Must you Romans spend all your time torturing people?"

"Well!" said the spy, swinging to her. He moved swiftly and struck her with his whip across her face.

She recoiled from him, gasping, putting a hand to her stinging flesh. "O God!" she muttered.

"How'd you like to have me take you away?" he asked, raising the whip again.

"If," said Sirena, "I must live in a world where the strong and the well beat the sick and the dying I don't care what in hell or out of it happens to me! But before you strike me again remember this, that I am a citizen of Rome!"

That dashed him. He let the whip sink. He stared at her several moments and said, "Well, citizen or not—"

"I said citizen!"

"And I say citizen or not you'll learn to keep your mouth shut!"

Joshua was on hands and knees, bent over, retching, though his stomach was empty of everything but bitterness.

The spy looked at him and again at Sirena. "Where are you people going?"

Sirena scorned to answer him. Joshua was unable. Zillah said: "He has a mother in Judea. We're going there."

"A mother? What is her name?"

"Miriam."

"Where does she live?"

"We gave all this information to a man at the baths."

"Never mind that! You'll give it to me now."

"In Bethany."

"Which road are you taking?"

"I haven't the slightest idea."

"Very well, woman, keep this in mind: this man is being watched. Be sure that he does not interfere in matters that are none of his business. Stay on the road and keep going, and when you get to Bethany, stay there."

Lucia had come running up and had heard the last words. She tried to remain quiet but the angry words burst from her: "When the messiah comes he'll take care of men like you!"

Slowly, deliberately, the spy walked over to her and squared off, one hand clutching his whip. "And just who are you, that you dare to affront one of Caesar's officials?"

"I—I am Lucia."

"Oh, so you are Lucia. Are you a Jew?"

"No sir."

"And just where are you from?"

"I have no home."

"Oh, you have no home. That's about what I thought. Is this your child in your arms?"

"Yes sir."

"You lie," he said, looking at her hair and at the babe's hair. "It's my idea that you're a runaway slave. Is that true?"

"No sir."

"You lie like a slave. Woman, we're going to keep an eye on you. Do you know what happens to runaway slaves?" He sneered at her and then looked down at Joshua. "Get him on his feet," he said, "and come with me." Sirena and Zillah helped Joshua rise and they all went with the spy and he stopped before Aza and Sarah and said: "Get up." They struggled and turned over to hands and knees, their faces grimacing. "Man, what's your trouble?—and don't tell me there's a demon in you!"

Aza got to his feet, his large cold eyes frankly hating the man. "There is," he said.

"Then why don't you have a wonder-worker cast the demon out?"

"I will," Aza said.

"Say sir to me."

"Sir," said Aza.

The man gave him an evil grin and then walked among these people, looking at them in turn. "What worthless rabble you are! It would be better for Rome if you were all lying out there with the Essene. You never work, you're no good. Waiting for a Jew-king. Waiting for a Jew who will overthrow Caesar. How can you be so damned stupid?"

Nobody spoke. All eyes were watching him.

"Well, you've heard my orders. You may stay here tonight but in the morning be on your way. Go to Bethany and stay there and keep your mouths shut." Then he left them, going toward a camp in the distance.

When the man was out of sight Joshua said, "Let us pray." He knelt, facing Jerusalem, his hands on the earth and his forehead pressed to his hands. The others gathered around and knelt by him.

"Our Father, we beseech you to look down and have mercy on your wretched and suffering children. Let your glory be exalted over the whole earth, and shine forth in the excellence of your great power, over all your people, that everything that has been created may be made sensible that you have made it, and watch over it; that everything formed may know that you formed it; that all who have breath may declare that the Most High, the eternal Father, reigns, with supreme power over all.

"Send us, our heavenly father, one to save us, to deliver the sick from their torments, the famished from their hunger, the slaves from their masters, the weak and helpless from the tyrannies of their rulers, that we may all rejoice and give thanks for deliverance from the evils that possess us. Send him soon, our Father; the whole earth cries for his coming. In the name of all your children who suffer, with none to pity them, send him soon!"

Joshua then went off a little distance to lie on his back, for he felt too weak to stand. Lucia went over to sit by him and brush the dust out of his hair. After a little while, Sibyl, speaking to no one, said that she was seeing heavenly things. She could see the Father's glory and the brilliant light of his heavens. She could feel his spirit in her and all through her, like a blessed healing, like roses soaked with rain, as though his hand had reached down to touch her hair and her heart.

She was looking up at the sky, and Sirena, Zillah, Aza and Sarah were watching her face. Levi was sitting back, looking at Joshua.

She could now see the messiah coming, Sibyl said; she did not know where he was, how far away or how near; but she could feel his glory coming before him like the morning and his light filling the heavens like daybreak. She could feel his power coming down from all the heavens to save his people. He was a gentle man and he was coming with love and healing to all the sorrowing of the earth. His face was obscure because of the glory but she thought he looked a little like Joshua. . . .

Lucia had come over and was now praying under her breath: "Protect him, God, and watch over him; for he is kind and good and he is not like other men. Bless him, Father, bless him and keep us. . . ."

Lying on his back and looking up Joshua was thinking: For it is a day of trouble, and of treading down, and of perplexity by the Lord God of hosts in the valley of vision, breaking down the walls, and of crying to the mountains
. . . .

How long was it till the ninth of Ab? On his fingers he tried to count the days.

XII

Convinced that Herod's or Pilate's men would bring
charges against him if he took the road followed by the
multitudes, Joshua turned westward with his group to
the hills and mountains of Samaria. The weather would
be cooler there, the odors more refreshing, and along their
way would be many fountains and streams of pure water.
He did not share the contempt of the Pharisees for these
people, who long ago had broken away from their fellows,
saying that Gerizim and not Sion was the mount of God
and the proper place for the temple. Of the Jewish holy
books they accepted, as Joshua now remembered it, only
those by Moses, and Moses himself they had exalted to
almost divine eminence. In the last days, the Samaritans
believed, a prophet like Moses would arise—possibly a
reincarnation of him, a one-who-would-return, the Re-
storer and Deliverer. After the Day of Judgment, they
said, the righteous would go to the Garden of Eden and the
wicked would be destroyed by fire. Like the Sadducees
they scorned the idea, so popular with the common people, of the resurrection of the body, and a few of them
denied any kind of life after death.

A strange people, Joshua thought, but still among God's
children and still Jews.

Joshua's group was following a poor road up a rocky
ravine that led to Bezek, Thebez and Sychar. Sirena had
observed that some members of the group were rapidly
failing in strength. There was poor Sibyl. For three days

she had been fasting and was now barely able to stand; but when Sirena had urged her to eat, Sibyl had said no, that God was preparing her for another vision. To see this in all its heavenly glory her soul would have to be as free as possible of the corruptions of the flesh. Sibyl now walked with such difficulty that she barely moved without assistance, her feet feeling their way around obstacles while her gaze remained fixed on the sky. She expected the messiah's appearance at any moment.

Sirena would look at Sibyl, remembering that the woman had been a whore, feeling pity, then shame that she should feel pity; for the more she fasted and suffered the more delicately lovely Sibyl became. In some moments, as in golden dusk, and in some moods, as when she felt closest to God, Sibyl seemed to Sirena not to be a woman at all but only an emanation. And by the way Joshua sometimes looked at her she must have been only an emanation for him.

All of them but the child were weak from hunger: Lucia had spent her last small coins on food for the babe. It was the harvesting season in Samaria's cornfields, and Joshua said they could use their ancient pluck-right. Corners of the fields would be left to the poor to glean, and possibly they would be allowed to glean in the fields themselves, after the sheaves were taken away.

Who had the right to glean? Sirena asked him.

All the poor, he said; the widows and the fatherless, yes, and even outlanders like her.

"We must get some pouches," she said. "Then we can gather the grain and make flour and carry the flour with us."

Yes, Joshua said, but his thoughts were elsewhere.

It was this in him, this indifference to his body's needs, or this unawareness, or it sometimes seemed this contempt, that annoyed Sirena, and Lucia a little, whose practical minds told them that the whole group would fall by the wayside and perish, if food were not found. They had left Galilee, where a half-dozen fish could be had for the cheapest coin. Around them now Sirena could see nothing that a person could eat, not even wild living things, nor any sign of a settlement, as far ahead as her gaze could penetrate the blue mists. They had escaped from the spies to find a more deadly enemy. This night they lay supperless to sleep and it was a night that none of them would ever forget.

Soon after dark a full moon came up beyond the Jordan and the world stood revealed in its light. It was an enormous and golden moon, like something ripened and edible; and when it first came in sight it seemed to be resting on a hilltop. Sibyl, exhausted by the day's journey, was lying on her back, her legs firmly together, her hands clasped over her breasts, her eyes wide open and staring and unbelievably lovely. She was slowly sinking into the trancelike state that possessed her when she looked into the heavens. As this mystical condition invaded her, obliterating her normal senses, she felt the very gradual disappearance of all boundary lines and of all sensations of touch and sight. Ideas came softly down streams of light, coalescing into bright meanings; and ideas and emotions all fused in a delightful haven of deep peace and quiet. She could never have said at what moment in this extraordinary experience she left the earth; she knew only at last that she could not feel the earth, that there was no sense of it against her body, that she was wholly withdrawn from it and was then lying on the atmosphere in space. For a while she knew that the earth was under her and around her and that she was resting above it, like one lying on a cloud; but as the trance deepened she lost all sense of the earth, it was gone, it was nowhere, and she was suspended under the heavens and was looking into them. It was when she was completely delivered from all natural confinements and taken up body and soul into the pure light of God's dominion that she began to speak. Her eyes never blinked while she was in this trance; nothing about her seemed to have human life. Her lips moved only a little when she began to speak; and in her face, even though she spoke for an hour or more, there was little change visible to those watching her.

Lucia was the first to observe that Sibyl had left this world. She whispered to the others, "Look, she has gone!"

They all gathered around Sibyl and looked intently at her face. She was somewhere between the earth and the heavens. The earth was flat, lying between the great underworld pit, into which the souls of the dead had departed, and the realm of light above. The heavens were concave above the earth and rested on stupendous pillars set at the extreme horizons. It was not a far distance between earth and the first heaven; the Egyptians had said that a man standing on the highest mountain could touch it with a long pole. Angels, who moved only at the speed of the fastest birds, traversed the space between earth and the first heaven in a few moments.

It was in this intervening space that Sibyl lay suspended. She saw angels and spirits everywhere around her, and presently she began to speak. She could see it, she said; it was a baby-soul, coming down to a body . . . it was a very tiny little soul . . . its face was round and smiling . . . it was a girl baby-soul, happy at the thought of being born . . . and now she could see two angels and they seemed to be fighting: one had struck the other . . . and now she could see a black face . . . it was smiling at her, it had strong white teeth, it had a very large nose. . . .

Lucia looked at Joshua and whispered: "Who would that be?"

Joshua did not know. He said it might be Azazel, or Belial.

The face had now come close to her . . . she could feel the body but could not see it . . . she could feel something touching her that was firm and eager . . . now the face was gone and the baby-soul was gone and she could see a white light. . . .

Lucia was trembling. "She's close to heaven!" she whispered.

Aza was swallowing hard, his big eyes full of amazement. Levi was looking more at Joshua than at Sibyl.

All around her now birds in bloom-drenched trees were singing . . . they were singing the praises of God, millions of birds . . . and there . . . yes, there it was, the heavenly chariot . . . it had sixteen wheels all made of light . . . its body was of opals and emeralds and twenty angels were riding in it . . . the chariot was racing across the floor of the first heaven. . . .

Joshua looked up at the sky. Possibly it was Ezekiel's chariot, he said. Lucia then looked up at the sky and for a moment thought she could see a baby-soul descending, and then a black angel stroking through space like a swimmer. She moved a little closer to Joshua.

"She's in the first heaven," said Sarah matter-of-factly.

As though she had heard and understood the words, Sibyl said she had now entered the gate of the first heaven . . . it was floored with marble . . . it had many lights and many birds were singing . . . she could hear the voices of children and smell incense . . . now . . . now she was floating upward, she could hear angry voices, she could hear angels weeping. . . .

Lucia made a sound of anxiety. She had heard that the second heaven was the abode of angels awaiting punishment. It was a dreadful place. Lucia had never understood why God had placed it between the first, where birds sang, and the third, which was so brilliant with light.

"I hope she doesn't stay there long!" she whispered.

Sibyl was now passing through the second heaven . . . everywhere around her angels were weeping . . . they were naked and ashamed and some were wet as if they had been bathing . . . they sat row on row as far as she could see . . . they were all bowed over and they were weeping and she could see their tears falling . . . then . . . yes, yes! she could see her parents there. . . .

Lucia gasped. She had not dreamed that Sibyl could see the souls of dead relatives, waiting in heaven. She wanted to ask, Is my husband there?—my children? She turned to Joshua, intending to beg him to ask the question, but then realized that Sibyl would not hear it, if it were asked. You could get right close to her and look into her eyes and she would not see. You could pinch her and she would not feel.

Her lips were moving so feebly that you could not be sure that they were moving at all. Nobody ate food in this heaven, they were saying . . . there were only faint lights here . . . like lamps . . . only gloom and sorrow here . . . this heaven was floored with black shining stones . . . now . . . now she was moving upward and could see a larger light. . . .

In a former vision she had described the third heaven: it seemed to be a kind of brilliant antechamber to the fourth: it was floored with topaz and had gleaming walls of aquamarine and lapis lazuli; and enormous draperies of light, like diaphanous silks, hanging from all its walls. Sibyl had not gone beyond the third heaven. Would she tonight?

"Will she go higher?" Lucia whispered.

"I think she's coming back," Aza said.

"Be quiet," said Sarah.

"She's going higher," said Lucia.

Sirena moved a little to get a clearer view of Sibyl's eyes.

Lucia looked up at the sky and thought for a moment that she could see Sibyl coming down. But possibly, she thought, unwilling to see her descend, she had seen only another baby-soul or a falling angel. Sometimes the angels fought in the second heaven and hurled one another into space, and then you might see an angel on the earth, wandering forlornly, corrupted with living matter and unable to ascend.

Sibyl's voice now said that she was far . . . far . . . and then had difficulty speaking at all. There was no emotion in her voice but they could tell that her lips refused to utter the words. Her lips would open a little and say, I am far . . . and say no more. Lucia put a hand to her throat. Even Sirena, most skeptical of them all, was deeply affected. . . When at last Sibyl was able to speak she said that she had come to a gate . . . she could barely see because of the brilliance of the light . . . it was much whiter than sheet lightning . . . she was looking at Aravoth. . . .

It was Joshua who gasped now. Aravoth? Aravoth was the seventh and highest heaven, the abode of righteousness and blessings and all the divine treasures. The souls were there who were to be given bodies; the angels were there who ministered to the Throne; and there, standing above the seventh heaven itself, was the Throne of God, and God sitting on his Throne. The splendors there, Joshua knew well, were too bright for mortal eyes. He supposed that Sibyl would return blinded.

She was looking into Aravoth, the lips said; but she could not see . . . no, she could not see, it was all blinding light . . . blinding like the sun but a thousand times brighter . . . no, no, she could not see, she could not see at all.

Of course she cannot see! Joshua thought. Was it not written that no person could look on God and live?

"She will now come back," he said.

"Can she see God?" asked Lucia.

"No."

"But you have said the pure in heart will see him."

"She's not pure in anything," said Zillah.

"But purer than we," Joshua said.

She could not see, the lips were saying; there was only light and she could see nothing in the light.

"Is it the seventh heaven?" Lucia asked Joshua in a whisper.

"If it is," said Aza, "she can't see it."

"Can she see the angels there?"

"If she could she'd tell us."

"She'll be blind now," Aza said, "and we'll have to lead her."

Sibyl's eyes had closed, as though for protection against the awful brilliance of the eternal. Her lips were moving

154

feebly but they made no sound. The group sat around her, almost too frightened to speak, only Sirena doubting that Sibyl had been to the heavens and seen their glory. How much to believe of these matters, how much to reject, she did not know, though the old Cynic would have said, Reject it all. She was a Greek, her greatest people had been rationalists, and to reject it all was her impulse.

Aza had said, She will be blind now and we will have to lead her. Was he right?

Sibyl had returned and had passed without speaking from the trance into sleep. Just before morning she had another vision: she saw the celestial son of man, robed in light and riding a white horse. He was somewhere in space and he was riding toward the earth. Even after she had come out of the vision she could still see him; she could look up at the sky and see him there, a figure of glory, riding a horse as white as snow. Lucia thought she could see the celestial rider.

Aza said: "Maybe I can but I'm not sure."

Sibyl said the mane of the horse was flowing out like cloud-silk and the hooves were flashing like white gilded birds.

"Is it the messiah?" Lucia asked Joshua.

Joshua was looking at the sky but he could see only its infinite blue.

"It's not the messiah," Aza said.

With contempt making a scowl of her entire face Sarah looked at her husband. "Papa," she said, "keep still. You're as ignorant as a pig."

"I know some things," he said.

"If it isn't the messiah," said Lucia, "who is it?"

"Elijah," Aza said.

Sirena said: "The messiah is to be a man, isn't he? If so, then he must be born. If he must be born, yet will show himself soon, then he is somewhere now, isn't he? And if he is somewhere now why does he wait?"

"Because Elijah has to come first," Aza said.

"And who is Elijah?"

"Papa," said Sarah, "you make me ashamed of you. Don't pretend that you know about these things."

"I know that Elijah was a prophet," said Aza, glowering at her. "I know he didn't die but went right up to heaven."

Sirena said: "Why does he have to come first?"

"To prepare the way and make it straight."

"Honest to mercy," said Sarah, "I've never seen you so stupid. Don't pay any attention to him, for he's an ignorant man."

Speaking to Aza Sirena said: "To make the way straight? Well, how long is that going to take him?"

"I don't know," Aza said.

"Of course you don't know," Sarah said. "Now be quiet."

"Will this Elijah come down from heaven?"

"Of course he will," Aza said.

"Papa doesn't know a single thing about it. All his life he has talked like a rab but he doesn't know anything."

"If he went up to heaven," said Aza angrily, glaring at his wife, "he'll have to come down from there, won't he?"

"I've never been so ashamed," said Sarah. "I just shouldn't let you go out in public."

Lucia looked up at the sky. "Then maybe it was Elijah she saw on the white horse." Agitated, she got to her feet. "If that was Elijah we'll see him soon!"

"Was it Elijah?" Aza asked Sibyl.

She did not hear.

Lucia turned to Joshua. "It wasn't the son of man she saw?"

"I told you," said Aza impatiently, "that he can't come until Elijah comes."

"Papa, if you don't be quiet I'm going to get up and go away."

"Joshua has never said anything about Elijah," Lucia said.

Sirena said: "If a celestial one comes he'll not be a mortal man, will he? He can't be a god if there is only God. Will he be an angel?"

156

"Now don't answer," said Sarah. "You don't know a thing about it."

"Elijah will be an angel," Aza said.

"Well, Sibyl ought to be able to tell the difference between an angel and a man. The king who is coming won't be a god or an angel, will he?"

"He'll be a king like David," Aza said.

Sarah looked helplessly round her. "I've never been so embarrassed in all my born days," she said.

"If we meet a learned Pharisee," Sirena said, "he'll answer all our questions."

"Papa will," said Sarah, "if you'll just give him time."

"When Elijah comes," said Aza, "he'll tell us. He'll come down from the highest heaven, right from the presence of God. He'll be an angel sent to make the way straight."

Sarah turned over to hands and knees and struggled to her feet. "Honest," she said, "I can't stand this."

"Where will Elijah come?" asked Sirena.

"To Jerusalem," Aza said.

"Oh, papa, in God's name! It is wicked for you to sit there and talk like a rab. Look at Joshua, he knows so much more, yet he says nothing."

"I know about Elijah," Aza said.

"If it was Elijah he saw," Lucia said, "he must be in Jerusalem now. Joshua, shouldn't we hurry along?"

"Maybe," he said, blinking hard and looking at Aza. "Do you say Elijah will come to Jerusalem?"

"I don't know."

"Papa, see! Joshua doesn't pretend to know when he doesn't know."

"Of course he'll come to Jerusalem," said Aza. "It's the holy city."

Joshua looked at Aza. "He can't walk, can he?"

"Don't worry about him," Sarah said. "We'll just leave him and he can talk to himself."

Lucia had bent over Sibyl and was pulling at her but Sibyl would not move. She would not speak. "Help me,"

Lucia said, appealing to Sirena, and the two women raised Sibyl to her feet but when they released her to see if she could stand she sank helplessly.

"She needs food," Sirena said, "but we have no food."

Lucia went to the small parcel which she carried, wrapped in an old cloth, and drew forth a morsel of bread and two hard figs. She had hidden this food for her child. She now knelt by Sibyl and asked her to eat, and when the woman paid no attention to her Lucia tried to force a fig into her mouth. "Help me!" she said, again appealing to Sirena.

Together they tried to force food into Sibyl's mouth but her teeth were clenched. Lucia looked up at Joshua. "Command her to eat," she said.

Joshua bent forward and with a finger gently opened one of Sibyl's eyes. "Why won't you eat?" he said. He knelt and said, "Sibyl?"

There was a change in her. She opened her eyes and gave Joshua a pale heavenly smile and began to chew even before she had food in her mouth. Lucia thrust between her lips a small piece of bread and a fig and Sibyl chewed them feebly only a moment and then swallowed them, choking and grimacing with pain. She ate all that Lucia gave her but when helped to her feet again sank helplessly.

Lucia shrugged and turned to Joshua. "Command her again," she said.

"Sibyl? Please get up."

At once Sibyl arose and again turned on Joshua a wan angelic smile. Zillah and Sirena exchanged glances. Levi in his grave and eloquent way was staring at Joshua, with the thought plain in his eyes that this was the messiah here before them.

"If someone will carry my child," Lucia said, bustling around, "I'll help her walk."

"And I'll help her too," Zillah said.

Joshua took the child and looked ahead at the road and the sky. He had forgotten that Elijah was to come before the king.

158

XIII

Lucia and Zillah helped Sibyl along but with difficulty, for they themselves were enfeebled, having eaten so little in recent days. Walking with them Sirena said bitterly, "If we don't find food we'll all die. We'll be eating grass like the Essene." Late in the afternoon they came within sight of a barley field that had been harvested and Sirena at once left the road and entered the field.

She thought at first that it had been stripped of every head in it. Joshua had said that the corners were left for the poor but the corner at which she looked had been sickled and the sheaves had been taken away. Falling to her knees she searched in the stubble and found a head and then another and shelled them in her hands. She put the kernels into her mouth and chewed as she crawled along, and after a little while she drew a part of her garment up to make an apron and dropped the heads into it.

Then Joshua and Lucia came out to glean with her and side by side on their knees the three of them moved over the field. Many more heads had been lost in the stubble than Sirena had expected to find and after an hour she had a hundred in her lap. One by one she had counted them. They also picked up stray kernels that had been knocked out under the sickle. When Sirena saw a locust she seized it and looked at it. She had never eaten locusts. The appearance of the thing, which seemed to be all legs and bloated abdomen, made her feel nausea, though she knew that locusts were a common food with the poor. Lucia had said that they were steeped in oil or sprinkled with salt or wood ashes and fried, or that sometimes they were eaten uncooked.

She held the wriggling thing in a palm and shuddered. "There are locusts here," she said. "Can we eat locusts?"

"I've eaten them," Lucia said. "You'll learn that when a person is hungry enough he can eat anything."

Joshua was now at a little distance from them, crawling along and gathering barley heads. Sirena went over to him and showed him the locust. "Shall we eat these things?"

"A lot of people eat them," Joshua said.

"But look at it. It's nothing but belly. Doesn't the sight of it make you ill?"

"It looks different when it's fried," he said.

And so they caught locusts, pinching their heads to kill them and dropping them into their laps with the barley heads.

They would have to make flour, Sirena said, but what would they use for a mortar and pestle?

Any hollowed stone, Lucia said, would do for a mortar; and for a pestle, a long thin stone or a piece of hard wood. "You've had an easy life," she said to Sirena, "if you've never had to make flour."

On returning to the road, having among them a bushel of barley heads and about two quarts of locusts, Sirena and Lucia searched roundabout for stones; and when they had found two with shallow basins and slender ones to use as pestles they sat with the grain, which the others had been husking meanwhile, and began to make flour. Making flour, Sirena discovered, was hard and exhausting labor. The barley kernels seemed to be as firm as grains of sand, and though she ground the pestle against them with all her strength she was unable to crush them.

"You do it this way," said Lucia. She was kneeling over her mortar, with her garment around it to keep the kernels from flying out; and she was jabbing at the grain, breaking it with short quick blows. When she had broken

160

the kernels she ground them round and round with the pestle until she had coarse flour.

Joshua meanwhile, with the fumbling help of Levi, was trying to kindle a fire, using stones to strike sparks into a pile of dry grass. He abandoned the effort; and with that dry humor which he so rarely revealed he said, "I guess I never learned to do anything but talk. I now see what a useless thing speech is in a crisis."

"Keep trying," Sirena said, "or we'll all starve to death."

"Look at the birds," said Joshua. "They take no thought for the morrow. God provides for them."

"They don't have to cook their food," Sirena said. "They have gizzards to make flour but we have only hands. Besides, in the winter months don't a lot of them starve to death?"

"You have little faith," said Joshua but he winked at Zillah.

"Oh?" said Sirena, who had not seen him wink. "Well, a Greek philosopher said that God helps those who help themselves. I don't think he's going to feed me if I just sit and wait for Elijah."

"He fed Moses," said Aza.

Sarah said: "Papa, are you going to start all over again?"

"What'll we eat in the kingdom?" Aza asked.

"In the kingdom!" said Sirena bitterly. "We'll not eat there. We'll just spend all our time singing the praises of God." She flung her hair back and looked up at Joshua. "Won't that become pretty tiresome after a while?"

"You're not very humble today," Joshua said.

"No? Well, I'm on my knees trying to make flour for you. The trouble with your philosophy, as I see it, is that those will be first in the kingdom who do least for themselves here. Is there no virtue any more in honest toil and thrift? Are we who try to care for ourselves to be less than those who are beggared by their laziness?" When Joshua did not reply she glanced at him and flung another taunt: "You seem to have the greatest compassion for those who have nothing because they are lazy or stupid."

161

"For shame!" said Lucia. "Look, Aza has made a fire! Soon we'll have warm bread and then we'll all feel more cheerful." Busy, skilled and devoted, she hustled around, finding a hollowed stone in which to mix the flour with water, and a flat thin stone on which to bake the bread and fry the locusts.

She fried the locusts first and all but Sibyl watched her. With the flat stone resting on other stones above the flame, she scattered a part of the locusts over it and sprinkled them with flour and with ashes from burned grass. With a stick she kept turning and stirring them, and when she sniffed their savor she said, "They smell good." She fried all the locusts and heaped them in a pile on a stone close by the fire. Sirena had been mixing the flour with water. The stone on which the locusts had been fried was now covered with grease, and over this stone Lucia poured batter, spreading it with a stick to thin it out. She spread the batter thin so that it would cook quickly, and when a loaf was brown she deftly tipped the hot stone up and slid the loaf off to another stone. Then she baked a second loaf, a third, a fourth. Under lowered lids Zillah was watching her with fascinated admiration. She had never seen a woman who knew so well how to do these simple things, who moved about her labor with such briskness and skill.

Lucia asked someone to find stones to use as plates and when these came she warmed them at the fire. While the bread and the locusts were still hot and steaming Lucia with two sticks divided and served the portions, carefully giving share and share alike. After she had served them she sat before her portion and took the child from Sarah's arms to feed it.

Sirena was looking at her fried locusts and contemplating the sensations in her stomach. In the heat they had shriveled and were now much smaller than they had been. She could see only fragments of legs on them. She had to admit that they smelled good but they did not look good. Joshua, she observed, was eating locusts with his fingers, picking them up one by one and plopping them into his mouth. He looked like one who was eating delicacies.

"Lucia," he said, "you're a fine cook."

"Thank you," Lucia said.

"Oh, there's no virtue," said Sirena, "in being a good cook. See the birds—"

"For shame," said Lucia.

"They taste mighty good," said Aza, smacking.

"A little like powdered peach-stones," said Sarah.

Zillah was eating slowly, as was her way, like one who found all food distasteful. Her eyes, sullen and intro-spective, looked at Joshua and softened, at Sirena and turned sharp and bright, at Sibyl and filled with dreamy quiet. Sibyl was eating, wholly unaware of what she was eating. Aza was wolfing his food down. The bread also, he said, tasted better than any bread mama had ever baked.

Before Sarah could speak Sirena said quickly, "See Lucia. She gave herself only as much as we have, yet she feeds two. I'd think that people like her would be first in the kingdom."

"Sirena, please."

"That is so," said Joshua. "None will stand higher than Lucia."

"How high will I stand?" asked Aza.

"Please!" Lucia cried, distressed. "Can't we be just friends and not think all the time who'll be first and who'll be second? I'd never want to be first anywhere."

"Lucia is like the fruit trees," said Joshua. "Their fruits are their witnesses. As my people say, it is by their fruits that we know them. Lucia also reminds me—"

"Joshua, please!"

"—of the parable of the stag that came in from the wil-derness and mixed with the flock; and the shepherd gave him to eat and drink and bestowed on him more affection than on his other sheep. The people asked, Do you lavish more on this stag than on the others? Why is that? And the shepherd answered, I have toiled long with my flock, leading them out in the morning and bringing them in at nightfall. All that I could do for them I have done. Yet this one, though lost in the wilderness and un-cared for, he comes to me. Shall I not love him then?

"Lucia—"

"Oh, Joshua! Won't you please talk about somebody else?"

"Lucia came out of the wilderness to my people, asking nothing but love. And love she will receive in boundless measure, for there are few people like Lucia. Of such is the kingdom. The Pharisees have an old saying that those who are well have no need of the physician, but those who are ill. By the ill they mean the abandoned and lost. Lucia was lost and she has come to the physician to be healed."

Lucia's eyes had filled with tears and she had bowed her head. If they had looked at Levi and seen the intense way he was staring at Joshua and the almost insupportable joy in his face they might have had a presentiment of things to come.

"Tell us some more," said Aza, rolling his big eyes. He had eaten his food and licked his fingers and now glanced slyly around him to see how much the others had left. "Mama," he said, "you eat too slow."

"I don't gobble it down like a pig."

"Tell us some more," said Aza to Joshua. "I'm still hungry and maybe your words will fill me up."

"Don't weep," Joshua said to Lucia. "My people have a saying that no man should ever make a woman weep, for God counts her tears."

"I can't help it!" Lucia gasped. To hide her tears she bowed her head lower and seemed to be busy with her child.

"Tell us a parable," said Aza, "and fill me up." To Sirena he said: "If a Jew couldn't talk in parables he'd die."

"Well, there was a man who led a wicked life. One day —"

"This means you," said Sarah to her husband.

Aza grinned. "Mama, this is only a parable."

"Just the same it means you."

"One day a friend told him he was doomed. The man went forth and sat between the hills and said, Mountains and hills, seek mercy for me. But they said, Before we seek mercy for you we must seek it for ourselves; for it is written, The mountains shall depart and the hills be removed. Then the man cried, Heavens and earth, beg mercy for me. But they said, Before we ask mercy for you we must ask it for ourselves; for it is written, The heavens shall vanish like smoke, and the earth shall wax old as a garment. Then the man said, Sun and moon, ask mercy for me. But they said, Before we ask mercy for you we must seek it for ourselves; for it is written, The moon shall be confounded and the sun shamed. Then he said, Planets and stars, implore mercy for me. But they said, Before we ask for you we must ask for ourselves; for it is written, All the hosts of heaven shall be dissolved and the heaven shall be rolled up like a scroll. Then the man said, I see now that it all depends on me; and he wept so long and loud that his soul went from him."

"Good heavens!" said Aza. "When are all these things going to happen?"

"When the world comes to an end."

"I never knew that," Aza said, looking up at the sky. "Well, Joshua, tell us another one."

"What kind should it be?" Joshua said.

"Something very Jewish," Sirena said.

"There was a father who said to his son, Go to the wise men that they may bless you. And he went to them and found them disputing and quarreling over the words in the holy books, the one saying, It means thus, the other, It isn't so. When the son told them why he had come they said to him, May it be his will that you sow and reap not, that you bring in and send not out, send out and bring not in, that your house be vacant and your abode inhabited, that your table be disturbed and you behold not a new year.

"Returning to his father the son said the wise men had cursed and not blessed him; but the father, hearing the words of the wise men, said, That you sow and reap not means that you beget children and not lose them; that you bring in and not send out means may you receive your daughter-in-law and not have to send her away because of your son's death; that you send out and bring not in means you will give your daughter in marriage and have no cause to take her back; and that your house shall be vacant and your abode inhabited means may your grave remain empty and your life long."

There was silence. Then Aza said: "I don't think I like that one very much."

Sirena said: "Joshua chooses his parables with delicate tact. Here are three women without husbands or children."

Aza looked in turn at the women. "I guess I'm just stupid," he said.

Sarah turned to Joshua. "Tell us why you left your home."

He was the second son, Joshua said. In Israel the first-born son had a right on his father's death to a double portion of all that his father had. For it was writen, He is the beginning of his strength, the right of the firstborn is his. If the portion of the second son was only a little he was privileged to take it and go into the world to make his fortune. "But I," said Joshua, "am one of the prodigal sons. I made no fortune. I return penniless."

"Why did you never marry?" asked Zillah.

"I couldn't afford to. A wife costs a small fortune."

"Not a wife like me," said Zillah. "I'd cost nothing. We have a little sister and she has no breasts: what shall we do for our sister in the day when she shall be spoken for? But look," she said, glancing wickedly at Sirena, "I am a wall, and my breasts like towers: then was I in his eyes as one that found favor."

Afraid that Zillah would become abusive or obscene Lucia spoke up. "We need a drink," she said and got to her feet. A hundred yards away was a small pool at which a farmer's beasts drank.

166

Aza looked up at the sky, for night had come. The demons would be out. "I'd better go," he said and picked up their skin-pouch.

"No, I'll go," said Lucia and took the pouch and hastenend away.

The principal night-demon was Shabriri and after a few moments they heard her crying, "Shabriri—briri—riri—iri—ri!" If you broke the name of a demon into segments you destroyed his power, for his power was in his name. In the holy writings of the Jews there were many words that had the power to abash and frighten demons, and to protect Lucia, Joshua now murmured the words of the ninety-first psalm.

"If Elijah has come," said Aza, "the demons will all be in their holes."

Lucia returned with the water and they all drank but Sibyl. Then, before they lay to sleep, Joshua recited other words to allay their fears and sweeten their dreams. The next morning they ate again, and, feeling nourished and strengthened, took the road to Thebez, pausing at every wayside field to glean and to husk the wheat or barley. Sirena went to a Samaritan farmer who gave her a stout close-woven sack in which to carry their flour. In Thebez she slipped away again and at one of the bazaars traded her robe for one of cheap but tough fabric and received in addition a handful of coins. Joshua seemed not to notice what she had done or to be aware a little later that Zillah also had slipped away to exchange her garment for a cheaper one.

Between Thebez and Sychar they gleaned and husked and pounded the grain into flour, until they had about thirty pounds of meal, which most of the time Sirena carried. With a coin she bought a little salt and some fruit, and along the road each day they caught locusts; and every day they ate two nourishing meals and they all felt more cheerful. They had climbed to the hills and though the days were hot the nights were cool, with a breeze moving across them from the western sea.

167

A little distance west of Sychar was Shechem, with cultivated plains lying all around it. It stood in the east-west roadway pass, with Mount Ebal on the north and Mount Gerizim on the south. It was along here, Joshua said, that the wicked King Ahab, slain and red with his own gore, was taken in his battle-chariot; and his chariot was washed by the pool of Samaria, while dogs licked up his blood. It was here that the priests of the abominable Jezebel had tried to confound the holy men of Israel. Possibly, he said, looking up, it was in this area that Elijah had ascended to heaven.

"Then this is where he might return," Sirena said. "Isn't it?"

"It may be," Joshua said.

Her practical eyes were looking round at the harvest fields. She proposed that they should glean here until they had another bag of flour, for it was still a long way to the holy city. What would they eat when there were no grain fields? And so it was that Sibyl went out to glean and wandered away from the others, finding herself at last by a dense hedge that fenced a wheatfield. Almost at once she felt the presence of someone; she looked first at the sky, thinking that an angel had descended; and when at last she saw a man standing back in the hedge, with only his handsome black face visible, she had no doubt that Azazel had appeared before her. The face was smiling, the eyes were hot and melting, the two rows of teeth were as clean as polished pebbles, and the black hair was a thicket of tiny curls like those she had seen on angels in heaven. While she looked at him he beckoned to her to come, and when she moved closer to him he reached out with an arm to draw her in. He drew her back into the hedge until they were hidden and with big wonderful hands he caressed down over her shoulders and body, his hot ardent eyes all the while looking full into her own. He did not seem to her to be a wicked angel. She felt the same bliss that had possessed her when, in a vision, she moved away from the earth and floated upward, drifting on cloudfoam

168

and light. After a while she was not conscious of his hands or of her garment, which was slipping downward; she was not conscious of his breath and lips on her throat. She fainted, and when she returned to her senses it was night and she was alone. She could not at once realize what had happened or where she was. Then in mists of light and beauty it all came back to her, enfolding her with pure emotion, and she knew that an angel had come down from the heavens to embrace her.

When, later, she told her friends what had taken place, most of them looked at her with wonder, but Sarah with horror, and Sirena with doubt. It was well known, of course, throughout the world that angels did come down and lie with mortal women, assuming the form and appearance of mortal man. In the legends of all people were tales of women who had been impregnated by these heavenly visitants. But Sirena, doubting, felt bitter mirth. Zillah was thinking, It would happen to her, good God, but never to me! Lucia was thinking, Though a whore she must be a holy woman, because only good women are visited by angels. Joshua was thinking of many things. There was some hidden meaning in this, some token, some sign, but his powers of divination were too weak to fathom it.

"You say he was black?"

"Yes!"

Many of the angels were black and Joshua knew the names of a few of them. Prince of all the black angels was Azazel.

"Did you know which one it was?"

Sibyl shook her head. She did not know.

"Will she now have a god-child?" Sirena asked.

Joshua missed the bitter malice. He said he did not know what this meant but Elijah would know. He turned to Sibyl, now sitting with hands clasped, looking as sweet and pure as one who had just come from heaven. "Was he alone or were there other angels?"

"He was wonderful!" breathed Sibyl. "Oh, but he was

169

handsome! All the brightness of the heavens was in his face and eyes. . . . There was a light all around him. It was dark but around me was light and I could hear music."

"Music? . . . Did you say music?"

"It was the angels singing."

Sirena was staring at her. *Could* it be? Had an angel actually come from heaven to visit this woman?

"The music!" said Sibyl, enraptured. "Listen!"

It was not music they heard but a low scream from Sirena. She was looking up at the night-sky and pointing. She had seen a star fall, had seen it come down in a path of flame and then vanish, as though it had plunged into the sea. And even while she pointed another star came, swift, but not as swift as lightning; it came in a long arc of golden fire and like the other went out.

Joshua was so agitated that he got to his feet and stood, trembling, and looked at the sky. Falling stars would be one of the signs and these stars were falling. He watched and waited. He listened.

"I have a feeling," said Aza at last, "that Elijah will come here."

XIV

None of them slept much that night and Joshua not at all. When daylight came they felt his eagerness. He was so boyishly expectant, so alive, yet so completely within the aura of naive and tragic adolescence that looking at his face was, Sirena reflected, like seeing his heart naked and beating. But she was not so skeptical this morning. She stared at Sibyl with fresh and insatiable interest, and up at the sky, and then around at the earth as though she expected Elijah to stand forth. Joshua was looking around too. He was eager to be off.

They passed Jacob's Well and followed the road that led to Lebonah and Gophna and all of them but Sibyl kept watching the sky. They could see Mount Gerizim ahead on their right, its summit almost three thousand feet above the sea. This was beautiful country, with its fertile plains and wooded hills and sweet water. Sirena looked at the loveliness and breathed deep of the cool air of morning and looked at the tidy fields and vineyards, the summits, the blue and lilac mists on distant hills, and felt that here as well as in the firmament God had revealed his hand. Why, she wondered, were Jews so indifferent to nature?

They had covered four or five miles without pausing to rest and the time was early afternoon when Sirena, walking ahead, saw by the roadside the body of a man. When she approached him he cried out, "Unclean!" and she knew that he was a leper. She waited for Joshua to come up and said, "A leper is there."

Joshua moved toward the man and he again cried out but Joshua went over nevertheless and looked down at him. He thought that perhaps this was the most hideous creature he had ever beheld. Not even at the baths of Hammath had he seen one so ravaged by disease and still alive. This man was naked but for a dirty rag over his loins and his whole body from his hair to his feet seemed to be one stench of rotting flesh. Parts of his face were not recognizable as human. Both eyes, though, seemed to be untouched by the sickness; they shone up at Joshua, clear and bright.

"You poor man," Joshua said.

"I'm done for," the man said and his ghastly face tried to smile. "Tell me, are you a son of Israel?"

The others had come up to look but all turned away but Lucia, pinching their nostrils, Lucia looked down at the creature and waited for Joshua to heal him.

"Has the son of David come?" asked the leper.

"I don't know."

"Elijah has come," Lucia said.

"Elijah?"

"We don't know," Joshua said.

"The stars are falling," the leper said. "I lie here and see them night after night. Elijah and the king must come soon. Doesn't Elijah have to come first?"

"I think so," Joshua said.

"And how long after he comes before the king comes?"

"My brother, I don't know." Joshua looked up at the sky and said: "I'm sure the messiah will come by the ninth of Ab."

"And what is today?" the leper asked.

"I'm not sure," Joshua said. "It's close to the end of Siwan or the beginning of Tammuz."

"And how many days to the ninth of Ab?"

"Maybe about forty."

Looking down at the man Lucia saw in his eyes a slyness that troubled her and she looked at Joshua and down at the leper, back and forth, wondering if Joshua could see what she was sure she could see. She was convinced that this leper was laughing at Joshua.

"You're sure," said the leper, his bright eyes on Joshua, "that the king will come on the ninth of Ab?"

"Pretty sure."

Yes, Lucia thought, the sly rogue was laughing!

"Is the one coming to be a king, a mortal man, or a savior-god?"

"A god?" said Joshua, shocked. "Man, there is only God. There is no other."

"Good. I wanted to hear you say that."

Lucia whispered to Joshua: "He's mocking you."

"What?" Joshua said, looking at her.

She took his arm and drew him away. "Joshua, that man is laughing at you. Why is that? Who is he?"

"Who is he?" said Joshua, staring at Lucia. "Just a man, isn't he?"

"He knows a lot more than he pretends."

"You think so?" said Joshua, frowning, blinking. He went over to the leper and said: "Who are you anyway? You're no common man."

Lucia had run over to the others. "The man there," she said, agitated, "he is not just a leper! He knows more than he says."

The others were sitting. Sirena got to her feet. "You don't mean he's Elijah!"

"He's someone," Lucia said.

Sirena and Lucia went over to Joshua, who turned as they approached, his eyes blinking hard and fast.

"This man," he said, "is a Pharisee. He used to be a rab. He is a very learned man."

"He was teasing you," Lucia said.

"He has read a book by Enoch. Enoch," Joshua explained, "went up to heaven without dying, the way Elijah did. Enoch says a savior will come, a son of man, who was hidden with God before the creation. But what about the root of Jesse?" Joshua asked the leper.

"Who are these women?" he asked.

"My friends and sisters."

"Do you journey with women? Man, you are wicked."

"Don't you call him that!" Lucia cried.

The leper looked up at her helplessly. He was a Pharisee and he knew that it was wicked to talk to women, but he could do nothing about it now, God had borne him down with an awful punishment, he had no choice. He closed his eyes to shut Lucia's face out.

A little later Lucia was gathering materials for a fire. They would cook a meal, she said, and they would feed the leper, even though he said horrid things about Joshua. They were all to forgive, she said; they were all to be kind. She baked bread and fried locusts and she spread a fruit paste on warm bread for the leper and took hot fried locusts to him but he would accept nothing from her hands.

"You'll have to give it to him," she said to Joshua.

Sirena said: "What things people are! They take their prejudices right to the door of death."

Joshua took the food to the leper and sat with the man while he ate. But he could not stand to look at the man. The leper's mouth or parts of it were eaten away and a part of his nose and he seemed to put the food not into his mouth but into his face. But he talked all right. He seemed to have his tongue yet and enough of his lips to say words plain.

"Will you eat some more?" Joshua asked.

"The warm bread is good. Yes, a little more, thank you."

Joshua went over to the group for another piece of bread and fruit paste.

Aza said: "I don't see how you stand that stink."

"Physicians do," Joshua said. "There are worse things."

When he was out of hearing Lucia said, "The leper tells him he is wicked, yet look, he sits by him and feeds him."

"He's a funny man," Aza said.

Joshua came again, with unpleasant odors clinging to his garments, and said, looking at Sibyl: "He knows the names of all the angels. He'll tell her which one came."

Lucia arose and seized Sibyl's arm and drew her to her

174

feet. Sibyl was in a stupor but Lucia pushed her or went ahead and pulled her and got her close to the leper. Now, she said to Joshua, they would find out which one!

"Last night," Joshua said, "an angel came to this woman. Or was it night before last?"

The leper glanced briefly at Sibyl and closed his eyes. "She thinks it was Azazel."

"Stupid woman. Azazel is the demon of the wilderness. He is buried under the stones of the holy city."

"She says he was black."

"Any angel can appear as a black man. Did he smell of sulphur?"

Both Joshua and Lucia turned to Sibyl, who stuporously and dreamily said the angel had smelled of incense. All around him, she said, there had been the light not of hell but of heaven.

The leper groaned with unbelief. It was not Machael or Gabriel or Uriel or Raphael, he said, for these were the angels of the Throne who stood before God. It was not one of the angels of the sun, for they did not come at night. It was not one of the four who stood at the corners of Jerusalem. It was not Kokabel, for he was the star of the Eternal. It was not Sahariel, who controlled the courses of the moon, but it might have been Gadreel, who betrayed Eve.

Immensely impressed by this Pharisee's learning, Lucia forced herself to ask a question. Did angels sometimes stay on earth and marry mortal women?

Yes, the leper said, but only rarely. He had known a woman whose husband was an angel. But after this angel became old and his hair as white as the snows of Hermon he returned to the realm of frost, for he had been one of its guardians. In a long-ago time, before the wicked Qeyon aroused most of the heavenly host to rebellion, angels came down quite commonly to marry, or to instruct and guide and foretell the future. All the great prophets had talked to angels.

"This woman," said Joshua, indicating Sibyl, "has visions and goes to heaven. She is sure she saw Elijah coming."

The leper groaned again. It was a dreadful indignity to lie helpless on the earth and listen to the silliness of women.

Lucia begged Joshua to ask this learned man when the messiah would come and Joshua put the question.

The leper drew a great sigh. As to that, he said, there were so many opinions! Some thought he had come long ago, that he had been a Persian king who was kind to Israel; and some thought he would not come for another thousand years. The most learned Pharisees, who had studied all the signs and prophecies and symbolic meanings in the sacred books, thought he would come soon.

"The ninth of Ab?" asked Lucia.

Oh, then possibly; or on the concluding day of the Feast of the Booths, or on the Day of Atonement, or at the Passover.

"What," asked Joshua, "will be the chief sign?"

Again, said the leper, there were as many opinions as heads of barley in a sheaf. One learned rab said that the wars of Gog in the land of Magog, as foretold by Ezekiel, would foreshadow his triumphant entry into the kingdom; but another said the chief sign would be darkness at noon, like the most utter darkness of night; and another that the sun would turn to blood and fall from the sky and the earth would split open across all the lands of wickedness, in a chasm as wide as the seven hills of Rome and as deep as hell itself; and still another—

"I have heard all those," Joshua said. "What do you say will be the chief sign?"

"Two. The despair upon Israel, because God can no longer withhold his mercies, when his people are under the heel of the harlot and cry out from the depths of their woes. The second, the appearance of Elijah."

"Elijah!" Lucia whispered, looking at Joshua. "Ask him how we'll know Elijah."

"By what sign will we know Elijah?"

176

"His wisdom and his righteousness."

The leper now seemed to shrink and subside. He was ill and he was weary. Sirena had come over with Zillah and had asked a question, and the leper turned a little, trying to see who had spoken.

"Another woman," he said. He looked up at Joshua. 'Please take them all away."

When darkness came Joshua said he would spend the night with the leper, for the man was lonely and no one spoke to him, now that he was ill. It would be a chilly night, Lucia said; she would bring some embers over and she would gather materials so that all night he could have a little fire. She called Levi to assist her and they went up and down the road and into the fields on either side, looking for twigs, pieces of wood, bark, dead grass. They laid several armfuls by the embers and Lucia started up the fire and Joshua sat by it and the fire warmed both him and the leper.

With reluctance Lucia went back to the group, who were sheltering under a tree. Would they need a fire? she wondered. She looked over and across the road at the tiny fire where Joshua sat like a shadow in the gathering darkness and she knew that he would learn many things tonight, which he would tell them tomorrow. The Pharisees, Joshua had said, were the wisest of all men and this leper was a Pharisee, an old Pharisee, for his hair and beard were gray and his hands were mottled with age. He was bald but for a fringe, and Elijah, Joshua said, had been bald when he went to heaven.

"Is anyone cold?" Lucia asked, glancing round her.

"A little," said Aza. "I've learned one thing, the old can't stand the cold like the young."

"Should we keep up a little fire? But if we do we'll have to go find fuel."

"Just move the fire around and warm the earth and then we sleep where the earth is warm."

"The earth is warm," said Sirena, putting a hand over it. "The sun has been on it all day."

177

Zillah had stretched out with knees drawn up to her belly, as was her habit, and seemed to be asleep. She had tucked her garment around her ankles and legs and snugly against her throat. Sibyl, indifferent to heat or cold, hunger, thirst or pain, had her back to the tree that sheltered them and was looking up among the broad leaves at the stars. Lucia thought she might have another vision tonight. Aza and Sarah sat together, warming each other. Sirena, her robe drawn tight around her and her face almost hidden, sat apart and alone and was silent. Levi sat apart too, his gaze on Joshua and the fire.

"See how bright the stars are tonight," Lucia said.

Only Aza looked up. "We seem to see more now that we're up in the mountains."

"And they're closer," Lucia said.

Joshua had also observed that the stars were brilliant and many tonight. From time to time he looked up to see if any were falling but he had seen none fall, or he looked over at the leper to see if the man was asleep. Because there was a slight breeze he had to be faithful in his care of the fire lest flames blow over and singe the old man. An hour passed, two, three and he could hear the leper's gentle snoring, and he himself dozed, lying on his side by the fire, his cheek on a palm. He waked after a while and saw that the fire was only a few golden embers and he laid grass and bark on them first and then wood. The fire blazed up and was a room of brighter light in the ghostly starlight. The leper seemed still to be sleeping. Joshua had wanted to talk to him most of the night, to ask questions, to learn, but of course he could talk to him on the morrow. He wondered if the man was not cold, for he had only the rag of a cloth over his loins, and he thought of giving him his own garment or of lying close to him and sharing it. He looked at him and wondered about him and nodded sleepily and he put a little fuel on the fire and shoved its circumference in, so that it would be small and compact and safe; and again he lay down and dozed.

178

He was awakened by something strange: had something touched him, had he heard an unfamiliar sound, or had there been exploding lights in the universe overhead? He sat up with a start, feeling anxious, feeling goose-flesh, and saw with amazement that the leper was gone. He did not believe this at first. He stared numbly at the spot where the man had lain and blinked hard and rubbed at his eyes and thought, Was he ever there at all? He got to his knees and rested on his knees, bending forward, staring, and at last reaching out to feel; but nothing was there, nothing but the earth. He sniffed, but no odor was there. Then he looked round him, thinking that he had confused directions; but no, there was the road, here was the fire, there the spot where the man had lain.

With something like terror numbing his mind he got to his feet. He looked all around him. He laid grass and bark on the embers and built up the fire so that he would have light, but in the light there was nothing, nothing but the empty earth, the stars and the smell of the night an hour before morning. He stood, blinking, staring, wondering and then ran across the road to his group. They all seemed to be asleep but were not. Aza said, "What is the matter?" His voice awakened the others.

"The man is gone."

Joshua's voice was so unlike itself that Lucia at once got to her feet. "You mean the leper?"

"Yes. He isn't there. There isn't even any smell of him."

They were looking at one another, as people will, especially in nighttime, when they are disturbed and chilled by a sense of menace and mystery. What, all but Sibyl wondered, could this mean?

"Let's go look," Lucia said, handing her child to Sarah and then touching Joshua's arm. They crossed the road. They looked at the fire and all around the fire and Lucia went down to her knees and rubbed over the earth with her hands, and she sniffed, at the air first and then closer and closer to the ground, until she had her face almost

179

against it. She got to her feet and turned wide fearful eyes on Joshua. "There's no smell," she said.

"I know it," Joshua said.

Then, it seemed to Lucia, the truth burst all around them, brighter than starlight. She stepped close to Joshua and looked up into his face, her own face a little paler now, her eyes astonishingly large. "Was this man wise and righteous?"

"I think he was," Joshua said.

"By what sign, you asked him, will we know Elijah? And he said, His wisdom and his righteousness."

Joshua was staring into her eyes. In a whisper he said, "You mean this was Elijah?"

"Was Elijah bald? Was he a leper?"

"A leper? No!"

But Lucia had turned and was running across to the group. She came up to them, crying hysterically, "It was Elijah! He has come!"

Sirena rushed up to Lucia and looked at her. "Elijah! You must be mad!"

"It will be the ninth of Ab," Lucia said, paying no attention to Sirena. "It will be the ninth of Ab, for Elijah has come! . . ."

XV

They were too deeply shocked to wait for daylight but set off at once, with Joshua and Lucia leading, their stride vigorous, too vigorous for Aza and Sarah, who soon fell behind. Walking together were Levi and Sibyl, though she was only dimly conscious of him, if at all. His gaze was on Joshua, Sibyl's on the sky. Next were Sirena and Zillah. Because Sirena found the bag of flour quite a burden Zillah said she would help her with it and they clutched on opposite sides a loose fold of the sack and suspended it between them. Before leaving their night-spot Zillah had gone to the ashes of the fire and looked all around it and up and down the road and up at the sky.

"Why do you suppose he went away?" she asked Sirena.

"I haven't any idea."

"Was he actually there?"

"Of course he was there," said Sirena. "We all saw him."

"We fed him, we made a fire to warm him, Joshua sat with him in the night, yet he went away. Was he Elijah?"

"Joshua says Elijah will not be a leper."

"Look," said Zillah, nodding toward Joshua and Lucia. Joshua was carrying the child and its head was above his left shoulder and it was looking back. "Father, mother and babe. Will we ever be one of three like that? Do you think the child is Joshua's?"

"Don't be stupid," Sirena said sharply.

"Look at Sibyl, a fading garden with no water. Have

181

you noticed how her eyes glow? She sits and sways, oh, so filled with raptures!—and you can walk right up and look into her eyes, as through windows at her soul, and she never knows it. She will just sit, swaying back and forth on her lustful bottom, with pale fires burning in her cheeks and with, oh, what memories! And Joshua says she's a virtuous woman! It's Joshua who is stupid."

Sirena glanced over at her and then shivered, for the morning was chilly. It was, she thought, only a few minutes before daylight; some of the stars were winking out and the sky overhead was fading into gray. It was at that time of night or early morning when she loved to breathe deeply, for it seemed to her that all the odors of earth and sky, of wind and water, were then present. On the eastern horizon was a warm glow, as though from fires down under.

"What do you think Sibyl has in that linen bag she carries?"

"I haven't the faintest notion."

"Money? No. Jewels? No. She has a pair of dainty slippers with silver clasps. Do you suppose she was a dancer some time? That's all she has, not another thing, and she hangs on to it for dear life. Oh, she'll entrust it to Lucia and Lucia will forget it and that's how I got to look into it. Do slippers mean something special to her?"

"I don't know."

Zillah stopped and relaxed her clutch on the bag. She opened the mouth of the bag and put a hand in and withdrew a handful of meal and began to eat it, her breath blowing meal away from her hand when she fed her mouth. They waited until Aza and Sarah came limping up.

"Joshua beckons to us," Sarah said.

They all looked at Joshua, who now stood on a hilltop against the morning light. He was beckoning to them to hasten forward. He and Lucia had seen a rider bearing down upon them, a man on a white horse, and at once Joshua got the notion that this was Elijah or a forerunner of some kind, for the man had come to them from the direction of the holy city. Before the others could hasten forward to Joshua and Lucia the horseman left them and came at a gallop down the road; and as he passed the group in which Sirena stood he waved his arms at them and shouted that Elijah had come.

"Elijah!" said Sarah, and overcome sank to the earth.

Joshua was shouting to them. "Come! Elijah is here!"

Sirena and Zillah hastened forward. Sirena thought Joshua was behaving very queerly; he acted like a man who did not know whether to weep or sing.

"Elijah has come!" he cried to them.

"Yes, so you said."

"He is on the Jordan!"

"But who is this man who told us? Can you trust him?"

"He saw Elijah. Tell Aza and Sarah to hurry along, we must go."

Aza and Sarah were coming as fast as their old bones would let them. After they had all come up and stood together in a group Joshua said to them, as though he had to repeat the words over and over to taste the full glory of them, "Elijah has come! He is on the Jordan river now!"

His soft smoky brown eyes filled with mist, and while they all looked at him but Sibyl they were astonished to see tears well over his lids and fall to his cheeks. For why should he weep? Lucia wondered.

With sudden energy that amazed them he shouted, "Sing, ye heavens, for the Lord has done it!" Impulsively he rushed over and kissed Lucia on her forehead and he kissed her child. He swung and kissed Zillah. He seemed for a moment about to kiss Sirena but instead kissed Sibyl. "Break forth into singing, ye mountains!" He took a dance step or two, flinging his arms out. "O forest, and every tree therein, sing, sing, for the Holy One has sent his prophet to prepare the way! Elijah has come!"

"You say he's on the Jordan, but where?" asked Sirena, staring at Joshua's rapt face.

"Sing, ye heavens! Elijah has come! Let the heavens

183

and the earth sing, and all the things under the earth! Why do we tarry here, for Elijah has come!"

"And he came on a white horse," said Sibyl.

"Yes, on a white horse, down from the sky!"

"But that man on the white horse," said Sirena, "was not Elijah."

Joshua was not conscious of her words. He now astonished them again. He began to hop around in a strange ecstatic way, his movements spasmodic and jerky, his head bobbing grotesquely but his eyes shining like things out of heaven. "Sing!" he cried. "All of us must sing!" With a sudden swift movement he clasped Sirena's waist and began to dance around and around with her, his own feet nimble, Sirena's stiff and awkward with astonishment. "Let us dance and sing! Come, all of you!"

The contagion spread. Aza seized his wife, saying, "Mama, let's be young again!" They sang and they tried to dance. Lucia was tripping back and forth, holding her child up and singing to its surprised and wondering eyes. Zillah rushed over and thrust Sirena away from Joshua and clasped his waist, and the two of them danced together, Zillah tossing her hair and breasts and leaping like a wild thing. Joshua did not know with whom he was dancing and he did not care; he was beside himself with joy and he kept shouting, "Sing, ye heavens! Shout, ye earth! The Lord has done it! God has sent his prophet, so let us sing! . . ."

They were all dancing now but Sirena. Sibyl had gravely sat and put on her dainty slippers and she was now doing a kind of ballet: she would run a few steps and fling her arms at the sky, as though scattering flowers, then poise, her arms reaching up; when, turning swiftly, she would run in the opposite direction, repeating the graceful movements. Aza and Sarah in spite of pain and swollen limbs were hopping around like mad. Lucia was waltzing with her child. Joshua and Zillah, both singing, were going frantically round and round, dizzy and entranced, until at last, exhausted, they fell and sprawled. In the moment of falling Zillah managed to keep an arm round him, and now lay on her back, an arm under his waist, her breasts rising and falling under her deep breathing. Then she moved over quickly and pressed her red ripe lips into his mouth.

That fetched him to his senses. He leapt up and looked down at her. "What are you doing?" he said.

"I just gave you a sisterly kiss," she said, her eyes innocent.

"Are you aware that Elijah has come?"

"Yes, and of much more."

"Get up," he said, observing that a part of her legs was bare.

"I can't," she said, tossing her arms out with abandon and remembering the warmth of his lips.

"Elijah has come," said Joshua, looking round him like a man dazed. He saw Sirena watching him with a faint smile, amused, a little pitying. "Did you know it?" he said, confused and bewildered by his uprushing emotions.

"But where is he?"

"On the Jordan!"

The others had ceased dancing and gathered round him. Lucia said, "Joshua, shouldn't we be going?"

"But where on the Jordan?" asked Sirena. "It's a long river, isn't it?"

"He's at Betharaba. Come, we must go."

Betharaba was the name for a ford, any ford or river-crossing, and any betharaba on the Jordan was a long way from where they stood. It was fifty miles or more but they all felt a wonderful strength; and Aza and Sarah surprised them by the way they set off, striding like two who were well. They all headed for Phasaelis, which was about twenty miles north of Jericho. Joshua was so eager to see the prophet that he went on ahead, sometimes vanishing in the distance; and time and again they thought he had left them but always he sat by the road and waited.

Joshua would have made the journey without eating and possibly without sleeping if the women had not scolded him; and as it was, he slept only a little and again and again in the night stood up, wishing that they could go. Sirena or Lucia would awaken and look over at Joshua and see him standing, looking toward the Jordan. They forced food on him and he would eat but he was hardly aware of his eating. He would say, "But why do we have to cook? We can eat the meal."

After they left Samaria they found multitudes of excited people moving south; and all of them told the same story, the same glad news, that Elijah had come to prepare the way and was baptizing in the Jordan.

Joshua had no doubt at all that it was Elijah and he was so shocked he was numbed when he heard the first man say that it was not Elijah at all.

"Not Elijah?" Joshua said, recovering his speech.

"No, it's a man named John."

"I don't believe it," Joshua said. "It is Elijah who has come."

The next day and the next he accosted strange men and said, "It is Elijah, isn't it?"

No, they said, it was a man named John.

Joshua was so disappointed, so stricken almost, that Lucia wept to see his face and the hurt in his eyes. "Never mind," she said. "Elijah is somewhere. There can be a John too."

"But John," he said, "who can this be? There is nothing written about John."

"Elijah," said Lucia, "is the one we'll find. He is on the river somewhere."

It was true that there was one named John, who was, some said, a Nazarite, but others said no, he was an Essene. Where had he come from? Out of the wilderness near Jericho, they said, preaching self-denial, repentance and baptism, a wild-looking man wearing a leather girdle and a ragged cloak of camel-hair. Because he wore camel-hair there were some who said he was surely a prophet, though Israel had not had a prophet in a long time. Others

186

thought he was the son of David, and still others, ignoring his name, that he was Elijah or Moses or Enoch.

"But if Elijah," said Joshua, "why would he change his name?"

Nobody had an answer to that.

"Maybe it *is* Elijah," said Lucia, giving Joshua a motherly pat. "We'll see."

Where was this man, this John, who might be Moses or Elijah, or even the messiah himself? He spent all his time on the river, they said, baptizing the multitudes and teaching. Sirena now asked Joshua about baptism: what was it for? The living waters, he said, drew their life from the holy spirit that dwelt in them, and those who plunged into such waters had their sins washed away. Then the one baptized began a new life.

"That seems an awfully easy way to get rid of sins."

"What?" he said, thinking of other matters.

"If sins can be washed away with water I'd not think them any great problem."

In reply to her Joshua said: "Who is this John?"

Yes, who was this John? There were thousands of ascetics who lived in the wilderness, clothing themselves with leaves or an old skin or with nothing at all; eating only wild fruits and locusts and honey, when honey could be found; and immersing themselves many times daily to wash away the evil of life. John was one of these. He believed that he had been called by the God of Israel to prepare the way for the son of David; and he was baptizing, he said, with water *and* with fire. He was telling the people what they must do to be saved. And because he put his emphasis on individual repentance, whereas the Pharisees put it on Israel's, meaning all Jews who kept the holy laws, the Pharisees would have nothing to do with him, but thought him an impostor.

On learning this, Joshua was again shocked. If the Pharisees, most learned of all men, rejected this John as an impostor, then would any be foolish enough to accept him? And why did he call himself John? "Why?" Joshua asked, looking unhappily around him.

"Probably," said Sirena, "because that's his name."

"It can't be."

Joshua was so bitterly disappointed that for two days he did not speak at all. He had never heard that the way would be prepared by one named John. He supposed that this man was only another charlatan, or if not, that he was hiding under a name that was not his own. Nor had Joshua ever heard that Jews thought baptism necessary to salvation. Where in the world had that idea come from to lodge in this man's absurd mind? From the heathen cults, of course: in them baptism symbolized the birth, death and resurrection of the god and of his initiates. But for Jews baptism was not a sacrament.

"This man can't possibly be Elijah," he said one evening. "And if he is a Jew he is a very strange Jew."

They all shared his disappointment and grief.

"Wasn't there an ancient prophet named John?" Lucia said.

"I know of none."

"They say he baptizes with fire. What does that mean?"

"Ask her," said Joshua, indicating Sirena. "It isn't Jewish."

"He must be a holy man," said Lucia hopefully. "They say he heals the sick."

Sirena said: "If baptism for Jews is not a sacrament then it doesn't wash sins away."

"I can't be sure," said Joshua. "I've forgotten some of these things."

"And why must everything be Jewish? It isn't Jewish, you say, as if God must do everything through your people."

"Hasn't he always?" Joshua said.

"The thing to do," said Sarah, "is wait till we see him. Then we can tell."

"If he isn't bald-headed," said Aza, "it's a cinch he isn't Elijah."

188

"That's right," said Lucia. "We'll see if he's bald."

The river crossing where John was laboring was north of Jericho. Joshua and his group left the road and crossed the hot tropical jungle to the river and found several thousand people there. Many of these were the poor and sick and outcast who had come down the river-road from the north and from the baths. The whole area was tense with the lightnings of hope and yearning and all tongues were talking about John.

They made their way with difficulty through the ghastly throngs, sprawled like beasts around them; and saw at last before them, standing by the water in his unclean garment, the long-haired wild-looking man who called himself John. His hair, a gray tangle of snarls, fell down his shoulders. His gray beard hung down his chest. At the moment he was calling on the people to come forth and be baptized and when a few went forth, Joshua's group observed that there was no laying on of hands: the persons simply waded into the river and plunged themselves under, and nobody touched them. John meanwhile was crying, in his deep wilderness voice, that he baptized in the name of water and fire and the son of David, who would soon come. He was making the way straight for Israel's king.

Lucia was staring at Joshua's face. Sirena, less overt, was also watching him.

Joshua was listening to John's words and studying his face. Had this one been sent by God? He doubted it. His doubt would have been sharper if he had known that for years John had lived like a beast in the wilderness caves, eating locusts and roots and punishing himself for his sins. He would have been shocked if he could have looked into John's heart and seen there his contempt for women.

Joshua saw that the man's ears and the skin of his face were like leather, that his eyebrows were extremely bushy, with black hairs standing among the gray, and that he seemed to have lost most of his teeth. His gaze was piercing.

Lucia had moved close to Joshua and she now touched his arm. "Is this the one?"

Sadly Joshua shook his head. "I don't know."

"Is he a holy man?"

"I don't know," said Joshua, and wondered by what signs a holy man was known.

John's dialect was difficult and for Joshua sometimes impossible to understand. He was calling the people forth to plunge into the living waters. That much was plain. He was baptizing them with water and with fire. That was plain too. He seemed to be telling them to repent and to accept the glad tidings, to wash away their sins, to be born again to a new life. Joshua was trying to recall what baptism meant to his people.

"Should we let him baptize us?" Lucia asked.

Joshua touched her shoulder. "My dear, yes, if you wish to."

"But not unless you say so."

"It can do you no harm."

There were people out in the river, plunging and rising and plunging again. Many stood on the shore in their wet garments, steaming in the hot sun; and others, still wet, were standing or sitting in groups. Joshua thought it an amazing scene. He remembered now that in Israel proselytes were cleansed with total immersion, at which there were witnesses; he knew that polluted souls, such as lepers, tried to wash themselves clean; but he did not believe that baptism was sacramental with his people, conferring spiritual grace, as it was thought to do in heathen rites. The Jewish word was tebilah, meaning an ablution. Sometimes the Levites were sprinkled with the waters of sin, after which they shaved and washed and made a sin-offering. But the kind of baptism Joshua saw before him was as foreign to Israel as belief in a savior-god. Only later was he to hear that baptism for the Essenes had become sacramental.

190

"He isn't bald," Lucia said.

"He could have a wig on."

She looked hard at John's hair but is was impossible to tell if it was a wig. "I'm going in now," she said.

Aza and Sarah said they would go with her. Lucia took her child and the four of them went to the broad river, and after a few moments Zillah followed them, though she did not want to leave Sirena alone with Joshua. At the water's edge she thought about it and came back.

"Aren't you going?" she said to Sirena.

"Oh, all right, to bathe but not to be baptized." They went away together and Sibyl followed them. Looking back at Joshua Sirena said: "Why don't you come?"

"Not now," Joshua said.

But he was curious to see what they did and he went down to the water. As he passed John he paused a moment to look at the man intently. Well, John certainly fancied himself as a prophet, or why did he wear camel-hair? He was a dreadfully emaciated man: through holes in the cloak Joshua could see his ribs like slats. The tendons stood out on his legs, arms, throat, and his cheek bones stood up above sunken cheeks. His eyes were black, fierce, piercing, wild.

When John saw Joshua looking at him he cried, "Go, plunge in! Man, wash your sins away! Why do you gawk at me like a Pharisee, you thing, clothed in wickedness! Go, I command you, plunge in!"

Joshua was not abashed. He said: "Are you a prophet?"

"I am John, come to baptize and prepare the way."

"But for Jews baptize and bathe mean the same thing. What do you mean that you baptize with fire?"

"Go. Plunge in. Cleanse yourself and repent."

"Are you an Essene?"

"Man, don't stand there and gawk like a Pharisee!"

"When is the son of David coming?"

"Soon."

"Will he come to the holy city first?"

"He will come to me."

"You mean here?"

"Here. Now go."

With his doubt stronger about this man, this strange wild thing from the wilderness, Joshua went down to the river and saw his group, including Levi, waist-deep, playing like children. Lucia had immersed her child and was now holding it up to the sun. Aza was trying to shove his wife under, for a part of her was still dry, and Zillah with both hands was hurling water into Sirena's face. Sibyl, like one voluptuously entranced, was rising and sinking and rising, going completely under each time. Feeling the need of cooling waters and a bath Joshua waded out to them and at once Zillah and Sirena rushed upon him and tried to shove him under. Sirena grasped his thick curly hair and Zillah strove to mount and bear him down.

"What women are you?" cried Joshua, offended by their hands.

"All right, then, you do it."

He sank gently to his chin and turned, looking round him; and when for a moment his back was to Zillah she put both hands on his head and pushed it under. He came up, gasping and sputtering and angry.

"Now your sins are washed away!" Zillah cried. "See them floating there, as big as monsters. You have broken every commandment, including the seventh."

Lucia came up to him with her child and said, "You baptize him for me."

"I know nothing about baptizing."

"Please, Joshua, for me."

"How? I don't know how."

"The way you do it that will be right."

Joshua took the child and with a finger and thumb closed its nostrils and quickly ducked it. The child slapped happily at the water and gurgled.

"Now push me under," Lucia said.

Joshua looked at her hair. "You've been under."

"Yes, but I want you to do it."

192

He put hands on her shoulders and she sank and went under. Then they were all clamoring to have Joshua baptize them. Sibyl floundered over and lay floating by him, her hair like river-moss. When Joshua thrust her head and shoulders under her feet came up.

"Her feet are still sinful," Aza said. "That's because she dances in fancy slippers."

"My slippers!" Sibyl cried. "Where are they?"

In trying to immerse her Joshua touched parts of her body that offended him. He backed away.

Zillah now flung herself down on the water, her eyes mocking him.

"Get up," he said.

"You must baptize me."

He turned away. He felt that the whole thing was becoming ridiculous.

Many people had been watching them, including John. He now waded out and shook a leathery finger at Joshua, crying, "Man, that is not the way! You don't touch them! And besides, I am baptizing these people, not you."

"We like to have him do it." Sirena said.

"Is he a holy one?"

"Oh yes, indeed."

"He cures the sick," Lucia said.

"You wicked woman. Go, all of you, leave the water."

They waded ashore and stood together, their garments clinging to their bodies. Sirena pulled her robe away from her on all sides, and, observing what she did, Sarah and Lucia tried to conceal their forms. But Zillah, who knew that she had a lovely figure, with a slender waist and high full breasts, let her garment cling, hoping that Joshua would look at her. Joshua was much thinner than she had thought he was. Lord, he was almost as skinny as John.

Sibyl was running frantically here and there trying to find her linen bag. She could not remember where she left it. She could find nobody who admitted to having seen it. "My slippers!" she cried. "Help me find them!"

Sirena had left the flour close by the water's edge and

had kept her eye on it. Nobody recalled having seen Sibyl set her bag down. Because her robe was wet Sirena asked Lucia to help her carry the flour and they both clutched the bag and held it between them. They moved away from the river and back toward the hills, with Aza and Sarah following, Sarah carrying the child; but Sibyl was still looking for her slippers and Joshua was again studying the man from the wilderness. Zillah and Levi stood back, waiting for Joshua.

He seemed to feel that by staring long and hard enough he could determine what sort of man John was; he was unwilling to accept his bitter disappointment, and so cast about him for signs of the man's holy mission. But what sign was there, except the camel-hair?—and was this to overweigh in the scales such things as his illiterate speech, his dirty and snarled appearance and his obvious contempt for women? Did God send prophets and fore-runners who behaved like tyrants and looked like old goatherds from the remote hills?

He could not believe it, not yet, but he turned away at last, sick inside and weary and sad all over. Around him were pilgrims who had come from northern Israel and from lands beyond, north and east; they sat or lay in the sands or among the stones above the sands, and while look-ing over the multitude of them Joshua remembered hav-ing heard that other men were here besides John, of whom some said, This is Elijah, or, Yonder is the messiah. He did not believe it but he began to wander aimlessly, and Zillah came up and then Levi and they walked with him, one on either side. Joshua saw no man who looked even faintly like the one, crowned with wisdom and clothed with light, whom God would send to prepare the way; and at last, despairing, he said to Zillah, "Where have they gone?"

"Over here," she said, and led him back to the hills above the river.

Lucia had warm bread waiting for him but Joshua said he could not eat. He stood in the sun, turning this way

and that to dry his steaming robe; and then, choosing a spot, lay down and closed his eyes. It's not long, he thought, till the ninth of Ab, yet the way is not being prepared, for no teachers are here, no, not one. . . .
a baptizer, yes, but as a teacher above all.

He had not learned that John looked upon himself as

XVI

In Israel a teacher usually stood on some eminence above his students and they sat around him. John had a huge rock with a flat top on which he stood and on which, it was said, he slept. The next morning at daybreak when Joshua and his group went over to see what John was doing he was already exhorting the people to come to the living waters. Again Joshua went up close to listen to the man and to study his face.

Joshua saw that by John's feet was a wooden trowel like the kind Essenes carried to bury their excrement. This man, then, was an Essene?—a member of that strange monastic sect in the wilderness, who spent the Sababth in bed, refusing on that day even to void themselves, much less to pull an ox from the mire. But would God send an Essene to prepare the way for the king?

When John paused in his furious speech and looked round him Joshua cried to him: "Tell us about the one who is coming!"

John swung his ragged head and beard and looked at Joshua. "What would you know about him?"

"Is he born of woman?"

"Yes."

"Then he must be alive somewhere now."

"That is so."

"Have you seen him?"

"Only in the spirit."

"Enoch says in his book that he will descend from above."

John shook himself impatiently. "I say he will be a son of David."

"Tell us about the kingdom. Will all people be admitted who repent?"

"No. The kingdom is for Israel. Wicked people will be overthrown and cast out. The Harlot will be destroyed." He meant Rome.

"Won't the kingdom be for all people who repent and humble themselves and love their neighbors and accept the Father?"

"I have answered you."

"Do you know where he is now, the messiah who is coming?"

"He's somewhere in Israel. More than that I don't know."

In Israel! thought Levi, looking at Joshua.

"Would you know him if you saw him?"

"I would know him."

What a fool you are! Levi thought.

"Is there some sign by which we can tell him?"

"The sign is in your heart. Repent and be baptized."

"Can you tell us when he will make himself known?"

"When I have prepared the way for him and made it straight."

"Are you an Essene? If you are, then you claim to know the secret Name. If you know it you can destroy the world. You—"

An angry man shouted, "Master, strike this fool blind, then he will believe!"

"Be still," said John to his disciple.

Sirena had come up and was no longer able to hold her tongue, though she knew the contempt in which Essenes held women. She said: "Will this king be a god?"

John turned his back on her. He looked over at Joshua, his black eyes flashing. "Man, why are you in the company of women?"

197

"They're my sisters. They're equal with men before God."

"Oh no they're not! Man was made in the image of God and woman in the image of man. There are as many levels between them as between the first and seventh heavens."

"You seem to me very arrogant," Sirena said. "Has God sent an arrogant man to prepare the way? And does an arrogant man ask us to humble ourselves?"

"Don't talk to me," said John, refusing to look at her. "Turn your face away and be silent."

"It is written," said Joshua, "that if the blind lead the blind they will both fall into the ditch. It isn't what goes into a man that makes him impure, but what comes from his mouth. I tell you that women will share equally in the kingdom; for look, I have one with me whose feet I am unworthy to wash, yet she is no daughter of Israel."

"Did you come to dispute," asked John sharply, "or to learn?" He turned his back on Joshua and again spoke to the people, calling on them to repent and be baptized and prepare for the son of David. He had a strong voice and his words carried far. He made large sweeping gestures, sometimes flinging both hands toward the people; or he would put a hand under his long beard and toss it up and out, as though to blow his words down the bridge of it.

Joshua and his group went away. They went back up the hill and sat beyond the sound of John's voice; and Aza, staring unhappily at Joshua, said, "Is he the one?"

"I don't know. Our Father works in mysterious ways and I am only mortal man. But John's words don't fill my heart."

"Why does he hate women so?" asked Sarah.

"Don't most men?" said Sirena.

"My husband loved me," Lucia said.

"Slaves," said Joshua, "have bigger hearts for love."

"Well," said Aza, his face becoming sly, "it's true of

198

course that a woman brought sin into the world. Adam was like God until Eve seduced him."

"You old fool," said Sarah. "Do you look like the image of God?"

"Whoever takes a woman," said Aza, "plows a field and sows it with salt."

Sarah said: "Go find some water and wash your mouth out."

Sibyl had been swaying gently and looking at the sky. "I don't see this man," she said. "He's not there."

"Is anyone there?" asked Lucia.

"There is still one coming on a white horse."

"We saw him," said Aza, "and he didn't do us any good."

A voice spoke and startled them and they turned to see a man, huge and ferocious-looking, with long black tangled hair and black eyes that seemed to throw off sparks and a thick black beard. For a moment Joshua thought it was John but this man's name was Judah; he was one of the leaders of the fanatical sect of assassins who hated Rome, despised the Pharisees and Essenes, and indeed all Jews who counseled peace and patience while waiting for the king. These men, the Zealots, believed that Jews should rise as they had risen under the Maccabees and throw off their yoke. The only king whom a son of Israel could accept was their God, who was their King, yet all the cowards and weaklings, said Judah and his conspirators, were teaching people to turn the other cheek, to walk two miles with Roman officials instead of one, and to give their girdle also if asked for their cloak.

He was looking at Joshua and his countenance was so menacing that in alarm Joshua got to his feet.

"What do you want?" he said.

"I heard you," said Judah's booming voice, "talking to the fool over there named John. Why do you waste your time with such weaklings and cowards? He knows nothing, this dung-burier from the wilderness in his hair shirt. He is ignorant, stupid, dull, cowardly and no good."

199

"I don't know what you mean," Joshua said.

"I mean, you pop-eyed simpleton, that the way to destroy the yoke is with the sword. Did Judas sit around and wait for a son of David when the Syrians enslaved Israel? By the God above us, no! He *was* a son of David. Did he bow his neck to the oppressor and ask to have it chopped off? By the God above us, no! He hacked him to pieces. Did Judas give his cloak and walk naked before his enemy? Man, you know what he did: he cut the damned enemy's head off and spiked it to the wall!"

"You mean the few people of Israel should wage war?—should march against the mighty Roman empire?"

"Judas had only a few men but they were men and not mewling boys like you."

"Don't you talk to him that way!" Lucia said.

"Woman, shut your lip."

"But Judas was killed," Joshua said.

"Is this the way a Jew talks? By God, he died like a man. He didn't sit around on his ass with women and stare all day at the sky. Simon won, didn't he? He littered the hills with the enemy's bones. Israel was again free, free, until the Beast of Babylon enslaved us! And Israel is enslaved today because the land is full of men like you!"

"Don't you talk that way!" cried Lucia, getting to her feet.

"But a son of David is coming," Joshua said, blinking hard at the man.

"O my God, always he is coming! Are we to sit around as slaves, waiting for this son of David? How many hundreds of years have we been waiting? How many more hundreds of years shall we wait if the damned cowardly Pharisees have their way? Is there no strength left in Israel? Are we unworthy of our God? Man, how King David would laugh at us if he could see us now!"

"But Shammai—"

"To hell with Shammai!"

"—said to wait, work, hate mastery, but not to fly in the face of the government set over us. Shammai—"

"If you say that word again I'll shove it down your throat. That limping Pharisee! There'll always be Shammais to say, Be prudent, wait, smile, bow, cringe! Why do you sit around here when there's an enemy to be slain?"

Wearied by the man's violence Joshua shrugged. "The Romans have legions," he said. "What have we? All our best men have been killed in the wars. We're only a handful against vast armies."

"You're a coward!" said Judah, breathing heavily through his hairy nostrils. "Man, Judah had only a few men against legions. That's all Judas the Maccabee had but the eternal God was on our side and we won. We can win again. One man against a hundred, that's all we need —that and the good right arm of our Father!"

Crushed before the man's anger and contempt Joshua was silent.

"Look at these women who follow you around. Of what use are they?"

"Hillel said—"

"So now it's Hillel, another of those damned Pharisees!"

"He said—"

"I don't care a piece of snot in a dwarf's nose what he said. Come, man, you're going with me."

Lucia rushed at him. "You brute, you leave him alone!"

He swung an arm at her, saying, "Get out of my way."

"We won't!" she cried, seizing his arm and tugging at him. "We're waiting for the king! He's in Israel now."

"You'll wait till your thigh rots. Do you know how many of these messiahs have been hung on trees to be the accursed of God? The fool over there on the rock will be dead in a week. He has come to prepare the way? Yes, the way to his own death. Yonder," said Judah, gesturing upstream, "is one who says he's the son of David. Tomorrow he is going to roll the river back. How long in God's name are we going to let dupes and imposters beguile and silence us?"

"Maybe he is the messiah."

Judah bent forward and blew great laughter into her face. "The messiah? My God, you lunatic!"

"But he might be," she insisted.

Zillah had softly risen and was standing behind Judah.

"The son of David will come," said Joshua. "How can you doubt it? Was it not foretold by the prophets?"

"No, not in a single instance. And do you say prophets? What have we Jews ever got from our prophets? Judas or Simon was worth all the prophets you could drown in the Jordan from Hermon to the Dead Sea."

"All the signs foretell his coming."

"Signs!" Judah snorted. "Israel sits around like an old woman waiting for signs! Come, I say, you must go with me. We have a camp back in the hills. We have a horse and weapons for you."

Joshua was backing away. "No," he said, "I'm a man of peace."

Judah lunged forward and with a huge hand seized one of Joshua's thin arms. In that moment Zillah leapt. She sprang up and both hands grasped Judah's hair and both feet kicked at his legs. She was trying to tear his hair from his skull. She was gouging and biting. Astonished, Judah turned round and round, trying to shake her off as if she were a bug.

"Get this thing off my back!" he bellowed.

Joshua and Sirena pulled the girl off. She ran away a few paces and crouched, facing them, her hands behind her back. Then, with a slow menacing gesture, her eyes fixed on Judah, she brought her right hand forward and into view and in it she had Judah's dagger. While riding his back she had reached under his girdle and withdrawn the weapon.

When Judah saw that she had his weapon his eyes opened wide with amazement. He advanced to retrieve it but Zilah raised it against him.

"Back!" she cried. She was grasping it by the haft and pointing it at him.

Judah turned to Joshua. "Who is this woman anyway?"

"I'm an assassin," Zillah said.

"Give his dagger to him," Joshua said.

"Oh, no. His big mouth has had a lot to say about cowards. He says they need to be only one against a hundred. All right, he's now one against a woman and we'll see if he dares to come in."

Judah's eyes were glowing with admiration. "Too bad she isn't a man," he said.

"Give him the dagger," Joshua said.

"Only if he promises to go away and leave us alone."

"All right," Judah said. "I misjudged this man, so what else can I do? Judas shall plow, and Jacob shall break his rod, but this man will sit in a garden." He advanced again to Zillah and reached out to take the dagger.

She drew it back and then with contempt hurled it at his feet.

Judah picked it up and carefully put it into the folds of his belt. He looked again at Zillah with admiration and said: "Why don't you put on a man's garb and join us?"

"You flatter me," she said.

Without looking again at Joshua or at any other member of the group Judah turned and strode away. They all stared at his broad back until he disappeared.

Then Sirena turned to Zillah and there was admiration in her eyes. "Would you have killed him?"

"Of course. Would you?"

"I guess I don't have that kind of courage."

"Greeks once had," said Zillah.

Lucia said hastily: "There's one up the river. Joshua, that might be the messiah." She hastened away to fill their water-pouch and after they had eaten of bread and water they decided to go upstream to see who this was who would roll rivers back.

They found him with a multitude around him. He was not the kind of man Joshua or any of them had expected to see. This man was not thin and gaunt and half-naked but wore a seamless tunic of fine linen, short-sleeved and fitted close to his neck. Over it he had a linen girdle wound many times round his waist, and on his feet he had leather sandals. He was sitting but they could tell that he was plump: his jowls hung over the tunic where it was tight against his throat, and his cheeks above his short beard were full and rosy. There was nothing about him to suggest the seer or wonder-worker, save possibly his eyes. His eyes burned with strong fires.

Joshua turned to a man and said, "Does this one say he is the son of David?"

"I think that is what he says."

"Has he proved it with signs and wonders?"

"They say he has cast out demons."

"But others do that."

"Yes, that is true. Well, tomorrow he is going to give a great wonder. He is going to roll the river back."

Well, Joshua thought, others had made such promises. Others had promised to throw down walls or raise Jerusalem nine miles above the earth or stop the sun as Joshua did or cast rods on the ground and turn them into serpents as Moses did or turn water into blood as Aaron did or make the ass talk as Balaam did or ascend to heaven without dying as Elijah and Enoch did.

"Have you seen him perform any wonder?"

"Not yet. But some say he has healed lepers and raised the dead."

"What does he teach?"

"I know only that he promises to roll the river back tomorrow. The day after he will perform a wonder even greater than that. And on the third day he will destroy Edom and usher in the kingdom."

"Only two days from now?"

"Only two."

"At what time tomorrow?"

"I haven't heard him say."

Sirena asked: "Can he turn water into wine, as Dionysus did?"

The man looked at her and said, "Is that a great wonder?"

"Well, then, can he walk on the water as Poseidon did?"

"That is no great wonder either."

"Can he raise the dead as Esculapius did?"

"You heard me say that some say he has done so. They say that a man somewhere here in the throng was dead but now lives."

Aza stepped up to ask: "Can he cast out demons?"

"Man, that is no great wonder. They say that he has cast out many demons and that they have plunged into the river and drowned. Some have seen them floating but I have not and can only tell you what they say."

Sarah asked: "Do you say he will roll the river back?"

"I do not say so but he says so. Tomorrow. He promises that the waves will be as high as city walls. The next day the earth will darken at noon when he destroys Rome. The day after that—"

"At what time tomorrow will he roll it back?"

"I don't know. Some say when the sun is a hand's breadth above Moab, and some, just at daybreak. When the sun is straight overhead tomorrow he will stop it. He will stop the sun, I mean. The earth will turn black and split open when he destroys Rome. I don't say that he will do these things. But the people say that he has promised to do them."

"How long," asked Joshua, "has this man been teaching here?"

"Quite a while, I think."

"Does he have a mother?" asked Sirena.

"You foolish woman, of course he has a mother."

"What is her name?"

"I don't know."

"Maira," said Sirena, "is the star of Isis. Maya was the virgin mother of Buddha. Myrrha was the virgin mother of Adonis. Maia was the virgin mother of Hermes. All these," she said, looking at the man and then at Joshua, "are the same name as Mary in your language."

"I don't know what you mean," said Joshua, frowning.

"You seem to be saying something that I don't understand."

"I'm only saying that if your messiah were like the saviors other people have he would be born of a virgin and his mother's name would be Mary."

"Is that what you've been trying to say all these weeks?" asked Zillah. "I thought you were saying that God is a woman with red hair and freckles."

"Ohh!" said Sirena and in that moment she hated her. "I was saying—"

"It doesn't matter," said Joshua. "Our messiah will be a king, not a savior-god."

As always when emotions boiled angrily at the surface Lucia interposed. "Joshua, do you think this might be the one?"

"No, I don't."

"Still, he might be. We could spend the night here."

"There's nothing here to make a fire," Sarah said. "We have nothing to eat."

"We don't need to eat if we are to see a river rolled back tomorrow."

"But if it doesn't roll back," said Aza, "we'd be twice as hungry."

Sirena smiled at his words. Her anger had cooled.

"We should be on a hill," said Lucia, looking round her. "Then we would see them if there are signs in the night. We could watch the stars. Think, when the moon comes up it might be as red as blood."

Aza looked over at the man with the fat jowls and the rosy cheeks. "I don't know," he said. "The more I see of some of these wonder-workers the more I think Judah was right."

XVII

Most of them slept, at least fitfully now and then, but with
an effort of will Lucia stayed awake to watch the heavens.
When the moon came up it was only half a moon, and as
pale as her own tired face. She saw no wonders in the sky
anywhere, though now and again she thought she saw
wonders, so deep was her yearning. At the first signs of
daylight she observed that people were stirring down the
hill, like strange shadows in the dusk, and she slipped
away to see what the wonder-worker was doing. He was
standing erect and looking into the east. She ran back
up the hill to tell Joshua.

He was asleep and she bent over him, whispering, "He's
getting ready to do it!"

Joshua sat up. "What is it?" he asked anxiously.

"The man, he's getting ready!"

Lucia ran from person to person to arouse the others
and they all got to their feet, looking ghostly, and Sibyl
more ghostly than any, and more lovely.

"What time is it?" Sarah asked, looking up from her
hands and knees.

"Almost daylight," said Lucia, taking up her child.
"Come!"

They went down the hill to the ragged famished multitudes most of whom were now awake and tense and expectant. The one who called himself the messiah was
standing stiff and still, looking out at the river's waters;
and with a sensation of something dead sinking into her

Lucia saw that he was squat and short. Joshua went up and fixed his gaze on him but Sirena with more of amazement than pity in her face was looking at the wretched people all around her. On her left was a little old woman, her form bent, her thin yellowed hands clutching convulsively at her breast; she kept swallowing but this was the only sign of the overmastering emotion that filled her frail body. Back from the multitude, alone, because they dared not mingle with their fellows, were several lepers; and at a little distance from them was a group of very old or very sick persons who were too ill or too feeble to stand. Sirena wondered how long it had been since most of these people around her had eaten; nowhere had she seen any sign of food and no one among them seemed to have built a fire. Lord, what a riddle it was! She sighed, marveling at the strangeness of mankind, its unquenchable fires of hope and faith. She did not for a moment believe that this little fat man would roll the waters back and throw down the walls of Rome.

Was he mad? Or who was mad, who sane, in the world now? She looked over at Joshua and saw hope in his face that on the previous day had expressed only disappointment. Hope was like a light in the face of Lucia but not in the face of Zillah; in the faces of Sibyl and Levi but not in the face of Aza. Zillah caught her glance and winked and came over to stand by her.

"What are you thinking?" Zillah asked.

"Just wondering if it is comic or pathetic."

"Which do you say?"

"I say I feel sick and queer and frightened. I feel as if I'll weep. I feel as if I would go away alone and weep a long time. For must people have miracles?"

"If he fails then what will they do?"

"Find another. There will always be another."

"As Judah said, endlessly, till we all die."

"Tomorrow and tomorrow and tomorrow."

"Forever?"

"Who knows? In the next century, the next, the next."

"What does it all mean?"

"Don't ask me."

"Would it be this way if God were a woman?"

"Don't ask me."

The golden warmth and light of the sun was on the hills beyond the river. Most of the people were looking at it and waiting for the sun. There was no sound, for even the children, feeling the tenseness in their parents, were hushed. The light spread downward over the hills, melting the shadows.

Then there came to them the strong voice of the man. They would all pray, he said, and he prostrated himself, not toward Jerusalem, as was the way in Israel, but toward the sun. Joshua observed this and was shocked. The man began to pray aloud but Joshua could not understand his words or even be sure of what language he was speaking. All those in his group seemed to be praying but Sirena.

She had remained standing and was now looking at the bowed forms around her. When she saw the man rise and go toward the river she said, "Joshua?" but Joshua was praying. He was lifting from Isaiah those noble words that seemed to have been spoken for moments like this:

"He will open the blind eyes to bring out the prisoners from the prison, and them that sit in darkness out of the prison house. He will pour water upon him who is thirsty and water on the dry ground; he will pour his spirit upon his seed, and his blessings upon his children—"

"Joshua, the sun is up. The light has risen."

"Get up!" Zillah cried. "The river is rolling back."

Joshua got to his feet. "Is it really?"

They now moved toward the water, their gaze on the sun which was now in clear view above the hill. Zillah with impish mischief was holding her hand up to measure its breadth between the hill and the sun. Lucia was moaning.

"Any moment now," Zillah said. "Let's all be ready."

"Yes," Sirena said bitingly, "any moment now!"

"Ye of little faith," said Zillah. She reached over and

clasped one of Sirena's hands and Sirena returned the pressure.

The man was standing by the water's edge, looking up at the sun like one who consulted a timepiece or waited for a signal. He then raised his right hand toward the heavens, and Sirena realized, with a start and a shudder, that she was not breathing. Nobody was breathing. The man was now speaking but Joshua and his group were too far back to understand what he said. The earth here sloped down to the river and they could look over the heads of those before them and see the Jordan's waters. The man had ceased speaking and again there was tense silence. A few moments passed. Sibyl gasped, sucking in her breath. Lucia was still moaning. Here and there a person overwhelmed by his emotions was fainting and falling. Someone pointed an arm downstream and a hysterical voice shouted, "See, the waters are coming back!"

The hysteria spread. Many voices were screaming and many hands were pointing. In the wild babble Joshua could understand only the words, repeated over and over, "The waters are coming back!" His eyes were wide and staring and he thought that possibly there was a change in the waters; but Sirena shrugged, for she could see no change at all. Gently rolling, the waters poured forward and down, forward and down, in their eternal journey to a dead sea. But around her were people who seemed to believe that the waters had turned and in a great boiling wall were rolling to the north. . . .

"Can you see any change?" she asked Joshua.

"I can't be sure," he said.

"O God!" Zillah cried. She pointed back up the hill. "Look!"

A dozen men were coming. They were Roman soldiers, with an officer at their head.

"Make way!" the officer was shouting, and the people were falling back. The men were striding fast, their heads up, their posture military. They strode past Joshua and his group and on down the hill to the man who had been commanding the river to roll back. They seized him by his arms and said, "Come!" The man tried to throw off their hands and the officer with the back of his hand smote him across his face and then the soldiers hustled him along. They came back up the hill, half-dragging the man, slapping and kicking him; and when they again passed, Sirena saw that the man's face was distorted with consternation and anger. They stared at the man's back as he was taken up and away and out of sight.

"May God have mercy!" Joshua said.

"What'll they do with him?" Lucia whispered.

"You've seen them before," Joshua said.

"On a cross? . . . Oh no!"

"The poor thing," Sirena said.

Lucia had begun to weep, and Sirena, looking at her, thought of the awful pathos of it. The wonder-worker was gone now, he would be dead tomorrow or the next day and some of the people would die here; with the fires of their faith and hope extinguished and with bodies too undernourished and weak to rise again they would simply lie where they had fallen and die. And what did it all mean? She looked over at the sun and the waters and at all the people around her, now wailing with bitter disappointment and grief. She looked at Lucia who had flung herself down and was heartbroken. She looked at Zillah. Then with Zillah's aid she helped Lucia to her feet and they led her away, and they all returned to the spot where they had spent the night. They all sat and none of them looked at one another now. Lucia wept until she could weep no more. Nobody spoke. There seemed to be nothing to say now, nothing to do. Lucia took the waterskin and went away to fill it and came back and offered a drink to each of them.

"How silly I was!" she said, speaking to Joshua. "You told us he wouldn't come before the ninth of Ab and that there will be many signs. Why in the world did I imagine that this was the messiah. I should have known better than that."

211

Sirena said: "You only thought what most of those people thought, poor things. They run from one to another
but they wouldn't if they had someone to teach them."

"Joshua could," Lucia said.

"But if he does," said Aza, "they'll hang him on a cross.
Is that what you want?"

"He wouldn't pretend to work wonders," Sirena said.

"It seems to me," said Aza, "that you forget what the
man said at the baths."

"Oh no, I don't forget him. But if nobody teaches them
what are all these people going to do? Pretty soon they'll
hear about someone somewhere and starving and dying
they will get to him some way. And he will be just another
impostor."

"They won't all be," said Aza. "There'll be one somewhere. Besides, it isn't our responsibility what all these
people do."

"You're selfish," Sarah said.

Aza rolled his eyes and shrugged. "Mama says I'm selfish
because I don't want them to kill Joshua. Let somebody
else be the teacher."

"We've seen nobody else who could."

Remembering what the spy had told him Joshua said
nothing but the next day he looked at the despairing multitude and wondered if he could quiet its grief and teach
it the few simple truths it needed to know. He had no
thought of getting involved with the passions and hungers
here when he began to talk to a woman who was weeping
bitterly. A man came up and then another, and soon someone was shouting, "He is here, he has come!" Joshua
wanted to flee then but almost at once he was fenced in
and people were begging him to talk to them; and though
prudence told him to excuse himself and go away he
yielded to pity and began to tell them what the signs
would be in the sky and the earth. He told them that the
son of David would not come before the ninth of Ab and
possibly not then and that they should pay no attention
to any man who before that day said he was the messiah.

They would know the messiah when he appeared; he would not look like mortal man, for he would be clothed with the majesty and power of God.

Joshua spoke, some of the people thought, like a learned man, even like a great Pharisee, even as the son of David might speak to them when he came; and the pathetic creatures began to push in around him, crying to be cleansed of evil, beseeching him to heal and to bless them, or striving, if unable to speak, to get close enough to touch his robe. Some became so frenzied in their demands and aroused to such a pitch of faith and hope by his words that Joshua began to look up the hill for the aproach of soldiers and to struggle to get away. He realized with despair that they had not understood him at all. He had asked them to repent, to be patient, to humble themselves, to wait, and his words had meant to them only that he was a wonder-worker!

Sirena had been watching the scene develop and was even more alarmed than Joshua. She had thought that the people would listen quietly and be sensible but some of them were behaving as if out of their minds.

She pushed her way through to Joshua and cried, "Come, we must get out of here!"

"Do you see them?" he asked anxiously.

"Not yet but we will if we stay here!"

They turned to flee and an old man followed them who bore the marks of a dreadful disease. "Master," he called, "why do you leave us?"

"Don't call me master!" Joshua said, flinging the words back at him.

"God!" said Sirena, hurrying along at Joshua's side. "It's not love the people want. It's miracles."

"If they ever find love that will be the biggest miracle of all."

They went to the other members of the group and then they all fled as swiftly as they could, with two of them helping Sarah along, and two of them Aza. They did not pause until the river and all its pilgrims were behind them and out of sight.

XVIII

They went south toward Jericho and on the way Sirena asked Joshua if there were teachers in the synagogues and if so, what they were teaching. Were they telling the people about the messiah who would come? Joshua did not know. He said he supposed the learned men were teaching, since synagogues were not houses of worship but of instruction. The instruction was chiefly on the Sabbath, in the morning and afternoon services, or on the second and fifth days of the week, the market days, when farmers came to town to bring their vegetables or fruits. Parts of the Torah were read or lessons from the prophets and of course they might be telling the people about the king and the kingdom.

"Would we be allowed in a synagogue?"

"Why should you want to?" he asked her. Did she understand that Aramaic had become the spoken language of the people, that because the Scriptures were written in Hebrew, which only the learned understood, it was necessary to have a Targoman or translator stand by the reader to translate for the people? Did she understand that the Pharisees were contemptuous of illiteracy and of imperfect pronunciations and of uncouth manners or dress, and thought it wicked for the ignorant to speak, yes, even to appear, in holy places? Did she realize that if he, Joshua, were to ask to speak he would be cried down?

"I just wondered," Sirena said, "what they are like."

Lucia said that if the wise men were teaching they ought

215

to go at least once to hear what was being taught; for all around them were the hundreds, the thousands, suffering and desperate, who did not know what to believe or to whom to listen; who could not distinguish between a learned man and an impostor; who would exhaust themselves and fall down and die. If the learned men were telling about the messiah would it not be all right for Joshua to repeat what they said? Would the Romans object to that?

If they all wished to go to a synagogue, Joshua said, he did not mind. They might not be admitted. If admitted, they might not be able to understand all that was said.

They were plodding up the hill in Jericho when Sirena observed that people were hastening past them. Why, she asked, did everybody seem to be running?

"My people," said Joshua, "believe that we should hasten to our holy places, to show our joy, but leave them slowly with dragging feet."

"Then let's go faster."

"Go on," said Aza. "Mama and I will get there some time."

In the court outside the synagogue was a large stone basin filled with water. Here, Joshua told them, they must all wash their hands before entering the holy place. After they had all washed he said to Sirena: "I suppose you know that women are not allowed in the same chamber with men. Your entrance is over there."

"Oh?" she said. She tried to laugh.

Zillah came up to her, saying: "Maybe this is what you were trying to say at the baths. But don't feel too bad, I'll sit with you."

"Over there," said Sirena. "On the side—removed—safely away from the men. I mean the men safely away from us!" To Joshua she said: "Can we hear?"

"I suppose so," he said.

"Oh well, if a woman can't hear, does it matter? Lucia's child is a male," she said to Joshua. "Shouldn't he go with you?"

"For shame," Lucia said.

Joshua entered and stood back by the door. A part of the congregation was already seated according to rank, with the lepers assigned to a special place in the rear. The furnishings of a synagogue were simple, Joshua reflected, looking at them; there was a closet in which were kept the rolls of the Torah and other sacred books, wrapped in linen cloths and laid in a case; and a reading-desk, sometimes with lamps. The one who would lead in prayer was standing, not on the platform from which the lesson would be read, but in a lower area near the scroll case. The ruler of the synagogue would appoint one to read from the Scriptures, another to offer prayer, and usually a third to teach. These persons would be chosen not only for their knowledge but for the quality of their voices. Members of the congregation sat but those who led in prayer or read the lesson or expounded the text all stood, as did the priest when he raised his hands to bless them. If he chose to the teacher was allowed to sit.

Feeling uncouth and ill at ease Joshua stood by the door and waited. He heard the reader of the lesson speaking in Hebrew, and the Targoman translating into Aramaic. These words came to him:

"If you will not observe the words of the Law that are written in this book, the Holy One will make your plagues wonderful, he will bring upon you all the diseases of Egypt, every sickness and every plague; the Holy One will rejoice over you to cause you to perish and to destroy you; he will scatter you among all peoples, and among these nations you will have no repose; these are the words of the covenant which the Holy One of Israel commanded Moses to make with the children of Israel in the land of Maob. . . ."

Joshua shuddered. He did not believe for a moment that God had ever been so vindictive and merciless. Had Moses been deaf or half-asleep? In how many instances had he misunderstood the Father?

The ruler asked if anyone wished to expound the text

and draw a lesson from it. Joshua wanted to but he did not dare. Inside he felt himself saying, I don't believe God ever spoke such words to Moses. I think our Father is filled with love and with pity. I don't believe he rejoices over our ignorance or would destroy us with dreadful punishments. For when have most of the people had a chance to become familiar with all the laws? No, I don't believe he would punish them with plagues and all the diseases of Egypt or drive them to such hunger that ravenous parents would eat their own children. I won't believe that such words came from God. . . .

Joshua knew that what he was feeling, what he was saying inside, in his heart, was blasphemy, the most dreadful blasphemy. He shuddered again.

But he went on speaking in his secret places. In synagogues all over Israel, he wished to tell them, as he was telling them, as he was telling himself, is a common prayer uttered by men. It says, Blessed are you, O Lord our God, King of the Universe, who have not made me a woman. Such a prayer could have come only from Satan. It is written in the Torah that God chose us to be a special people unto himself, above all other people that are upon the face of the earth. I don't believe it. Our Father in heaven is the Father of all people, of Israel and of the lands beyond Israel; of the sick and the poor and the oppressed, as well as of the rich, yes, even more than of the rich; of the slaves as well as of their masters; and of the ignorant as well as of those who teach them. . . .

With horror Joshua realized that he was speaking aloud! With shocked disbelief he heard himself saying: "Our Father does not punish the poor man who has never learned to read, and so does not know all or even a part of the hundreds of laws that the Scribes and Pharisees with marvelous and prolonged meditation have evolved. He does not punish the man who is too poor to afford the sin and trespass and other offerings. Our Father—"

"Silence, you arrogant dullwit!"

Were they commanding him to be silent? Had he been speaking aloud?

"If you wish to expound the lesson," an angry voice was saying, "come up here!"

"I don't wish to."

"Then why were you **speaking** without permission? Who are you anyway?"

"I came to ask one question," said Joshua. "Yonder on the Jordan are thousands of people. Why don't you go teach them?—tell them that the son of David will soon come—and that he will not come with a sword to smite or a breath to destroy, but with love, to lift up the weak, to console the sorrowing, to call the homeless children to him, to heal the sick, to feed the hungry, to teach the ignorant, and above all to love the unloved. Why don't you—"

"Silence!"

Any member of the audience had the right to silence the one who expounded the lesson, if he took liberties with the text. There were those demanding that Joshua be silenced, those demanding that he be allowed to speak.

"If we are to teach the people then let us teach them that the messiah will bind up the wounds—"

"Silence!"

"Silence yourself, you pig! Let him speak!"

Several voices were now calling on him to leave the building. They were telling him that he had profaned God's holy words. They were calling him an impostor, a fraud, an abomination.

"You abomination from hell, get out of here!"

Joshua was looking into an inflamed face. "All right. I'll go."

"You bet you'll go or we'll throw you out!"

"I'll go," he said and he turned and left the building.

At once a part of the congregation poured out after him and a voice was crying that surely this was the son of David. Standing back, Levi looked hard at Joshua a long moment and then quietly slipped away in the direction of Jerusalem.

"Son of David—'

"Don't call me that!"

People surrounded him, including women who had left their chamber; they were pressing in, some staring at him dumbly, some trying to touch him, some begging him for healing or forgiveness or blessings. "O Lord!" Joshua said, looking round him for his group. The people were becoming hysterical and they were fighting one another in their eagerness to get close to him. A man then touched him and cried in a loud voice that he had been healed; and he hastened away toward the city, shouting to all who would listen that the son of David had come.

While Joshua was vainly struggling to escape, Sirena fought her way through the mob and took his arm to draw him after her; but rough hands thrust her aside and she narrowly missed being knocked down and trampled. These were stronger people than those at the river. She called to Joshua, telling him to fight his way out. . . .

Then Zillah was fighting madly to get to him. "Joshua!" she shrieked.

A group of officials had come running from the city and were shoving their way through the mob toward Joshua. They seized him and were taking him away when Sirena ran crying after them.

"He did nothing!" she said, clutching a man's arm and trying to hold him. "He doesn't pretend to be any king or wonder-worker or messiah! Listen to me!"

The man flung her arm off and she was furious. "I'm a Roman citizen, I'll have you know! You'd better be careful what you're doing here!"

The one who seemed to be the leader now faced Joshua. "What were you doing?"

"Nothing," Joshua said.

"Do you pretend to be king of the Jews?"

"No sir."

"What did you tell these people to arouse them so?"

"I told them God will not punish the ignorant just because they are ignorant."

"What else?"

"I told them that God is love."

"Didn't you tell them a king is coming to overthrow Rome?"

"No sir."

"Isn't that what your people believe?"

"Some of them, yes."

"Do you make offerings to the Emperor?"

"Sir, I have nothing to offer."

"Where are you going?"

"Up to Jerusalem to see my mother."

"Is this redhead your wife?"

"No sir."

"Your concubine?"

"No sir."

"Weren't you out by the river the other day?"

"Yes sir, we were there."

"Did you see the one who was going to roll the river back?"

"We saw him."

"And the one who called himself John the baptizer?"

"We saw him."

"Such men ought to be a warning to you. Do you wish to be crucified?"

"I wish to be a good citizen."

"Then by the gods, man, you'd better be. Stop exciting this rabble. We have enough trouble with them as it is. Stay away from them."

"Yes sir. We'll go to Jerusalem."

"To see your mother, you mean?"

"Yes sir."

"It's a good thing for a man to see his mother. All right, be on your way."

When they were on their way Sirena and Zillah walked with Joshua. They had been lucky, Sirena said; this official had been more decent than a lot of Romans. Would the Pharisees now be watching him?

"I suppose," he said, deeply troubled.

221

"Then isn't it too dangerous to go to Jerusalem?"

"Is it safe anywhere?"

"But there are more of them in Jerusalem." They were silent a little while. Then Sirena said: "Remember what I told you when we first met?"

"You said a number of things."

"The first evening by the sea—that a philosopher said that what people love they destroy."

"I recall it but I don't believe it."

"That love makes us weak before our enemies, hate makes us strong."

"Hate makes us tyrants. Only in love is there real strength."

"My God!" cried Zillah, looking behind her.

"What is it?" Joshua asked.

"Levi. He has left us."

They stopped and looked back. When the others came up Joshua said: "Have you seen Levi?"

"He was at the synagogue," Aza said. "He stood with me just outside the door."

"Was he a spy?" Zillah said. "Has a spy been with us all this time?"

Wondering about Levi they all looked at one another.

"I don't think he was a spy," Joshua said. "I'll trust him. He'll catch up with us."

They went on up the road, a desolate hill-country road, known as the Bloody Way because of bandits who preyed on the defenseless. Joshua thought his group was too ragged and destitute to be of interest to brigands. Anyway, they were all too weak from hunger and excitement and the fatigue of their long journey to care much, as they slowly climbed the hills, pausing often to rest. This, Sirena thought, was God-forsaken country around them, scorched and dead under the late summer sun. It was waterless, treeless, empty. In the twenty miles to the holy city, they would have to climb, Joshua said, several thousand feet, going up and up into the gray sky and the rocky hills. On reaching the crest of a hill Sirena hoped to see

222

before them the towers and walls of the city, but always there was only another hill and the dusty road, always the same.

"We'll never make it," she said. "Our food and water are both gone."

It was toward evening of their third day, and choked with thirst and gray with exhaustion they went over to a rock ledge and sank to the earth. To the north they could see the misty depths of the Jordan valley and the fertile oasis of Jericho, and beyond them the mountains of Samaria, the haze above Galilee's sea. They had no water for their thirst, no food for their hunger, and almost too weary to say a word they lay down and fell asleep.

XIX

Hours later they were awakened by the sound of a man's voice, and on looking up, Sirena saw a huge brute of a man, whose dagger-blade shone in the moonlight. He was thrusting at her with a foot and he was saying, "Get up."

"Who are you?" Sirena asked, rising to her feet.

The man grinned at her. He went over to Joshua, who was now sitting, and peered at his face. "Give me your money," he said.

"We have no money."

"Get up. All of you get up."

Joshua arose. The man reached under his robe to search for weapons and a money-belt and then pulled the robe up to examine its hem. He looked at the garments worn by the others and cried, "God's curses on them, these people are beggars!" Lucia at that moment was trying to hide her child and the man saw her and he went over to her and said, "Give it to me."

Lucia screamed. With the child in her arms she turned, frantic, and made a move to run but with one bound the man seized her. He tore the babe from her grasp and felt over it to learn if it was male or female.

"The little bastard's a boy," he said to his companions. He held it up to the light. "It looks strong and healthy. How much could we sell it for?"

Lucia rushed at him, screaming and fighting. One of the men hurled her to the earth. She was up at once and was attacking them all with her feeble strength. Trembling, wondering what in the world he could do against such evil and powerful men, Joshua glanced round him, trying to see a club or a stone that he could use as a weapon.

Lucia was calling to him now to save her child. She had thrown herself on the man who held the babe and with a foot he pushed at her and she fell. Again she was up, shrieking. "Joshua! O God!"

The man went off a few paces, holding the child up, which now was frightened and crying. "Shall we bother with it?" he asked his companions. Lucia tried to rush after him but another man seized her and hurled her down. The third man was looking in turn at the women, with rape in his eyes. He fixed his gaze on Zillah. Reading his mind, Zillah feigned idiocy: she made her mouth loose and open and slobbering and she crossed her eyes and bugged them at him, rolling them grotesquely.

"Holy Moses!" he cried, staring at her. He turned to Sirena, trying to make out her shape.

Sirena now hastened over to the man with the child and knelt to supplicate him. "Please don't take it!" she said.

"What'll you give us for it?"

"My body!"

He sneered. "What in hell could we do with that?"

One of the men perceived that Joshua was searching round him for a weapon and that Zillah had picked up a stone. "Let's get out of here!" he cried.

And suddenly they were gone, with Joshua, Zillah and Lucia running helplessly after them. They had left their horses by the road; quickly mounting they galloped down the hill, with a cloud of dust rising to hide them, with the wailing of the child coming out of the dust. When the man hurled Lucia to the earth she had fainted but had come to her senses and was now rushing down the road, screaming, a woman out of her mind with grief. Joshua ran after her, a stone in either hand, and Zillah

225

and Sirena ran after him. They overtook Lucia and fetched her back, half-dragging, half-carrying her, as she kicked and shrieked. They set her down on the earth and held her and talked to her but she would not listen and she did not hear. She would weep and beat her hands on the ground and suddenly she would scream; and she poured out her bitter woe until, exhausted, she fainted again.

The experience had made all of them ill. Joshua sat bowed over and seemed to them to be praying. The other women, gathered around Lucia, wept softly, wept from exhaustion, terror and hopelessness. Aza was moaning and cursing. When, O Lord, when would the son of David come! As for the brigands, he said, you could never find them now, not in all the years of the world. They would go far, perhaps into another land.

On returning to consciousness Lucia started up and would have run away if they had not held her. She screamed and tore at them and reproached them. She turned bitterly on Joshua.

"O my God, why didn't you save him?"

Joshua looked up, and they saw that his cheeks were wet with tears.

"There's nothing Joshua could have done," Aza said. "Just one move and they would have put a knife through him."

"Oh, but he could have saved him! He cast out a demon, he healed the sick, he could have saved my child!"

"Nonsense," Aza said.

"He healed the sick!" Lucia cried, shaking a face haggard with grief.

Sirena said: "They only thought they were healed. Now please say no more."

"Her child will come back to her," Joshua said.

"When?" asked Lucia.

"When one comes to bind up the wounds and call the orphans to their mothers."

"Yes, yes, always when someone comes, always somewhere in the future!" She fought to loosen Sirena's grasp on her arm. "Let me go!"

"Now look," said Sirena. "Can't you be a little reasonable? You can never find him, never. They are far away now on fast horses, far away."

Lucia bowed forward, moaning, "My poor baby!"

A little later Lucia seemed to sleep. She had lain down on her side and had pulled her gray hair over to cover her face; and they heard her weeping behind the hair and then she was still. The old people had dozed off.

Sirena said: "You may as well sleep. I'll stay awake and watch her."

One by one they slept and then Sirena nodded and her head sank. When they awoke Lucia was gone.

Sirena leapt up crying, "She has gone!"

They searched behind the stone ledges and they went to the road and looked both ways. Her tracks were there, made by small bare feet. They followed them down the road and saw where she seemed to have fallen.

"I guess she fainted here," Sirena said.

They went to the next hill to look beyond, and to the next hill, but there was no sign of Lucia, save her footprints in the dust.

"Should we go on?" Joshua said.

"We could go on and on," Zillah said, "and never catch her."

"Let's go to the next hill," Joshua said.

They went down to the next hilltop but it was the same: there was nothing ahead of them but another hill and an empty road and distance.

"We have to go one way or the other," Sirena said. "We've no food, no water."

"Which is closer?" asked Zillah.

"Jerusalem," he said.

"We have to go back anyway," Zillah said. "Sibyl and the old people are waiting for us."

"She has no food or water," Zillah said. "She will die."

"If we don't do something," Sirena said, "we'll all die."

227

"Well, let's climb back."

They climbed back up from hill to hill and at daylight came to the spot where they had slept. Sarah said they would have to go find Lucia, they could not leave the poor thing to the brigands.

Sirena had sunk to the earth. "How? She has the strength of a desperate mother. What do we have?"

"The strength of friends. But for her we might all be dead."

Joshua said: "We'll all go find her."

Sirena shrugged. "Talk is easy but do you know how far back it is—and with neither water nor food."

"Papa and I will go find her. The rest of you go on."

"I can see us finding her," Aza said, "choking to death and staggering down the hills."

"You big strong ox," Sarah said.

Hopeless, despairing, they were considering the problem when there came over the hill above them a man riding an ass and leading two beasts laden with goods. With sword and dagger flashing from his girdle he drew up before them.

"A beautiful morning," he said. "Why do you look so sad?"

They told him what had happened and the smile left his face.

"We can't go after her," Sirena said. "We've nothing to eat or drink."

"Well now, if that's all you need I have both."

"But we have no money."

"Nobody is asking you for money. Are you all going back to find her?"

"I'm going," Sarah said.

"We haven't decided," Sirena said, "who will go."

"Well, I was thinking that if only one or two of you go I can let you take turns riding my beast. A little walking will do me no harm."

Joshua had been studying the man and his speech. "Are you a Samaritan?"

"You said it."

"And you would befriend us, whose people hate your people?"

The Samaritan pretended not to hear. He had dismounted. He now led his beasts away from the road. Digging into his cargo he brought forth a pouch filled with water and several parcels of food. He turned to them.

"After you've eaten you'll feel better. Hungry people always do." He laid the parcels by the pouch. "If one of you—?" he said, looking at the women.

Sirena went forward. Kneeling, she opened the parcels and found in one of them cheese, in another various dried fruits, and in a third, bread and a piece of roasted flesh. The Samaritan handed her his dagger and she sliced off meat and cheese. After drinking in turn from the water pouch they sat to eat.

"Better eat and drink all you can," the Samaritan said. "I have plenty." For a few moments he watched them eat. "Would you know these brigands if you saw them?"

"I would," Sarah said.

"Well, I don't think you'd ever find them. They probably have a camp away back in the hills or even across the river."

"Lucia will track them," Sarah said.

"You can't follow tracks over stones." He saw Sirena looking at the cheese. "Slice off some more, eat all you can, take some with you."

"The messiah is coming soon," Aza said, looking at the Samaritan.

"The one who'll overthrow Rome?"

"You don't believe it?" asked Sirena, looking at the man.

"My dear woman, I'm no longer a child. I don't believe in fables."

Zillah said: "But his coming is foretold in books."

"Well, a lot of them have come, haven't they? We've had several in Samaria. Just how many have they crucified anyway?"

"Do you think the end of the world is near?"

229

"Oh, by the beard of Moses!"

"It is foretold," said Joshua, accepting another piece of cheese.

"Just about anything is foretold, if you can read it that way. As I see it, here we are and we don't know why and some day we'll be no more. That's about all there is to it. Well, who is going with me?"

Sarah struggled to her feet. "My husband and I," she said.

"Should we all go?" Joshua asked, looking at Sirena and Zillah.

"I don't see why," Sarah said. "We'll find her."

The Samaritan had been observing Sarah. "You'd better ride. You don't look like you could walk very far."

"It's him," she said, indicating her husband.

Sirena asked: "When'll we see you again?"

"When we've found her," said Sarah.

"I'm a merchant in Schechem," said the Samaritan to Joshua. "When this king comes let me know. You're sure you won't take some food and water?"

"No, thank you," Sirena said. "We'll be fine now."

"It's not very far," he said.

They all said goodbye and then they helped Sarah mount and the Samaritan walked ahead to lead the two beasts with cargo and Aza led the beast on which Sarah rode. Joshua and the women stared after them until they were out of sight.

Then they turned up the hill, walking together, and a little after noon they could see the walls of Jerusalem. Having lived there, Joshua knew, as the others did not, that the city's patricians, proud of their sophistication and their wealth and their ceremonial purity, looked with contempt on the poor and the ritually unclean and resented their entering the city. Even the craftsmen and petty merchants, though landless and seldom prosperous, shared the contempt. He was thinking of these things as they trudged up the hill, their gaze on the distant towers.

How, Sirena asked, did it feel to be coming home?

230

He felt sad and wretched, he said. He could not forget Lucia and her child.

"We all feel sad," Zillah said.

Sirena asked: "Are people like me welcome in the city?"

Joshua responded with a tired smile. None of them were welcome, he said, and he least of all, for an unclean Jew was a pig.

"Won't it be better if we leave you at the gate?"

It would make no difference, he said. They were all outcasts anyway and they might as well stay together. It would not be like this after the messiah came.

They passed through the gate and Sirena's first impressions of the city were unpleasant; looking across it, she could see that it was very unlike Antioch and Athens and Rome. The parts she could see seemed to her to be barren and ugly. How, she wondered, could anyone believe that this was to be the most splendid of all cities, this hot and dusty and treeless place, with its waterless environs and stony hills! And when Joshua pointed out the temple her astonishment was boundless: compared to the great temples which she had seen it was nothing at all.

"Has your city always been like this?"

Zillah said slyly: "It's the navel of the world."

"Why didn't they build it in Galilee? It's so much nicer."

Joshua said: "Only when you've seen Jerusalem can you understand Jews."

They were looking at the temple when a man in immaculate garments passed, without indicating any awareness of their presence. After he had gone a hundred feet or so beyond them he stopped. They had turned to watch him, and now they saw him stand with his feet close together and bend low. It was said, Joshua told them, that the Pharisee in prayer ought to bend so low that every vertebra in his back would stand out separate, or in any case until the skin over his heart would fall in folds. This man had bent until his head seemed almost to touch the earth.

In a low voice Sirena said: "What is he doing?"

"Getting ready to pray."

"He's humbling himself," said Zillah and winked at Sirena.

Sirena choked back a laugh.

They stood for several minutes, watching, and the Pharisee still prayed. Joshua explained to them that the prolix prayer was believed to promote health and prolong life. Glancing round her, Sirena saw other men in awkward attitudes. She asked about them, and Joshua said that when the moment for prayer came, a devout Jew instantly interrupted what he was doing and began his prayers. Some of the learned Pharisees said that if a man happened to be sitting on a horse he must not dismount; or if up a tree gathering fruit he must remain there until his prayers were done; and even if a serpent was climbing his body he must pretend to be unaware of it.

Sirena was looking at his face. Having never known Joshua to make a jest she supposed that he was serious. "Shouldn't we stand still out of respect?"

It didn't matter at all, Joshua said. For those ritually unclean, prayer was like precious ointment poured on a dunghill. Did they know, he asked, that the Pharisees believed that God read the Torah every Sabbath?

Again Sirena looked at him sharply, but no, he was not jesting. "How do you tell a Pharisee?"

By their garments, he said. They had rich silk girdles with extremely wide borders. Yonder was a man and this man was a slave: he was marked as a slave by the fact that he had no beard, and he had no beard because he was not allowed to wear one, and he was not allowed to wear one because for Jews hair was godlike.

"Are you teasing us?" Sirena asked. She looked at Joshua's beard. It was short and curly and had never been trimmed, so far as she knew, since she first met him. It had never been anointed or scented. She turned to Zillah. "Is he?"

"Oh Lord, no," Zillah said. She poked Joshua in the

ribs. "You'd make a handsome Pharisee. You'd **pray all** the time."

"You think I'm jesting?" Joshua asked, blinking at Sirena. "Listen. If a clean Jew leaves an unclean Jew grinding meal in his house, the whole house becomes unclean if the mill stops. But if it goes on grinding the house becomes unclean only as far as the unclean one can reach by stretching his arms."

Sirena stared at him and then looked at Zillah. Zillah winked. She said: "You know who figured that out? Why, most likely the one who said that the spirit of God dwells only in Judea, for Judea is the grain, Galilee is the straw, and everything beyond Israel is chaff. Sirena is chaff. I am straw."

Joshua said, "Look! I think this is the High Priest coming, the one they call the Holy Father. Notice his garments."

A proud and haughty man, dressed for beauty and for glory, was coming toward them but he did not see them, he would not see them. While he slowly sauntered past, at a distance of a hundred feet, Joshua was whispering to them about the priest's robes and ornaments: his ephod was made of gold, of blue, of purple, of scarlet, all of the finest linen, and his girdle also; and upon the shoulders of the ephod were precious stones; and his chains were of the purest gold; and his breastplate was set with four rows of jewels, one of which was diamonds. He had enough wealth on him, Joshua said, to feed all the poor by the river.

"He's magnificent," Sirena said.

"The mites of ten thousand widows and ten thousand beggars bought that magnificence."

"Just the same, Joshua, you have to admit that his robe is beautiful. Or don't you?"

Joshua looked at her and shrugged. "Would you think a purse beautiful made from the hide of a man skinned alive?—or a necklace of teeth knocked from a slave's mouth?"

"Look, Joshua, things can be beautiful in themselves."

"They aren't," he said.

"They sometimes are. The rose is fertilized with dung, isn't it? The form of the tiger has been nourished and shaped by a hundred defenseless gazelles. The greatest philosopher or poet may be a bastard child conceived in a brothel. Isn't that the riddle of life?—how beauty can come out of evil?"

"I don't find such things beautiful," he said.

"Beautiful in themselves, I mean."

Zillah said: "Can a jewel be beautiful that is paid for with orphans? Is Lucia's lesson of love one you can never learn?"

Sirena flushed a little. "I suppose," she said, "it is the difference between Greek and Jew. I say beauty is beauty, no matter how many orphans it took to produce it."

"And we say," said Joshua, "there can be no beauty without righteousness."

"Why, good heavens!" cried Sirena, so vexed that she lost her temper. "We have the proof right here with us, don't we? Which is the most beautiful one among us and what made her so?"

Joshua shook his head sadly. "Come," he said, "we must find a place for the night."

XX

They all wanted to go with Joshua when he saw his mother but he said he wished to go alone. He recalled the words of the Roman in Jericho, It is good for a man to see his mother. But was it good, when the mother had one way of life, the son another? To see her again would be an ordeal and he dreaded it. He had thought many times of the old Cynic's words, When you see your mother, feel shame for yourself, for me, for all men, because it is a man's world and a man's arrogance that have given bitter tongues to women. That, he admitted, might be so, but was not arrogance also natural to a woman? A woman, like a man, could become inflexibly and inexorably set in rules of conduct, in rigid ceremonials and rituals, handed down from father to son or from mother to daughter. Or had such women, as the Cynic said, grotesquely reshaped themselves in the image of men?

She would peer at him in the intent and searching way she had and she would say, "You are still a wicked son." She would reproach him. She would say he had been her favorite and he had disappointed her. She would feel the warmth and the tears of self-pity. She would again wish to shape him to her will. Mothers were that way with their sons but had men made them that way or was it a weakness in mothers? Had the old man seen all the truth?

Saying that he was going for a walk he slipped away one morning. Bethany was a few houses on a small tableland

235

in the wilderness, a mile or two east of Jerusalem. His mother's house, as he remembered it, was a small ugly thing of mudbrick, with almost no furnishings but some straw mats and goatskins for bedding, one rickety bedstead of olive wood, a few cooking pots with round bottoms, a water pouch made from the skin of a kid, and a small storage bin. She had had three or four goats and a few olive trees, and with these she had managed a frugal living, after her husband's death. Why, he wondered, did wives complain incessantly about their health, yet in most cases outlive their husbands? He thought there must be in Israel ten widows to every widower.

When he came in sight of the village he stopped. He saw the house. It had not changed at all. He looked round him at the bleak ravines, the outcroppings of stone, the waterless earth as far east as he could see, as far north or south. He recalled Sirena's question, "How can a person live in this country and ever smile?" and Zillah's reply, "They don't." Still, that was not true. In a way his people were a people of deep and abiding joys.

While he stood there a woman framed herself in the doorway. He knew that it was his mother. She looked old and gray and bent. Even from a distance he could see that her face was dreadfully wrinkled and he felt pity for her, knowing that she was alone and lonely, old and ill and abandoned. He went forward and she came out to meet him. He stood before her and said simply, "It is Joshua, your son."

She was peering up at his face. Her sight was failing her and she could not see him clearly. "Yes," she said, "it is Joshua. I can tell by your voice. Do you now have a beard?"

"Yes, mother."

"Where have you come from today?"

"The city."

"Do you know what day this is?"

Did he? "No," he said.

"It is the Sabbath."

There it was again. After years he had come home, but deeper in her than joy at seeing him was consciousness of all the holy rules and laws, that had overgrown her motherhood as a thicket might overgrow and conceal a garden. In her was the fear that he was not observant. There were her eyes again, the same eyes, peering at him, searching him for evil. But he felt no evil.

Her laugh was short and bitter. How many times had he heard that laugh as a child?

"The same wicked son," she said. "You have profaned the holy Sabbath day."

"Yes, mother."

"Didn't you hear the horns blowing last night?"

"Yes, mother, I heard them."

"And you've already walked farther than the holy laws allow you to. Do you always profane this day?"

"Mother, I suppose I do."

"Have you eaten?"

"No."

"Have you said your prayers?"

"No, mother."

"Have you washed your hands?"

"No, mother." Joshua sighed. She was the same mother. She had not changed at all.

"What things have you touched?"

"I don't remember. Mother, must we go over all this again?"

"Your father and I taught you," she said bitterly. "We taught you to say all the prayers which our Father commanded us to teach our sons. Blessed be he. But you have forgotten all that we taught you, haven't you?"

"Not all of it, mother."

"Which is the greatest of the commandments?"

"Hillel said it. Don't do to others what you'd not have them do to you."

"Oh, no," she said, shaking her gray hair. "This is the greatest: Hear, O Israel, the Lord our God, the Lord is One. How could you forget it?"

237

"I found a greater one, mother."

"Oh, no. Of the commandments which is the second?"

"Mother, I don't know and I don't care."

"You don't care!" she cried, aghast. "The same wicked son. After your father departed I taught you, even then. And now, here I stand, myself sinning, for it is a sin on this holy day to talk to one who is impious. The hours I spent with you, the hours I wasted!"

"Yes, mother. Don't weep."

"I taught you to fast for the Day of Atonement but do you?"

"No."

"I taught you to give thanks to God at every hour of the day and night. My son, do you?"

"I give thinks in my own way."

"Have you been with the heathen?"

"Yes, mother."

"Have you touched a heathen woman?"

"Not in the way you mean."

"But you have been with them!" She was working herself into a tantrum. All the bitterness of her lonely years, all her disappointment in this strange son who had been her favorite, were coming upon her like the night. "You've been away in the heathen world," she said, her eyes accusing and reproaching him, "and you'll never be clean again! Why have you done this to your old mother?"

"Mother, listen."

"No, I won't listen!"

"Listen a moment. Are you aware that the son of David is coming?—and soon?"

"Of course I know it! But he's not coming to people like you, never to people like you!"

"You don't understand," Joshua said patiently. "He is coming to all people. He is coming to bind up the wounds, to open the prisons, to bring orphans—"

"Oh, no!" she said, shrinking from him. "He's coming to his own holy people. He's coming to destroy all the wicked people."

"No, mother. He's coming to all people who will come to him."

"You say such things on this day of all days!"

"On this day of all days, yes. Mother, will you listen? The one who is coming, the messiah—"

"Shall I listen to a wicked man who lives with the heathen? I taught you, Joshua, I devoted myself to you—but you ran away to the godless people. And now, after all these years, when at last you come home how do you come?" She was on the verge of tears.

"But it won't be as you think it will be, as you hope it will be."

"Please! Don't speak any more wicked words on this Sabbath day!" She opened her eyes wide and looked at him with horror, and in the horror he saw tears.

"I'd only like to tell you," he said, "why the son of David is coming."

"*You* would tell *me?* You, a friend of the heathen, would tell a daughter of Israel? Do you know that you have broken your mother's heart? Do you know that you have desecrated my yard? Do you know that you have heaped shame upon my gray head?"

"Do you want me to go?"

She hesitated, looking at him. "Yes, go."

He turned away but at once turned back. "May I come again?"

"Only when you have returned to your people and re-pented your wickedness."

Still he hesitated, looking at his mother but she turned and left him and went into her house. He saw her bent form and her gray hair and again thought of the Cynic's words. Yes, it was nice for a man to see his mother if motherhood was more than a physical relationship, more than the tyranny of a will, more than a mind abandoned to rituals. He did not feel that this was his mother or that he had a mother. . . .

He turned back to the city, feeling pity for this little old woman, so lonely and embittered, feeling that he would never see her again. He blinked, and felt tears fall from his lashes to his cheeks. He also was lonely and sad and when back in the city he stood alone, looking around him, trying to believe that all this was a part of him and that a part of him had never gone from it. The devotion to it of pious Jews was as intense and all-embracing as their devotion to their holy books; but for him, long ago, it had been a city of strangers, and the holy books had had in them much that was evil. If I forget you, O Jerusalem, let my right hand forget her cunning! If I do not remember you, let my tongue cleave to the roof of my mouth; if I prefer not Jerusalem above my chief joy! With what outpouring of prayer and praise the pilgrim greeted his holy city, when returning to it from far places! And that was good. But it was also written, Their houses shall be spoiled and their wives ravished. It was written, Let their wives be bereaved of their children and be widows. It was written, Let his children be fatherless and his wife a widow. Let his children be vagabonds and beg . . . Let there be none to extend mercy unto him; neither let there be any to favor his fatherless children . . . Their children shall be dashed to pieces before their eyes . . . Had his mother fixed such wicked words in her heart? Did she really believe that God had given such commands to his children? Where was the roof above Lucia's child? he might ask her; and what would she say? It was written, Hath he not sent me to the men that sit upon the wall, that they may eat their own dung and drink their own piss? Where was the house of fellowship? It was written, And you shall take them as an inheritance for your children after you, to inherit them for a possession; they shall be your bondmen forever. Where was there pity for the slave?—where in all the words of the holy books, from end to end! Were these the things to which his mother turned in her loneliness?

Looking round him with sad hurt eyes Joshua remembered that this was indeed the holy Sabbath: yes, it was true that his mother had taught him many of the laws but these had lost their meanings as he wandered among other people and observed their customs. There were so many hundreds of these laws to be obeyed; besides all those in the Torah there were countless others which learned Jews had evolved; or various subtleties and refinements upon those that were old. On this day, for instance, there were thirty-nine kinds of work prohibited, including singing and playing music, or matters as trivial as the tying of a knot in a string. The devout among his people were so confined by the multitude of rules that they were no longer free, but moved as imprisoned creatures in the infinite complexities which their own ingenuity had created. It was, it seemed to Joshua, a monstrous travesty on holiness. For was there any holiness in his mother?

He went around to the temple, which he would not have dared to enter, being unclean, and saw above a gate these words in Greek:

> Let no foreigner enter within the balustrade
> and embankment about the sanctuary. Whoever
> is caught makes himself responsible for his
> death which will follow

This interdict had been put there by the Roman governor in deference to Israel. Joshua had heard that ignorant persons, such as those unable to read, not even in their own language, much less in Greek, had ventured into the courts and had been killed. He had no doubt of it. There was no more fanatical and murderous person in the world than a religious bigot who saw his sanctuary defiled. . . .

Joshua had no wish to go in. He did not believe that this was God's house or that holiness was to be found in buildings, and least of all in a building with fabulous treasure in gold and jewels and furnishings, while most of the people starved. He did not believe that a spirit of holiness dwelt in the hearts of those proud and arrogant men arrayed in rich robes, embroidered with gold and emblazoned with precious stones. What had Sirena meant? God was with the poor, the sick, the defenseless and the homeless. He was with those who needed him. His spirit was under the sky and by the waters and in the fragrant groves. It was with Lucia now.

Well, the ninth of Ab would soon be here, when all devout Jews would fast, and lament the destruction of the temple long ago by heathen hands. Would the king of love and compassion announce his presence on this day? If he did, who would recognize him, who accept him? Joshua did not believe that he would come with lightning and thunder, a flaming sword in his hand, his nostrils spouting fire. He did not believe that he would come as an avenger to destroy the heathen peoples and enthrone Israel above all the nations of the earth. He did not believe that a vast and celestial Jerusalem would descend from the heavens, or that this city would be lifted nine miles above the earth, to shine there with streets of gold and with walls encrusted with jewels.

No, there would be a greater miracle, the miracle of love. The messiah would come with great power but it would be the power that dwelt in pity and compassion. He would come to bind up the wounds, to heal the sick, to comfort the widows and orphans, to bring the blessing of peace and goodwill to all who would accept it. He would come with God's power upon him but it would be the power of tenderness. He would come with love, and for whom more than for the Lucias and the Sibyls?

Joshua went over and sat on a hillside and looked at the Mount of Olives. Some night he would go over there and pray, pray that his people might lay aside their arrogance and humble themselves; that they might accept all people as their neighbors and their brothers; that they might understand with Philo, the great Alexandrian Jew, that not all wisdom and goodness was to be found in their books; and that, more than anything else, they might soften their harsh contempt of women and realize that they were sisters and mothers and not the sinful daughters of Eve.

While trying to formulate a prayer that he would utter, over there among the olive trees, he wondered if he would dare to use the prayer as a text and a lesson. Would he dare to tell his people that they, who of all people had suffered most, who so many times had been conquered and enslaved, were best fitted of all people, by reason of long suffering and example, to offer the world a nobler idea of the messiah? Should he or some man of greater learning try to soften their proud and impassioned and fanatical hearts, and make them understand that God, the Father, was not the petty vengeful tyrant who harangued Moses? But if he or another man tried to do that what price would he pay? Should he keep the prayer in his heart and wait for the ninth of Ab or the Day of Atonement?

He supposed he should. He turned away at last, thinking of Lucia, a desperate woman alone somewhere trying to find her child; of Sibyl, who had not been with them for two days; of Sirena, wavering between faith and doubt, between Jew and Greek; of Zillah, with her overmastering need of love; and of all the thousands upon the Jordan, and of the fierce Zealots who would lead Israel to disaster if they could. He thought of the strange man who called himself John the baptizer, now dead—and then of the whole incredible picture of Israel, with its anxieties and terrors and hopes, in these last days before the end of things. Though unhappily aware that this was the Sabbath he began to walk aimlessly; and at last was descending into the vale of the cheesemongers, where they now spent their nights, when he saw Sibyl.

Looking more lovely than an angel and more unearthly she was hurrying along, her arms filled with parcels.

"Sibyl?" he said.

She started and choked back a scream. "Oh, Joshua, you frightened me!"

"You have been gone from us. Where have you been?"

"Away."

"And what do you have there?"

"Food for all of us."

He went up to her and tried to look into her eyes but

243

she lowered her gaze. He put a finger under her chin to tip her head up but she would not look at him. "Where did you get all this food?"

"An angel gave it to me," she said.

"An angel? A man?"

"An angel like a man."

"Sibyl, you are lying to me."

Then he knew. Why, he wondered impatiently, had he not known from the first? Sibyl, the harlot of Migdal, who looked into the heavens and saw visions, who had seen the radiance of the celestial spheres, who had lain with an angel, the very sight of whom would make his mother ill —Sibyl the whore—but who was he to reproach her for her devotion, in whom it was so easy to see the mother! Should he not instead touch her gently and bless her? What did the Father think of such a woman as Sibyl?

"Joshua, are you angry with me?"

"No, Sibyl. I am not your judge."

"I am wicked," she said, looking at the parcels.

This woman, the mother, called herself wicked, and his own mother, turning him away from her door, thought herself holy. What did the Father think of them?

"You did this for love of us?"

"Yes, Joshua."

"And you did it on the Sabbath?"

"The Sabbath, then, is not a day for love?"

"But this—"

"Yes, Joshua." She looked down at the parcels. "I will take them back," she said.

"They are not the kind of things that can be taken back."

He was asking himself, Who is more worthy in the sight of God, the harlot who sins to feed those she loves?—or the Pharisee who will not sit with a Lucia?

He took from her most of the parcels and they went down the hill and found Sirena and Zillah sitting by the goatshed waiting for him.

With astonishment the two women looked at the parcels

but before they could speak Joshua said: "With my people there is an old saying: Judge not, lest you be judged also. Let us eat and rejoice and leave her soul to heaven, for where the mother was supposed to be she was not and where she was supposed not to be she was." He looked at Sirena. "Isn't that a darker riddle than any the old philosopher gave us?"

XXI

As the ninth of Ab drew near Joshua was unable to sleep, almost unable to eat. He searched the heavens for signs, he prowled the city, he talked to a few of the common people; and he learned to his astonishment that the most learned men had never expected the messiah on this day. He would come, they said, in one of the two holiest seasons, the Day of Atonement or the Passover. On the eighth of Ab Joshua felt crushed.

"But the learned men could be wrong," Sirena said.

"If they are wrong," said Joshua, "who are right?"

People were wailing and crying all night but they were the common people. Joshua refused to eat and until dark he walked up the hill and over the city and down, and up and down, staring with the common people at the sky, at the earth; praying with them that the messiah would come on the morrow; and at last returning to the goat-shed but not to sleep.

They were in the deep ravine between Jerusalem's two hills, known as the vale of the cheesemongers because of the many small dairies there. In one of these Sirena had found work to earn their food. She had also found a stable in which they could sleep; in one end of it were goats, in the other a pile of clean barley straw. None of them had had a bath since they left the Jordan, and when Sirena wondered if they could find a place to bathe, Zillah said there was not much water in Jerusalem. King Herod Antipas, known by those who flattered him as Herod the

Great, but by devout Jews as that Hasmonaean slave, who had inherited from his brutal but imaginative father a love of display, of magnificent buildings and of women, had aroused the Jews to wild revolt when he built an aqueduct to bring water to the city.

Joshua was sitting by the shed and looking up now and then at the sky when the three women came to sit with him.

"Hear them crying," Sirena said, looking up the hill. "Will Lucia know that tomorrow is the ninth?"

"I hope not," Joshua said.

Sirena fell to thinking about the attitude of pious Jews here toward the heathen. When she tactlessly asked for work in a Jewish dairy the owner had refused to talk to her. Later she learned that milk drawn from beasts by unclean hands could be used only by the unclean. She learned that a devout Jew would no more have sat to eat with Joshua than he would have cursed his own father. For whom was the messiah coming anyway?

She had found work in a heathen dairy at the north end of the vale and daily her astonishment grew. She learned that ritual offenses were far more wicked than moral ones: it was a worse sin to omit a fixed prayer, such as the Shema, or to enter a synagogue with unwashed hands, or to walk more than two thousand cubits on the Sabbath, than to beat a slave to death or to cast a wife out who had burned her bread. It was a worse sin to touch one of the holy books with unclean hands than to leave an unclean Jew by the wayside to die. It was a worse sin for a ritually clean Jew to eat cheese made in the dairy where she worked than to stone to death an ignorant man who unwittingly wandered into the temple courts. . . .

Joshua said the messiah was coming to the unclean but she thought it was the clean who needed him most. For she had perceived how wide was the gulf between Joshua and clean Jews. She now realized what awful blasphemy it was for Joshua to say that the God of Israel was the Father of all nations and loved all people. She understood at last why he was afraid to enter the synagogue to teach, why if he did so he might be killed.

"Have you seen any signs?" she asked.

"Not one," he said. "But how can he delay his coming?"

"For the reason that Elijah hasn't yet come. Or perhaps for the reason that no teacher has risen. Preparing the way and making it straight, what can it mean but teaching?"

The night passed and the ninth came and no messiah announced himself in the holy city. Sitting by the shed, Joshua was turning over and over in his mind Sirena's words, Preparing the way, what can it mean but teaching? He was afraid to teach yet he became more and more convinced that someone would have to teach the ignorant or the messiah would never come. If Elijah came would he teach them, and if so, why did he tarry? Joshua prayed for guidance and struggled with his inner torments and postponed an ordeal which he felt deep in his heart must come. How long till the Day of Atonement? Sirena asked. Joshua tried to count the days: after Ab came Elul, and after Elul, Tishri, with the new year, and the Day of Atonement was the tenth of Tishri, or about fifty-seven days, he thought, after the ninth of Ab.

"It will come," he said bitterly, "and find me a coward, eating the labor of women."

"That doesn't matter," said Sirena quickly. "I understand now why you must not teach. It would be your death."

"If none teaches, then will the messiah come?"

"Let Elijah teach. You know, Joshua, if Elijah is coming to the poor and the outcast, then won't he come to Galilee? Have you thought that perhaps we should go back there to wait for him?"

"But this is the holy city," he said.

"For a Greek," she said, "that depends on your point of view."

Every day Joshua went forth to observe the people and one evening he became aware, with gooseflesh tingling all over him, that he was being followed. Was this a spy? Should he swing back and face the man or should he pretend not to have seen him, and so discover his purpose in the days to come? Prudence told him to go on but anger spun him and he went back. He was too astonished for words when he saw that it was Levi.

He stared at the little man several moments before he was able to say, "You? You, Levi? What is the meaning of this?" When there was no response, no change in the face or the eyes, Joshua said: "Why did you leave us at Jericho? Is it true that you were spying on me all that time?"

"No."

"But you are spying on me now. Why?"

"Only to protect you," Levi said.

"Do I need protection?"

"There is one who spies on you," Levi said, "whom you may never see, for he is cunning."

"Who is this, Levi?"

"Master, I don't know. I think he is one of Herod's."

"Don't call me master. I am only Joshua, a man like you. How long has this spy been watching me?"

"Since Jericho."

There came over Joshua again infinite sadness, and with it, helplessness; for what could he do? He could be a coward and flee. Or he could remain here and comfort and counsel in his humble ways and face the punishment that probably would come. He thought Levi was looking at him almost worshipfully and he did not like that.

"Levi, have you been watching me every day?"

"Yes."

"Well, we are down there," said Joshua, pointing. "Come this evening and eat with us."

One day he brought home with him a piece of papyrus on which was one of the Jewish Sibyls, based on prophetic books of the heathen; it told what would happen as the dreadful day of judgment drew near.

He read it to them: "From heaven shall fall upon earth

swords of fire; immense torches shall fall also, and flame in the midst of men. The earth, the great mother of all, will in those days be shaken by the hand of the Immortal. The fishes of the sea, all the beasts of the earth, the innumerable families of birds, all the souls of men, and all the seas shall tremble. All will be terror. The Immortal will break down the scarped summits and the high cliffs of the mountains, and black Erebus will appear to all eyes. High as the abode of the winds shall be the caves in the high mountains filled with corpses; and rocks shall drip blood and form torrents which shall inundate the plain. God will judge the people by war, by the sword, and by a deluge. From heaven will fall stones, a terrible hail, and brimstone. The moans and clamor of the dying will rise in all the earth; then all, silent and prone, will lie bathed in their blood, and the earth will drink the blood of men, and wild beasts shall gorge themselves with their flesh."

With a wan smile he laid the thing aside. "That's what some of them are telling my people. Do you hear their wailing? They have heard these things, these lies from the mouth of a lying prophet. They are afraid. And if none stands up to teach them their terror will destroy them."

"But not you."

"I am not worthy. But where is the man? Are we to wait until the people are prostrate with terror and dying of fear? Men go around the city proclaiming these terrible lies and that seems to be all right; but if one says the messiah will be a prince of love and peace, that is not all right."

"That," said Sirena, "will never be all right."

"Not even the most thorough cynic among the Cynics could believe that."

"Do many of the people accept these things, these lies?"

"Most of them."

"Are some dying of fear?"

"Some of them."

Joshua looked up to see a man standing before him. The vale of the cheesemongers was so densely peopled

that the huts and barns and stables and shops stood
jammed together, with streets, which were only paths, so
narrow that a beast laden with flax could barely get
through. Artisans lived here, traders, petty merchants, and
many of the poor. When Joshua and the women sat in
the stable to talk they could be overheard if they did not
whisper by people all around them, who also were housed
in stables and sheds. This man had heard them talking.

He was middle-aged and he looked very sad and weary,
with sorrowful inflamed eyes. The parts of his lips that
were visible in his thin black beard looked sickly; his
hands at his sides were shaking with tremors; and his voice
shook when he spoke.

"Are you the one they tell about?" he asked, staring at
Joshua.

"Who tells?"

"They tell in the city. Are you the one who was born
in a stable?"

Perplexed, Joshua turned to Sirena. "Can you imagine
what he means?"

"The heathen savior-gods are born in a cave or a stable
but this man is a Jew, isn't he?"

"You teach among the beasts," the man said, still looking at Joshua.

"I wasn't teaching," Joshua said. "I was reading."

"I've heard you teach many nights."

Sirena said: "The god-baby lives with beasts and they
adore it. But where has he heard these things?"

"Such things are to be heard everywhere."

Not to be put off the man said: "He was uttering prophecies just now. I heard him."

"I was reading," Joshua said, beginning to feel anxious.

"What is your name?" asked Zillah.

He did not look at her, he paid no attention to her.

"We wish to be alone," Sirena said. "Will you please
leave us?"

Slowly, as one who would not be put away, as one who
had sought long and not found, the man sat, his sad eyes

251

never leaving Joshua's face. He was determined not to be shut out from the good news, if there was good news in this stable. He sat like a dumb thing that had all of time on its side and looked at Joshua and waited.

Sirena asked: "Is it in Israel that you heard about a holy man in a stable?"

He did not look at her, he seemed not to hear.

"Talk to him," said Zillah, "and then he'll go away. It's plain that he doesn't like women."

Sirena shrugged. "Do you mean King Cyrus?" she asked the man. "He played in the ox-stalls as a babe. The god Attis was nourished by a goat in a shed. Poseidon, another god, was born in a cave and fed by a ewe. Are these the ones you mean?" He refused to look at her. "Gods are born in stables and the beasts adore them but not in Israel. In Israel there is only the Father." She turned to Joshua. "Why in the world are heathen gods born in stables? I'd never thought about it."

"I don't know," Joshua said, wishing the man would go away, wondering if he was in any way associated with the spy. "Do you know Levi?" he asked.

"I know him," the man said. "He knows that you are teaching in a stable but he doesn't know why and I ask you why."

"He was only reading," Zillah said.

"I heard his prophecies," the man said. "Has the son of David been born in a stable?"

"I have no idea," Joshua said.

"Will he be a god?"

"By the merciful one, no! Can a son of Israel think such wickedness?"

Sadly, patiently the man studied him, and he startled them the next evening by walking in with Levi. At first the women, or Sirena and Zillah at least, were annoyed by the presence of these men, the one called Levi and the other called Simon: they were so dumb in their humility, so patient but also so persistent in their need, so transparent and child-like in their faith. They got used to them, though they refused to let them sleep in this shed or to remain long. The two men gave them no trouble. They never looked at anyone or spoke to anyone but Joshua.

Joshua had told the women what Levi had told him, that a spy was on his trail and that Levi was spying on the spy.

"I wouldn't trust him," Sirena said.

"I wouldn't either," Zillah said. "And as for the other spy I'll find out who he is."

"Levi says he is one of Herod's men."

Sometimes Joshua came in from his wanderings with strange things to tell. There was the man who for years had walked up and down in the city, crying in a voice as loud and clear as a trumpet, "Woe, woe to Jerusalem!" The people said he had repeated this cry every few seconds, day and night, and had never grown hoarse or weary. He had never raised his voice or lowered it. He had never uttered any words but those.

Another man, while fasting for the ninth of Ab, had seen wonders in the heavens, like those which foretold the defeat of Hannibal by the Romans. The sun and moon had fought together, throwing off vast sheets of flame and assaulting one another with lightning until the sky was swimming in stupendous seas of fire; and the sun, torn in two and bloody and dripping, had hastened to his setting. Then stones as hot as flame had fallen into the dead sea, and people as far away as Hebron had heard the seething of the waters. Two moons came up that night, filled with blood, and moved slowly across the heavens, with blood pouring from them. The man, it was said, had gone out and found trees on which blood had been spilled and had shown them to his neighbors. He had found an ass shedding floods of tears and praying with a human voice. . . .

There was the man who had been healed. For thirty years this poor creature had lain by one of Jerusalm's pools, unable to move more than his hands, with which he dipped up water to drink or ate what was thrown to him. He was covered over with leaking sores and huge swellings, which the people could look at when they lifted the filthy rag that covered him. Day and night his lips had moved in prayer. Then—only the other day, it was said—someone had healed him, a wonder-worker with divine powers; and there were those who believed that the messiah had secretly entered the city.

But did Joshua think so? they asked him. Joshua said that possibly he had, but that in any case such wonders foretold his coming. There could be little doubt now that he would come, if not on the Day of Atonement, then at the next Passover. Sibyl made a little sound of distress. She was looking at Joshua. She had been acting strangely of late, as though possessed of a deep and silent grief. She seemed to be fading, to be thinner and paler, and to have some secret, denied to the others; but when asked what she was thinking or why she cried out as if in distress she would say nothing at all.

They were all becoming strange, it seemed to Sirena, as the Day drew near. An immense hush seemed to have fallen upon the city, even, she thought, upon the beasts, for the goats she milked seemed more subdued and their language softer. The hush fell a little before the first day of the new year, and deepened as the Day of Atonement approached. Joshua said that the people were not talking, or if they talked it was in low voices; and that they seemed to step more softly, lest they disturb the silence with footfalls. The number of people who thought the messiah was already here seemed to be growing, though among them he knew of no learned man, no rab, no priest. A light snow was falling.

As they sat together the evening before the Day Joshua told them there would be spectacular rituals in the temple and its courts; there would be praying and singing; and the sins of Israel the past year would be placed on the head of a goat, the goat for Azazel, and it would be taken across the wilderness to the east and hurled over a precipice. The assembled host would almost faint and some would gasp and shudder and some would stifle screams when the High Priest went into the Holy of Holies, to perform the sacred rites there, to sprinkle incense. The Holy of Holies was such a dreadful place, so filled with the presence of God and with his majesty and his power, that it was never known if the High Priest would come out alive; and the multitude held their breath until they saw him again. Yes, there would be these very impressive ceremonies but not for the common people; they were sitting in their huts or tents or in sheds and barns or under no shelter at all and there was no absolving of their sins, no goat for them, but only the messiah if he would ever come!

"You can almost hear the hush," Zillah said. "Is that music?"

Joshua listened. He thought possibly they were hearing music from the temple courts, or it might be music from the heavenly spheres.

"The messiah is already here," Levi said. He was as usual staring at Joshua.

"We don't know," Joshua said.

They all listened. They thought they could hear music. They talked, they listened, they waited, until one by one most of them fell asleep. Joshua could hear gentle rain falling on the shed roof and after a while he slipped away and climbed the hill; and he walked in the rain till daylight. He saw many people who were not asleep and they looked at him, their lips mute but their eyes speaking; and he went now and then past the temple, to see its lights and hear its music; and at the break of day returned to the shed, thinking, *This* is the Day of Atonement, has he come?

Had he come? "Well, I'm not going to sit around any longer and wait," Zillah said. "I'll get a job too." She found work in a dairy and she and Sirena bought warmer clothes for them, as well as blankets for bedding. They never had a fire. They ate cold food, chiefly goatmilk and cheese and dried fruits. They worried over Lucia and the two old people and now and then they went beyond the wall to the road, as though they expected to see them coming. They talked about them and about the weather and about many things but they never mentioned the ninth of Ab or the Day of Atonement.

Joshua was more thoughtful, sadder, thinner. Now and then on a Sabbath he would wash his hands at the basin before a synagogue and go inside, not to teach but to listen. He liked to hear the psalms, which were chanted antiphonally to music, the congregation repeating the words after the precentor. At the conclusion of the psalm the leader would say, "And you say amen!" and the deep voices would respond, "Amen! Amen!" The musical instruments were cymbals, psalters and harfes, all of which sounded forth in a kind of free fantasia at the breaks.

He liked to hear the congregation respond to the reader.

"We will sanctify your Name in the world even as they sanctify it in the highest heavens, as it is written by the hand of your prophet: and they cried one to the other and said—"

"Holy—holy—holy is the Lord of hosts; the whole earth is filled with his glory!"

"To those over against them they said, Blessed—"

"Blessed be the glory of the Lord from his Place!"

"And in your holy words it is written, saying—"

"The Lord shall reign forever, your God, unto all generations! Praise the Lord!"

"Unto all generations we will declare your greatness, and to eternity we will hallow your holiness; and your praise, O our God, shall never depart from our mouth, for a great and holy God and King you are! Blessed are you, O Lord the holy God! . . ."

One Sabbth after another he listened to the teaching.

"While the angels were disputing and discussing with one another, the Holy One, praised be he, created man. He created him with wisdom, for he created first the things necessary for his life. Then the angels spoke before the

256

Holy One, praised be he: Lord of the world, what is man that you are mindful of him, and the son of man that you visit him? Why should this sorrow be created? Then the Holy One, praised be he, said to them: Why have all sheep and oxen been created, the fowl of the air and the fish of the sea—why have these been created? A castle with all good things, and there are no guests; what pleasure has the owner who takes his fill? Then the angels said, O our Lord, how excellent is your Name in all the earth! Do what seems best to you. . . ."

Why should this sorrow be created? There, Joshua felt, his people spoke when their souls were closest to heaven. There was Job . . . Jonah . . . Isaiah!

He heard:

"How does the holy city sit solitary? Jeremiah asked it. It is like a noble woman who has three friends: one sees her in honor, another in abandon, a third in sorrow. Moses saw the children of Israel in their honor, Isaiah saw them in their abandon, Jeremiah in their sorrow. And in sorrow she is still solitary. . . ."

There again, it seemed to Joshua, his people were at their best—in their astonishing talent for parable. In sorrow she is still solitary: how beautifully it was said! He had almost forgotten that the great prophets had been great poets, and great prophets only as great poets are. When aglow with pride in his people he even enjoyed the casuistries.

He heard:

"Seven garments, the Holy One, blessed be he, has put on, and will put on from the time the world was created until the hour when he will punish the wicked Edom. When he created the world he clothed himself in honor and majesty, as it is written: You are clothed in honor and majesty. When he forgave Israel's sins he clothed himself in white; for it is written, His garment was white as snow. When he punishes the people of the world he puts on the garment of vengeance, for it is written: He put on the garments of vengeance for clothing and was clad with zeal as a cloak. The sixth garment he will put on when the son of David comes; then he will clothe himself in a garment of righteousness. The seventh garment he will put on when he punishes the heathen, and it will shine from one end of the earth to the other. . . ."

In another synagogue he heard:

"Blessed is the hour when the son of David will come! Blessed is the womb out of which he will come! Blessed will be the people who will see him come. . . ."

But a few minutes later the same Rab or Hacham, meaning the learned one, was describing the veil which hung before the Holy of Holies: it was only a hairbreadth in thickness, and was woven of seventy-two twisted plaits, each consisting of twenty-four threads. Six threads were white, six were blue, six were scarlet and six were gold. The veil was forty cubits long and twenty cubits wide, and was made of eighty-two myriads. It took three hundred priests to immerse a veil before it was used. On and on he talked, explaining the wonderful mysteries, embellishing, exaggerating, all for the glory of God.

When a statement was made that seemed to him blind with folly Joshua would leave the building and walk; as when it was said, "The Law is the tree of life." He wanted to say, "No! The tree of life is love. Hillel said it." But he did not dare to speak, not yet. He was being watched possibly day and night; Zillah had never been able to see the spy, if there was one, and concluded that the whole thing was in Levi's fancy. But Joshua sensed that he was under the watchful eyes of a spy and he remembered every day the admonitions of the Roman officials. He knew it would be more prudent if he did not enter a synagogue at all. He knew that he could not forever hold his tongue.

One day he heard:

"Why did the Holy One, blessed be he, make a distinction between Israel and all other people? For the same reason that he distinguished between the sacred and the profane, darkness and light, holiness and evil. Blessed are you, O Lord, who have made a distinction between these things! Better for the wicked to cut off their hands and pluck out their eyes than that they should commit a sin no larger than a grain of mustard seed. The distinction made between Israel and all other people. . . ."

Hearing such teachings Joshua came to that hour when he could no longer be silent. When the ruler asked if any person wished to comment, Joshua stiffened and said, "I do."

There was silence. Joshua was standing in the rear. He said: "In all the synagogues where I have listened I have heard the learned men of Israel talk about vengeance but never about mercy; about the splendors and treasures of the temple but never about the poor who cry for food; about the righteousness of those who observe the commandments but never how their riches came from the toil of the weak; about the wickedness of the heathen but never about the arrogance of their judges. And how tiresome to be eternally told that Israel is as the light, all other people as the dark; Israel as holiness, all others as evil!"

People all around were staring at him. He was alarmed by his boldness but boldness seemed to beget boldness; he was miserably conscious of the risk he was taking but seemed to love the risk. Just the same he might have sat down if he had not seen on the platform the gray beard of a Pharisee nodding gentle approval.

"You command the people to come forth to bring their tithes and firstfruits and all the other taxes on which the priesthood has grown fat; but where is your sympathy for all the common people who have been robbed and cast out? I hear things that make me ashamed to be a son of Israel. There is an old saying in our books, that some strain out the gnats and swallow the camels. This they are doing in every synagogue in this city."

An inner voice said, Be silent, go now—for some were looking at him with anger, some with amazement. A voice cried to him to sit down but a graybeard up front said, "Let him speak."

Joshua looked round him a few moments. "Hillel was a

great and learned Pharisee. Has Israel ever had a greater? When asked to state the Law what did he say? What offends you, do not to your neighbor. That, he said, was the whole Law, all of it, and everything else was commentary. All the rest, he said, was the sophistries of men who miss the spirit while devising subtle ambiguities in the letter. As the end draws near we must prepare ourselves to receive one greater than Moses, greater than Isaiah. How will he come? With a flaming sword? No. With anger and vengeance? No. With mercy, forgiveness and love."

There was outcry. Angry voices were demanding that Joshua be silenced and ejected. They were calling his words abominable and blasphemous in the holy house of the Lord. But the old graybeard, one of Israel's patriarchs, leaned over and spoke to the ruler; and the ruler thundered, "Silence! Let this man speak!"

Trembling, Joshua waited until the clamor subsided. Trying to speak gently he said, "Not a flaming sword, but forgiveness. Not vengeance, but love. He will come not to destroy but to heal; not with the pomp and splendors of kings and tyrants, but as the physician among us, to bind up the wounds, to proclaim peace and justice throughout all the lands of the earth.

"Then why don't we teach these simple truths and prepare the way? Will he have time for sophistries and subtleties, when so many of his people beg for bread? Will he not come like the disciples of Aaron, who, said Hillel, love peace and pursue peace, loving all creatures of the earth, drawing them all together in fellowship? Will he not say to us, as it is written, Love your neighbor as yourself, be kind to those who ill treat you, forgive those who would do you harm? Will he not come saying, as it is written in one of our books, that we shall love the Father with all our life, and one another with a true heart?"

He looked round him again at the hostile or wondering faces. He moved his tongue over dry lips. He said to the ruler, "Perhaps I should sit now, though I have much that I'd like to say."

The ruler turned to consult with the old patriarch and then said, "You may go on."

"I wish to ask you learned men, my superiors in all things, this question: why don't you teach kindness and love, instead of vengeance and destruction for most of the people of the earth? Why don't you teach the best of what is written in our books, instead of the worst? Why don't you teach as that great Pharisee Hillel taught?—or as Philo has taught? Philo was a son of Israel. He was a very learned man who wrote forty books. Our Father, said Philo, is not the vindictive one Moses wrote about, but the divine intelligence; the power that contains all powers; the idea that embraces all ideas; the goodness that is the sum of all goodness; all these, and love. The Law, said Philo, was given to all nations, not alone to us. The children of Israel, he says, are not God's special and chosen people, but those people are who share his goodness. The greatest good, Philo says, is not quibbling about tithes and blood-sacrifice and sin-offerings, nor how many heathen souls it takes to equal one righteous soul in Israel—"

The storm had been gathering and suddenly it broke. A hand seized him and Joshua turned to the hostile faces around him.

"Just one more word!"

"No more, you abomination!"

"Just one—"

"Throw him out!"

Men were rising to their feet and were demanding that this wicked one, who had profaned a holy place, should be thrown outside. Strong hands grasped his arms. Strong men propelled him toward the door and then hurled him out bodily. Most of the people poured out after him, some angry enough to kill, others asking, Is this the one who is to come? Joshua had sprawled and then had got weakly to his feet and was brushing himself off. Loud voices were now denouncing him and hands were shoving him back and back. He retreated before the enraged faces

261

and the bitter words and went ashamed and crestfallen
back to the shed.

XXII

He did not tell the women that he had spoken in a synagogue and had been thrown out and denounced. He did
not tell them that he felt his life to be in danger. He continued to wander unhappily about the city, listening, observing, waiting for the Passover, and knowing all the while
that he was being shadowed, though whether the spies were
Herod's or had been set on him by his own people he had
no way of telling. Never once was he able to catch a
glimpse of a spy but Levi said they were watching him.

"More than one now?" he said.

"Sometimes more than one."

"Herod's?"

"Yes, Herod's."

One evening he was passing the temple when from a
high tower he heard a trumpet, and realized that this was
another Sabbath eve. The trumpet was a signal to the
righteous to put away their work. In other parts of Israel, he was thinking, sextons had climbed to rooftops to
blow six blasts. On hearing the first sound, those in fields
nearby would wait for those farther out, and then together
they would all march into the town. At the second call of
the trumpet the shops would close; at the third, pots would
be taken from stoves and wrapped to preserve their heat,
and the Sabbath lights would be kindled. The devout
would then remove their talisman, and after a short in-
termission there would be three other blasts, announcing
that the Sabbath had begun. While trying to imagine the

stirring all over the land he was deeply moved; there was something fine, he thought, in holy customs that could unite a people in their devotional hours.

After the final trumpet sounded Joshua went down into the vale and on coming to the goatshed was surprised to find a light burning within. Zillah had bought oil and a lamp and had kindled the Sabbath light. She had bought two Sabbath loaves and a cruse of wine and some salted fish.

Joshua entered the shed. "Who has done this?" he asked.

"I," Zillah said. "Do you mind?"

He looked at the light, remembering his childhood. "No," he said.

"I thought it would be nice to have a Sabbath meal," she said. "As head of our house will you sanctify and bless our food?"

He looked at the three women. They were sitting in straw to their waists and had blankets over them, for it had been a cold day and would be a colder night. On short planks laid before them and serving as a table stood the light and food. He sat across from them and buried his legs in the straw. Zillah arose and draped a blanket over his shoulders and brought it up and shaped it to form a hood round his face. She patted him on his curly hair and said he now looked like a patriarch.

Sitting, she said, "Now you can bless our food."

"I don't know the blessing."

"Didn't your father teach you?"

They heard a sound and looking over at the entrance saw Levi. Shivering in his rags he was looking at the light and feeling the cozy warmth of the shed.

"Don't ask him in," Sirena whispered to Joshua.

Joshua said: "Come on in, Levi. How are you?"

Levi came over and stood behind Joshua and looked at the light and food. He said to Joshua: "He followed you here today."

"He did!"

"Who?" asked Sirena.

264

"Did he then go away?"

"Yes," Levi said.

"Well, sit down and pile the straw around you. It'll be a bitter night. Are you hungry?"

"No," said Levi, who was famished.

Joshua was looking at the food. "May God bless our food and bless us and bless all people." He said to Zillah: "Will that do?" He broke a loaf of bread into five portions. "We have no cups."

Zillah fetched cups up from the folds of her lap. She had only four.

Joshua poured wine into the four coups and gave one to each of the women and one to Levi. He gave bread to them.

Zillah handed him her cup, saying, "Sirena and I will share one."

Levi clutched his bread and cup of wine and stared at Joshua. "I heard you in the synagogue," he said.

Sirena gasped. "In the synagogue! Joshua?"

"He is teaching now," Levi said.

"Joshua!"

"Only once," he said, his gaze fixed on the light.

"They threw him out and cursed him," Levi said.

"O my God!"

"I thought they would kill him," Levi said.

Sirena and Zillah were staring at Joshua. Sibyl seemed not to hear. Trying to speak quietly Sirena said, "Why did they throw him out?"

"They hated him for what he taught."

"And what did he teach?"

"Love. He told them the messiah will come with love and peace."

"Did they denounce him for that?"

"He said Israel is not a chosen people but only those who love their neighbors."

"Joshua, why did you do this?"

"Was it the same spy?" Zillah asked.

"No."

265

"You mean there is more than one spy now?"

"At least two," Levi said.

Sirena and Zillah looked at Joshua. He looked at the light.

When they had finished their meal Sirena hoped that Joshua would send Levi out but he told the man to lie down and then covered him with straw and an old blanket. Afraid that the lamp might kindle the straw and burn the shed he snuffed the light. The darkness was then complete. Around them was the sound of the beasts, and above them on the western hill was singing. They sat under their blankets, shivering, listening, or trying in the gloom to see the face of one another.

At last Levi said: "Do you see?"

"Do we see what?" asked Zillah.

"How his face shines."

"Oh, go to sleep!" said Sirena.

"Can't you see the light?"

"I can see it," said Sibyl.

Sirena looked round her but could see nothing, not even the faintest image of a face.

"I can see him in the light," Levi said.

"He is standing on something tall," said Sibyl. "There is a light all around him and it is brighter than the sun."

"Can you see anything?" Sirena asked Zillah.

"No, nothing."

"Is Joshua standing up?" Levi asked.

"I'm sitting," Joshua said. "You'd better go to sleep now."

"He is standing in the light," said Sibyl. "There are people all around him now."

"Where is he?" asked Levi.

Sibyl said, "Can you hear the music?"

Sirena shivered. Zillah reached over and clasped one of her hands.

"Has Joshua left us?"

"I am still here," Joshua said. "Go to sleep now."

She could see him very clearly, Sibyl said, and he looked

266

like one who had just come from heaven. He looked like an angel but he was taller.

"Is Joshua still here?" Levi said.

Sirena choked back a scream. "Joshua," she gasped, "please send him away!"

"You'd better stop talking now," Joshua said.

"The whole sky is lighting up," said Sibyl. "There are multiudes of people around him now. Listen to the music!"

"O God!" Levi cried and went groping through darkness to the entrance. Because a soft snow was falling in the pale moonglow he thought the whole sky was kindled; and he called to them to come see. Zillah went out and looked up at the luminous beauty of the storm.

Speaking into the entrance she said, "There is a great light. Come and see."

Then the others went out and they all looked up at the sky.

"It's only a snowstorm," Sirena said and went shivering back to her blanket.

After a few moments Zillah followed her and then Joshua; but Sibyl, now clothed with the vision and yielding her will to a higher will, stood in the night, crying softly to all who would listen that the son of man was coming to the earth. Sometime later, when the others were dozing, she returned, wet and chilled, and crawled under her cover; but Levi spent the night going from friend to friend to tell them that the one they waited for had come. At daylight he appeared with two other men and they looked into the shed and Sirena was awakened by their whispering. The other men like Levi were ragged, ill-nourished, dirty, solemn, childlike. One was named Zabdai and the other Kepha. They all stepped timidly into the shed and peered down at Joshua.

"He is still here," Levi said to them. "He is the one who in the synagogue confounded the wise men."

"Joshua," said Sirena, "wake up!"

"Now what is it?" asked Zillah, stirring.

"It's that man again."

Joshua sat up in the morning dusk and looked at the three men who were staring at him. Levi had told them that there had been a great light around Joshua and with pathetic eagerness the three of them waited to see what Joshua would do.

"He snuffed the lamp," said Levi, "but there was still light."

"Ah!" said Kepha.

"This stable was filled with it. Then this woman—"

"Send them away!" Sirena cried, feeling hysterical.

"Please go away," Joshua said.

But they would not go away. They continued to stare at Joshua and to whisper among themselves about the wonders he would soon perform and the glories that would fill Jerusalem, until Sirena, almost beside herself, got up from the straw and went over to them. They backed away from her and they went outside and out of sight but they waited; and during the days that followed the three of them with Simon trailed Joshua when he left the shed. If he turned impatiently to ask why they spied on him they would fall back, abashed, but the faith in their eyes never wavered. And one day they beheld the miracle they had been waiting for.

Joshua at the moment was standing at some distance from a synagogue, and the four men, who had come to think of themselves as his faithful disciples, were not far away, watching him. Then there came down the street a funeral procession, with women going before the corpse, with men behind it, accompanied by torch-bearers, musicians with drums and flutes, and the hired mourners who were skilled in feigning grief. It was a law in Israel that a person who met a funeral procession, or who happened to be standing by the way when it passed, was obliged to fall in with the mourners and go with them for some distance. Even meditation on the Torah was interrupted for this duty.

Joshua walked with the mourners, hearing the sounds of

sorrow and the shrill cries of those extolling the deceased. A priest shouted from time to time, "Overspread and cover yourselves with darkness, you mountains, for he was a descendant of Israel!" These words evoked each time a tremendous outburst of wailing. The procession paused now and then and a loud voice proclaimed, "His reward will be great for he has done homage to the Torah! It is a consolation that this man has become a child of future bliss! Brothers in Israel, listen. . . ."

Joshua had been trying to slip away but had got lost among the mourners, and when the cortege came to the public cemetery he was not far from the bier. A man who stood close to the coffin was then heard to gasp. Joshua looked at him and saw his face slowly turn ashen white and his eyes almost pop from his skull. A picture of complete horror, the man was trying to back away. Then another, sensing that something was wrong, peered at the corpse and blanched. Joshua pushed forward to get a view of the dead man and was astounded not only to find one eye open but to observe that the eye was looking at him. A moment later the other eye opened and both eyes looked at Joshua. Turning to the people around him Joshua cried, "This man is not dead!" There was a rumbling of amazement, of terror and awe, as the man shook himself free and stood up, his face bloodless and drawn but his eyes flashing with the fires of life. Levi and his companions saw the man rise from his bier. They had no doubt that Joshua had raised him from the dead and they hastened away to tell their friends. They found Sirena and Zillah at their bench in the cheese factory and Levi slipped up and whispered to them:

"Joshua has raised the dead!"

The two women could only stare at him and then at one another. Sirena felt chilled first and then tremulous with panic.

"What are you saying?"

He told them the wonderful tale. They were taking this man to his grave and Joshua went up to the bier and uttered the man's name and said, Arise! and the man stood up.

"O God, have mercy!" Zillah gasped.

"He is mad!" Sirena said.

Levi and his companions, triumphant now in their faith, embellished the story, until before nightfall they were saying: "Joshua followed the bier and there was a bright light around him and a halo around his head. We saw him praying as he walked along. When the dead man came to the grave Joshua raised a hand to silence the mourners. He then touched the dead man and in a loud voice said, Brother, arise! Cover yourselves with light, you mountain! Then everywhere there was light that was blinding and the man stood up in his grave clothes and said, Hail to the son of David, King of Israel, who has raised me from the dead!"

"What *did* you say?" asked the astonished Sirena later.

"Only that the man was not dead."

"Well, was the man dead or not?"

"Am I the one to know?"

"If he was dead, what made him live again?"

"Yes," said Zillah, her wide wondering eyes fixed on Joshua. "What did?"

Joshua shrugged and said nothing.

Levi and his friends, still embellishing, were telling all who would listen that Joshua the son of David went with the procession, but his feet did not touch the earth, not really, nor Joshua, but stood above it in a cloud of light; and the sun came down low and was like a great fire just above him; and Joshua prayed as he walked in the light, calling to the Father, saying, Grant me powers that I may give the people a sign and usher in the kingdom! The people, knowing then that the son of David was with them, began to sing; and again Joshua spoke in a loud voice, commanding the mountains and the earth to throw off their darkness and to cover themselves with glory; and he said to this man, Your reward will be great, for I will raise you from the dead as a sign to Israel! Then the whole

270

universe burst, as with light flowering; and walls fell down; and the seas rocked in their deeps. The man then leapt up from his coffin and began to sing and all the heavens were singing, as it was written in the psalms. . . .

XXIII

The people were hushed on the Day of Atonement, for it was a day when, God willing, their sins were taken from them; but the Passover season was a time for rejoicing. This was the greatest of their holy weeks, when thousands from all over Israel and from the lands beyond came to their city. It was a time not only for rejoicing but for breathless hope: Elijah on this occasion was believed to visit every house, and doors were left open so that he could enter. Many believed that Moses might also come, or Abraham or Isaiah or David. And they were all waiting for the son of David, the king.

The Passover fell in the spring month of Nisan, from the fourteenth to the twenty-first; and by the middle of Adar, the preceding month, preparations had been made. Sepulchers were whitened, roads and bridges were repaired. The poor searched round them in the hope of buying at a bargain a Passover lamb, for after the multitudes came in the cost of sacrificial beasts soared. Zillah, unknown to her companions, had slipped away to find a male lamb, the son of a year, and to pay for it, as well as to place an order for bitter herbs.

Before the first of Nisan the early pilgrims began to arrive, particularly those with relatives or friends in the city, whom they wished to visit; and then the people began to come by the hundreds, by the thousands, in greater numbers than had ever come before, because in this season, they had heard, the son of David would reveal his presence in Israel and then proceed to the destruction of Rome and the elevation of Israel above all nations. Those who had homes in the city were expected to offer hospitality and shelter to the pilgrims, who in turn would give them the skin of their slain beast. Soon all the houses were filled. Then tents were set up in all the squares and open places, small tent-cities began to form outside the walls; and every foot of space in every hillside cave was occupied, every stable and shed; and still the pilgrims poured in, many of them bringing with them their beasts. They were not only Jews but Jewish proselytes from every land in this part of the world, and Jerusalem was such a babble of alien tongues as no city had ever been. Merchants came with caravans of wares which they hoped to sell. Camel-trains from eastern countries came with spices and herbs, fine rugs, cloths and raiment. Caravans came down from the north and up from Egypt and from coast harbors, where they had taken their cargoes off ships from western lands. Before the fourteenth of Nisan and the beginning of the Passover the city was an incredible bedlam of noise and confusion and color. The principal streets and paths were filled with people day and night, jammed shoulder to shoulder; and on both sides the streets were lined with tables, stands and booths, which offered for sale cakes made of wheat from Mount Ephraim, fish from Lake Kinnereth, jewelry from Alexandria, and a hundred other products from a hundred other far places. Lining the streets also were the butchers, the wool-combers, the cobblers and tailors; and milling around and back and forth were the multiudes buying their beasts from the cattle stalls near the mount of the temple; haggling over the price of trinkets; shrieking with delight when they saw the faces of old friends; pausing to utter their prayers or to meditate on holy words; scanning the heavens for signs; staring at the priests or Levites who passed—for a great many priests, including all twenty-four courses, had come to the city; seeking places to void or to rest their weary bodies; or pouring into the synagogues to listen to words of the wise.

Sirena had been in a number of the great cities and had seen multitudes on festival days, but she had never seen such unresting tides of humanity or heard anything to compare to their ceaseless babble. Herod had hundreds of spies and policemen here but in these throngs they were as helpless as struggling men in a rolling sea.

By noon of the first day of the holy season everyone had ceased working, including even those repairing sandals or cutting hair; and the multitudes, leaving their lodging-places, swarming through the city, dragging or carrying their bleating and terrified beasts, each of them eager to be among the first to enter the temple courts. When the great outside court was filled the gates were shut, Levites sounded a threefold blast on the trumpets, and the slaughter began, while outside other thousands clutched their beasts and waited. Toward evening the gates were opened and those in the courts came out, rushing toward their homes, carrying their butchered animals wrapped in their skins, their own faces and garments smeared with gore. They would dash to their homes and spit their beasts from anus to mouth with a staff of fragrant pomegranate, if they were lucky enough to have it, and then roast the carcass in the courtyard of their homes. Evening had come and a full moon; and inside the temple court other beasts were being inspected and slain, while those who had entered with the first course were feasting and drinking in accordance with their holy laws.

When Zillah confessed to Joshua that she had bought a lamb and suggested that he should take it to the temple court to have it ritually slain, so that the four of them might roast it and eat unleavened bread and bitter herbs in the way of their people, Joshua looked at her a long moment before speaking.

"God doesn't want all this slaughter," he said at last. "Nor all the blood and fat burning in altar fires."

Zillah had been looking forward to a feast after a cold lean winter. She was now angry. "Aren't we going to eat at all?"

They were standing before the goatshed. "Hear the gluttons," said Joshua, meaning all those who were feasting up and down the vale. "Some of them will be as drunk as a Roman. What will the son of David think of them?"

"All right, what?" she cried impatiently.

"He will say to them—"

"Oh, to hell with your pompous words!" she shouted. "He will say unto them! I say unto you that I shivered in the cold, I toiled for the coins to buy a lamb and bread and herbs, so that we might eat—and these I hid from you, thinking you would be pleased! But no! You can only tell us that he will say unto them!"

Joshua's temper had risen a little but he tried to speak gently. "Would you be a glutton and a drunkard to welcome him, or a penitent with a humble heart?"

"Humble heart! By Aaron's rod haven't I been humble?

Sirena said, "If we're not to eat it what shall we do with it?"

Joshua sniffed. From the hillside all around them came the odor of roasting flesh, and the sounds of feasting and rejoicing.

"Sniff!" Zillah cried. "Then pretend you don't like it."

"But do you realize that he may reveal himself any moment?"

"And what if he does? Is it so sinful if he should find us eating?"

"But so many will be sotted with drink, so many sick from gluttony."

"It seems to me," Sirena said, "that there is something very fine in all this—in all these people worshiping God in the simple way of their fathers."

"Oh, but not for Joshua!" Zillah cried bitterly. "We can love him and labor for him until our hands are raw but he will never love us, no, but only the idea of love. We toil for him and he toils for the Father. All winter long—'"

"Hush," Sirena said.

"Damn you, don't you tell me to hush!"

"Zillah, Zillah!" Joshua cried. "You've been sweet for such a long time."

"To hell with the sweet! Joshua, you're self-righteous and I hate it!"

"You're just upset," said Sirena. Joshua turned as if to leave them and she asked quickly, "Where are you going now?"

"Just around the city," he said.

"Aren't you going to eat with us?"

"Not now."

"Do you promise not to enter synagogues and to stay out of trouble?"

Joshua said he would; but when he was beyond hearing Sirena said to the other women: "Maybe one of us should go with him. He seems troubled. Zillah, have Levi take our lamb to the court and we'll feast later. I'll be back soon."

So many tents had been pitched, each with its flap open to let Elijah enter, that the streets and paths were almost filled, and a man found walking difficult, especially after dark. Joshua moved by moonlight and by the lamplight that shone out from tents and huts and caves, listening to the sounds of revelry, smelling the odors, pausing now and then when he heard disputing voices. Some of the voices spoke languages unfamiliar to him.

Near the top of the hill he heard angry words and stood by the tent to listen. The men inside were arguing over a phrase in the twelfth chapter of the books called Exodus, which said, literally, that the lamb was to be slain between the two evenings. One man argued that it should be slain at dusk; another, that the first evening began when the sun passed the meridian; and a third, that the first evening was the sunset, and the second evening was twilight of the same day, after the first stars appeared.

"You idiot," one of them cried, "how can there be two evenings in one day?'

Joshua sighed and went on, and by another tent he heard:

"I tell you it is written that the man who is clean and not on a journey, and yet fails to perform the Passover, his soul shall be cut off, he shall bear his sin, because he brought not the offering of the Holy One in his appointed season."

"Yes, so it is written, but what did Hillel say? I tell you any man could pretend to be on a journey."

"You don't know what a journey is. Listen. . . ."

Joshua moved on, and again paused. Inside a tent a man was disputing over the matsos, or unleavened bread, saying that it should never be baked thicker than the breadth of four fingers, and always should be baked by three women, one to knead the dough, one to roll it, and one to bake it; but another said it might be as thick as all the fingers on one hand, but should never be made of barley flour; and still another argued that the poor were allowed to use barley flour, if they could not afford wheat.

"I don't know about that part of it," said the first voice. "When I get home I'll find out. But I do know—for I have heard our teacher say it—that no loaf should ever be thicker than four fingers—and that means four ordinary fingers, not four fingers on a fat hand, and not counting the thumb, ever, but only the fingers, including the little one. As to why the water to be used in baking must be drawn beforehand and kept over night, I can answer you. When the sun goes under the earth it heats the water, but we must never use warm water in the matsos, because the heat in the water might cause the dough to ferment, and then it would be leavened dough. As to why there must be three women. . . ."

Joshua sighed again and passed on. In a tent he heard singing and recognized the Hallel and knew that the fourth cup of wine was being drunk. He paused to listen and heard the customary prayer: "All your works shall praise you, our Lord. And your saints, the righteous, who do your good pleasure, and all your people, the house of

277

Israel, with joyous song let them bless and magnify and
glorify and exalt and reverence and sanctify and ascribe
the kingdom to your name, O our King! For it is good to
praise you. . . ."

Joshua was walking among the tents on the eastern hill,
wondering if he ought to go see his mother and if she
would admit him to her house, or if he ought to go alone
to the Mount of Olives and sit there and meditate, when
he heard feet behind him and turned to face Sirena.

"Are you following me?"

"Joshua, won't you come eat with us?"

"I'm not hungry," he said.

"Why are you troubled?"

"I don't think the son of David is coming in this season. The people are too wicked."

"Do you call this feasting wickedness?"

"But you do not hear their disputes. Shall the Passover
lamb be killed at sunset, at dusk, when one star appears,
or seven, or not until morning? Shall the unleavened loaf
be as thick as four fingers?—and if so, whose?—a woman's?
—a fat man's or a thin man's?—or a child's? How old
should the lamb be?—for he is a son of the year, as written; but does this mean a yearling or one six months old,
or may it be older than a year? What are its bones to be
crushed with?—and may the bitter herbs be endive and
lettuce?—or succory and horehound? What are charcha-
vina?—beets or eggplant?"

"Joshua?"

"If the herbs are dipped into salt water or vinegar the
first time, shall they the second time be taken with charoseth? And if so, is charoseth a compound of dates, raisins,
and vinegar only, or should it contain some red wine?
Why do the Samaritans refuse to drink wine at the Passover? Can it be—ah, what wickedness!—that God's chosen
people took the custom of wine-drinking from the Greeks?"

"Joshua, please!"

"Are my people to save their souls by splitting hairs
and swallowing camels—as when they decide what to do

278

with the part of the lamb that touches the oven?—because never, oh never, must they eat that part! Or when they decide which wood, if they cannot afford pomegranate, they may use? In thrusting the stick through the dead beast, should you enter by the mouth or the rear vent? Should you—"

"Joshua, what is wrong with you?"

"Should you—"

"Don't say it! You're feeling bitter."

"What's wrong with me?" he said, blinking at her. "I tell you, said Hillel, the earth was created first; but no, said Shammai, the heavens were first, and God planned by night and created by day; but no, said Hillel, God both planned and created by day. Do you not know, said Shammai, that the sacrificial lamb *presses* down the sins of Israel, because the root word for lamb and for press is the same. Not so, said Hillel: that which is pressed down rises up, and so the sins would be released. What nonsense you talk, said Shammai—"

"Yes, and what nonsense you talk! Are you trying to drive yourself crazy with all these quibblings? Who cares about them anyway?"

"Israel," he said, looking at her strangely. "My people. That's the way they are. How thick should the matsos be? Do you suppose God cares?"

"No. Now come eat with us."

"My people—"

"Yes, yes, Joshua, your people! Will you come?"

He turned to her and said gently, "Woman, why do you worry about me?"

"*Man,* because I love you."

"Did you say love?" he asked, blinking. "But what is love? My mother is drinking her four glasses of wine and singing the Hallel and praying; and she thinks God loves her for that. She'd watch the death of an unclean Jew or a heathen and never lift a hand. But if you—"

"Don't say it. Now please come with us."

"You are going to eat, very well, but I must walk among

my people, to observe again how with them the spirit has flown from the letter. I'll listen to their arguments, their over-subtle refinements, their absurd logic, their worship of the written word, their devotion—"

"All right, all right, then I'll go with you."

"I'd rather go alone."

"Is it that you wish to suffer?"

"My people, Sirena, have to suffer. If they had no reason to suffer they'd not know what to do."

"The prophets can rant, teachers drink hemlock, gods hang on trees, but people will go on being just about what they are. You can't give them love, for love is not what they want. You can't make them see things as you see them. So come on, Joshua, and eat with us. We need you."

"What do you mean by we? Does the Greek need the Jew?"

"Yes, good God, and the Jew the Greek."

"But I'm not hungry."

"Why go from tent to tent to listen to this mischievous silliness about the thickness of a loaf or what time to slaughter—"

"Sirena," he said, "leave me. You don't understand and I don't think I could make you understand."

"Will you come to us later?"

"Yes, of course."

Sirena turned away but almost at once came back. "Joshua, if you wander around tonight I'm afraid you'll get in trouble. You'll get into arguments. Or you'll begin to talk to the people and then the Romans will take you away. That's not what you want, is it?"

"I only want to be alone."

"And you promise to come to us later?"

He moved up and looked into her face and said: "My people have a custom at this season which I've never told you. It's a terrible thing."

"If you wish to tell me then tell me," she said, watching his eyes.

"They crucify a criminal."

"Oh no!"

"I've wondered why they do it. There are heathen people who hang a god in a tree at this season, or a god effigy or a man who represents a god. It's an old custom."

"Just when do your people do this?"

"I don't remember."

"Well, you can't stop it, so why worry about it?"

"Because it's wicked."

"Yes, and so are many things."

"Did you ever see people crucify a man who symbolized a god?"

"No."

"I once saw it. They dressed him in purple and put a mock crown of thorns on his head and a mock scepter in his hands; and they scourged him and crucified him. On the cross above his head they put a derisive sign."

"Well, they do it in many places—at Rhodes, at Salamis. But why talk about it?"

"They pierced him with a lance," Joshua said.

"Oh yes, and in India they hang the god symbol between two thieves. Men do terrible things but why in the world must you talk about them, and tonight of all nights?"

"Yes, tonight of all nights. I was thinking of what Isaiah said, that he is despised and rejected of men, a man of sorrows; and he will pour out his soul unto death and bear the sin of many."

"Who will?" asked Sirena incredulously.

"The man of sorrows."

"You mean the one who is to come?"

"Isaiah meant Israel."

"Joshua, I don't think you are yourself tonight. I wish you would come and be with us."

"The one the Lord bruised and put to grief and offered up for the sins of the wicked. He was brought as a lamb to the slaughter—"

She put a palm to his mouth to silence him and he backed away, still speaking.

"The one despised and rejected. For the sins of the peo-

281

ple, said Isaiah, this one would be stricken. He will bear
our grief, said the prophet, and carry our sorrow; he will
be wounded, and those who see him will find no beauty in
him. Israel. And isn't Israel wounded?"

"You mean another goat for Azazel?"

"Another what?"

"Joshua," she cried, beside herself, "I don't know what
we can do with you!" She turned abruptly and left him
and ran back to the shed.

XXIV

Sirena ran to the shed and said to Zillah, "I think Joshua is out of his mind! He is muttering about some man of sorrows who'll be killed for the sins of Israel."

"What man of sorrows?"

"What man of sorrows do we know?"

"You mean Joshua, I suppose."

"I think we should go find him."

They hastened to the eastern hill and they searched all night but they did not find him.

"What did he say he was going to do?"

"Pray and be alone."

"Where could he be alone in this city?"

"Would he go to his mother?"

"I don't think she would admit him."

At daylight they returned to the shed and they were eating milk and cheese when Levi burst in on them. The little man was so agitated he could barely speak. He gasped out to them that Joshua had been arrested and he smote his thighs as a sign of grief.

Sirena and Zillah both leapt up and they shoved Levi out of the shed to have a clearer view of his face.

"Who arrested him?"

"Roman soldiers. They took him away."

This was Levi's story. He had followed Joshua after Sirena left him. Joshua had gone first to look at his mother's house but he had not disturbed her; and then he had gone to the Mount of Olives where he had prayed and sat as if in thought. Toward daylight he began to talk to a group of people and a multitude gathered. Then the soldiers came.

"Where is he now?"

The soldiers, Levi said, were taking him to the Procurator.

They turned back to ask Sibyl if she was coming and then the women followed Levi up the hill to the Citadel of Antonia, thinking Pilate would be there; but they were told that he was in the palace of Herod and that King Herod himself was in the city. At the palace they were told that Joshua was to be brought before Pilate in the Praetorium, which Jews called the Gabbatha, meaning the stone pavement or platform. Many of those who had seen Joshua arrested were now waiting for the trial.

The women and Levi pushed through the mob until they could see the judgment-seat which Pilate would occupy. They looked all around for Joshua but there was no sign of him. They waited, and the sun was an hour and then two hours above Moab, when they heard cries from the guards, as the Roman governor came in from the rear. Armed men now came forward, bringing Joshua with them, and Sirena thought she would faint when she observed that he was bound. She reached for Zillah's hand and found it trembling and then Zillah hid her face against Sirena and wept. They were well up front, and so were able to see Pilate clearly and to hear what he said.

After seating himself and arranging his robes Pilate looked for a few moments over the heads of the people. He would speak in Greek but he had an interpreter by him who would translate his words into the language of Israel. He asked: "Where is the accused?"

"Here," a centurion said, and he and his companions took Joshua forward.

Pilate looked at Joshua and seemed to be studying him. "Of what crime is this man accused?"

"Blasphemy!" a voice said.

Another voice said: "Insurrection and rebellion!"

"Blasphemy," said Pilate, "is no concern of this court. Who accuses him?"

Sirena began to feel relief. She thought Pilate's manner that of a judge determined to be impartial and wise.

One who might have been a priest stepped forward and said: "I accuse him."

"Of what crime?"

"Of blasphemy against the Holy Name."

"Blasphemy is no concern of this court but is something for Jews to settle in their own way. I know nothing about it." Pilate studied the accuser a moment. "How did he blaspheme?"

"I have heard that he says God has a son."

"You have heard? And God has no son, you say?"

"The Lord our God, the Lord is One!"

"Very well, blasphemy has nothing to do with this court, nor hearsay. What is the name of the accused?"

When Joshua did not speak, a soldier standing by him spoke up, saying, "The man is called Joshua."

"Is this man a Jew?"

"Yes, your honor."

"Bring him a little closer." They shoved Joshua forward and Pilate said, "Joshua, look at me." When Joshua did not look up a soldier prodded him. "Joshua, there seem to be several charges against you, one of which is blasphemy. Have you been telling the people that the God of Israel has a son? . . . Speak up, man! This is a court of truth and judgment and it is my duty to determine the facts. Tell me what you said."

There was complete silence when Joshua's voice was heard, low and firm: "I have not said that our Holy One has a son. That would be blasphemy. A learned Jew in Alexandria, named Philo, has written that God has a son."

"Philo? I have heard of that man. But do you say that the God of Israel has a son?"

"I say that we are all his children, and in that sense I am his son, or you."

"Well, in any case blasphemy is no concern of mine. Who else accuses this man?"

"I accuse him!" said one. "This man has taught that the God of Israel does not want the slaughter of beasts, or blood on his altars."

Pilate looked round him and Sirena thought he seemed amused. "I can understand that that might be thought a crime. The priesthood draws a part of its living from the sacrificial beasts and priesthoods always protect those customs that enrich themselves." He turned to Joshua. "Have you said that the offering of beasts on the altars of Israel is a sin?"

"A prophet of Israel said it. He said that God does not take delight in the odors of burning flesh."

"What do you say?"

"I say that God is love and mercy, and his delight is in good deeds, not in the rituals of Moses."

"Hear!" cried a voice.

"If the only charge against this man is blasphemy I can find no great fault in him. Is there any other charge and are there any witnesses?"

"I, my lord," said Herod's spy who killed the Essene.

"Speak. What do you know about this man?"

"My lord, I have been watching him for months. He is a rabble-rouser who pretends to work wonders and miracles."

"You lie!" Zillah cried.

"Be silent there," said Pilate, frowning. To the man: "Go on."

"He used to be up in Galilee, agitating among the people there; and then he was on the river by Jericho, where he professed to heal the sick."

"He did heal!" cried a woman's voice.

Sirena and Zillah looked at one another. "My God!" said Sirena. "It's Lucia!"

"Then he came to this city, where he was thrown out of a synagogue."

"Yes," Pilate said. "Anything else?"

"My lord is aware that the Jews expect a king to come, a son of David they say, who will have more than human powers and will overthrow Rome and enthrone the Jews above all nations. This man has been teaching this treasonable falsehood. He is an enemy of Caesar's government which has been established in this land."

"Is all this true?" Pilate asked Joshua. When Joshua gave no reply Pilate said sharply: "Man, answer me! Have you been teaching that a Jew-king will come and that he will overthrow Rome?"

Sirena spoke. "My lord," she said, her voice shrill and frightened. "I am a witness for the accused and I beg to be heard!"

"And I!" Zillah said.

"And I!" said Levi.

"Come forward," Pilate said. When Sirena stood before him he asked: "Are you a Jew?"

"No, my lord. I am a Greek and a citizen of Rome."

"A Roman citizen?"

"Yes, my lord."

"Tell me what you know about this man."

"I have journeyed with this man and with other friends almost a year. I know that he is a good man. He does not teach violence, but only gentleness and love. There is no evil in him."

"He sits with lepers!" said a disgusted voice.

"Be still," said Pilate. Then, to Sirena: "Do you love this man?"

"I respect him and admire him."

"You haven't answered me. Do you love him?"

"Yes, my lord."

"That makes you a pretty poor witness, doesn't it?"

"That makes me a good witness, for only love can read the human heart."

He smiled and turned to Zillah. "And you also love him, I suppose."

"Yes, my lord."

"And you?" he said to Sibyl.

"I love only God," said Sibyl.

Pilate turned to Levi.

"He raised a man from the dead," said Levi.

"You're stupid!" Sirena cried. "My lord, this man is ignorant and doesn't know what he is saying."

"He raised a man," said Levi, scowling at her. "I saw it."

"Very well," said Pilate, "tell me about it."

"They were taking this man to bury him and they came to the cemetery; and then Joshua went forth and touched the man and said, Arise; and the man stood up. I saw it. And all around Joshua there was brilliant light like the glory of God, and the man was well and strong and he said, Glory to God, and to this man, his prophet, who has raised me from the dead! And he healed a man in Jericho."

"This stupid man lies," Zillah said. "We have fed him and been kind to him and now he is our enemy."

"A woman back there said she saw him heal. Where is she?"

"Here," said Lucia.

"Come forward."

She went forward, with Sirena and Zillah staring at her, with Sirena thinking that she looked smaller, frailer, grayer.

"Did you see this man healing someone in Jericho?"

"Yes," said Lucia and lowered her head.

Pilate turned to Herod's spy. "And you saw him?"

"Yes, my lord."

"You actually saw him do it?"

"No, my lord, but I saw the man who said he had been healed. I talked to him."

"My lord," said Sirena, "I was there and I saw it. I was with him at the baths, I was with him in all the places. He pretended to heal no one. Ignorant people sometimes think that they are healed or that they see wonders but they are deceived. This man has taught only one thing, that God is love. He has never—"

"Just a moment," said Pilate, raising a hand. "Let me hear what he has to say for himself. You women seem to be conspiring to keep him silent. Joshua, have you been healing the sick?"

He hesitated. Could he know whether or not God had been using him as an instrument? He said quietly, at last: "I have pretended to no such powers."

"But you raised a man from death," Levi said. "I was there and I saw you do it. And when he came to the stable all the stable was lit up, there was a light—"

"Yes, our little Sabbath light!" cried Zillah, disgusted.

"And the light of a storm," said Sirena. "That was all."

"There was a light outside," said Sibyl. "It was like the light in the heavens and there was one coming on a white horse."

"Just a minute," said Pilate, a worldly and skeptical man. "Where's the horse now?"

"I don't know," Sibyl said.

"Joshua, have you been riding a horse?"

"No, my lord."

"Let me tell you," said a voice, "about his blasphemy!"

"Be quiet," said Pilate, "or I'll have you silenced. I've told you that blasphemy or consorting with lepers is no affair of this court. Take such matters before your Sanhedrin, according to the religious laws of your people. This court has jurisdiction over civil crimes and no other."

There now came through the throng a woman, and with her a man; and the man said: "This woman wants to speak."

"Very well, woman, what have you to say?"

"This man," she said, pointing to Joshua, "is the one who healed me."

"Where?"

"At the baths. I was sick with the falling weakness and I touched him and I was well."

"And he raised the dead," said Levi. "He made a light stand in the sky. He turned water into wine. He lives in a stable, as it is written—"

"Take this man away," said Pilate to a guard. After

Levi had been hustled out of sight Pilate turned to the spy. "Did you see him heal this woman?"

"My lord, no. But I think this is the woman who leapt up and ran away shrieking. She was sure the Jewish king had come."

Pilate put a hand to his face and looked thoughtfully at the witnesses. At last he fixed his gaze on Sirena.

"Though a poor witness you seem to be a woman of some education. Why have you journeyed with this man almost a year?"

"My lord—" she began and was silent.

"Well, don't you know?"

"I met him near Capernaum. I had come down from Antioch because I had been told that a king with great powers was coming to Israel. Many people were coming. I met this man and saw that he was kind to the sick and to beggars and to the old—even to slaves, even to the lost. Then—"

"Then what?" asked Pilate, gazing at her steadily.

"Well, I suppose I liked him most of all because he seemed to have no contempt for women. He didn't believe that women brought sin into the world. He treated us as his equals. Once he said—"

"Yes, yes, go on, what did he say?"

"He said we're all equal before God. He said the meek will inherit more than the arrogant, the slave more than kings."

"Inherit more what?"

"More in the life that follows this."

"You seem to be saying that everyone should be meek and poor. Have you anything else to say?"

"Though he is a Jew and I a Greek I never thought of us that way and I'm sure he did not. We were brother and sister under one God."

"Who else traveled through Galilee with this man?"

"These two women with me, and one named Lucia, over there, and an elderly couple who are not here now."

"Where are they?"

"Lucia's child was stolen by bandits and she went to find it and the old people went with her."

Again he studied Sirena. "As a Greek you must believe there are many gods. Or don't you?"

"No, my lord. Some of the great philosophers, including Plato, thought there is only one."

"And who is he? Does he have a name?"

"The Jews call him Yahweh."

"But what about Hermes, Dionysus, Prometheus, Zeus, Jupiter?"

"Euhemerus said that in the beginning they were only men."

"Well, tell me, was Augustus Caesar a god or not?"

"My lord, must I answer that?"

"You're not on trial here. There's no charge against you."

"I don't think he was."

"Has this man Joshua ever pretended to be this Jewish king?"

"No, my lord. I swear it."

Again Pilate seemed to be studying her. He turned to Zillah. "Why have you journeyed with this man?"

Zillah's lips curled. "My lord, I have no learned defense like hers. I came with him because I loved him."

Pilate looked over at Joshua, as though wondering why women found him attractive. "Are you a Jew?"

"Yes, my lord."

"Do you think a Jew-king will come and overthrow Rome?"

"I believe as Joshua believes."

"How is that?"

"In peace and obedience. He doesn't believe with the Zealots, who would make war on Rome, but has said, If a man asks you for your cloak, give him all you have. If a man asks you to go a mile, go ten. These are teachings of the Pharisees."

"Is this man a Pharisee?"

"No."

"What is he?"

Her words startled him. She said: "He is a man of sorrows."

"Oh?" said Pilate, looking again at Joshua. "And what kind of man is that?"

"Israel. But I'd rather Joshua would answer you."

Joshua all the while had cast his gaze down. Pilate now turned to him. "Joshua, are you a man of sorrows? If so, what do you mean by it?'

Joshua looked up and said: "Our prophet Isaiah has written that a man of sorrows, one despised and rejected, would bear the griefs of people and be wounded—"

"He meant Israel," a voice cried, "and not a man!"

Pilate turned to a guard. "Take him out." To Joshua he said: "Are you this man of sorrows?"

"No."

"Is this man of sorrows the king who is coming?"

"I don't know."

"What say your wise men?"

"Some say no and some say yes. Some think he meant Israel; some, a king."

"Well, tell me this, if you can. Why can't Jews live as other people in the Roman provinces? Why must we be forever plagued with these agitators and trouble-makers? How many of them must we destroy? Will there never be an end of these rebellious men in Israel? Can you answer that?"

Joshua moved his tongue over dry lips. He looked at Pilate and said: "It is written in our holy books that we must have no king but God."

"And you believe that?"

Sirena moved to silence Joshua but fell back, despairing.

"It is a holy commandment," Joshua said.

"But all people have to live under a ruler, don't they?"

Knowing that Joshua's replies would leave Pilate no choice but to condemn him, Sirena forced herself to speak. "My lord, the Jews believe—"

"Who is better qualified to tell what Jews believe, you, a Greek, or this Jew before me? Let him answer."

Did Joshua sense that his answers would cost him his life? He hesitated. He glanced over at the women, at Lucia, and at Pilate.

Pilate said, "Will you answer my questions?"

"We believe," said Joshua, trying to speak quietly, "that we are a unique and a chosen people. We believe that we should be the subjects only of our Lord and his laws."

Pilate leaned forward. "Then at heart you are all rebels against the rulers placed over you. Is that correct?"

"I'm no rebel. Most of my people believe in peace. They don't believe that we should revolt against the rulers placed over us. As Hillel said—"

"You're not consistent. If you believe you should be subject only to your God, then how can you in your hearts be law-abiding citizens? And if a king is coming who is a man of peace how will he overthrow the might of Rome?"

Joshua met Pilate's eyes and said: "With love."

"With what?" asked Pilate, astonished. "You tell me that someone will overthrow the Empire and all its legions with love?"

"I mean that love will conquer."

"I must have before me a madman," Pilate said. He looked round him like a man in deep confusion and turned to Sirena. "Is this man mad?"

"My lord, I don't think that love is madness."

"Perhaps not, but such blind infatuation with it must be." He turned again to Joshua. "I wish to be very sure that I understand you. Did you say that love will overthrow Rome?"

"Yes."

"You mean that love will conquer soldiers with lances?"

"Even those."

"And an emperor with a hundred armed legions?"

"Even those."

Pilate was silent. Looking now at Joshua, now at Sirena or Zillah or Lucia, he seemed to be thinking. At last

293

he said: "If you came from Galilee you should be in the court of King Herod. Do you want me to send you to him?"

"No."

"Be sure. You may have your choice."

"Can it matter whether I am stoned for blasphemy or hanged for treason? I believe that love and only love can conquer the evils in the world. If that is an offense I am guilty."

"I've been wondering if you have a wish to be found guilty. Have you?"

"No, my lord."

"You don't seek death?"

"No."

"Have you a secret belief that you may be this man of sorrows?"

"Only as every Jew is."

"Yet you do believe that a king will come who will overthrow Rome. You have confessed to that, as I understand you. Am I right?"

Again Joshua looked at him and Sirena thought he turned a shade paler.

"My lord—"

"Joshua, just give me a plain answer. Is that your belief?"

"Yes, my lord."

Zillah gasped and reached for Sirena's hand. Dizzy and swaying, Sirena closed her eyes.

Again Pilate was silent while he studied Joshua's face. He said at last, "I've done my best to give you a fair trial. Now listen well to what I say. You don't seem to be a vicious person. If I were governor in another province and a man were brought before me who said that he owed no allegiance to the emperor, but only to the god of his people; and if he said further that his people are a chosen and unique people, and so entitled to special privileges above all other people, could I acquit him? This is a court of justice and judgment. You may feel no allegiance

294

to the government that rules over this part of the world but I am its servant and it is my duty to see that its laws are obeyed. If those who teach revolt were freed in Israel, or even those who teach that their people owe no allegiance to the governing powers, then those who may teach similar doctrines in other provinces would have to be absolved of all charges against them; and if this were done, there would soon be no government, nor organized law anywhere, but only revolt and insurrection and anarchy.

"His majesty, the Emperor, has already granted to your people special privileges above those granted to any other people. No coins in this city bear the image of the Emperor. No ensign with his image flies from the towers. It has been recognized that in some ways you are indeed a peculiar people, and for that reason you have been granted special rights; but there must be a limit to these things, and that limit is reached when the sovereignty of the Empire is challenged.

"Joshua, have you anything to say that you haven't said, or any more witnesses to speak for you?"

"No, my lord."

"I am sorry, then, to say that you leave me no alternative. You have pled guilty to a charge that compels me to sit as your judge. Love may be and in fact is a fine thing but love is not the point here: if one man would overthrow his government with love, another may wish to do so with hate, and in a court of law we cannot distinguish between the means, if the purpose is the same. You have made it clear that you feel no allegiance to the lawfully constituted authority which rules over this part of the world, but tolerae it only because you must. And all the while you are waiting for one who will overthrow it. If I were to turn you free, even though you might give a man your sandals as well as your cloak, or go with him ten miles instead of one, it remains a fact nevertheless, according to your own admissions, that you believe a king is coming, one of your own people, who with love or with some means will destroy the government which now prevails over you; and that you will continue to teach such doctrines; with the consequences that the people of this land will be kept by such men as you in a condition of unhappiness and expectancy, for which there can be, if this madness is persisted in, only the eventual destruction of your cities and your people.

"I am sorry that you Jews can not or will not be good citizens. That you can not or will not because of some ancient belief of your people is a matter that can have no validity under Roman law. You force upon me the judgment which as the Emperor's servant I must now pronounce. You have nothing more to say in your defense, no more witnesses to call?"

In a low voice Joshua said, "No, my lord."

Zillah now burst into hysterical weeping and flung herself down before Pilate; and Sirena knelt, supplicating him, begging to be heard.

But Pilate silenced her, saying, "I have heard you. The evidence voluntarily offered here proves that this man is a rebel, no matter how gentle in his actual life, and dangerous to the peace and well-being of that government under which we all live. I have no choice but to condemn him to be hanged in the manner prescribed for rebels." He motioned to the guards and said, "Take him away."

There was outcry in the court, from those who approved the sentence, from the few who were wildly begging for mercy; but at once the guards seized Joshua and took him out. Pilate arose and left the court. Zillah had fainted and Sirena was now kneeling by her; and Lucia had come over and was looking down at them.

XXV

They took Joshua outside the city walls to an area used by Jews for stoning to death those condemned by their high court, and by Romans for the execution of political criminals. The degree of brutality in crucifixion depended on the manner of it. In its most merciful form there was affixed to the upright beam a small platform, on which the condemned man stood, with his wrists bound to the crosspiece: and he died in this case, sometimes after many days or even two or three weeks, from starvation, exposure and exhaustion. In another form a stake was thrust out from the upright beam, and this the man straddled, resting his crotch on it to help support his weight and to ease the burden on his arms. In the most cruel form his wrists were bound to the crosspiece or his hands were spiked to it, and his ankles were bound or his feet were spiked to the main beam; and with no platform to stand on or stake between his thighs he was suspended from his arms and suffered the most dreadful agonies. Sometimes when hanged in this position the man's thighs after a few hours were broken, so that with all his weight hanging from his arms a great burden was placed on his heart and he died more quickly, from hemorrhage and suffocation. Sometimes also the crucified person was given a drink of frankincense in wine or some other opiate to deaden his sensibilities; and in Jerusalem certain Jewish women, moved by compassion and mercy, vied with one another in providing the drug. The more hideous forms of death on the cross were imposed only on implacable robbers, brigands, rebels and the ringleaders among revolting slaves. Pilate had decreed that Joshua should suffer the mildest form of punishment and should have a drink to deaden his pain.

It was the custom to scourge the condemned man before he was hanged, and sometimes those physically weak were dead before they were put on the cross. After Joshua was taken outside the city he was stripped naked and scourged with leaded whips, until his whole back was bloody and his breathing was difficult. Then he was laid down, with his torn back against the main beam; his wrists were bound to the crosspiece and his ankles to the upright post, with his feet on the platform; and men then hoisted the cross and set it in the earth. All crosses were short; Joshua's feet were only a few inches above the ground.

A mob had followed to watch the scourging and the crucifixion. The four women were in this mob, struggling to get to Joshua or at least to see him; but the guards drove them back. They did not see the scourging. They did not see Joshua at all until some time after he had been hung up and most of the people had turned away. Even then they were not allowed to approach him but were forced to stand back a hundred yards or more. They could see him hanging there, or standing, for his feet were on the platform; they could see his arms flung out above him; and Sirena thought she could see bloodstains over his face and chest. His head was bowed and his body seemed to sag with weariness or death.

What were the women thinking? Lucia, poor thing, had believed from the first that with some miracle Joshua would free himself; and now her face, thin and gray with fatigue, was a picture of wonder, of doubt, of astonishment, all these emotions playing over her features; and her eyes stared at Joshua, as she turned her head this way and then that, like one trying different perspectives. Zillah's emotions were such a turmoil of bitterness and hate, of impulses toward vengeance, of suffocationg tenderness that she was unable to think at all or to see clearly, but stood trembling and moaning. Sirena, by far the most rational one, was thinking many things. Men hung on crosses were usually left there to the birds of prey, until only their skeletons remained. She was hoping that they would be able to claim the body and bury it. She was recalling the words which almost a year ago she had spoken to Joshua by the sea of Galilee: "A philosopher has said that people create gods only to destroy them." She had asked him, then or later: "But if the messiah comes, won't the people destroy him?" She had said to him, "People don't want love, but hate, for hate gives them strength, but love makes them weak before their enemies." She recalled how agitated Joshua had been, how he had fled from her, to sit with his feet in the water. . . .

What was Sibyl, the Migdal harlot, thinking? She had not wept in the court or since then and she was not weeping now. A part of the time she stood with her eyes closed, swaying gently like one going to sleep and about to fall; and when she opened her eyes she looked up at the heavens. When his soul ascended she thought she would see it. She thought she would be able to follow it. . . .

"He will not die!" Lucia was whispering.

Weeping quietly, Sirena turned to her, "What are you saying?"

"He will not die."

"He's dying now."

"I tell you he will not die."

Armed guards had been left with Joshua, lest his friends try to take him down; and these men now sat at a little distance from the cross and seemed to be casting dice. There was nobody in the whole area now but Joshua, the guards, and the women. Feeling exhausted by grief Sirena went forward, wondering if she could bribe the guards or move them to pity; but at once a big ugly fellow arose and shouted at her, "Back, you fool!" She returned to her companions and after sinking to the earth reached up and took one of Zillah's hands to draw her down. Zillah collapsed and fell fainting, and Sirena drew her across her lap and held her. From time to time through tears she looked at Joshua but there had been no movement in him; he still stood as before, sagging, his chin sunk to his chest. She wanted to call his name or a word of love but was afraid the guards would send her away. She looked down at Zillah's face, wet and white and ghastly; at her closed eyelids and quivering lips; and gently she put a hand to Zillah's brow. "Zillah?" she whispered but Zillah made no response. Sirena looked up at Sibyl who, still standing, gazed at the sky; at Lucia, who still gazed at Joshua.

Another hour passed and there was no change. Another hour and a third, and Sirena thought she heard Joshua utter a cry. She was sure of it when she saw that the guards were looking at him. One of the men arose and went over to Joshua and stood by him, looking up at his face. Then he returned and sat with his companions. A little later Sirena saw a convulsed movement in Joshua; he was tossing his head up and back and from side to side. Then he seemed to be trying to hold his head up, but slowly, very slowly, it sank, and she thought he shuddered and slipped downward a little. A few minutes later he was still.

He is dead! Sirena thought. She whispered: "Zillah."

"What?"

"Are you all right?"

"Who is all right in this stinking world!"

"I think Joshua is dead."

"Would to God I were dead with him!"

Lucia turned to whisper to them, "He will not die."

"Maybe Lucia knows," Sirena said.

"She did this to him," Zillah said.

"No, love did it."

It was toward evening when one of the guards went over to look at Joshua's face. He returned and spoke to his fellows. They then seemed to be discussing some matter, to be disputing while they all stared at Joshua; and at last they went over and stood by the cross. One of them

300

reached out and seemed to touch Joshua. Another picked up a lance. He put the sharp point of the lance against Joshua's side and appeared to be pushing gently with it. After prodding several times with the lance the guard set it upright in the earth.

Sirena thought dully, without feeling, He is dead. "Zillah?"

"Yes?"

"He's dead, I guess. What'll we do now?"

Zillah sat up. With an angry movement she flung her hair back but she did not look over at the cross. "How do you know?"

"I saw them prodding him with a lance."

"How can you stand to watch it?"

"How can you stand not to!"

Again Zillah burst into tears. "There's no God!" she cried bitterly. "There's no God!"

"Hush, Zillah. The men are watching us."

"To hell with them!"

The guards heard her cry and one of them, who seemed to be the leader, now came over. He was a big man, with the hard seamed face of a warrior. His eyes were blue and cold.

He looked at the women and said, "What are you doing here?"

"Waiting," Sirena said.

"Who are you?"

"His friends."

"Waiting to steal the body, you mean?"

"No."

"Then why are you here?"

"Because we love him."

"Love a criminal?"

"He was no criminal!" Zillah said.

Looking at the man's cold blue eyes Sirena asked," Is he dead?"

"That's none of your business."

"I'm a Roman citizen and I'd think it might be my business."

"If you're a Roman citizen why are you here?"

"I have told you. May we have the body?"

"No."

Sirena and Zillah had saved a part of their wages. Sirena wondered if she could bribe the man. "Will you leave him there all night?"

"You'd better go," the man said. "We don't want you here."

"Please, we'd like to stay."

"I don't want you here."

"May we have his robe?"

"It belongs to us," the man said, "but it's worthless."

"Then may we have it?"

"If you'll go away and not come back."

Sirena considered a moment. "All right. But we'd like to wait here until he is dead. May we?"

"He's dead now."

"Oh no, he isn't!" Lucia said.

"A little while ago he said something. Would you tell us what he said?"

"I don't know."

The guard went back and stood by Joshua, looking at his face. He took the lance and again thrust at him, putting the point to his thigh and to his chin and under one arm. He dropped the lance and picked up the robe. He came over and flung it at Sirena's feet.

"There's your rag. Now get out of here."

Darkness had come. Hours had passed since Joshua was hung on the cross and now he was dead and the world was lonely. Sirena picked up the robe and folded it and hung it over her left arm. She reached down to Zillah.

"Come, we must go."

"That's what he said so many times!"

Zillah arose and was about to spit at the guard when Sirena cried out sharply. She seized Zillah's arm and swung her. She put an arm around Zillah and led her away, and Sibyl followed; and when Lucia made no move to follow the guard pushed her roughly and told her to be gone. He stared after the women until they were out of sight.

The three of them went to the shed, where everything was so poignant with the presence of this man who had been hanged for love, and was now what Jews called an accursed of God on a tree. Zillah flung herself down on the barley straw and tried to weep out her desolate grief. Sirena, as pale and quiet as death, looked at the garment over her arm and wondered why Lucia had not come. The loneliness in her was almost more than she could endure and she flung herself down and for a few moments cried into the straw, "Poor Joshua! Poor dear Joshua!" Then she got up and knew that she was done with weeping and when a little later Levi came shuffling along, smiting his thighs, she turned on him with bitterness.

"So you come back! After lying to get a man hanged you come back!"

"Where is he?"

"Yes, great God, where is he!"

"He isn't dead," said Levi. "I've seen him."

"You've never seen him. People like you never will."

"It's people like you who haven't seen him. I have, and Simon and Kepha and Zabdai."

"What do you mean?" she asked, beginning to feel that the whole experience was unreal.

"I mean that you didn't see him."

Her bitterness ebbed. Feeling strange and strangely stupid she looked at Levi's gentle face. "You mean you saw him?"

"We saw him. We still see him."

"I don't know what you mean," she said weakly and looked back into the shed at Zillah and Sibyl. "Or at last, possibly I do. Where is he?"

"Back in Galilee."

She ran over and sank by Zillah, crying, "Zillah?"

"Now what?" asked Zillah.

"What are you going to do?"

"Wait for the king, of course."

"Shall I tell you what Levi says?"

"No. He is crazy."

"Possibly he saw more than we saw."

"He saw nothing. He's as crazy as Sibyl."

"I'm not so sure. Zillah, have we been fools?"

"I'm going over to see Joshua."

"But he isn't there."

"I want to touch him, just once."

"I tell you he isn't there."

"You don't want me to touch him?"

"We touched him but never knew it, saw him but did not see. Levi saw."

"Oh, in God's name, don't give me your pompous words now! I tell you I'm going to Joshua."

"But you can't, Zillah, not that way."

"I won't listen to you! Before daylight I'm going over to touch Joshua!"

"Very well, I'll go with you."

They spent the night here but they did not sleep. Sibyl sat by them and murmured over and over to herself, like one who had found the tower beyond tragedy, "I will be with him soon." When Sirena thought daylight was coming she went with Zillah and they climbed the hill, taking their way among the sleeping people, and went to the field of stoning. The guards or other guards who had relieved them had built a fire and were sitting around it; and just beyond them in firelight was the dim figure of Joshua, sagging downward, all his weigh on his arms.

"Look!" Zillah whispered.

"Don't look. I don't want to see him."

Zillah ran forward until she came to the firelight. Then slowly she approached the men and spoke.

"May I go over to him?"

"What do you want?"

"Only to touch him."

"Woman, he's dead."

"Not for me. I only want to touch him, once."

"She must be mad," the man said, looking at her.

Boldly, then, Zillah went up to the guard and proffered a gold coin. "I just want to touch him."

"All right, then, go touch him and then get out of here."

While the guards watched Zillah went softly to the cross and stood there, feeling suffocated, feeling that she was close to something, yet terribly alone and desolate. "Poor Joshua!" she murmured. "Our poor Joshua!"

"Hurry up," the guard said, "and get away from there!"

With a gesture of infinite love or of infinite renunciation Zillah bent down and kissed one of the cold feet. Her hot tears fell to the flesh she had kissed and her hair spilled over the tears.

"That's enough," said the guard. "Now get away."

Zillah turned, blinded, and ran back to Sirena.

XXVI

Lucia did not come but Levi came again, and gently, with faith that nothing could put aside, he told them that Joshua was in Israel and at the moment in Galilee. Sirena and Zillah looked wonderingly at one another. Was Levi mad, or were they? They decided to leave at once. Should they try to find Lucia? Zillah said no, that Lucia, now that she had been disappointed in the only kind of miracle she could understand, would go again over the hills, looking for her child. And even if she did not, they would see her again. Because Sirena and Zillah had hoarded a part of their earnings they were able to hire passage to Jericho, and there for a day or two they tarried, to look round them for Aza and Sarah. To people they met they described the two old ones but nobody had seen them.

Knowing that Joshua had buried some coins in Galilee and that Lucia knew the hiding-place Sirena thought Lucia might go there; and they hired passage again and went up the river road, pausing in Tiberias to search. To search for Joshua? Yes, they were looking for his face. The baths were almost deserted; the only people who had remained were those too crippled or ill to walk. One old woman said she had seen Joshua, looking very sad and walking alone.

They went north again, walking now, going up the road down which they had come. Sibyl was so weak that they had to support her. At each spot where they had spent a night with Joshua they paused to feel his presence. For

Sirena and Zillah the memories were almost too poignant to bear, as they recalled that in this spot Joshua had prayed; in that, he had blessed a cripple; and in still another he had taught them his gospel of love. Sibyl seemed unmoved as she looked at the waters or up at the sky, or gave them her pale mechanical smile when they did her a kindness. One night at dark she went away alone and on returning, after an hour or two, she said that Joshua had appeared to her and had spoken.

"As a man?" asked Zillah.

"As Joshua."

"What did he say?"

"That he was the Passover lamb used in the slaughter."

Sirena and Zillah looked at one another. Sirena said: "Is that all?"

"He said, Wait for me and tell the people, for I'll come again."

"O my God!" Sirena gasped. "How stupid we have been!"

"What do you mean?" asked Zillah.

"Didn't you hear?—I'll come again. Levi saw the same truth."

"You mean that Sibyl sees a truth that we do not?"

"Yes."

"You mean Joshua actually stood before her?"

"What is actual? Have the philosophers answered that? If she saw Joshua, does it matter how?"

Sirena was looking at Sibyl, a pale creature of ghostly loveliness who had been fasting for days, preparing for a vision or an ascent.

"You mean Joshua will come again?" asked Zillah, her astonishment and confusion growing.

"Do you ask that question, whose people have looked deepest?"

"I am only a stupid one among my people."

"All that matters is that he should be recognized when he comes."

Sibyl said she could hear music. Barely alive now, she

307

was lying on her back and listening; and somewhere at a great distance above her, or far away in Galilee, she could hear music that was very lonely and sad. She closed her eyes, as though to sleep.

Sibyl now surrendered to a vast and holy quiet, to the great love that had been the soul of Joshua; she gave herself up to it completely and after a while seemed not to be breathing at all. She knew that she was no longer on the earth, but above it, and slowly ascending; she was among the clouds now; she could hear the flutes passing with soft harmonies into the heavenly choirs. Somewhere ahead of her she saw Joshua, waiting.

"I guess she sleeps," said Sirena at last.

"Do you think she saw Joshua?"

"In her way."

"I don't understand you."

"Can you hear music?"

"Music? Well, yes, I seem to."

"What is it like?"

"Very sad and very far away."

"Then you do understand," Sirena said.

Some time later they lay back and clasped hands and slept. In their dreams they heard music and when they awoke at daylight birds were singing round them in the trees. Sirena sat up, wondering for a moment where she was. She looked over at Sibyl. Her gaze at first was curious because of Sibyl's loveliness, but then she sensed a slow gathering of horror, of unbelief, of amazement; and she knew without touching the woman that Sibyl was dead.

"Zillah?" she whispered. "Look."

Zillah sat up and followed Sirena's gaze to Sibyl. "She still sleeps," she said.

"Yes, she sleeps." Sirena looked at Sibyl's thin bloodless face and open staring eyes and felt chilled. Yet what *was* death, after all? "You recall what she said last night?"

"About Joshua?"

"She said that Joshua told her, Wait for me, I shall come

again. Did Joshua say that to her? Well, no, not really; and yet he did in another way, which we never understood. Levi, I guess, understood it—or did the experience for him rest at a lower level? Did Lucia understand it?"

"You mean that the messiah will come?"

"No, Zillah, not that. Don't you see that he has come?—again? Can't you understand it now? He has come in the only way he will ever come—as he came a hundred or a thousand years ago; as he will come again next year, or a hundred years from now, or a thousand years hence. Don't you see? He has come, he will come again, he will keep coming, until in this world there are no more Lucias hunting for their lost children, no more soldiers with lances by dead men in the night . . ."

NOTES AND COMMENTARY

As with the Notes to former novels, to save space the full names of the authorities, titles of their publications, and page references are omitted. The scholars following include many of the greatest in the New Testament field. Where these letters appear, OT indicates Old Testament; NT, New Testament; CE; *Catholic Encyclopedia;* JE, *Jewish Encyclopedia* and EB, *Encyclopedia Biblica.* The materials appear in order under the following topics.

AGE, the   It is difficult for us today to project ourselves into the Palestine of 1900 years ago. McCown: "The Occidental who would understand Jesus must put himself into a completely different atmosphere from that which Jeans, Eddington, Millikan and Whitehead breathe, into the atmosphere of the *Arabian Nights* and the apocalypses." Conditions were so primitive, says Sachar, that "men used scythes and sickles for mowing; their ploughs were of wood, rarely shod with iron; and threshing was done laboriously with the clumsy flail. Small, undersized oxen, hardly as large as modern calves, dragged the ploughs back and forth, barely scratching the surface of the earth. . . . All Orientals regarded labor as a curse and the early Hebrews were no exception." As for his misfortunes, the peasant, says Finkelstein, "never stopped to theorize about the reasons for suffering or divine punishment. It was sufficient explanation of evil to say that the 'anger of God was kindled' . . ." Palestine, says Hunkin, was filled with abnormal types—"quacks and vagrants and street-corner preachers. The less educated masses listened to their babble until their minds were reduced to a state of uneasiness and confusion." Budde: "Solon and Brutus are the classical examples of how, in antiquity, insanity, idiocy, abnormal mental conditions of every sort, were ever the best cloak under which to preach and prepare without arousing suspicion." Klausner: "Galilee was filled with the sick and suffering and with those pathological types which we now label neurasthenics and psychathenics . . . especially hysterical women and all manner of 'nerve cases'—dumb, epileptics, and the semi-insane were numerous." Angus: "The cry for salvation was loud, persistent, and universal. . . . Men sought deliverance . . . from the burden of grief and sorrow, from the reign of death, the universal power of demons and the malefic astral deities, from the oppressive tyranny of fate, the caprice of *Sors,* or *Fortuna,* the pollution of matter, the consciousness of guilt, the wasting of disease, from the *taedium vitae.*" As for public morals, says Kennett, "the successors of Hyrcanus who assumed the title of king were so unutterably vile that no one with a particle of respect for religion could have desired the continuance of their rule." Workman: "Crucifixion, the punishment of slaves, was one of the commonest sights of life." Easton: "Morally, conditions were bad because venality, cruelty, and sexual license were uncondemned by public opinion." Though Mosheim says the "wiser part of mankind" looked upon religion as a "just object of ridicule and contempt," Goodspeed points out that "our modern scientific attitude of mind was of course unknown." Roztovtzeff: "In the ancient world the mass of the population never attained, either in the East or the West, to a scientific and rationalistic way of thinking." Willoughby: "The supernatural realm was conceived to be far more important than the natural world. . . . Most men . . . tended to think of events as the result of the more or less capricious activities of spirits or demons." Glover: "Fancy, ritual, mysticism, unsound science, are triumphant." Case: "Gods, angels, demons, and the souls of men seemed accessible to mortal eyes and audible to human ears. . . . Man had no real privacy; angels and demons kept an ever-watchful eye upon him." Cumont: "People could no longer take a bath, go to the barber, change their clothes, or manicure their fingernails without first awaiting the proper moment." Bevan: "the febrile fancies and unwholesome imaginings which sprang up in such rank abundance." Zeller: "a deep distrust of man's capacity of knowledge prevailed." Farrer: "The time of the origin of Christianity was marked by a state of great mental fermentation, the political agitation of centuries having reduced multitudes, especially in the East, to a condition bordering on actual craziness." Scholars point out that Tiberius was the slave of astrologists; Domitian lived in fear of the fulfillment of Chaldean prophecies; Aurelius surrounded himself with magicians. An age, says Fiebig, steeped in Oriental mythology that had a "formative influence on the story of Jesus." And the masses of ignorant people, says Dibelius, "expected the end of the world any day." Silver: "The crash and doom of the world was at hand . . . there was no longer time for the ordinary pursuits of life." Guignebert: "men's minds were occupied with lurid and fantastic descriptions of the events which would occur when the present age gave place to that which was to come." Trattner: "Palestine in the times of John and Jesus was agog with vivid expectation of a cataclysmic change."

BAPTISM   We still don't know, says Bowen, what the baptizer did; Lightfoot says those who came to John *plunged themselves* into the river." Brandt says in Aramaic and Hebrew there is no difference between baptism and bath; the title of baptist meant only "one characterized by the practice of bathing." Bousset: "We know too little of the baptism of John to be able either to affirm or deny that it had a sacramental value." Oesterley and Box point out that it was believed that holy spirits dwelt in water. Scott finds it strange that Jesus "began his ministry by submitting to the baptism of John." Most scholars reject the assumption that John baptized Jesus.

BUDDHA   On the many parallels between Buddhism and the Gospel story see A. J. Edmunds. CE, a *very* conservative source, admits the "striking" parallels. Farrer says it is difficult to believe that Buddha's teaching had not traveled "at least as far as Greece and Italy."

BURIAL   Josephus: "All who pass by when one is buried must accompany the funeral and join in the lamentation." If Westerners are shocked by the violence of such scenes, Orientals, says Mackie, would be no less shocked by our "apparent callousness."

CROSS   *Peloubet's Dict.*: "The emblem of a slave's death and a murderer's punishment." Hannay: "The cross, ages before Christianity, was simply the conventional phallus."

CRUCIFIXION   Schultze says that as "regards the means employed (the cross properly so-called), stake or gibbet, and for the method of attaching the victim thereto, the executioners seem to have had the greatest liberty allowed." On the crucifixion of Jesus much dreadful nonsense has been written; e.g., Lambert: "The blood and water that gushed out have been held by some medical authorities to justify the opinion that the Savior died of a broken heart."

DEMONS   Harnack: "The whole world and the circumambient atmosphere was filled with devils . . . every phase and form of life was ruled by them. They sat on thrones, they hovered around cradles. The earth was literally a hell." They had, says Case, "an insatiable appetite for the human soul." The belief was worldwide, says

313

Oesterley, "that all diseases, sickness and infirmities were in-flictions of demons." Romanes says if Jesus had denied pos-session "he would have been giving evidence of a scientific knowledge . . . beyond the culture of his time." Stevens: "special wickedness, popularly conceived as the result of the indwelling of demons in men." Weiss: "man no longer had the mastery of sin, but sin of him." Lippert: "Among the diseases which appeared longest to be consequences of pos-session belong sudden epidemics, mental disorders, epilepsy, hysteria, gout, rheumatism, St. Vitus's dance, paralysis . . . even deaf-mutism." Harnack: "It was as exorcisers that Christians went out into the great world." As for spirits, says Cheyne, "the world was conceived, by both Jews and Christians, to be subject to 'ministerial spirits'." Cumont: "swarms of the in-fernal spirits rose to the upper world through the natural openings of the earth, or through ditches dug for the purpose of maintaining communication with them and conciliating them with offerings." Justin said Jesus had been made mortal to destroy demons; Origen, that with prayer "we expel them from the souls of men, and even sometimes from the bodies of animals." Egyptians divided the body into 36 parts, each hav-ing a special demon which needed to be propitiated.

DREAMS   Cicero: "Let this divination of dreams
                be rejected. . . . For . . . that superstition,
spreading through the world, has oppressed the intellectual energies of nearly all men, and has seized upon the weakness of humanity." Blunt: "Anyone who was subject to frequent dreaming was looked on as a special medium of divine energy, and many sought to produce the state by artificial means, e.g., fasting or the use of drugs."

EMPEROR   Case speaks of that "astonishing phen-
WORSHIP   omenon still withus": e.g., Hitler, Stalin,
                Roosevelt. Latourette: "The longing
for a savior who would bring peace to the earth had seemed to have fulfillment in Augustus." Renan: "The worship of Augustus had become the principal religion of the provinces." Worship of the emperor, says Willoughby, was a "well-estab-lished and generally accepted phase of imperial policy." Pius said of himself, "I am Lord of the world and the Law of the sea." Statues of Antinous, Hadrian's paramour, rose in every

314

market-place, temples were built in his honor, and his cult was maintained for a century. Farrer: "It was with no shock to Christian feeling that Constantine and his successors were divinized by the senate, and had temples raised and priests appointed to them; and if with the emperor Gratian the custom ceased, the Christian emperors were for some time afterwards still spoken of as gods." Only to the Jew, says Box, was worship of the emperor "the blasphemy of blasphemies."

ENOCH,
  BOOK OF

This was one of the most important books in shaping early Christianity. Renan: "The hostility between the good and the bad . . . led him to an eschatology that was absolutely ferocious. . . . Dante had in him a true forerunner. Enoch delights to relate these hideous torments; he even invents them. . . . The angelology of the Book of Enoch is perfectly ridiculous. . . . he knows a whole race of celestial beings, whose names he fabricates in the most audacious fashion. All this is pure nonsense."

ESSENES

As recently as 1947 Marcus has said that scholars today know no more about them than former scholars "nor has any scholar convincingly shown whether Jewish or Greek or oriental influence is paramount in their beliefs and practices." Kohler: "the enigma of history." Lightfoot: "the great enigma of Hebrew history." Schurer: "The origin of the Essenes is as obscure as their name." Philo said their number was 4,000; soon after his time they completely disappeared from history. Edersheim thinks the name means 'the outsiders'; Baur, Keim and others, physician; Lightfoot and others, silent ones; but Morrison, Julicher and most scholars argue for 'the pious'. Zeitlin thinks the word was derived from Hasidim; others from haseh, meaning holy or pure. The great majority of modern critics, says Guignebert, think it "largely indebted to foreign influence," though Reuss argued there was none. Some have seen a Buddhist influence but that, says Schurer, is "far-fetched"; for Hilgenfeld they were originally a non-Jewish tribe; Lightfoot and others see a Persian influence; Baur, Keim, Julicher and others, a Greek; for Zeller it was a reflection of Pythagoreanism; for Bentwich, a "mingling of Jewish and Pythagorean ideas." But Cheyne says they were an offshoot of the Pharisees "and carried the Pharisean doctrines or tendencies to an extreme." Only an exaggerated Pharisaism think Margolis and Marx, Schurer, and Finkelstein; but Case says that *like* Pharisaism it "sprang from anti-Hellenistic Judaism." The fanatical atmosphere of the time, Finkelstein points out, gave rise to many sects—the Morning Bathers, the Water Drinkers, the Worshipers at Sunrise, etc. Though Ewald called it "the noblest and most memorable development" in ancient religion, they held women in contempt, as Lightley says. "Women-haters," says Enslin, and quotes Josephus: "they guard against the lascivious behavior of women, and are persuaded that none of them preserve their fidelity to one man." They were thought, says Philo, "to pervert man's moral dispositions." Kuenen: "Ascetic communism." Enlow: "mystics, ascetics, and communists." Rhees: "they were found in nearly every town in Palestine," leaving their own settlements, says Schechter, for the "purpose of exhibiting their supernatural powers."

FORMALISM   Though Friedlander says in the Bible "there is no indication of a fixed ritual" Scott says: "Religion, to the ancient mind, was not so much a matter of belief as of praxis; liberty was allowed for an endless modification of doctrine, while the ritual was inflexibly maintained." M Joseph: "No religion has more clearly recognized the value of ceremonial than Judaism." But, says Finkelstein, what "we regard as ritual and ceremony was living reality to the ancients"—and E. Carpenter: "Early man felt the great truths and realities of life—often I believe more purely than we do—but he could not give form to his experience. That stage came when he began to lose touch with these realities; and it showed itself in rites and ceremonials." A study of the history of law (Macmillan, Robson, *et al.*) reveals to what extent formalism prevailed in more than Judaism. If a beast injured your vines and you sued you'd lose if you called them vines for in the Twelve Tables they were designated as trees; you would lose if you called a bull a bull —he was the leader of the herd; or a goat a goat—it was the browser upon leeks; etc. But Levitical legislation, Toy says, fixed "men's minds on ceremonial details which, in some cases, it put into the same category and on the same level with moral duties." Hooke says Jeremiah rejected "the very core of the ritual system" and Whittaker thot such rejections "found no permanent response." Snaith: "the devotion to the temple of the priests in these latter days knew no bounds." Lietzmann: "Shammai and Hillel, and their disciples, disputed whether the evening prayer was to be offered in a standing posture or lying in bed; what was the appropriate order for prayers after a meal; whether the towel used for drying one's hands was to be placed upon the table or upon the cushion used as a seat . . . and so on *ad infinitum.*" Lightley: "The Rabbis counted 248 classes of things to be done, and 365 of things forbidden. . . . The Mishnah lays down no fewer than 39 principal classes of prohibitions, and from these many others are deduced." See also *Pharisees.*

GALILEE   Bauer: "Galileans grew up . . . in considerable freedom from the Law." Filson: "a land of mixed population." Carus: "Galileans were a people of mixed blood." Klausner estimates half a million non-Jews in Palestine, and Guignebert says "a large part of the Jewish population of Galilee was composed of recent converts, old inhabitants of the country, forcibly driven to circumcision . . ." Oesterley and Box: "It is well known that the racial purity of the Jewish population of Galilee was not above suspicion; the very name 'Galilee of the Gentiles' suggests that the region so called was the borderland between the Jews and Gentiles."

GARDEN
  OF GETH.   Barton: "The fact is certain that the Garden of Gethsemane lay on the western slope of the Mount of Olives. Since the 16th century the Roman Catholics have shown a little garden, which lies just above the Kidron, as the Garden of Gethsemane. More recently the Russian Church has walled in the space next above it as the real garden. There is no certainty that the garden was on either site. To the Jews of the first century a garden was not a place for flower-beds, but an olive orchard, and such an orchard may have extended widely over the hillside."

GENNESARET   The Rabbis derive the name, says Edersheim, "either from a harp—because the fruits of its shores are as sweet as the sound of a harp—or

317

else explain it to mean 'the gardens of the princess', from the beautiful villas and gardens around." The original name of the sea of Galilee seems to have been Chinneroth from the Hebrew word for harp. Josephus refers to it as Gennesar. Lake of Gennesaret occurs only in Luke. In John it is the Sea of Tiberias.

GOD Jehovah, which most Christian scholars persist in using, was arrived at by taking the biblical letters JHVH and adding to them the vowels of Adonai (Lord). The *New Stand. Bible Dict.* says "the form Jehovah is impossible, according to the strict principles of Hebrew vocalization"; and Rabbi Landman calls it an "etymological misadventure." By the time of Jesus, says J. E. Carpenter, the Jews had "long ceased to use the ancient divine name Yahweh" because, as Hunkin says, "it was too holy to be pronounced."

GOLDEN RULE The saying, says Klausner, 'what is hateful to thyself do not unto thy neighbor' may not have been Hillel's invention but "was current in Palestine from the time of the Book of Tobit." In other words it did not originate with Jesus. The Notes to my next novel will dwell at some length on the authenticity of the sayings of Jesus.

GREEK INFLUENCE In this novel there is obviously Greek influence on my character Joshua. "The supreme factor which influenced the Judaism of the Dispersion," say Oesterley and Box, "was Greek thought. . . . Utterly unlike the traditional attitude of intolerant prejudice towards the Gentile world which was characteristic of the strict Palestinian Jew, his brother of the Dispersion regarded the larger world with a kindly eye, ready [to] associate with his Gentile neighbors."

HILLEL Hillel and Shammai were two famous Jewish teachers just before the time of Jesus. They established two schools and differed, says G. F. Moore, on "more than three hundred" matters of Law. Hillel encouraged his disciples to read Greek literature; Shammai was a rigorist. Bentwich: "If any man can be said to represent that which is best in rabbinical and Pharasaic tradition, it is

Hillel." Waxman: "set himself to the task of standardizing the methods of interpretation of the Law." Sekles: "raised the study of the unwritten law to a very high reputation." Some have thought Hillel influenced Jesus.

IMAGES   Klausner: "Images of the Emperor . . . were not religious but only political emblems, yet the Jews deafened the whole world with their protests against them."

JESUS   Duff: "It is a serious fact that virtually all men are wondering just what Jesus was." More than 60,000 books have been published about him in 800 languages and dialects; in the 4-year period, 1928-32, the Cumulative Book Index listed nearly 900 entries on Jesus and related subjects. No wonder Schubert has said: "No single school can ever master every section of this immense field. But . . . when the W. Durants and H. G. Wellses can communicate to the world their amateurish visions of the centuries and millenniums it is not only possible but also urgent that the professional stay not too far behind." Bruce Barton's book on Jesus Trattner calls "nothing more than a misshapen phantom." In the brief space here I will give as full a picture as possible of Jesus as the scholars see him. Danby has said that for "a critical knowledge of the Jewish background of the Gospels the Christian can never wholly dispense with Jewish scholarship"—nor should ever wish to. I have read all the Jewish scholars available to me. If any reader wonders why I quote no Catholics, Prof. J. H. Cobb gives the answer: "the Catholic scholar begins with Scripture and tradition, the total deposit of the faith as, and only as, this is officially interpreted by the living *magisterium* of the church . . . . when the Catholic scholar writes about Jesus, messianic prophecy, and the doctrines expressed in the various NT books, he is controlled at every point by loyalty to the teaching church." But today, says Riddle, "all disciplines make their contribution to the attempt to undersand and interpret the NT correctly"; and as long ago as 1917 G. McCown summarizes it: "The 19th century ended with the destruction of its characteristic 'liberal' portrait of Jesus. It would appear that after nearly forty years, the 20th century has discovered none at all of its own. The light-headed wanderings of mind to which humanity is eternally subject and the ponderous inertia which delays human progress leave the major problems still unsolved. Indeed a large majority of Christians do not know such problems exist. Even in the most progressive and most literate countries the vast proportion of Christian people have not allowed science to infect their religious ideas. They have one foot in the fifteenth, the other in the twentieth century . . . . Worst of all the greater part of the writers who essay to settle the practical problems of civilization and the church still write in blissful ignorance of all principles of Synoptic criticism and historical interpretation." Bearing in mind the paucity of the evidence we must stand aghast at the dogmatism in men past and present: for Celsus and Compte, Jesus was an impostor; for H. S. Chamberlain, Delitzsch, Haupt and Haeckel he was not even a Jew but had 'an Aryan father'; for Gore he was "the consummation of nature's order" but for de Loosten he was a hybrid tainted at birth; for Hirsch, a paranoiac; for Benet-Sangle, a case of religious paranoia; for Lomer, a man subject to delusions; for Frenssen, a man with monstrous thoughts and visions; for Rasmussen, an epileptic; for Holtzmann, an ecstatic; for Neitzsche, a sickly and contemptible weakling; and for Daab he rejected both religion and morality. De Jonge argued that he was a widower with a son; Voigt, that he was baptized on the 10th or 11th of January in the year 27! Some have seen in him a propagandist for the Essenes; some, a sentimental moralist; some, an eschatological fanatic. For Dobschutz he was "in no way an ascetic"; for Wrede, Brandt and others he was a rabbi; for Otto, "a charismatic evangelist who was also an exorcist"; for E. Meyer, Wellhausen and others a teacher who opposed formalism in Judaism. But we don't even know what language he spoke! Schweitzer thinks Meyer proved it to have been Aramaic but McCown says he "doubtless spoke Greek." For Eisler he was only a revolutionary who for a time seized and held the temple. And so on, ad infinitum.

The trouble obviously is that too many scholars are the victims of their prepossessions. An instance is the luminous detachment of Oesterley when he deals with the OT and his naive bias when he deals with the NT. Loewe wrote to Montefiore (both are Jews) : "I quite agree with your point that Jewish scholars sometimes quite unfairly suppress unfriendly

passages and sometimes argue merely from the friendly ones."
Montefiore: "Mr. Loewe, generously anxious to champion the
Rabbis, and to weaken any difference between their teaching
and that of Jesus, if the teaching of Jesus appears superior to
theirs . . . ." Well, as Schweitzer says: "The critical study of
the life of Jesus has been for theology a school of honesty. The
world has never seen before, and will never see again, a
struggle for truth so full of pain and renunciation as that of
which the Lives of Jesus of the last hundred years contain the
cryptic record." NT research says Schubert, "has always suffered from a curious inability to be thoroughly historical in
method and in aim . . . this inability has been increasingly
obvious in recent years." Instances are Craig who says everything depends on the significance we find in the faith; or Dodd
who says that in the NT there is "an impression of truth
which lies beyond the flux of time." Giving high praise to
Loisy (than whom few deserve it more) Gilbert Murray says
that "Previous historians of Christianity have generally been
theologians, convinced of the miraculous nature of their subject and consequently, however learned, compelled to be uncritical"—as the reader will observe again and again in the
pages to come. Typical of what Murray censures is Brandt:
"We hold Joseph of Arimathea to be an historical person; but
the only reason which the narrative has for preserving his
name is that he buried Jesus. Therefore the name guarantees
the fact." Or Beyschlag who says Jesus' spirit "was a holy
energy which excluded from the first that sinful predominance
of the flesh, which is in all other men the basis of sinfulness."
Or Cornill who saw in Jesus "the end and turning point in
the history of humanity." If you want the true spirit of Jesus,
says Farrer, "you will find more of it in the fragmentary literature of paganism than in all the works of the Fathers put
together; and more not merely of its spirit but of its actual expression."

Writing of Eratothenes Draper says "he hoped to free history
as well as geography from the myths that deform it, a task
which the prejudices and interests of man will never permit to
be accomplished." Says Hatch: "I feel that I should fail of
my purpose if I did not linger still upon the threshold to say
something of the 'personal equation' that we must make before we can become either accurate observers or impartial

judges. There is the more reason for doing so, because the study of Christian history is no doubt discredited by the dissonance in the voices of its exponents. An ill-informed writer may state almost any propositions he pleases, with the certainty of finding listeners; a well-informed writer may state propositions which are as demonstrably true as any historical proposition can be, with the certainty of being contradicted . . . . most of us bring to the study of Christian history a number of conclusions already formed. We tend to beg the question before we examine it." Thus wrote one of the greatest of them. Schubert: "dangerous . . . is the resurging insistence on a religious and theological interpretation of the NT . . . the NT itself is a product of a long and well-known historical process, a process which began with the very beginnings of Christianity and was not yet finished by A.D. 200." Nor even by the Middle Ages. Clemen: "my readers' time and my own is too valuable to be spent on the criticism of popular writings that do not even endeavor to prove their stupendous assertions"—such as Will Durant's. Lake: "if the history of religion has any clear lesson it is that a nearer approach to truth is always a departure from orthodoxy." Percy Gardner wrote that he could not hope to "escape the opposition and anger which have always greeted any attempt to apply to the Christian creed the principles which are applied freely to other forms of faith." Or Eichhorn: "The NT writings are to be read as human books and tested in human ways." Or Nash: "the sense of fact has triumphed over the dogma of infallibility in all its forms"— or anyway is still trying to. The outstanding fact in modern NT scholarship, says Scott, "is the dominance of the historical method. It made its way with infinite difficulty in the face of the settled belief that Christianity, as a special revelation, cannot have been subject to the ordinary laws of development." But that "long and arduous adventure of the spirit," wrote McCown in 1940, "even now is far from finished."

Historicity of Jesus Was Jesus of Nazareth a historic person? We do not know, and unless documents turn up of which we have no knowledge we cannot hope ever to know. Montefiore, who rebuked Loewe above, says petulantly: "If eccentric scholars like to argue that Jesus never existed, let them do so." And Klausner, another Jew, says it is "unreasonable to question" it. But says Schmiedel: "the view that Jesus never really lived

322

has gained in ever-growing number of supporters. It is no use to ignore it, or to frame resolutions against it." Weigall: "Many of the most erudite critics are convinced that no such person ever lived." Among those so convinced, some of them internationally known scholars, are Bauer, Bohtlingk, Bolland, Bossi, E. Carpenter, Couchoud, Depuis, Drews, Dujardin, Frank, Hannay, Heulhard, Jensen, Kalthoff, Kulischer, Loman, Lublinski, Matthas, Mead, Naber, Pierson, Robertson, Rylands, G. Smith, W. B. Smith, Stahl, Van Eysinga, Virolleaud, Volney and Whittaker.

For such as Volney he was an astral myth and for Depuis, the sun; for Kulischer, a vegetation-god. Bauer was perhaps the first great scholar to deny the historicity; for him Jesus was a personification of certain ideas and ideals then current. Kalthoff's argument is similar: every movement of the folk-soul demands an ideal person and creates an illusion of reality more compelling than fact itself. Jensen tried to find parallels in the Gilgamesh legend. Drews, W. B. Smith, Dujardin and others argue that there was a pre-Jesus Jesus-god-cult and point out that Paul knew nothing of an historical Jesus but only the Christ—that is, the god. Robertson argues this thesis as plausibly as any: see *Christianity and Mythology*. G. Smith: "I believe the legend of Jesus was made by many minds working under a great religious impulse"—which is essentially the position of many scholars who accept the historicity. Couchoud and others argue that Jesus was the name of the god in a mystery-drama (see MYSTERY); Jehua-Joshua-Jesus (all the same name) mean, they say, Jahweh the savior. Dujardin reminds us that Frazer said the rite creates the god: " 'Passion' is the technical term that one finds in all the religions of mystery." Hannay: "a great deal of useless discussion has taken place as to the historicity . . . of Jesus, but we know that nineteen-twentieths of his supposed acts and teaching were attributed to various gods all over Asia." Those on *this* side have some strong arguments which their opponents have not yet demolished.

Of the abler scholars who accept the figure as historic nearly all follow Renan, Arnold and others in rejecting the supernatural elements. These elements, they say, all came from pagan cults. Schmiedel has a famous thesis, that there are nine unflattering statements in the gospel stories which prove the historicity of Jesus—for unflattering things would not have been inventd. *But we need to know if these meant to people then what they mean to us.* Loisy speaks for a great number when he says: "Jesus the Nazorean is at once an historical person and a mythical being who, supporting the myth and supported by it, was finally made by it into the Christ." Like many others he rejects everything in the gospel story but the historicity of the central figure. For readers unfamiliar with the field possibly it ought to be said that the only evidence supporting the historicity is the Gospels, for what they are worth. The passages in Josephus are now admitted even by Catholics to have been forgeries. There is no allusion to Jesus in any work contemporary with him known to us, Jewish or gentile; and the Gospels were not written down until long after his death, and contradict one another on a great many details.

One group of scholars accepts the eschatological view, popularized by Schweitzer: that he preached repentance believing that the end of the world was near. C. F. Moore: "The core of the preaching and teaching of Jesus is the 'kingdom of God,' the coming time in which He shall be owned and obeyed by all men as king." Keim argued that Jesus expected the end to come any day. The eschatological view was first advanced by Reimarus at the end of the 18th century, his essay being, says Schweitzer, one of the greatest events in the history of criticism. Jesus, said Reimarus, "had not the slightest intention of doing away with the Jewish religion and putting another in its place." His whole teaching was summed up in, Repent, for the kingdom of heaven is at hand. Schweitzer says the first alternative laid down by Strauss (1835) was *"either purely historical or purely supernatural.* The second had been worked out by the Tubingen school and Holtzmann: *either* Synoptic *or* Johannine. Now came the third: *either* eschatological *or* non-eschatological." Those rejecting the eschatological view have included Bousset, E. Haupt, Schürer, Wernle, Brandt, Wellhausen, Hilgenfeld, Jülicher.

Popular in recent years has been form-criticism, defined by Prof. S. E. Johnson as the doctrine "that community interests controlled the formulation of the Gospel material," and championed by such as Bultmann and Dibelius. They point out that traditions about Jesus are *not* Jesus. Form-criticism explains the many contradictions and differences in the Gospels:

the stories developed in different cities widely separated, under different conditions and needs: this explains the enormous difference in spirit between, say, Mark and John.

As for Jewish scholars Graetz thought Christianity arose out of Essenism. Salvador (a Jew on his father's, Catholic on his mother's, side) pointed out, as Jews have since, that ethical precepts ascribed to Jesus were commonplaces of his time. He finds the Sermon on the Mount in Sirach, as Kalthoff did later. Montefiore thinks most of the ethics in the Gospels can be found in other Jewish writings but thought the form in the Gospels superior (he gave no credit to the King James translators), an opinion some Jews have hotly disputed. Answering him Friedlander set out to prove that the whole Gospel system of ethics stemmed from earlier Jewish writings. If any reader is curious to know which among so many books he might read, I find Guignebert's Life best on the whole; McCown, *Search for the Real Jesus,* has excellent summaries; phoney doctrines are set forth in Goodspeed, *Strange New Gospels;* on Christian origins few are more brilliant than Loisy; on form-criticism, Dibelius or Bultmann; on the eschatological view, Schweitzer. If the reader is curious to know what my opinion may be after more than thirty years of reading in this field the answer, in regard to the historicity, is simple: I have none. Either side can make out a plausible case—and I would say almost equally plausible.

Some Jewish Opinions of Jesus For Montefiore he was a prophet teaching men to prepare for the coming catastrophe and he was "indignant that any ritual law should stand in the way of . . . the higher law of compassion and loving kindness. I think Rabbinic teaching *was* defective about the love of the foreigner and the idolater, and that Jesus might very well have said, 'You all consider your neighbor to be only your fellow-Jew, but I tell you that the neighbor whom you are to love includes all men' . . . I would not cavil with the view that Jesus is to be regarded as the first great Jewish teacher to frame such a sentence as: 'Love your enemies, do good to them who hate you, bless them that curse you, and pray for them that ill-treat you' . . . . to deny that he opened a new chapter in men's attitude toward sin and sinners is, I think, to beat the head against the wall." He thinks a few of the NT sayings have no parallels in other Jewish writings, such as Matt. xi, 25; xv, 11 and 20; xix, 10; and xxiii, 34. No other Jew known to me has written so glowingly about Jesus as Montefiore. For Israel Abrahams, Jesus "in his attitude towards sin and sinners was more inclined to take the initiative . . . . One might put it generally by asserting that the Rabbis attacked vice from the preventive side; they aimed at keeping men and women honest and chaste. Jesus approached it from the curative side; he aimed at saving the dishonest and the unchaste." He thinks Jesus did a service to Judaism when "he ejected the sellers of doves from the Temple" but other Jewish scholars say it is a calumny to say that doves or anything else was sold in the Temple. Klausner is very generous: see his *Jesus of Nazareth*. For Loewe, "essentially the preaching of Jesus was that of the Rabbis, but the method differed . . . . My attitude towards Jesus and the Gospels is as follows. I regard him as a saintly artisan, of Hillel's type. Unlike Hillel, he did not study, consequently he took no part in the *Halakhah* . . . free to devote himself to popular ethical teaching . . . His is a simple message . . . . I do not believe that Jesus called himself 'son of God' in a different sense from 'children are ye to the Lord our God', that he rejected the Law . . . . I do not believe that he claimed a mystic or supernatural power." For Paul Goodman it is being "gradually recognized that Christian morality is in reality Jewish, and had, with an incomparable power and grace, been proclaimed by Jewish prophets and psalmists many centuries before Jesus." But "the charm of his personality has sent its rays all over the world, and infused countless human hearts with the spirit of love and self-sacrifice . . . . It is not fair to take the denunciations of the Scribes and Pharisees in the NT at their face value . . . . there is no utterance, however striking or characteristic, emanating from Jesus (with the sole exception of the idea of non-resistance) which cannot be traced, often in identical words, to the teaching of the Jewish schools." Jesus was not only a man "with very human failings" but "was liable to gross errors." Friedlander says that "Probably 1900 years ago, a teacher and a claimant to the Messiahship, named Jesus, the son of Joseph and Mary, lived in Galilee. His apocalyptic dreams and his eschatalogical discourses induced his followers to recognize his Messianic claims, and this led to a conflict with the ruling authorities, i.e. the Roman Procurator . . . . In the early years of the second century the

Gospels were written and Christianity arose as a new religion . . . . Not only is the baptism story apocalyptic" but so is practically all the teaching ascribed to Jesus. "The Beatitudes have undoubtedly a lofty tone but let us not forget that all that they teach can be found in Isaiah and the Psalms." The picture of the Pharisees in the NT is a "ludicrous and monstrous caricature." The Lord's Prayer "is quite Jewish in structure . . . a type of the seven-fold Jewish prayer (Birkath Shiba) that was in vogue"; it "grew out of the 36th chapter of Ezekiel (verses 23-31) . . . By all means let us admit that the Golden Rule in the positive form . . . is of the greatest value. But let us be honest and acknowledge that it had been uttered in its *positive* form by Jewish teachers centuries before Jesus was born." For Hirsch, "All of us are agreed that Jesus was a noble character" and for Sachar, "Few had ever prayed and taught with such charm and power. His radiant personality, his tenderness and humility, captivated the masses . . . . As a teacher he was superb." He was not, says Greenstone, "very learned in the Law, he attracted to himself, by his sympathetic nature and his lofty spiritual attainments, the great multitudes of the lower classes . . . . Only to a few select and devoted disciples he revealed himself as the Messiah." For Louis Israel Newman "His purpose as a religious reformer was not to abrogate it [the Law], but to soften its seeming severity and to elicit its inner spirit." Enelow points out that "Jews, whether modern or ancient, Reform or Orthodox, do not acknowledge the divinity of Jesus . . . . It is understood that Jews could not do that, and still remain Jews, as the very foundation of all Judaism is the unity and the spiritual nature of God." He put, say Margolis and Marx, "morals above ritual, inward piety above ceremonial." His essential mission, says Abba Silver, "was apocalyptic, not prophetic. He was more of the mystic than the moralist . . . . He sought to save men from the birth-throes of the Messianic times. The ethical counsel which he gave to his followers was for a world *in extremis*." (Jewish scholars have been more generous toward Christians than Christians have been toward Jews.)

A Biography of Jesus Can a biography of Jesus be written? Obviously not—for as Kalthoff says, "Jesus has been made the receptable into which every theologian pours his own ideas." Wrede: "It finally comes to this, that each critic retains what-

327

ever portion of the traditional sayings can be fitted into his construction of the facts and his conception of historical possibility and rejects the rest." Or Kohler: "The history of Jesus is so wrapped up in myths, and his life as told in the Gospels is so replete with contradictions, that it is difficult for the unbiased reader to arrive at the true historical facts." Or Guignebert: "only a firm resolve and an intense desire to extract information at any cost from a witness who has nothing to tell, could discover in a few meager phrases of Tacitus, Suetonius, Pliny the Younger, Celsus, and a false Pilate thrown in, an assurance of the historical existence" of Jesus. Or Rhees: "Our evangelists cared little . . . about the requirements of strict biography." Or Burkitt: " 'We know Him right well' says Prof. Weinel. What a claim!" Or Dodd: "From sources outside the NT there is little to be learned of Jesus . . . . It is idle to attempt to write anything like a biography of Jesus from our Gospel sources." Or Inge: "Whatever confidence we may place in the good faith and substantial accuracy of the synoptic Gospels, it remains true that we cannot construct a biography of Jesus." Or K. L. Schmidt: "There is no life of Jesus in the sense of an unfolding life story, no chronological outline of the story of Jesus, but only single stories, pericopes, which are placed in an (artificial editorial) framework." Or Berr: "the reading back of the deification of Jesus into his career involved the asumption of a miraculous life and messianic utterances . . . what ought to have happened did happen; what ought to have been said was said." Or Reinach: "the *myth of Christ,* the evolution of which can be clearly traced from the time of Paul and the Fourth Gospel, must be distinguished from the *history of Jesus.*" Or McCown: "no biography of Jesus and no geographical or chronological outline of his ministry are possible." Or Josiah Royce: "I have a right to decline, and I actually decline to express an opinion as to any details about the person and life of the founder. For such an opinion the historical evidences are lacking." (Prof. Royce's choice of words amusingly highlights the confusion: the most reputable scholars say Jesus was *not* the founder). Or Lake: "historical criticism shows that the points in the story of Jesus which played the greatest part in commending C to a generation asking for private salvation are those which are not historic . . . . the Jesus of history is quite different from the Lord assumed as the founder of Catholic C." That the Lord and Jesus, said Lessing, are "one and the same person is inconceivable." Schechter: "It is now more than half a century since Renan put the question, 'Has Jewish tradition anything to teach us concerning Jesus?' This question must be answered in the negative." Though Philo, a contemporary, left some fifty works that survived, in them says Guignebert "it is impossible to find even a single allusion to Jesus and his followers." And Schechter points out that though the Jews "are supposed to have been both the target of his wrath and the object of his pity and prayers" the literature of the Jews of his time "has not left us a single reference to this controversy." (Compare that with Sachar and Greenstone, that he attracted the multitudes!). Loisy: "We must now renounce writing the life of Jesus. All the critics agree in recognizing that the materials are insufficient." But some, including Goguel, Easton, Scott, Taylor, Dodd, think there is in the gospel story a kernel of fact. Wendland, whose reputation was great, says arrogantly that anyone "who failed to recognize a living, religious personality in the Four Epistles of Paul and in the underlying framework of the Synoptic Gospels is not qualified to undertake any historical investigation of this period." Neumann says that in all history never has a "character so clearly outlined, so vivid, so uniquely original as that of Jesus been invented." Scholars retort by pointing to Hamlet. Olmstead in his 'biography' cries triumphantly: "At long last, Jesus makes his own appearance in the full light of history." He gives the year of his birth as 20 B.C. and says flatly: "For almost half a century Jesus lived an obscure life." He says Nazareth "for close to half a century remained the home of Jesus"—though that there was a Nazareth has not been proved. He rebukes the Camb. Anc. Hist. for no longer attempting a portrait of Jesus. (The reader can contrast Prof. Olmstead with the first statements in this paragraph). Lagrange, a Catholic, admits: "The Gospels are the only life of Jesus Christ that can be written." And O'Brien, commenting on the 'Lives' by Fillion and Fouard, concludes: "Guess if you can; choose if you dare."

Bearing in mind that no life can be written we shall look at some items that usually go into one. It is still said by some pretending to scholarship (Lundberg and Farnham) that "Jesus was an Essene." Ginsberg, Graetz, Conybeare, Bugge and

N. Schmidt have argued for it but most scholars reject it. Guignebert finds the notion "incredible." Toy: "The supposition that Jesus was an Essene must be pronounced to be baseless and even bizarre." Then Toy says that Jesus "apparently began his career as a disciple of John"; but many scholars, including Wernle, Soltau, Gruppe, Usener, reject the relationship as unhistorical. As for the Last Supper, the details as given in the Gospels have been rejected by nearly all the greater scholars; the notion that the bread was his body, the wine his blood, came from the pagan mystery cults—which see. As Guignebert says, it was "an extremely common belief in the ancient world that by drinking the blood, or later on, by immersion in or sprinkling with the blood, it was possible to absorb the qualities of the god . . . . (Jesus) did not use the words attributed to him, with some variation, by the three Synoptic Gospels. These words can only represent a cult legend." Many Jewish scholars have pointed out how repugnant the thought would have been to a Jew. Klausner: "it is quite impossible to admit that Jesus would have said to his disciples that they should eat of his body and drink of his blood . . . . The drinking of blood, even if it was meant symbolically, could only have aroused horror in the minds of such simple Galilean Jews." It has also many times been remarked that the assumption that Jesus was tried and executed on 14th Nisan is "incredible"; or that Simon, a pious Jew, came in from the country on that day; or that on this day they bought a shroud. As for the meal as given by Mark it has no similarity save in one detail to the Passover meal. As for the trial, Jews have been justifiably incensed over Christian acceptance of the gospel account. Baron: "the alleged earlier sentence pronounced by the high priest (Mark 14) would have been altogether impossible under the then-prevailing legal conditions." Edersheim (Catholic Jew) admits that "in their treatment of Jesus, the Sanhedrin violated not only the law of God, but grossly outraged every ordinance of their own traditions." Kohler points out that none of the charges against Jesus was "a mortal sin according to the Law." N. Schmidt: "We have really no authentic information as to what took place at the trial of Jesus." Guignebert: " 'I am innocent of the blood of this just person, see ye to it'. And the Jews cried with one voice, 'His blood be on us and on our children'. Few of the sayings of the Gospels have done

330

more harm than these, and yet they are only the invention of the redactor! . . . The Gospel account of the arrest, trial and condemnation of Jesus swarms with impossibilities, improbabilities and inconsistencies, and is quite unintelligible from the juridical point of view." Dujardin: "As for Pilate, he is an inconceivable caricature of a Roman magistrate." One of the best books on the trial is Prof. Husband's: "I would reject the current opinion that Jesus was formally tried by the Sanhedrin for an alleged offense against the Hebrew criminal code . . . . The case against Jesus . . . could under no circumstances be tried by any tribunal except that of the governor . . . . All four Gospels must be wrong in stating that the trial occurred on the day before the Sabbath, for it was forbidden to hold court on that day . . . . The traditional view of the history of the trial of Jesus endeavors to establish two impossible theses."

Hirsch, Montefiore, Klein, Chwolson and practically all Jewish scholars and most Christian reject the notion that he died at the hands of the Pharisees. Case: "it was not a custom among the Jews to persecute messianic claimants; they left that work to the foreign ruler." Whittaker: "a surviving annual rite at Jerusalem in which usually a condemned criminal played the part of a dying god." Robertson: "If the reader, cowed by the truculent negations of some of the anti-mythologists, should reply that there is no documentary ground for the hypothesis of a pre-Christian Jesus-cult, let him be assured that he has been deceived." In other words, the Robertson school argue that if Jesus was a historic figure he possibly was delivered up as a god-substitute at the annual rite. As for the 'Twelve' Streeter says: "Peter was not 'a witness of the sufferings of Christ'. Neither he nor any of the Twelve were present . . ." Stevens: "The crucifixion of Jesus was, for the first disciples, the principal obstacle to belief in his messiahship." Schweitzer: "the whole account of the last days at Jerusalem would be unintelligible, if we had to suppose that the mass of the people had a shadow of a suspicion that Jesus held himself to be the messiah." Sorley points out that for the Jews a dead messiah was an "impossibility . . . . The disciples must either relinquish their belief in Jesus as the Messiah or they must also believe that in his own person he had conquered death." Guignebert: "We have dwelt at length on the growth of legend round the story of the death of Jesus, because the details are so familiar, and their very familiarity seems to render criticism superfluous. But none of the details will bear close examination, and all in the end fall outside the realm of history." *If* Jesus lived we do not know when he died: the Asiatic Christians said the 14th Nisan, their opponents the 15th, and after long and bitter controversy the pagan Easter time was chosen—that is, the sun-god's resurrection at the spring equinox. Some placed the year as early as 21; Irenaeus between 40-50; and so on. As for the tomb, Loisy says Mark arranged the account "with surprising artlessness. Never had fiction more childish found so many to believe it true." Reinach: "The discovery of the empty tomb is the less credible in that Jesus, once put to death, would have been thrown by the Roman soldiers into the common grave of malefactors." Dodd: "Some critics hold that the story of the empty tomb is a later addition."

The resurrection is of course rejected by practically all the greater scholars. Easton says: "Persons who think they have seen a dead man appear to them may be divided into three classes . . . . the medically insane . . . . the temporarily deceived . . . . [and those who think they see] a specter or ghost . . . . To the naive thinking of the class of men to whom the earliest disciples belonged such visitations were always possible." Weiss: "is it not a depressing thought that these fundamental facts of the Christian religion were no more than delusions, fancies, hallucinations?" Pfleiderer: "we are probably at liberty to suppose that the gentile Christians of Antioch retained their old customs, in accordance with which they had previously celebrated the death and resurrection of Adonis, their lord, and that they now merely transferred them to their new lord, Jesus." Gunkel: "Is it a casual occurence that Jesus should be alleged to have risen from the dead on *this* day in the calendar, on this most sacred Sunday, when the sun rises from the night of winter?" Grant: "the romantic theories which trace the resurrection faith to Mary Magdalene are perfectly impossible." Case: "Had not the disciples of Jesus been 'unlearned and ignorant men' (Act. 4:13) —Galilean peasants and fisher-folk—they might have had more scruples against believing that Jesus had actually appeared to Peter." Loisy: "Then came the shining day when he thought that Jesus was visibly, and perhaps audibly, before him. His faith filled the vision with

332

all he longed to believe and gave him the assurance that what he saw was a reality. Neither historian nor psychologist need inquire further." Guignebert: "people were then generally incapable of distinguishing a *subjective* experience, an hallucination or even a dream from a really *objective* experience . . . . *in the history of religious enthusiasm nothing appears more contagious than visions.*" The two principal explanations then are: (1) that some of the disciples had hallucinations (2) that the later Christians merely transferred pagan cult ideas to their new god.

Jesus in Legend We will now consider a few other aspects of the traditional Jesus. As for his name, Dujardin says "Jesus is in Hebrew Ieshouah, or Ieshou. But 'salvation' in Hebrew is Isehouah. Jesus is therefore literally Salvation." Van Eysinga: "Justin Martyr, in his Dialogue with the Jew Trypho, shows that Joshua is the name of God himself." As for his appearance, Kautsky says: "concerning the person of Jesus, nothing definite can be said." G. Stanley Hall: "He has been represented as very young and prematurely old, stout and slender, dark and light, with the racial features of every people in Christendom." Draper: "Among the early Fathers—Justin Martyr and Tertullian—there was an impression that the personal appearance of our Lord was ungainly; that he was short of stature; and, at a later period Cyril says mean of aspect 'even beyond the ordinary race of men'." Justin said he had neither beauty nor dignity; Irenaeus characterized him as infirmus, inglorious, indecorus; Origen said he was small, insignificant, ill-favored; Commodian, that he looked like a slave, an opinion with which Tertullian, Cyprian, Hyppolytus agree. One early tradition claimed he was a leper. Bishop Eusebius said 'a razor never came upon his head, he never annointed with oil, and never used a bath.' On some early Christian sarcophagi Jesus is represented with distinctly Jewish features but later, as Glover says, he was idealized. The dispute over his appearance lasted for centuries; in the end Jerome, Augustine and myth-making won and he became beautiful. Of the influences on him Guignebert says, "Most critics believe that he remained free from any profound Hellenistic influence." On Jesus as 'messiah' there are various schools of thought. Wrede, Robertson, Berr, Lake, Dodd, Guignebert, Klausner, Whittaker and others think he never so regarded himself; that he did so regard himself as been held by Bousset, Schweitzer, Nock, Burkitt, Latourette and others; that he was only a preacher of the kingdom but not a messianic pretender is the position of Case; and there are those who, as McCown says, advance a "thorough-going apocalypticism which defines Jesus' echatology in a different way from Schweitzer": to this group belong Otto, Von Dobschutz and McCown. Berr: "He did not believe himself to be the messiah"—but Nock: "Jesus claimed in some sort a messianic position." Dodd: "Jesus never did put forward explicitly a claim to be Messiah"—but Latourette: "It is clear that Jesus thought of himself as the Messiah." Lake: "never claimed the authority of any special office or function such as that associated with the word 'Messiah' "—but Tyrell: "his messianic consciousness was the main determinant of his action and utterance." Robertson says he did not claim "to be the Messiah in any sense whatever"—but McCown: "Jesus probably did believe himself to be the true but hidden messiah." And so on. For most Jews the messiah was to be a son of David or one like unto David. For Christians the word messiah means son of God. Lake: "It is quite clear that the writer of Luke and Acts, and the editor of Matthew, identified Jesus with the expected son of David, but there is room for doubt whether this fully represents the thought of the first disciples . . . . Christian scholarship has in general greatly exaggerated the amount of evidence, especially for a Davidic king." On Jesus as a pacifist Lake says: "If Jesus intended to lay down a general principle of conduct we have to admit that he was wrong, or adopt the pacifist position . . . . it is futile to argue that when he said 'resist not evil' and 'love your enemies' he sanctioned the patriotic pursuit of war." In those days prudent Jews counseled non-resistance. On Jesus and the 'Law' Manson says: "if with St. Peter (Acts xv, 10) we describe the Law as 'a yoke which neither our fathers nor we are able to bear', we should have to regard the 'New Law' of the Sermon on the Mount as a still more intolerable and impossible burden." Volkmar: "He had learned to fulfill the law as implicit in one highest commandment and supreme principle . . . but he never, as appears from all the evidence, declared it to be abolished." On Jesus and women we shall take only the opinions of two eminent Jews. Kohler: "a redeemer of men and an uplifter of womanhod without parallel

334

in history." Montefiore: "To talk to a woman, to look at a woman, indeed to have anything to do with a woman, was regarded as dangerous and objectionable [by pious Jews] .... He is a great champion of womanhood." On Jesus and marriage it has been suggested that he never married because he could not afford the price. Finkelstein: "bachelorhood and celibacy were not infrequently the enforced lot of those who were kept out of the market by poverty."

As for his "pessimism" Bevan says: "it is recorded that he wept, but never that he laughed." Of his pessimism, says Tyrrell, "it is vain to deny that this note is as true to the Gospel of Christ as a cheerful belief in the world is doscordant from it." On Jesus and formalism Wrede says: "Jesus' attack on the character of the Law is always of a moral kind." Holl: "Jesus reverses . . . the usual relation of religion and morality. Every other religion, at least of the higher kind, makes the personal relation to God depend on the right conduct of man." Wernle: "our Savior from the theologians." Though many Christian scholars write of him as the 'founder' of Christianity, Wellhausen: "He did not preach a new faith." McGiffert: "Jesus remained a loyal Jew and had no thought of breaking with the faith of his fathers and founding a new religion." Bacon: "Nobody in Jesus' time accused him of attempting to found a new religion. Least of all did he so regard his work." EB: "It would be a great mistake to suppose that Jesus himself founded a new religious community." Loisy: "had no intention of founding a religion; the idea never entered his mind." Reinach: "Jesus taught no dogma of any sort, nor anything resembling the sacraments of the Church." Enslin: "the view, which still persists in some circles, that Jesus' aim was to found a Church, distinct from the Synagogue, is quite improbable." Lake: "Few things are more certain than that Jesus had no intention of founding a new society outside the Jewish Church." Norton: "Jesus established no forms or ceremonies, nor formulated laws." Goguel: "Jesus did not create the Church; he did not trouble about establishing institutions or laying down rules." Moxom: "Jesus wrote no book, appointed no officers . . . and established no institutions." Glover: "There is a growing consensus of opinion among independent scholars that Jesus instituted no sacraments." Peters: "left no writings of any description, no code of law, no

335

form of thology." Klausner: "never intended to found a new religion . . ." Trattner: "had no message except for his own countrymen; not did he ever dream of any but Jews sharing in the heavenly kingdom." Kohler: "he was not the founder of Christianity, as he still is regarded by many." It is the opinion of most scholars that the famous verses in Matthew on which the Roman Church rests were a later addition.

In view of what we have seen so far it is absurd to ask what he taught. Many have taken the position of Steudal: "I shall be obliged to any theologian who will bring me a saying of Jesus which I cannot prove to have been already in existence in his time." If it is pointed out that the *form* of the gospel saying has more grace of style Rabbi Feldman reminds us that "it must be remembered that the NT parables, as is generally admitted by Christian scholars, have in the course of transmission . . . been subjected to editorial embellishments." (See Moffat, *The Parallel New Testament*). Harnack says everything in the gospels "was also to be found in the Prophets, and even in the Jewish tradition of their time." Even Guthrie, a theologian, admits: "The very words of Jesus were in many instances suggested by sayings current in his day, more or less as unconscious quotations from the Testaments of the Twelve Patriarchs." Forgive us our debts as we forgive our debtors was, says Moore, a commonplace in Jewish literature. So were the materials of the Lord's Prayer; the version I have Joshua use is that of Olmstead slightly modified. Clemen: "Wetstein, always the most exhaustive investigator in such fields of inquiry, cites numerous parallels to the Beatitudes." Schmiedel: "It is at once evident that the great groups of discourses in Matthew . . . were not arranged in this order in the source, still less by Jesus himself." Von Soden: "In the composition of the discourses no regard is paid in Matthew, any more than in John, to the supposed audience, or to the point of time in the life of Jesus to which they are attributed." Loisy: "It may be said without a trace of paradox that of the teaching he actually gave no collection was ever made . . . . Just as a legend has been built up for him so too there has been built up for him a body of teaching, and it has been done by borrowings from many quarters." Guignebert: "It is agreed that the Gospel discourses attributed to him are . . . the work of redactors . . . . It is hardly reassuring to remember that before being written

336

down they had a wide oral circulation, that they had been adapted to the purposes of apologetics, and that they had served as controversial weapons." His disciples reshaped whatever sayings there may have been "in a messianic light" and "dropped many recollections which did not harmonize with their present belief." He agrees with Harnack, Von Hartmann and many others that whatever message Jesus may have had was "for Jews alone." Some scholars have derived most of the gospel sayings from non-Jewish sources—Seydel for instance from Buddha (there will be additional notes on this in my next novel). Bousset, Zimmern, Gunkel, Jeremias and others derive 'Can the sons of the bridechamber etc.' from an ancient myth. Similarly, the miracles are traced back: M. Müller, Seydel, Van Eysinga and others remind us that Buddha walked on water—and so did Poseidon and other gods. Holl, Goguel, Otto and others have argued that the sayings contain some original elements; many other scholars deny this. Particularly significant, I think, are the next two statements. Manson: "It is more and more coming to be realized that what Jesus offered to men was not good advice or even a good example, but good news—the announcement of the Kingdom of God as a present and beneficient reality. As such it comes primarily saying not 'Thou shalt' and 'Thou shalt not', but 'Ask and you shall receive; seek and you shall find; knock and it shall be opened to you' . . . . the task which Jesus took in hand was not the reform of the Torah but the re-creation of men and women who could not obey the Torah, much less the Sermon on the Mount." Lake (italics supplied): "The thoughts and words of Jesus . . . were borrowed from his own time and race . . . . *No historical reconstruction can make them adequate for our generation, or even intelligible except to those who have passed through an education in history impossible for most.*" (For the reader curious as to the credentials of these two scholars: Kirsopp Lake, Professor of Ecclesiastical History, Harvard; T. W. Manson, Professor of Biblical Criticism and Exegesis, University of Manchester). Worth pondering too is Schmidt: "It is a significant fact that none of the historic creeds of Christendom devotes any attention to the great ideas that occupied the mind of Jesus." Beauful is Tschaikovsky's tribute: "What eternal poetry and, touching to tears, what feeling of love and pity toward mankind in the words: 'Come unto me all ye that labor and are heavy laden'."

And so at the conclusion of this long section we ask, What do the scholars leave us? and in all honesty, must answer, Little more than the name. Still, there are the profound words in the Foreword which precedes this story—the myth which for the thoughtful must always be of far greater importance than the facts.

JEWS — Grant: "even after twelve centuries of settled life he was still a son of the desert . . ." Klausner says the effect of the conditions of the time "was to beget either utterly fanatical seekers after freedom who turned into actual rebels, or utterly despairing visionaries, extreme moralists and mystics, who waited for nothing less than the mercy of heaven . . ."

JEW vs. GENTILE — Orthodox Jews still maintained their aloof and exclusive position of a chosen people, though in Asia Minor, says Tarn, there were Jews "who tolerated mixed marriages and dropped circumcision." Case: "Judaism grew sterner and more exclusive under the pressure of Graeco-Roman life, and the scribes increased the number of cases in which any intercourse with a Gentile would defile a Jew."

JOHN THE BAPTIST — Rabbinic literature, says Abrahams, "contains no reference to John the Baptist." Loisy: "the account of the martyrdom of John in the first two Gospels has few marks of historicity." Friedländer argued that the Apocalyptists, from whom John is supposed to have come, were the real leaders among "the people of the land." Klausner: "should baptize with fire (such is the correct reading, and not 'baptize with the Holy Spirit', which is not a Hebrew form of expression." Origen said later: "The Jews do not associate John with Jesus." Most scholars believe that the gospel treatment of John shows an effort to play him down, Jesus, up; because, says Bowen, John was "an embarrassment" to the gospel chroniclers and "they are moved to minimize him largely to suppress the significance of his work." Parsons says "it is indisputable" that the John movement was of "greater vigor, magnitude, and importance

338

than uncritical Christian thought has imagined. It had enough vigor to perpetuate itself in some form for centuries."

JOSHUA   Readers will not find in this novel representations of the people in the gospel story. Joshua is not intended to be 'Jesus of Nazareth'.

JUDAISM   Gressmann: "Judaism turned away from Hellenistic religion and became a rigid legal religion . . ." Guignebert: "It has long been acknowledged that in the time of Jesus Judaism had already become a syncretistic religion." Klausner: "It feared compromise, because all its advantage lay in its determined opposition to compromise. For what it claimed and taught and believed was that its truth was unique in the world, that its Torah was absolutely without parallel, and that its ethics could not be equaled in any other nation. But Philo comes and says that there is truth in the books of the pagans, that their philosophers are also saints and holy men, that Greek morality is very lofty and comparable in its basic principles to Jewish morality . . . . The instinct of self-preservation and of the Jewish nation and of the Jewish religion, which indeed are one and the same thing, whispered to orthodox Judaism that it must not admit this compromising doctrine into its house."

JUDAS   Reminding us that such prudent scholars as Julicher and Klostermann think the Judas story a later (Christian) invention, Guignebert says the betrayal "appears wholly useless and inexplicable." What need, asks B. Smith, had Jesus' enemies of Judas and his kiss? "None whatever." Bauer dismissed the story as a myth based on Psalm xli, 9 and Zech. xi, 12. Volkmar says "the Jews needed hardly even a spy, much less a traitor." Cheyne thought him unhistorical. See Robertson, *Jesus and Judas*.

KINGDOM OF   Easton: "In NT days practically all
HEAVEN   Jews expected the final salvation to
                come soon; 'the kingdom of God was at hand'." Case: "the kingdom of God was to be a kingdom of Jews." Trattner: "the fifth millennium was soon to end . . . and the sixth millennium 'the kingdom of God' was at hand." Silver: "The Messianic hopes were rife in Israel at this time, not only because the people were suffering under Roman op-

pression, but also because their chronology led them to believe that they were on the threshold of the Millennium." Enslin: "the cataclysmic end of the present age. Attempts to soften or alter his message to make it more acceptable . . . are utterly superfluous." Dujardin: "Competent Jewish scholars admit . . . it was concerned to impose on the whole of humanity, not only the religion of Jahveh, but also the domination of the Jewish people." McGiffert: "The Assumption of Moses, a work written about this time, represents the kingdom as just on the eve of establishment . . ." Tasker: "the teaching of Jesus centered upon the idea of the kingdom of God." Ginsberg: "the expression 'Kingdom of God' belongs to the religious language of the Jews; in Matthew's 'Kingdom of Heaven' we still have the exact rendering of the Hebrew Malkut Shamayim. A feeling of reverence led the Jews at a very early date to avoid as far as possible all mention of the name of God, and Heaven is one of the usual substitutes for it." The Kingdom, says Toy, is Judaism's "most distinctive peculiarity." It meant, says Stevens, "a spiritual commonwealth, embracing all who adopt certain principles and motives of life." Schechter: "What exact relation the terms 'the world to come', 'the Kingdom of Heaven', and 'the days of the Messiah' bear to one another, and in what order they follow, and in what places they shall be experienced, are all questions which have been variously disputed by Jewish scholars without any very satisfactory results." Otto: "the chief thing is that the kingdom of heaven is a pure *mirum*, a pure miracle." Lake: "It means primarily the sovereignty of God in the world . . . . coincident with . . . . the Golden Age." Many Jews, he says, "were looking for the End of the Age and the Resurrection, rather than for the restoration of the kingdom of David." For those expecting the restoration a king "would appear, destroy all opposition, and reign for four hundred years. He and all mankind would then die. The world would come to an end and be restored to primeval silence. Then would follow the Resurrection and Judgment and the beginning of the Age to Come." Manson: "The essential thing for the understanding both of the ministry of Jesus and the theology of Paul is the doctrine of the two kingdoms: the kingdom of God and the kingdom of Satan . . . . at the beginning of the Christian era there was scarcely a devout soul in all Israel that was not looking for the coming

340

of the kindom." For Paul the gospel is "what *God* has done. *Ex hypothesi,* man can do nothing to free himself. He is too deeply enmeshed in the toils of sin by heredity, environment, and his own acts." Schmoller, Weiss, Bousset and many others maintain that Jesus taught only the coming of the kingdom; that is why his preachments are so negative—less ethics than penitential discipline. Renan, Harnack and others had said the deepest teaching in the NT is Luke xvii, 20-21: there has been much dispute over two Greek words in this passage: do they mean the kingdom is *among* or *within?* Few scholars believe that Jesus taught the noble idea that the kingdom is within you; Ritschl has argued Jesus meant that but the idea is pagan, not Jewish. As Dill says, Plutarch "asserts as powerfully as any Stoic that life takes its predominant color from the character, 'the kingdom of heaven is within' . . ."

| LAYING ON HANDS | Jayne: "The laying-on of hands was regarded as a most efficient means of transferring the divine power for healing." |

Jastrow: "Diseases continued to be 'drawn out' long after a belief in possession had waned. A similar idea gave sanction to the laying on of hands, to the King's touch . . ."

| LEPER | Hall: "A leper colony even today is too horrible for uncensored description." |

In Scripture leprosy meant not only elephantiasis (supposed to have been Job's disease) but also psoriasis, vitiligo, ringworm.

| MAGIC | Adeney: "Magic was widely practiced by its pretenders and widely believed in |

by its dupes."

| MARY | Guignebert: "The oldest tradition believed, probably rightly, that the mother |

of the Master was called Mariam." Weigall: "There is no certainty that the name of the mother of Jesus was Mary. In a 2nd century Jewish source her name is Miriam."

| MARY MAGDALENE | She was probably so called, says Grierson, as one belonging to Magdala. Of the one 'possessed by demons' Nevius |

says: "The subject is often thrown into paroxysm more or less violent and falls senseless to the ground." Klausner: "Mary

Magdalene, 'from whom seven demons had gone out', that is to say, a woman hysterical to the point of madness." Under devil-possession, says Glover, modern medical science distinguishes four classes: insanity, epilepsy, hysteria major and the mystical state. Hannay conjectures that she was called "Mary of the Almond to symbolize her as a temple harlot."

MESSIAH   In the OT, says Abrahams, "there is no indubitable instance of the use of the term Messiah as a personal description of the instrument of the future redemption." G. F. Moore: "There was . . . no Jewish 'doctrine of the Messiah' such as Christian scholars have often tried to construct . . ." Joseph: "the word 'Messiah', as used in the Hebrew Bible, has not that half-supernatural significance which it has come to possess. It means only the 'anointed one' . . ." As for *the general expectation*, Ramsay says "It was part of the ancient view that there could be no remedy for the evils of the world except through the help of divine power." Plato: "We will wait for One, be it a god or a god-inspired man, to teach us our religious duties, and . . . to take away the darkness from our eyes." Suetonius: "There had spread over all the Orient an old and established belief that it was fated at time for men coming from the East to rule the world." Murray: "It was not a mere Jewish Messiah that the world hungered for; it was a Savior of mankind. And such a Savior must, according to all Greek precedent, be the son of a God by a daughter of Earth, and she, on the analogy of many myths, a Virgin of royal birth, made fruitful by the divine Touch . . ." Boklen, Bousset, Moffatt and others have pointed out that in the Persian expectation there would reappear pious men of antiquity, announced by forerunners. Lietzmann: "The ancient yearning of the orient was mixed with Greek belief and Etruscan augury when Virgil . . . prophesied a savior who would descend upon earth as a divine child, wipe out the sins of the past, and introduce the golden age . . ." E. Carpenter: "During the first century B.C. there was a great spread of Messianic ideas over the Roman world, and Virgil's 4th Eclogue, commonly called the Messianic Eclogue, reflects very clearly this state of the public mind." Rostovzeff: "Neither ancient religion nor ancient philosophy drew a hard-and-fast line between the divine and the human. Hence the belief in a

Messiah—in the incarnation of divine power in a human form on earth, in order to save and regenerate perishing humanity." H. T. Fowler: "At the opening of the Christian era two great hopes characterized the religion of Israel—the hope of the messianic kingdom for the nation and the hope of the resurrection for the individual." Oesterley and Box: "It is characteristic of Judaism in all its manifestations that it looks to the *future* for the full realization of its hopes . . ." Justin Martyr attributed to the Jew Trypho the saying, We all await a Messiah who shall be a man born of man, and this, says Guignebert, "was probably the current idea." How widely the yearning prevailed among Jews we do not, says Latourette, know. Schweitzer: "We do not know whether the expectation of the Messiah was generally current or whether it was the faith of a mere sect." Most scholars think it widely prevailed. Weiss: "The broad mass of the people awaited the coming of a powerful earthly king . . ." who would, says Bokser, "usher in for them a period of national glory," a yearning that was strong, says Vogelstein, because of "the horrors of the civil wars." "The Zealots tried to hasten the coming with force." There is, says Grant, "an intimate connection between crushing oppression . . . and hopes of men for divine intervention." Morrison: "the hope of being ultimately rescued from Roman rule . . . The stranger would be trodden down; Israel would be consoled, and the Messianic Kingdom with its center at Jerusalem would suddenly burst on the world." Silver: "Messianism thrives on suffering . . . . The pathetic eagerness to read the riddle of Redemption and to discover the exact hour of the Messiah's advent. Biblical passages which seemed to point . . ." Calculations based on these "were so authoritatively delivered as to cause the migration of whole communities to the Holy Land . . ." A huge apocalyptic literature, say Oesterley and Box, "developed during the two eventful centuries that immediately preceded . . ." In that of Enoch, says Pfleiderer, the messiah is a "supermundane, semi-divine person, the mysterious 'son of man' . . ." In the Psalms of Solomon he is "described in the manner of the ancient prophetic ideal—a man of the earth, of the seed of David . . ." Such books, says Bentwich, "filled their readers with wild ideas and nourished dangerous expectations." As for the nature of the messiah, the Jews, says Clemen, "remod-

343

eled their idea . . . after Babylonian patterns . . ." McCown: "Among the Jews there was an almost infinite variety of opinion as to the nature of the anticipated Kingdom of God and messiah. It is perfectly clear that Christianity was a messianic movement." There were many false messiahs. Says Klausner: "To speak of the *King*-Messiah, of a *political* Messiah, was very dangerous in those days of Roman rule." Lightley: "Of Messianic 'impostors' there were probably many . . ." Whittaker: "Many supposed messiahs had been executed . . ." Guignebert: "Each visionary who arose . . . could count on a following who would be ready to hail him as the long-awaited Messiah." Ebersheim: "such was the infatuation of fanaticism that, while the Roman soldiers were actually preparing to set the Temple on fire, a false prophet could assemble 6,000 men, women, and children, in its courts and porches to await then and there a miraculous deliverance from heaven."

MIRACLES Walker: "No conception of what is now called natural law had penetrated the popular mind." Trattner: "In that age supernaturalism was a commonly accepted mode of thought." Miracle, says Brown, was "as much a part of the primitive view of the world as the universality of law is a part of the universe of modern science." If the miracles of the first century, says Sanday, "had been wrought before trained spectators of the twentieth, the version of them would be quite different." Warschauer: "In judging of such tales of the marvelous, whether ancient or modern, we never fail to make allowance for these facts, *viz.*, the unfamiliarity of our witnesses with the conception of natural law, their lack of training in accuracy as we understand it, and, above all, their natural liking for the extraordinary." Abrahams: "All ancient religions were based on miracle . . ." Renan: "There was never an age so childlike in its credulity." Even the clearest Roman minds, says Cumont, "accepted the chimeras of astrology and magic." Wonders, says Milman, "were speedily superseded by some new demand on the ever-ready belief." Hall: "It was a peculiarity of the Jews that any great leader to be accepted must accredit himself by working miracles." All the features of the NT miracles, says Dibelius, "recur in popular miracle stories over and over again." Some of those relating to Buddha, says Pfleiderer, "are pre-

344

cisely analagous to the miracles of the Gospels . . ." Mc-
Cown: "When once it comes to be recognized that almost every heathen shrine boasted its miracles, that
stories of miraculous healings were told of almost every heath-
en deity and semidivine hero, and also that the Jewish rabbis
worked miracles by calling upon divine aid . . . the problem of
the Gospel miracles is subjected to a new illumination."
Schechter: "The student of the Talmud finds that such marvels
as predicting the future, reviving the dead, casting out demons,
crossing rivers dry-shod, curing the sick by a touch or prayer,
were the order of the day, and performed by scores of Rabbis."
For Jesus, says Reville, "as for every other Jew, miracle was the
natural mode of divine activity." CE: "One need only refer
to the 'Ellados Periegesis' of Pausanius, or glance through the
codices collected by Photius in his 'Bibliotheca', to recognize
what great importance was attached to the reports of miracles
in antiquity by both the educated and uneducated." EB: "the
desire of Peter that Jesus should bid him to come on the water
is, literally speaking, simply childish." Latourette: "Several
of the diseases healed seem so like nervous disorders which we
now know to be subject to sudden cure . . ." (See Ryle, 'The
Neurotic Theory of the Miracles of Healing', Hibbert Jour.,
April, 1907). As so frequently, G. Stanley Hall says it best:
"True miracles are things which are absolutely false. They
never happen . . . . Why then the persistent credulity of so
many who should know better concerning this class of marvels?
The answer is, because these records are so overdetermined by
the higher meanings which they embody . . . . All discussion
of whether the nature of miracles of the NT were literally performed or not represents a low plane of crass religious material-
ism."

MYSTERY   Cumont: *"It is always with difficulty
                 that men resign themselves to dying
wholly."* In the mystery cults they shared the immortality of
their god. The most important of these, says Angus, were
"Eleusinia, the cults of the Cappodocian Men, the Phrygian
Sabazios and the Great Mother, the Egyptian Isis and Serapis,
and the Samothracian Cabiri, the *Dea Syria* and her satellites,
the Persian Mithra." Christianity, as my Notes to the next
novel will show, became a mystery religion. The secrets of

these pagan cults were so well-kept that "not one account" has ever reached us; their books of ritual were apparently destroyed by the Christians. Sacred sacramental meals were common to some of the mystery cults. Reitzenstein: "Osiris, Attis and Adonis were *men* who died and rose again as *gods*. If we unite ourselves with them, take them up into ourselves, or clothe ourselves with them, we have the certainty firm as a rock of our own immortality, and indeed *deity*." Bousset: "mystical union of identity with the deity"' and as in the Attis rites the mystic "becomes Attis." Willoughby says it has been the habit with Christian writers "to deprecate the ethical significance of the mystery religions"—notes to my next novel will have more to say about this. Marcus asks: "How seriously are we to take the thesis championed some twenty years ago by L. Cerfaux that certain Jews in Alexandria were organized into a Jewish mystery cult and practiced a non-normative Kyrios mysticism?" The answer is to be found in the works of Prof. Goodenough. On the moral values in the mysteries scholars have differed, Rhode, Ramsay, Farnell finding them negligible; Glover, Lake, Legge being neutral; while Cumont, Gruppe, Kennedy, Anrich, Wobbermin, Dill, Loisy, Jevons, Vollers, Bigg and others regard them highly. All mystery gods were savior gods. Case: "Participation in the life of the god was realistically attained by drinking the blood and eating raw the flesh of the sacred victim in which the god was assumed to be incarnated"—such as the bull or lamb, of which the wafer is a refinement. Among the greatest authorities on the mystery religions are Toutain, Farnell, Gasquet, Loisy, Boulage, Anrich, Wobbermin, Reitzenstein and Gumont.

MYSTICS   A rich source for the study of mysticism is the 'lives' of Catholic saints, though many things in the record are baffling to ordinary persons: why Marguerite Marie cleaned up vomit with her tongue, why others could not resist licking the most repulsive spittle; etc. William James: "mystical states, when they are well developed, usually are, and have a right to be, absolutely authoritative over the individuals to whom they come." Hocking has argued that mystics in meditation may recall "those deepest principles of will, or preference, which the activities of living tend to obscure." Clemen: "As Bousset has shown the idea prevailed in Persia that the soul after death, accompanied by angels or daemons, wanders through the various heavens, and can, in fact, even before death visit these in states of ecstasy." Rohde: "In ecstasy, in the freeing of the soul from the hampering confinement of the body, in its communion with the deity, powers arise within it of which it knows nothing in the daily life hampered by the body." Cumont: "A whole system of fastings and macerations placed the mystic in a fit state to attain to ecstasy." Leuba: "The term 'mysticism' comes from a Greek word which designated those who had been initiated into the esoteric rites of the Greek religion . . . . union of self with a larger-than-self, be it called the World-Spirit, God, the Absolute . . . . Inge has published 26 definitions of mysticism . . . . William James affirms that 'personal religious expuerience has its root and center in mystical consciousness' . . . . Their [mystics'] writings are marred by an inexactness approaching at times deliberate falsehood . . . . there is still in certain quarters a surprising inability to appreciate the profound significance of Christian mysticism." He says their "doctrine of humility, self-surrender and passivity should not blind us to the presence in them of a tremendous energy of self-affirmation." He quotes Hugel who found in them "a great self-engrossment of a downrightly selfish kind; a grouping of all things round such a self-adoring Ego." He lists six traits in the mystic: need of self-affirmation and self-esteem; for affection and moral support; for peace; for sensuous satisfaction, which usually takes a strong sexual coloring. The "greater and better the lover, the more complete the satisfaction. Thus to be loved by God . . . the delights said by your great mystics to transcend everything which the world and the senses can produce, involve some activity of the sex organs . . . extravagant carnal imagery used by the mystics to describe their intense enjoyment of divine love . . . . We must surrender to the evidence: the virgins and the unsatisfied wives who undergo the repeated 'love-assualts of God!'." Though he quotes with approval Hocking that they realize a uniquely divine life, and Murisier that guidance by the idea of a divine person was the main characteristic of mysticism, Leuba is fully aware that repression and egoism are the heart and source of it.

NAZARETH   Some have argued that there was no such place; such a theory, says Klausner, is contradicted "by the 'Lament' or Ha-Kalir containing the name 'Natzrath' and based on an ancient *Barita,* and the adjectival form *Notzri* and *Natzari* in the geography before the 4th century . . ." Guignebert: "No ancient pagan or Jewish writing mentions Nazareth." W. B. Smith says the root of Nazareth, NSR, occurs 63 times in the OT as meaning a protector; Na-Sa-Ru is found 7 times in the Code of Hammurabi. The Syrian form Nasaryu means God is protector. A scholar of the eminence of Cheyne rejected it as historic. Whether so or not, Mathews puts it straight west of Tabor, O'Brien straight north; Barton says it was just 3 miles SE of Sepphoris; and Enelow says it was "densely peopled"!

PASSOVER   Hooke: "The eating of bitter herbs belongs to the same category of ritual actions, and finds an illustration and an explanation in the Athenian spring festival of Anthesteria, a festival which has several interesting parallels to the ritual of the Hebrew Passover, and I have no doubt that both can go back to the same source ultimately."

PHARISEE   Oxford Dict.: "a self-righteous person; a formalist; a hypocrite." Burkitt: "Generations of Christians have only heard of 'Pharisees' as opponents of Jesus . . ." Marcus suggests that gentile scholars might "strive to maintain that disinterested and sympathetic attitude toward he Pharisees with which liberal Christian scholars like Strack, Moore and Herford have sought to replace the narrowly prejudiced attitude of earlier scholars like Wellhausen and Charles." Parkes: "the Christian church has been, and in large measure still is, profoundly, ignorant of the nature of Pharisaic Judaism." Such scholars as Glover, Schücher, Reville, de Pressense, Renan have presented a distorted picture. McCown puts his finger on it: "the injury and opposition which the early Christians suffered during the period when the Gospel traditions were taking shape must inevitably have tinted the portrait of the Pharisees with unduly lurid colors." Wenley: "Judaism has frequently been taken at its lowest, in the bickering sects in the time of Christ." Riddle (see his *Jesus and the Pharisees* for the best account to date) : "It has been generally assumed that the portrayal of the Pharisees in the NT . . . is consistent, sufficient, and trustworthy . . . . It is easy to demonstrate that the sources contain confused traditions . . . . Mark, as the earliest Gospel, does not have a definitely anti-Pharisaic tendency . . . . Obviously, there was a growth of tradition of Jesus and the Pharisees from the appearance of Mark to the period of the 4th Gospel . . . . there is little correspondence with fact in the gospel portraits of the Pharisees, and in the relation there alleged as existing between them and Jesus . . . . the portrait of the Pharisees in the Gospels is inconsistent, incomplete, and incorrect." He reminds us that Lightfoot searched "long and vainly" for a use of the trumpet in alms giving in Rabbinic literature! With the bitterness that characterizes some of his pages Schechter (a Jew) says the Pharisees "are no longer condemned *en masse* as so many hypocrites. It is even admitted that there were a few honest men among them." Too many statements on this subject are at one extreme or the other. Though Guignebert points out that Chwolson, Abrahams and Fullkgrug argued that the hatred of Jesus by the Pharisees was the invention of a later time (as it probably was), he says: "the Pharisees pursued Jesus with an unrelenting hatred; they devoted themselves to an unceasing attempt to oppose, embarrass, compromise, and finally to exterminate him"—a preposterous statement by a famous professor in the University of Paris, and typical of too many Christian scholars. At the other (Jewish) extreme is Dembitz: "They had the courage to add to the 248 positive commands found in the Pentateuch their own further commands." Courage is hardly the word for it. Glover: "The Pharisee was essentially an actor—playing to himself the most contemptible little comedies of holiness." On the other extreme, Zitlin: "Others hold that some of the leaders of the Pharisees were even arrogant and boorish. Needless to say, such statements are not only baseless . . . ."

So we must ask: what *were* the Pharisees? They said: "This multitude that knoweth not the Law are accursed." Of Rabbi Meir (2nd cen.) it was said that he could give 150 reasons to prove it 'unclean'. R. Jacob (same cen.) : "He who walks by the way and studies and breaks off his study and says, 'How beautiful is this tree, how beautiful is this fallow' Scripture counts it to him as if he were guilty against himself." And so on—such sayings were many; but they were *not* hypocrites; they were fanatics. R. Akiba (most famous Jew of 2nd cen.c.e.), who rose from the common people, confessed that in his earlier years at the sight of a Pharisee he wanted to "tear him to pieces like a fish." That was so, as Dembitz admits, because "a sharp difference was developed between the Pharisees and the common people." A lexicon to the Talmud says: "A Pharisee is one who separates himself from all uncleanness and from eating anything unclean." Most scholars have thought the word means 'separated' and Loewe accepts Finkelstein's theory that the separateness was from sin. But Lightley, Leszynsky, Oesterley, Lauterbach, Box and others doubt that the word meant 'separated'. Josephus said of them: "they take a pride in the scrupulous observance of the religion of the Fathers and think to themselves that God loves them more than others" —as God should have done if the 248 commandments in the OT are his. Now for typical opinions, first Gentile, then Jewish.

Case: "In thought it led to infinite devotion to details and preternaturally refined distinctions and warnings. In religion it led to the formation of a . . . church within a church." Elsewhere he says: "God himself became a rabbi, read every Sabbath in the Bible, and became entangled in an all-embracing scholasticism." They sought, says H. T. Fowler, "with pathetic devotion to carry out the will of God as prescribed in his law." Norton: "a cold, iron-bound legalism, or rather a combination of literalism, legalism, and formalism." Rhees: "its beginning was intensely earnest, but in the time of Jesus the earnest spirit had died out in zealous formalism." Easton: "they were at least frank and outspoken enemies [of the early Christians]; whatever the nature of their 'hypocrisy', every one knew exactly where they stood." Moore: "That many who bore the name Pharisee were a disgrace we have on rabbinical testimony." Schurer: "the true Israel, which was related to the remaining bulk of the people as these were to the heathen." Nash: "They abstained even from table fellowship with the heathen as being an abominable thing." Lake: "Taken at their best they probably represent the highest form of a religion based on codified ethics . . ." Herford: "To study Torah was, to the devout

Pharisee, to 'think God's thoughts after him', as Kepler said."
Toy: "Whatever the shortcomings and the crimes of the Pharisaic party (and they were great), its functions and its mission
were broad and noble." Lagrange: "organized for the purpose
of observing Law with even greater exactitude, and of impos-
ing it on others." Strange that the Christians, who so closely
copied them in this, should have hated them so!

JE: "Liturgy was and still is the field on which the different
parties within Judaism . . . fight their battles with more or
less bitterness." The Pharisees, says Waxman, were the teachers who developed "the views and activities of the Sopherim,"
that is, the scribes, in a direction, says Bosker, "of individual-
ism and universalism in both its elements—theology and ritual." It is true, says Kohler, that the Talmud itself "charges
five classes out of seven of the Pharisees with being hypocrites"
but nevertheless, says Ginsberg, "it is well-nigh impossible for
one of today to penetrate into the soul of a Pharisee of 2000
years ago." They have been, says Enelow, "much-maligned."
The ideal of some of them, says Sachar, was a "life consecrated
by religious rites, a life in which every step, from the eating of
a meal to the wearing of a new cloak, was a sacred act," but
all this "had degenerated into a blind, fanatical adherence to
forms." Abrahams: "To assert that Pharisaism included the
small and excluded the great, that it enforced rules and forgot
principles, that it exalted the letter and neglected the spirit, is
a palpable libel." Schechter: "Just as the Christians perceived
in the devotion of the Pharisees to the Law only a means to
insinuate themselves into the good opinion of the people, so
the Jews regarded the Christians' claims to a superior holiness
only as an excuse to emancipate themselves from the common
duties of life." Yet, says Klausner, "the casuistry and immense
theoretical care devoted to every one of the slightest religious
ordinances left them open to the misconception that the
ceremonial laws were the main principle and the ethical laws
only secondary." "That such insistence upon external observance," says Rabinowitz, "opened the door to hypocrisy
cannot be denied, nor that there were hypocrites among them."
Ginsberg asks *which* branch should be considered—"the
apocalyptic or the legalistic? And if the latter, of what shade,
the progressive or the conservative? And again, what are the

sources which we may draw upon for an unbiased and fair presentation." Some Jewish scholars have pointed out that some Christian scholars (e.g. Strack and Billerbeck) have criticized Ormah, that is, subtlety in casuistry, but are silent on Kawwanah, the inner intention, and Lishmah, the serious intent without calculation, which the Mishnah makes an inseparable part of the Law. Rabbi Meir said: "All depends upon the Kawwanah of the heart."

PHILO   Philo was the great Jewish Hellenist who tried, says Barton, to interpret "away the literal [and offensive] meaning of biblical passages." Hatch: "the writings of Philo . . . contain the seeds of nearly all that afterward grew up on Christian soil." Such Jews as Heinemann and Cohn have argued that he was more Greek than Jew; and M. Stein, that he did not even know Hebrew. Klausner says he produced "only an eclectic system in which Hellenism and Judaism lie together in confusion . . . . Judaism rejected Philo and C drew near to him precisely because of the compromise which Philo made between Judaism and Hellenism." See Goddenough, *The Mystic Gospel of Hellenistic Judaism*.

PILATE   Case says he seems to have been a man "very much in earnest" who strove to give a "good administration." That Tiberius left him in office ten years speaks well for him. Tiberius said: "The officials of the Roman provinces are like flies on a sore; but those already sated with blood do not suck so hard as the new-comers."

POOR, THE   Who was an am ha-arez? One, said R. Eliezer, who did not say the Shema morning and night; one, said R. Joshua, who did not wear the phylacteries; one, said Ben Azzai, who did not wear fringes on his garment. Finkelstein: "the vehement excoriations of Jesus against the Scribes was mildness itself compared with the almost savage ferocity which the am ha-arez of the following century felt for the cultured group." R. Meir: "whoever marries his daughter to an am ha-arez might as well bind her before a lion." Another rabbi said: "the am ha-arez is despicable, and his wife is like vermin, and to his daughters may be applied the verse, 'Cursed be he that lieth with any manner of beast'." The am ha-arez were, says Finkelstein, simple, naive people of the soil, "ready to receive the imprint of the first teacher who ministered to them. They were beneath the attention of a priesthood more concerned with Temple ceremonial than with service to the people." *Talmud*: "A Jew must not marry a daughter of an am ha-arez because they are unclean animals and their women forbidden reptiles . . . . the hatred with which the Amei ha-Ares hate a scholar is greater than the hatred of the heathens against Israel, and their women hate still more ardently." Klausner: "a class of poor, destitute and unemployed, and landless peasants, side by side with a class of wealthy farmers, great landed proprietors and rich bankers. The former waxed poorer and poorer, sinking into mendicancy, crushed and depressed, hoping for miracles . . ." Oesterley and Box: "Judaism has very little sympathy to offer to the unlearned, the ignorant, the weak, the fallen, the sinner"; but as Whittaker says, "exaltation of the poor and oppressed . . . had long been a distinctive feature of Hebrew literature." Leitzmann thinks Jesus was an am ha-arez. Grant: "The civil or political taxation was imposed over and above the religious dues demanded of the Jewish nation by the Law . . . . *therefore, there was a twofold taxation of the Jewish people, civil and religious; each of these had been designed without regard to the other* [his italics]." Renan: "wealth in those days had hardly more than one source—the priesthood." Strack and Billerbeck say the "Amme ha-Aretz were by no means always people who were wanting in earthly goods . . ." The poor were despised by the Pharisee, as Case says, "not so much because of their poverty as because of their indifference to the Law." Poverty in those days, says Oesterley, "was more terrible than anything experienced in modern times." Mommsen: "To be poor was not merely the sorest disgrace and the worst crime, but the only disgrace and the only crime"—he means in the Roman world in general.

PRAYER   Seneca: "So live with men as if God saw you, so speak with God as if men heard you." The more enlightened pagan attitude toward prayer was given by Maximus of Tyre: "He that prays either is worthy of the things he prays for, or he is not. If he is, he will obtain them, even though he prays not; and if he is not, he will not obtain them, even though he prays."

PROSELYTE   Derwacter: "The surmise that proselytes
                 to Judaism were numerous in many
quarters in the 1st century A.D. is borne out by the testimony
of Josephus . . . . Mixed marriages were common." Gilroy:
"drawn from heathenism by the higher ideals and the purer
life of Judaism."

SABBATH   Abrahams: "All things considered, it
                 would seem that Jesus differed fun-
damentally from the Pharisees in that he asserted a general
right to abrogate the Sabbath law for man's ordinary conven-
ience"—but most scholars think the abrogation came later after
C became a gentile movement. Kohler: "the Sabbath became
for all time the most significant characteristic of Judaism . . . .
was hedged in by ever new prohibitions, so as to incrust the
kernel with an almost impenetrable shell hiding the very
spirit that made the day one of elevation and sanctification."
The Christians, of course, eventually adopted the sun's day.

SADDUCEES   Josephus said they were "rather boor-
                 ish" and "able to persuade none but the
rich." They originated, says Edersheim, "in a reaction against
the Pharisees." They represented, says Kohler, "views and
practices of the law and interests of the Temple priesthood
directly opposite to those of the Pharisees." Hölscher calls them
"the scoffers." A. T. Robertson and others say they expected
no messiah, but Leszynsky and others dispute this. In any
case they did not believe in the resurrection and personal immortality. Edersheim and Derenbourg derive the name from
the Hebrew adjective zaddik, meaning righteous; other schol-
are accept the derivation from Zadok, though Cowley traces
it to the Persian Zindik.

SAMARITANS   Jews ancient and modern have denied a
                 close blood relationship, a question on
which scholars are divided. Edward Robertson: "Most modern
investigators see in the Samaritans only a semi-Jewish sect
which first appeared on the stage of history at the Return under Ezra, when their proffered cooperation in rebuilding the

354

temple was declined . . . . Dr. Gaster, himself a Jew, has repeatedly attacked this view." Oesterley: "The Samaritans were publicly cursed in the synagogues; and a petition was daily offered up praying God that the Samaritans might not be partakers of eternal life." Abrahams: "It is indeed remarkable how many stories are to be found in the Rabbinic sources of conduct very like that of the Good Samaritan." I have been unable to learn why observant Jews of that time hated them with such ferocity.

SIN   Oesterley and Box: "the Christian doctrine of sin cannot be adequately understood or taught without a study of the Jewish doctrine; the significance of the Christian teaching can only be apprehended when its contrast to the Jewish is realized . . . . in almost every case [in OT] ritual offenses were regarded as more grievous than moral ones . . . . The Jews do not believe in Original Sin; the idea that Adam's sin in any way affected the status of the human race is quite alien to Jewish teaching."

SON OF GOD   N. Schmidt points out that if Jesus had been the son of God the demons which he cast out would have known him for that: "No unmistakable Messianic title, such as 'Messiah', 'Son of David', or 'King of Israel' is ever put upon the lips of the possessed." Abelson: "a Hebrew idiom, which conveys nothing more than the truth of the spirituality of man." Dulk: "The Galilean teacher, whose true character was marked by deep religious inwardness, was doomed to destruction from the moment when he set himself upon the dizzy heights of the divine sonship . . . . Religion as a whole can only avoid the same fate by renouncing all transcendental elements." But of course most scholars (see Jesus) think the idea of divine sonship came later from paganism; it is inconceivable that a Galilean Jew would have thought of himself in such blasphemous terms, if not infected by pagan concepts.

SON OF MAN   This difficult term which occurs 81 times in the four gospels is still unsettled. Since Genebrard and Grotius said it meant merely man many scholars have followed them. A few have thought it a substitute for the pronoun I. Herder, followed by Schleiermacher, Neander and others thought it was intended to teach the human as distinct from the divine nature of the messiah; Hilgenfeld following Baur, that it indicated a lowly position; others, that Jesus invented the term (*bar nasha*), which seems improbable; still others try to trace it to Ezekiel. A few including J. E. Carpenter have thought Jesus used it as a symbol of the coming kingdom, a thesis now abandoned. Holtzmann and a few others thought Jesus used it to suggest but conceal his messianic destiny, but Eerdmans, Oort, Wellhausen and others see in it no messianic meaning whatever. The view that the term means simply man has been adopted by Leitzmann, Pfleiderer, Marti, Bevan, Schmidt and many others; but scholars of the eminence of Driver, Van Manen, Charles and Dalman dissent. Mills, the great Zend scholar, says: "The Son of Man again, as in Daniel, recalls Vohuman who represented man." Torrey says, "a definite and recognized messianic title" but Burkitt: "means 'the human being', 'the man'." H. W. Robinson thinks it "designates the 'corporate personality' of the saints of the Most High" but Otto, "a celestial man, of a quite unique sort." Grill, Völter, Cheyne, Porter, Gressmann, Bertholet have tried to show it means an angelic being; Bousset, Reitzenstein have tried to trace it to an ancient mythman. Case, Wellhausen, Patton, N. Schmidt and others think Jesus never applied the term to himself; but Klausner says, "Jesus always called himself 'the son of man', i.e. simple flesh and blood." And Reinach: "Jesus calls himself the son of man, which in Hebrew is synonymous with man . . ." And Dodd: "The title which Jesus seems to have preferred is 'The Son of Man' . . ." But Bacon: "To place the title in Jesus' mouth as applying to himself . . . a manifest anachronism." Reitzenstein says he did apply it to himself in an eschatological sense; but Kohler: "none of the passages in which Jesus speaks of himself as the Son of Man in the eschatological sense is genuine." Briggs says Jesus hid behind the term his messianic claims; but Oesterley: "as Dalman has shown . . . among the Jews the expression was never used as a current designation of the Messiah." Stevens refers us to Psalm viii, 4. What *did* it mean? Some like Finkelstein go to Ezekiel, thinking he invented the term "for God's address to him, to signify that even the divine messenger appears before his Master as only one of the multitude." Some like Beyschlag go to Daniel: "The son of man is the divinely invested bearer of the Kingdom that descends from above . . ." Moore: "in eschatological contexts . . . the Son of Man is plainly the figure of Daniel's vision . . ." Case: "Daniel's Son of Man . . . a type of the kingdom of the saints that should arise from the revolt against Syrian oppression." Accepting this view Schweitzer thought the problem "has been solved." But Davies says Daniel was referring to Israel (most probable), and Barton that it was not there messianic. Hurst thinks that as a definite title it appears first in *Enoch*. There is another view, as given in a brilliant work by Legge: "the Phrygian Ophites, where 'a Man and a Son of Man' were said to be the origin of all subsequent things, as in the Avestic literature of Persia where Gayomort, the son, . . . is made at once the pattern and the source of the whole human race." And Gunkel has pointed out that 'the man' is a figure in Babylonian mythology. Loisy: "The 'Son of Man' is a mythical conception . . . earlier than the apocalypses of Daniel and Enoch . . . . Its origin is pagan, probably Chaldeo-Iranian." Gilbert Murray says the Gnostic redeemer "has various names which the name of Jesus or 'Christos', 'the Anointed', tends gradually to supersede. Above all, he was in some sense Man, or 'the second Man' or 'the Son of Man' . . . . He is the real, the ultimate, the perfect and eternal Man, of whom all men are feeble copies." Lake: "There seems but little doubt that 'Son of Man', which in Greek is an unintelligible phrase rather than a title, was quite as obscure to the generation of Greek Christians which produced the present gospels as it is to ourselves . . . . the phrase 'Son of Man' may itself belong to the embellishment rather than to the body of tradition." And Weiss points out "how favorably inclined was the Hellenistic-Roman era toward the idea of the divine man."

SOUL   Cumont: "primitive and universal belief that the soul is a breath, exhaled with the last sigh." Note our 'the breath of life.'

TEACHERS   Klausner: "It was a common sight then in Palestine to see teachers ('Rabbis') atracting disciples in large numbers and publicly expounding the Law." There were also wandering teachers from other lands and peoples.

TEMPLE   Olmstead: "To the sophisticated Gentile tourist, who with his own eyes had looked upon the Rome of marble left behind by Augustus, the chaster beauties of Athens, the strange enclosure at Baalbek with its stones of unparalleled size, and the huge agglomeration of gloomy temples at Egyptian Thebes, the little Jewish shrine must have appeared poor and even tawdry."

UNCLEANNESS   Finkelstein: "the men of Jerusalem found an impassable religious barrier set up between the provincials and themselves in the Levitical laws of purity . . . . The scholar, who had merely despised the peasant when he was at a distance, found him unbearable in close proximity." He says that when an ignorant man approached the temple with unwashed hands R. Eliezer sprang at him crying, 'I swear that even if the High priest were to come near the altar with his hands unwashed, his head would be split with a log!' The Galileans "had never submitted fully to the biblical laws" and whatever they touched shared their defilement and "could neither be eaten by the pure nor used for sacrifice."

WOMEN   Israel in the time of Jesus, says Delitzsch, "regarded with suspicion and contempt every trade which necessitated an intercourse with women." Jewish ritual contained a morning prayer for husband and son in which they thanked God "that he was not made a woman." Among those who could not give evidence women were listed with slaves and idiots. Christians took over this attitude. Donaldson: "the Church never assigned any ecclesiastical functions to women, as they were deemed in every respect inferior to men . . . . The highest post to which she rose was to be a doorkeeper and a message-woman, and even these functions were taken away from her during the Middle Ages." On the woman taken in adultery Nicholson says: "it is not likely that they had any thought of really stoning the woman. They might not put to death without leave from the Roman governor, who would hardly give it in such cases as this."

ZEALOTS   Lake: "in the first half of the first cen-
                tury a steadily growing menace to all
organized government, willing to destroy but unable to build
. . . . Much of the teaching of Jesus becomes intelligible only
when we place it in contrast to the Zealots." Wellhausen:
"fanatics for God and the fatherland . . ." Case: "To one who
believed sincerely that this territory was a holy land, which
God had promised by irrevocable covenants to deliver to his
chosen people for their perpetual possession, Roman domination seemed clearly to represent a temporary stay of the divine
purpose."